"Stone is a stone cold thriller genius."

GARETH L. POWELL award-winning author of *Ragged Alice* and the *Embers of War* trilogy.

"An exceptional thriller from one of the best in the business."

KEALAN PATRICK BURKE Bram Stoker Award-winning author of *Kin* and *Sour Candy.*

"Tightly woven with suspense and vivid, compelling prose, this third book of the series is proof of Ms. Stone's talent as a master storyteller in the Thriller genre."

S.J. PIERCE international bestselling author of the *Alyx Rayer* mystery series.

"D.K. Stone's masterfully crafted Fall of Night takes readers on a deep dive into the murky waters of the mountain park, where secrets from the past are revealed, concealed and unearthed again."

PAM CLARK award-winning author of *Kalyna.*

FALL*of*NIGHT

a novel by
D. K. Stone

Stonehouse Publishing
www.stonehousepublishing.ca
Alberta, Canada

FALL*of*NIGHT

a novel by
D. K. Stone

Stonehouse Publishing
www.stonehousepublishing.ca
Alberta, Canada

Stonehouse Publishing Inc is an independent publishing house,
incorporated in 2014.

Cover design and layout by Janet King
Printed in Canada

Stonehouse Publishing would like to thank and acknowledge
the support of the Alberta Government funding for the arts,
through the Alberta Media Fund.
National Library of Canada Cataloguing in Publication Data
Stone, D. K.
Fall of Night
Novel
ISBN: 978-1-988754-30-7 (paperback)

Disclaimer: Although Waterton Park is a real location, the
characters, situations and events portrayed in this series are all
fictious. Any resemblance to any real persons, living or dead, is
purely coincidental.

For Frank and Linnea.
Always, always…

"Life went on without you. Of course, it did. Of course, it does. It was just an ending, they tell me, not the end."

Lang Leav

CAST OF CHARACTERS

Annabelle Rice: New York socialite; wife of Edward Rice.

Annie Parcelle: A local retiree and long-time Waterton resident.

Arnette Miles: A local business owner; wife of Murray Miles.

Audrika Kulkarni: The owner of Fine and Fancy, and one of the most forceful businesspeople in the Park; married to Vasur Kulkarni.

Barry Goldman: A business associate of Mr. Edward Rice.

Ben Grayden: Officer on the Pincher Creek Police force; school friend of Jim Flagstone.

Brendan Miles: One of the two local seasonal workers who work in Lou's Garage, son of Murray and Arnette Miles.

Brian Howe: One of Waterton's police force.

Bryce Calhoun: Great-nephew of Levi Thompson; cousin to Colton Calhoun.

Colton Calhoun: Infamous Waterton murderer; deceased.

Darren "Dax" Xavier: Known felon; wanted by the U.S. Department of Corrections.

Delia Rosings: Reporter for the Calgary Sun newspaper.

Edward Rice: Businessman with various investments, legal and illegal; husband of Annabelle Rice and father of Gabrielle Rice.

Elaine Decker: A local business owner; wife of Fred Decker.

Fred Decker: A retired hotelier; husband of Elaine Decker.

Gabrielle Rice: Rich's ex-girlfriend.

Grant McNealy: Head Warden for Waterton Park.

Hunter Slate: Outgoing and well-liked owner of Hunter's Coffee Shop, the unofficial meeting place for Park business.

Jeannine Barton: Wife of Park Superintendent Sam Barton.

Jim Flagstone: A police officer with strong ties to Southern Alberta and the ranching community; deceased.

Jordan Wyatt: Newest, least experienced member of Waterton's police force.

Levi Thompson: Oldest man in the Park, and descendant of one of the original settlers to the area, Levi runs a ranch outside the Park's boundaries.

Liz Moran: Receptionist for the Waterton police station.

Louise "Lou" Newman: Owner of Lou's Garage; she was born and raised in Waterton.

Margaret Lu: A local business owner. She is Audrika's biggest competitor, but she can be counted on to side with Audrika in a fight.

Mila St. Jean: A seasonal worker in Lou's Garage.

Murray Miles: A local businessman; husband of Arnette Miles.

Oscar Hycha: One of Waterton's police force.

Prischka Archer: The director of Coldcreek Enterprises and Rich's one-time supervisor.

Rich Evans: Prior manager of the Whitewater Lodge, now attempting to immigrate to Canada.

Ronald Hamamoto: A local retiree and long-time Waterton resident.

Russell Durnerin: A local rancher; father of Shawna Durnerin.

Sadie Black Plume: A police officer whose family comes from the nearby Blood Indian Reservation.

Sam Barton: Park Superintendent, and the go-between for Parks Canada and the Chamber of Commerce; husband of Jeannine Barton.

Shawna Durnerin: A local rancher.

Stu Callaghan: A New York lawyer and Rich's college roommate.

Susan Varley: One-time owner of the Bertha Mountain Bed and Breakfast; deceased.

Tom Farrel: An investigator from New York, hired by Gabrielle Rice's family to locate their missing daughter.

Tyrone "King" Fischer: New York mafia and rumoured associate of Darren "Dax" Xavier.

Vasur Kulkarni: A local businessman; husband of Audrika Kulkarni.

PROLOGUE

One year later.

Tuesday dawned sunny and bright. No clouds scudded the sky reflected in the windowed office on the 23rd floor of the Flatiron Building where Rich Evans sat. It was a picture postcard kind of morning, all saturated colours and deep shadow. A perfect New York day. The sort of weather photographers and tourists ached for.

Rich straightened his tie, fighting the urge to remove it. Two years ago, he would have reveled in such a morning. Today, irritation prickled under his apparent calm. He rolled his shoulders in the stiff suit and checked his watch—8:39 a.m., twenty minutes to go—then settled back against the leather armchair.

Rich's meeting with Prischka Archer didn't start until 9:00 a.m., but in his effort to be on time he'd come early. His one-time boss was already in her office and likely had been since dawn. Prischka *could* call him in—there was only one other person in the waiting room, and she'd shown up after Rich had—but he knew she wouldn't. Prischka worked by clockwork, her days marked by the passage of time. That had never bothered Rich before.

It did today.

There was too much riding on this meeting. His application for permanent residency, allowing him to stay in Canada, had been de-

railed by the arson trial. While his existing work permit allowed
him to remain in Waterton until December, staying in Canada after
that point was another matter. He'd applied for an extension to his
"skilled worker" permit, but there was a good chance they'd turn
him down. Rich was no longer a manager. The only place he had
worked since the Whitewater had burned to the ground was Lou's
Garage and he could hardly ask his girlfriend to write him a refer-
ence. That would look worse than being unemployed. But barring
pumping gas and trying to stay out of jail, he'd done *nothing* since
Coldcreek Enterprises had terminated his employment. On paper,
Rich didn't look like much of a candidate. He tugged at the sleeves
of his shirt and the metal cufflinks—tiny Xs, a gift from someone
he could no longer remember—twinkled on his wrists. That's why
today's meeting with Prischka was so important. A word from her
could change everything.

He'd just put his hands back on the armrests when he felt his
phone buzz. He fished it from his pocket and flipped it open. Seeing
the 1(403) prefix to the number, a smile broke across his clean-shav-
en jaw. *Louise.* He put the phone to his ear.

"Hey Lou," he said. "What's—"

"Rich. Oh my God. You're okay." Her panicked voice rang
through the ear-piece. "I was so worried."

"Lou? What's—"

"I had a dream. I—I had to call you."

Rich switched the phone to the other ear. "You've got to slow
down, I can't—"

"I had a dream," Lou said, "a *terrible* dream. One of the—" Her
voice broke. "The ones that aren't *just* a dream."

"Jesus." Rich's gaze skittered nervously around the waiting room.
Prischka's assistant sat, quietly typing at the beige comput-

er, his head down-turned. A woman in a business suit, sat by the far window, staring down at her clasped hands. As much as Rich had worked toward accepting what Louise told him when she had a 'feeling' about things, this *wasn't* something he could discuss in these people's presence.

"Are you okay?" he asked.

"No. I—" Lou cleared her throat. "I needed to hear your voice."

"It's okay. I told you to call any time. I meant it." The secretary's gaze flicked to Rich as he spoke, then moved away just as fast. "What time is it in Alberta?" Rich asked.

"Quarter to seven." Louise sniffled. "Wait... Oh God. You're not *in* your meeting right now, are you?!"

"Not yet. The meeting is at nine." Rich checked his watch—*8:41*—then stood from the chair. "Hold on a sec, sweetheart. I'm just going to step out of the office so we can talk."

"I'm so sorry, Rich. I shouldn't have called."

"No, I'm glad you did." He pushed open the office door and crossed the hallway. "I *always* have time for you."

"Thank you." She gave a teary laugh. "God, it makes me feel better just to hear that."

"That's my girl." Rich thumbed the elevator's button, smiling through his worry. Louise was on the line. She was okay.

"But seriously, Rich. Do you have *time* to talk?"

"Yeah. A few minutes anyhow. I'm just going to step outside."

"Outside?"

"Uh-huh. Going to grab a breath of fresh air." He laughed. "Okay, not *fresh* exactly, but fresher than indoors. I've got a little time before the meeting."

"Are you sure?"

"Absolutely." The elevator door opened. There was a letter carrier on his way out and Rich stepped past him. When the doors closed, he spoke again: "You sound scared. Talk to me, Lou."

"I—I am… or I *was*, at least."

"About…?"

"About *you*. That's why I called."

The elevator dropped, Rich's stomach following a moment later. "Tell me about this dream."

"It wasn't *just* a dream. I had a vision."

Rich flinched. "I… okay." He pinched his nose with his free hand, wishing desperately that she was next to him, not a country away. "Then let's figure this out. Talk to me."

"Well, it started like any normal dream," Louise said as the elevator shuttled downward. "I saw shapes and colours. Unimportant things. Bits and pieces of my day at the garage. Levi in his truck and Hunter saddling a horse, and then all of a sudden, I saw a city street *really* clearly. Like I was *there*, Rich. I saw you walking down the sidewalk."

The hair rose on the back of Rich's neck. "Me…?"

"Uh-huh. There were people all around you. You were dressed in a suit. A real fancy one. I could see every detail, from your shoes to the shirt, to your tie."

Rich's eyes lowered to his navy pin-stripe jacket, one of three he'd brought along on the visit. "What kind of suit?"

"Black, I think," she said, and Rich's chest eased. "No, wait. Not black, but *blue*. It was pin striped. Navy with lines, and you had little silver buttons on your wrists. They looked like tiny crosses. A red tie."

A shiver ran the length of Rich's spine. "What else did you see?"

"You were in New York."

"Yeah, but you already know that, Lou." He forced a laugh he didn't feel. "I mean, you helped me pack."

"That's not the weird part."

The elevator hit the bottom and Rich's stomach lurched. "It isn't?"

"No," she said. "There was… something wrong. Like, a fire in a couple of the buildings, I think. But I'm not sure. Oh God, Rich. The sky was black. I—" Her voice broke and she began to cry.

Rich stepped out of the elevator, pushing through the entrance door to the street.

"Hey. Hey! Lou. *Breathe*, baby. Just hold on. I'm okay. It was just a dream." He forced his voice to be light. There were still too many people standing near the Flatiron building… too many people who *might* know Prischka. "It's gorgeous here," Rich said as his feet carried him south toward Washington Square Park. "The sun is shining and—"

"There were people dying!" Lou cried. "Clouds of smoke! Fire and ash, plumes of it filling the sky."

"It's perfectly clear." Rich continued up Fifth Avenue, his eyes on the distant spires, glittering jewel-like in the morning brightness. "Hardly a cloud in the sky, never mind smoke."

"But you're not listening, Rich. I could see them! They were trapped."

"*Who* was trapped?"

"The people from the buildings."

"Okay. Back up. *Where* was this happening?" He glanced both ways, then crossed the next street, heading south. Morning traffic moved along beside him like a river.

"I… I don't know where. But *you* could see it."

"Okay." Rich jogged across another street, putting more distance between him and the Flatiron building. "Tell me what you saw."

"Buildings. Two of them on fire."

"What kind? Sky scrapers? Office buildings or—"

"Really tall ones. And there were people, Rich. People trapped by the fire. I could see them jumping. You were standing down on the street. Watch—" Her voice broke.

"Watching?"

"Yes." She took a sobbing breath. "You saw the bodies fall."

Rich paused at the crosswalk then crossed another street, the buildings of the financial district sharp on the horizon. "Lou, just listen. I'm not saying I don't believe you—*I do*—but what if it was just a nightmare? It might—"

"It's a warning!" Her voice cracked. "Don't you understand?!"

"But Lou—"

"Something *bad* is coming, and I don't know what it means or how to stop it, but you need to be careful!"

In the split second before he could think of how to answer, a glittering dart in the sky caught Rich's eye, a plane flying above New York, far too close to the buildings.

"There's a plane," he said.

"What?"

"A plane flying over Manhattan."

"No, no, NO!"

"It's too close, Lou. It's going to—"

In the distance, the 93rd to 99th floors of the World Trade Center building exploded in a fireball.

CHAPTER ONE

October 15, 2001

In the dim light of the bedroom, Louise Newman stared at the ring on her hand. Outside the window, the wind moved branches and the light followed, tiny explosions of light—blue, red, and yellow—flashing through the solitaire. Lou smiled. As a mechanic, she knew exactly *zero* about the design of engagement rings, but she knew that Rich had gone through the trouble of having this one created for her. Unlike every other ring she'd seen in her life, this one had the diamond *inset* in the band. *"So it won't catch on things while you're working on a car,"* Rich had said. *"I want you to wear it, Lou, not look at it."* It didn't change the beauty of it, but it increased its personal value.

It hadn't left her finger in six months.

Smiling, Lou curled her hand into a fist, letting her lashes flutter closed. On New York time, Rich would almost certainly be up by now. He had a meeting today, one he swore should *"definitely be the last"* and Louise knew he likely wouldn't pick up his cell. She didn't want to jinx it by trying to call him. Not after what had happened a month ago. She'd just started to doze when the 'snooze' on the clock abruptly ended and the alarm blared back to life. "Take it to the Limit", an Eagles ballad from Louise's childhood began mid-song.

She groped across the bedside table, knocked a book about the French Revolution she'd been reading the night before to the floor, and silenced the alarm. For several long seconds, she stared at the ceiling.

"No use thinking about it," she muttered.

Lou pushed the covers back and swung her legs over the side of the bed, bedsprings groaning. The sound held the memory of Rich, here together every night since the Whitewater had burned. She wished he was home with her today. That he was here *right now*, giving her a reason to stay in bed and be late for work. The ache in her chest—which followed the scar of the gunshot that had nearly killed her two years ago—twinged and she pushed her sadness away. *Rich would be home soon,* she thought. The travel bans were affecting everyone these days, not just him.

Lou dressed in silence. Her inner life had changed since Rich Evans had come to Waterton; her happiness was now tied to *his happiness*, and their unplanned separation pulled at both of them. Lou knew, with certainty, that he *would* come home to Waterton. She'd seen that future. But when his one-week trip back to New York to deal with the permanent resident paperwork had stretched out to more than four times that, she'd found herself growing impatient.

She grabbed a button-down shirt, shivering as the cool cotton slid over her skin. Soon she'd be shifting into her winter flannels, but as cool as this morning was, it would be scorching by mid-morning. That was part of the truth of the mountains. October could be a moody season, but this year had been unexpectedly balmy. If only Rich was here to share it with…

The phone in the kitchen rang.

"Rich," Lou breathed. She jogged from the room, taking the stairs two at a time. The black rotary dial-up hanging on the wall jangled for the second time. She grabbed the handset and put it to her ear. "Hello?"

"G'morning, gorgeous!"

"Rich," she laughed. "I was hoping it was you."

"Lucky you, then, 'cause it is. I didn't wake you up, did I?"

"Not at all. Just got dressed."

"Wish I'd been there to help."

Lou grinned. "Mmm... yeah. I can imagine how that helping would go. I would've liked that."

He groaned and the sound was so crisp, so *clear*, that it felt like he was in the kitchen with her. "Don't remind me."

"Oh, I *will* remind you. Can't have you disappearing on me forever."

"I promise I'm doing everything in my power to get home."

Louise's grin brightened. *Home.* That was his word, his definition. "I know," she said. "I'm just teasing you."

"I know. The weather still holding out there?"

"Uh-huh." Her eyes lit on the uncurtained kitchen window and the mountains beyond. "It's beautiful today. The leaves are turning."

"Wish I was there to see that."

"I wish you were too."

"Not to worry though, it should be soon. Just got out of—" A vague sound, like an intercom, interrupted for a spit-second. "—my meeting. I think I've finally got things in order."

"What?!" Lou squealed and Rich laughed. "But that's amazing!"

"Yeah, Prischka was true to her word. She pulled a few strings. The guy I met with told me the immigration office is processing my permanent residency application already. I'm heading over to the office this afternoon. Need to pick up some kind of temporary document while things are being processed." He chuckled. "So I hope you weren't kidding about wanting me there, 'cause I was looking at flights for Thursday."

"Thursday... as in *this* Thursday?!"

"Uh-huh. If that's okay with you."

"Oh my God, yes. Yes!" Lou laughed. "Lethbridge or Calgary airport?"

"Lethbridge if I can make the connections work."

"I'll be there to pick you up. Just give me the word."

"I will and I..." He paused. "I was wondering if you'd be willing to swing by the Registry before we came back home to Waterton."

"Sure. What for?"

"I thought we could pick up the marriage license at the same time."

Lou's smile widened until her cheeks hurt. "I guess we could. But... we haven't even set a date yet. I mean... it seems a bit rushed, doesn't it?"

"Not to me. I've been wanting to marry you since the day I met you."

Lou giggled. "Hardly."

"No, really. At least since the *week* we met then. And this whole thing with the World Trade Center really shook me up."

Her smile dimmed. "Yeah. Me too."

"It put things in perspective. I mean, if Prischka's office had been *there* in the Twin Towers, rather than three miles away, I could have died."

"Rich, don't—"

"No, listen. I need to say this. I love you. I want to be with you, and I'm *tired* of waiting."

"Me too."

"So, let's get the license when I get home. Let's make a date."

Again, in the background, an intercom interrupted—he had to be calling her from a train station or subway—but Rich's words carried on over top of it. "Let's stop pissing around and do this. Okay?"

"I… Okay."

"Awesome! I was just talking to Stu about coming home when we had lunch yesterday…"

Louise chewed her lower lip as Rich carried on. Something *else* had happened, but she couldn't tell what.

"…so I told Stu he ought to keep his plans open. Winter wedding in Waterton."

She smiled. "Winter, huh? Um… Rich. Can I ask you something?"

"Sure, sweetheart."

"Don't take this the wrong way. I *want* to get married, but…"

"But what?"

"Why *now*?"

He laughed. "I told you. I've *always* wanted to marry you."

"I know that, but…" She swallowed the words she wanted to say: *there's something you aren't telling me.* And went with a half-truth instead. "Are you sure this is right? To rush in, I mean? I'm not going anywhere. You're not going anywhere. There's no reason we need to—"

"I want to marry you, Louise Newman. Done deal."

She giggled. "Me too."

"So let's do this." His voice grew serious. "Will you marry me, Lou? Not in the summer, not the summer after that, but this year. This winter even? Do you want to get married?"

Joy pushed past the last of her hesitation and she grinned through tears. "Yes."

* * *

Lou was on her way to Hunter's for dinner.

Very little hinted at the lateness of the year other than the length of the shadows that stretched out across the sidewalk and the cool wind that whistled through autumn leaves, carrying with it the fresh scents of September. Waterton was closed for the season, the tourists long gone. On Main Street, only a skeleton crew of businesses remained: Lou's Garage, a few touristy shops trying to mop up the last of the fall trade, and Hunter's Coffee Shop. All other businesses had windows covered with plywood, their peeling paint announcing their owners' departures as much as the hand-lettered signs that said '*Closed for the Season, back next year!*'

Tonight, Louise barely noticed the quiet of the town. Her thoughts were on other things.

How many times in her life, Lou wondered, had she walked up this driveway to visit Hunter Slate? How many moments had they shared? With her father's death, Hunter had become more than just a friend. He was her surrogate dad. And on nights like tonight—when Louise felt uncertain—his jovial nature was the balm she needed to soothe her nerves. His phone call, inviting her for dinner, had been a welcome surprise.

In the warm light of early evening, Hunter's squat one-level house appeared dwarfed by the soaring mountains that surrounded it. An older-model truck was parked on the street, a web of cracks on its windshield, Hunter's orange truck behind it. Otherwise the road was bare. Lou jogged up the sidewalk, smiling. This cabin, almost as much as Whispering Aspens, felt like *home.*

She had just lifted her hand to knock on the front door when an explosion of barking erupted from the other side.

"Enough!" she heard Hunter shout. "Get down! You dogs go on!"

She grinned. Hunter's cougar hounds were as much 'him' as the coffee shop that he ran. The dog's bellowing dropped to half-decibels and she heard footsteps approach the door. It swung inward.

"You know, Hunter," Lou said. "If those dogs of yours were any louder they'd…"

Her voice faded as she caught sight of the scowling white-haired man who stood on the other side.

"Levi," she said. "I… I wasn't expecting *you* here."

The dilapidated truck she'd seen on the street now made sense; it was Levi's.

"Disappointed?" he grunted.

"Not disappointed. Just… unexpected."

"Best close that door," he grumbled. "Dogs'll get out otherwise."

"Right." She closed the door behind her, frowning as her eyes caught on a neatly pinned sling. "What happened to your arm, Levi?"

He glanced back from the kitchen doorway. Annoyance, like a shadow, rested across his wrinkled face. "Tripped in the yard while I was saddling a horse," he said. "Damned thing nearly trampled me."

"I'm glad you're okay."

He made a sound of irritation as he pulled out a chair with his good left hand and settled into it. Hunter's dogs—three cougar hounds of varying size—sat in a semi-circle next to the stove where Hunter stood frying meat. The steaks looked like beef, but the scent was sharper. *Venison*, Lou thought, smiling. It had been a childhood staple. She stepped around one of the dogs, who whined at her intrusion, and gave Hunter a quick hug.

"You're right on time!" he said. "Meat's almost done."

"Good to see you, Hunter."

"You too, hon." He flipped a steak. "Grab a chair, I'm almost done."

The dog, whose view she was blocking, pawed at Lou's leg and whined. She laughed. "You've got quite the audience here."

Hunter smiled and pushed the cast iron skillet off the burner. "Oh, just nudge 'em with your toe if they won't get out of your way. You know how they are about deer meat."

"As they should be." Lou reached down and ruffled the dog's silky ears. "Who's a good dog?" The mutt ducked his head out from under her hand, intent on Hunter. "I know, I know." She laughed. "You have other interests."

Lou caught Levi's eyes as she stood. The elderly man broke her gaze, the mask of irritation dropping back into place between one heartbeat and the next. He glared down the hallway, ignoring her. Lou sighed. Levi was Levi and there was nothing she could do about it. She just wished he hadn't dropped in for dinner. He and Hunter had been friends for years; the two men relied on one another.

She forced a bright smile and took her place. There were three settings and she took the far end of the table, giving Levi the distance he needed.

"Haven't seen much of you around Waterton lately, Levi," she said.

"Was waiting for the tourists to git out. Got no use of 'em."

"Ah… of course. How's the ranch these days?"

"Ranch is fine."

"Your arm." She pointed. "Is that a problem with—?"

"I've *got* ranch-hands," he snapped. "They can handle things."

"Of course they can." Louise let out a slow breath. "Did you drive in tonight?"

"Does it look like I'm drivin'?" Levi lifted his arm. "Had the neighbour take it into town for me."

"Levi's staying here for a while," Hunter said. "Coffee shop is only open a few hours a day. And the dogs don't like being alone, so it all works out…" He flipped the steaks. "One of the Calhoun boys—"

"Bryce," Levi said.

"—will be watching over the herd while Levi's here," Hunter finished. "And when his arm is healed, he'll head on back."

"Calhoun," Lou repeated. The name was an unpleasant reminder of the murders years before, but Levi's family was sprawling. It wasn't a surprise that he'd asked one of his relatives to take over while he healed. It *was* a surprise that he'd holed up with Hunter.

"Yeah," Hunter said. "One of the younger Calhoun boys, I think." He glanced at Levi. "That right?"

"Mmmph. Bryce, Alanna's oldest boy."

"Bryce doesn't mind spending his winter out at the ranch?" Lou asked. She tried to pull Bryce's face to mind, but couldn't get more than a freckled youth who'd followed her and Colt around when they'd been kids. "He doesn't mind the time away from home?"

"Course he doesn't mind," Levi grumbled. "Family keeps after family. Besides, there's more'n enough to spare from that brood."

Hunter chuckled. "Bryce'll carry on at the ranch while Levi's arm heals. Works out for everyone."

"I just hate imposing," Levi said sourly.

"You're *not* imposing. The dogs need someone 'round the house. You're doing me a favour, if the truth be told. Not sure how I'll manage after your arm's healed." Hunter grinned. "You could stay *longer*, you know."

"What d'you mean?"

"With Waterton as quiet as it is in the winter, I could use the company."

Levi said nothing.

"C'mon," Hunter said. "It'll be fun!"

"Well, if you're sure."

"Of course!" Hunter's braying laughter filled the small kitchen. "Let's plan on it then. Stay the winter in town for once. Won't that be great, Lou?"

Lou wilted. *So much for neighbourly visits.* "Yeah," she said, hoping her voice sounded more excited than she felt. "Of course. It'll be nice to have the company."

"Well, if it's no bother—"

"It's none at all!" Hunter said. "I'm already looking forward to it."

As they chatted, Hunter carried bowls to the table. Lou filled the glasses with water, ice-cold straight from the tap. She'd just sat down when the sound of nails skittering on the linoleum floor filled the kitchen. Hunter did a two-step, the final plate, piled high with venison, held over his head while three dogs circled his feet. Duke, the youngest, bayed and jumped. The two others followed.

"Sit down!" Hunter said in a laughing voice. "Not for you. Nope! You'll get yours after." He set the plate on the table and three dogs sat down so fast their haunches bounced.

Lou ruffled the head of the nearest dog. "Impatient, aren't you, boy?"

"They're *all* impatient, but Duke's the youngest. That makes him the worst," Hunter said. "You'd think I never fed 'em, the way they act around game."

The corner of Levi's mouth crooked up. "You feed 'em too much," he said. "They're fat, the lot of 'em. Don't look like work dogs no more."

Hunter laughed rather than argued. "Well, save the bones, would you? They think if they're well behaved, they'll get something." He offered Louise the steaks and she speared one. "They're all burned on the outside, medium in the middle."

"Just like I like them," Lou said.

Hunter pushed a steak onto Levi's plate. "You heard from Rich lately, Lou?"

"He called this morning, actually."

Levi grumbled. He and Rich had history too. Rich had told Lou about Levi's poaching, and him saving him from the bear. But saving someone was one thing. *Liking them* was something else entirely.

"Spuds, Lou?" Hunter asked.

"Thanks." She reached for the dish of potatoes.

"Any luck getting his application finished up?"

"Uh-huh. Things are moving along." Lou set the bowl in front of Levi who glared at her, then took the bowl of peas from Hunter's outstretched hand. "Rich got his temporary papers today."

Hunter thumped his hands down on the table, whooping as the silverware jumped.

"Well, that's wonderful!"

"It is," she said with a smile. "He's coming home Thursday."

Hunter cheered and the dogs barked. Lou couldn't help but grin.

"Thursday, huh?" Levi repeated.

Her gaze flicked across the table. Hunter had begun cutting up Levi's meat. "Uh-huh. Rich and I are…" She dropped her chin. "We're… we're actually thinking of moving the wedding day up a bit."

"Oh, Lou, hon," Hunter said, dropping Levi's cutlery and pushing back from the table. "That's great news!" He came to her side and pulled her into a bear hug made awkward by her sitting. "When's the big day gonna be?"

"Not sure, exactly. Rich wants it soon."

"Young love," Hunter teased. "Always in a rush."

"We're hardly *young*, Hunter."

He laughed. "Younger than me, at any rate." He ruffled her hair, then sat back down. "Why the change of plans?"

"As much as I'd like to think it's impatience," Lou said, "I think it's because of the attack in New York. It affected him."

"Course it did."

"I figured we were going to be married anyhow, and since I'm not one for standing on ceremony, we're just rushing it a bit. Nothing wrong with that, is there?"

"Nothing at all!" Hunter crowed.

Levi said nothing, just rolled his eyes.

Dinner carried on. Hunter talked about getting a sheep tag and Levi groused about not being able to go hunting on account of his arm. Bryce, it seemed, would be Hunter's partner this year. Lou found herself wishing that Levi *wasn't* Hunter's guest, and then felt guilty for thinking it. When dessert rolled around, she excused herself, gave Hunter a tight hug, and headed home.

It was sunset. Lines of shadow stretched across the sidewalk, while overhead a brilliant ripple of red and gold played over the westernmost peaks. Darkness rose in the east.

Levi just doesn't like Rich, Lou thought. *Never has, never will.* It bothered her more than her own prickly relationship with him. Somewhere in the distance, a nocturnal bird burst into flight while in the thicket to her side, a deer moved skittishly through the brush. Lou barely noticed. It was Waterton's quiet season. With the tourists gone, animals took their place.

As she reached the cabin steps, she heard the phone ringing and Lou's heart leapt. *Rich!* She pushed open the door and kicked it closed behind her. Half a second later, she grabbed the phone from its handset. "Hello?"

"Hey, sweetheart."

"Rich!" she laughed. "I almost missed your call. I just got back from dinner with Levi and Hunter."

"Well, I'm glad I caught you. You got a minute to talk?"

"Of course I do."

"I've got the flight booked. You got a pen?"

She reached for the jar next to phone.

"Got it."

In her excitement, she didn't see the shadowy figure standing in the shadows of the yard. Nor did she see him move to a new vantage point on the street so he could watch her through the kitchen window.

* * *

The Rocky Mountains where Waterton lay had a lingering twilight hour. With the sun gone behind the jagged peaks, light leeched from the sky, shifting from lavender, to dusky purple, and eventually to chalky blue. Sadie and Jordan were in the cruiser on patrol when a crackle broke through the CB radio.

Liz, the dispatcher's voice, followed half a second later.

"Constable Black Plume and Constable Wyatt," she said. "This is dispatch. Come in please."

Sadie was driving. Sadie *always* drove. So Jordan pulled the handset from its cradle. "This is Constable Wyatt. What's up, Liz?"

"Pincher Creek RCMP just contacted me about a body a couple of hunters found. They need you to check it out."

Sadie's mind flashed to a dark memory from two years ago. *"Officer Down."* She blinked and it was gone.

"A... a body?" Jordan said.

The CB crackled. "Yeah. Woman, late-twenties or early thirties," Liz said. "Two guys were hiking around in the forest reserve east of the park and they saw her floating face-down in a small lake."

"So why're they calling *us* about it?" Jordan said. "If the guys were hunting in the forest reserve, then that's Pincher Creek's domain."

"'Cause the little lake where they saw her is just inside the park boundary..."

A trio of lines appeared between Sadie's brows. It wasn't the first time someone had used the park as a dumping ground. She turned onto Main Street, shuttered business fronts flashing past on each side.

"...which means that Waterton police have to deal with it."

On Mountview Road Sadie flicked on the lights but not the sirens.

"Ask Liz where they want us to meet them," she said.

"Liz, where are we supposed to go?"

"Officer who called it in said they'd meet you on the road that goes in past the buffalo paddock. There's a trail and a little lake there. They have an ambulance waiting to take the body away once you're done with it."

"Got it," Jordan said. "You can tell them we're on our way. Constable Wyatt out." He returned the handset to the cradle. For a long moment he said nothing, but as they neared the turn-off heading out of the park, he turned to Sadie. "You think maybe this is a murder?"

Sadie *did* think it might be. It was fall, after all. No one was in town. And a body shouldn't just show up in a bog outside the buffalo paddocks, not by accident anyhow. She didn't say that. Instead, she shook her head.

"Let's keep the guesswork out of it and do our job. Get the evidence. Figure it out from there."

With the highway in view, the light bleeding from the sky behind them, she flicked on the sirens and drove into the gathering darkness.

* * *

Lou hung up the phone and grinned.

"Coming home," she whispered.

She'd thought it—*hoped it!*—a thousand times since he'd been told there was a *"hold up with the permanent residency application."* It was happening now. Thursday was only a few days away.

Her mind rushed through the things that needed to be done. The garage's business was down to a trickle. Today, Vasur Kulkarni had brought in his second-hand delivery truck to have the muffler replaced, but she could put that off. Lou's Garage had no other pressing repairs, and oil changes were easy enough to squeeze in during the evening hours. An unexpected day off would be fun! Mila and Brendan could cover the front of Lou's Garage for her. *Rich's flight was coming in on Thursday morning,* Lou thought as she crossed the kitchen. There would be lots of time to swing over to the Registry and pick up a marriage license.

Lou giggled, the joyous sound contained in the small kitchen. *Married.* Such a small word, and one she hadn't expected to give her such happiness, not after years of living alone. Just a few more days and they'd be together again. Reaching the door, Lou slid off her jacket and hung it on the hook. *If she got up by six,* Lou thought, *she could leave Waterton at seven. She'd be able to be on the outskirts of Lethbridge by—*

Through the door's narrow window, a silhouette caught her gaze.

The hair rose on the back of her neck. In the darkness stood a man. He was at the end of her driveway less than fifty feet from her door.

Watching.

CHAPTER TWO

Lou's heartbeat surged. With the streetlight behind the man, she couldn't see his face... but she could *feel* him. A sliver of ice ran the length of her spine as a realization hit: The lights in the kitchen meant he almost certainly *could* see her.

Hands shaking, she turned the lock, bolting the door. She stepped sideways—her eyes tracking him—and fumbled blindly along the wall until she found the light panel. She flipped the switch. The room fell into velvety blackness and Lou bolted to the window above the sink.

She peeked out. From this angle, the man was closer, but with the screen of trees she could see fewer details. He hadn't moved. His imagined gaze still rested on the door where she'd entered, his body postured toward the house, stance wide. Lou rubbed sweaty hands on the sides of her jeans. Had he been waiting there when she came inside? She didn't know.

She needed to call the police.

Lou was leery to leave the window, but there was only one phone in the house. Terrified, she crept to the black rotary in the hallway and dialed. She stretched out the cord to tiptoe back to the window as it began to ring.

The man's silhouette remained in place.

"Waterton police station. How may I direct your call?" a woman's cheerful voice said.

"Liz, hi. It's Louise Newman, over on Evergreen Avenue. I think I've got a prowler."

"A prowler." The woman's tone changed abruptly. "Inside or outside of your house?"

"Outside. He's watching the house, as far as I can tell, but he hasn't moved in about five minutes. I don't think he realizes I know he's there."

"I'll send someone over right away. Just stay on the line while I contact Sadie and Jordan." There was a pause and Lou heard Liz talking to someone. There was a mumbled answer, then: *"WHERE outside the park?!"* Another, muffled reply. Lou leaned toward the window. In the darkness a small red eye winked as a cigarette rose like a firefly to the man's mouth. He breathed in and the ember flared. Lou leaned closer, trying to catch something—*anything!*— and the top of the phone's receiver banged the window.

The man jerked at the sound, his gaze swiveling toward the panel of glass behind which Lou stood, phone in hand, heart beating its way through the cage of her chest. Before she could move, the man turned and jogged away in the direction of the downtown. In a heartbeat, he was gone.

"Lou? You still there, honey?" Liz's exasperated voice returned.

"Still here," she said, "but I should tell you—"

"Sadie and Jordan are out at a crime scene right now. I tried their radio, but they're not answering. I'm going to call Constable Hycha for you. Oscar's off-shift, but he should be able to get there in—"

"It's okay, Liz. Forget about it. I'll just swing by tomorrow and make the report. The guy's gone."

"But you said he was outside your—"

"He was. I saw him take off. I don't know what he was doing here, but he's gone now."

"Lou, it's really no trouble for Oscar to swing by," Liz said. "He won't mind."

"I know he won't, but I will."

She sighed. With the figure gone, her anxiety faded like smoke. Lou had been on edge all week.

It could have been someone stopping for a cigarette, she thought. Rich being away was getting on her nerves.

"There's nothing to see," Lou said. "Honestly."

"Well… if you're sure."

"I am."

"You come by tomorrow and write up the report. Okay?"

"Got it," Lou said.

"And I'll mention it to Sadie and Jordan once they're done with the crime scene. They could swing by your house then."

"Sure. But honestly, it's fine, Liz. I'm good."

"Well, call if anything changes," Liz said. "Oscar's just a phone call away. You know that, right?"

"I do. And thanks."

"Not a problem. G'night, Lou."

"'Night, Liz."

For the second time that night, Lou hung up the phone and went to the door. She double-checked the lock. She checked the windows and doors in the rest of the house, then flicked on the outdoor porch light before heading upstairs. When she glanced out the window just before she crawled into bed, the street was empty.

* * *

The sky had darkened to slate gray by the time Constable Black Plume and Constable Wyatt reached the parking area next to the

Buffalo Paddocks. Sadie parked their vehicle in front of a line of sandstone slabs, pocketed her keys and climbed out. The rocks were the park's way of preventing people from driving onto parkland and while Sadie appreciated the environmental approach, she was also annoyed that they couldn't drive the rest of the way.

There was a body to deal with.

Constable Ben Grayden from the Pincher Creek police service waited at the far end of the line of vehicles. He looked up as Sadie stepped from the car. He was auburn haired, his nose freckled and peeling, and he had the same tall, raw-boned physique of the ranchers who lived in the area.

He strode to Sadie's side and stopped, grinning. "Constable Black Plume?"

She nodded. "That's me."

"Thanks for coming out. I know it's not ideal timing," he said, waving at the darkening sky, "but I didn't want to waste any time. Body's got to be moved before the animals get to it."

"Appreciate you calling us," she said, then glanced to where Jordan was pulling the camera and evidence kit from the back of the police vehicle. "Hey, Jordan. While you're back there, can you grab a couple spare pairs of gloves?"

"You got it, Sadie."

She turned back to Constable Grayden. Behind him, an ambulance waited alongside a police cruiser labeled "Pincher Creek Police."

"I'm Ben, by the way." The officer offered his hand and Sadie shook it. His fingers were warm despite the chill, his grip strong but not crushing. "I was friends with Jim Gladstone back when we were in school," he added.

Jim's name was a kick in the gut. Sadie jerked her hand back, smile disappearing. "Right."

"You used to work with Jim, right?"

Sadie gritted her teeth and nodded.

Ben rocked on his heels. "I was sorry to hear about—"

"So where's this body at anyhow?" she interrupted. "I want to get started."

"Over there at the edge of the foothills." Ben pointed. "Where the slope starts to rise."

"That'd be Indian Springs," Jordan said. Sadie nodded as he came forward, the camera bouncing on his chest, both arms full of equipment. "It's a little lake on the edge of the park. Some drought years it dries up entirely."

"Interesting." Sadie took the evidence kit and turned to Ben. "You ready to go, Constable Grayden?"

"Ben, please."

She stared at him for a second. "Okay, Ben," she said. "You ready?"

"You bet. I'll tell the EMTs to grab their gear and follow us. They can take the body into Lethbridge for an autopsy once you're done."

"Thanks." Sadie scanned the horizon. The mountains were black shapes against the dulled silver of the sky. Night was falling. Even with the lights they carried, they'd soon be wandering around in the dark. "Better get moving," she said. "Want to get as much of the scene tagged as we can before we lose the light."

They walked for a few minutes in silence before Sadie said: "We'll need to mark off the entire area, Jordan. Block off the whole lake from hikers."

"Oh, my team already secured the perimeter," Ben said.

Sadie frowned. "You did *what*?"

"Wanted to secure it in case anyone else saw our lights and came to snoop around, but… I figured you'd want to do your *own* assessment too."

"It's *our* jurisdiction," she said. "Something gets missed, it's *my ass* on the line. Not yours."

"Uh… yeah." Ben laughed nervously, then fell silent.

Jordan, two steps behind them, said nothing.

"The light's almost gone. We can discuss this later," she grumbled and then sped up again.

On they walked; Sadie, Ben, and then Jordan. A few steps behind, the EMTs followed, a stretcher and body bag in hand. An uneasy silence pressed down on the small group, the hush of the night air and darkness pushing aside any conversation.

Twenty minutes in and Sadie's back was slick with sweat, her neck itchy. The small group was surrounded by flying, biting insects, and she swatted them as she trudged through the overgrown grass. Mosquitoes whined in her ear. *Ben should have contacted them the minute he got the call about the body,* she thought. She didn't want to be out there, running around in the dark. And then, almost as quickly, Sadie thought of Jim, her one-time partner. Even now, years after his death, he popped to mind on a daily basis. She knew what he'd say in this situation: *Relax, Sadie. You're just worried because it's a body.*

And she was.

Probably nothing to it, Jim would tell her if he was here. *Some outback hiker who got lost and died of exposure.*

That was entirely possible. It had happened in Waterton before. But another, less confident voice niggled at the back of her mind. The voice of doubt. *What if that wasn't what happened? What if this wasn't an accident?* Then she and Jordan—a kid just three years out of the academy—had a murder to investigate and she'd done too many of those in the last few years.

Sadie wiped a line of sweat from her brow as a small lake—a pond, really—finally came into view.

"How'd the hunters find the body?" she panted. "They would have had to hike past the park boundary even to *see* her out here. If they were hunting, they *shouldn't* have been inside the park."

"They say they saw the body through their rifle sights," Ben said.

"And you believe them?"

"They're a couple of kids from Hill Spring," he said. "Never been in any trouble before. Never stepped out of line."

"You interviewed them both?" she asked.

"I did."

"Anything seem strange? Anything that didn't add up?"

Ben frowned. "Nothing. They were out together when they saw the body through the scopes. They had their hunting licenses, and they were out following a herd of deer." Ben shrugged. "Good kids. Respectful. They'd even asked permission to cross the Durnerin ranch to reach the forest reserve."

Sadie pursed her lips. "So you believe them?"

"I've no reason *not* to believe them. Like I said, good kids."

Sadie shook her head. She knew too well how the people who hid in plain sight were the most dangerous. "Not sure I have your confidence," she said. "Still seems pretty suspicious to me."

"At least they called in the body," Jordan said. "If they hadn't, well…"

He left the thought hanging like a thread between the three of them. Sadie's gaze flicked back to the flat shimmer of the pond. It was hidden in the elbow of the mountains on the park's east side, completely separate from any roads. Barring this overgrown trail, there was no access. No way to even get here.

"If those hunters hadn't called," Sadie said. "No one would have found the body until spring."

"Except the bears," Ben said. "We're deep in grizzly territory here. Ranchers are riled up this time of year, 'cause the bears are taking their cattle. But they'll feed on anything they can find, dead or alive. If those hunters hadn't called, well, I doubt there'd be anything to find come spring."

"Right." Her feet slowed as they neared the boggy edge of the lake. The scent of water-logged carrion rose in a wave. Sadie swallowed hard and began to breathe through her mouth. Behind her, she heard Jordan gag.

Ben cleared his throat. "C'mon," he said. "The guys and I made note of a few things, but, uh…" He ducked his chin. "Like you said, Constable Black Plume, you'll want to check it yourself."

"Thanks." She flicked her braids back behind her shoulders. "So Jordan, you want to document the scene or tag?"

"I, uh…" His gaze moved skittishly to the body and then away again. Even in the half-darkness, he looked green. "I'll handle the camera, if that's okay with you."

"Fine with me," Sadie said. "Let's start with the body then. We can check the trees tomorrow when its light, but we should get the body out of here before anything else finds it."

"Right." Jordan lifted the camera. "You tell me what to take."

Sadie nodded. She walked slowly to the body, forcing her mind into that white space she went to when she needed to deal with a gruesome crime scene. Like the day that Jim had been killed and she and Jordan had responded. Her mind took in the pond and the dead girl with a lack of emotion, her clarity hatched out of the horror she analyzed.

Look at the pieces, she remembered Jim telling her the first time they'd analyzed a crime scene. *Don't let yourself look at it all. Just go bit by bit. Look—really look!—at what you already have rather than searching for something else.*

She reached the edge of the pond where the body lay. The mud was churned with footprints, but they'd been worn down to pockets of undefined mud by the rain of the last days. *This isn't an accident.* Seeing a single line of prints—a police officer's shoes, if she had to guess—her lip curled. She glanced back over her shoulder. "You guys look for any footprints before you walked up?"

"We did." Constable Grayden nodded. "Took photos too," he said. "I'll get them to you." He stepped up to her. "These two sets here," he said, pointing down at the clean-edged prints in the mud. "Those ones are us. The rest are left over from whoever brought her here."

Sadie's gaze drifted to the others. They were lumpy and indistinct, blurred away by the passage of time. She swore under her breath. "I was hoping we'd have something a bit clearer."

"I figure the girl's been here a few days at least," Ben said. "Might be closer to a week."

"The rain last week must have blurred the prints."

"Uh-huh." Ben took a step closer to the body. "It's shit like this that makes me hate my job."

It was an unexpected comment—something *Jim* might've said— and the words unsettled Sadie. She forced a tight smile.

"Well, someone's got to do it. Right?"

"Guess so. Just wish…" He sighed. "People can do some pretty fucked up stuff."

"Yeah. They can."

For a split-second, Sadie was standing in Susan's kitchen, stinking of burned eggs and blood, as she stared down at Jim's body. The image seared. She shook her head to dislodge it.

"Night's falling," she said. "I better get on with this." Sadie peeked over her shoulder. "Jordan, photograph the girl just as she was found. Then I'll check for evidence."

"Got it," he said, and the snap-flash of the camera began.

Sadie slid on a pair of latex gloves and shook out an evidence bag. She waited until Jordan had taken photographs from all sides before she moved toward the body.

"I'll get you some light, Constable Black Plume," Ben said.

"Thanks." She looked up. "And it's Sadie."

He jogged away from her, returning a few minutes later with a large police light. It shone a wide beam over the corpse, lighting the twilight scene with the intensity of a movie set.

"I appreciate that," Sadie said as she leaned in. The smell of rot rose to her nostrils and she swallowed bile.

"Tell me if you need it pointed somewhere else," Ben said.

"That's fine."

The dead girl was small-framed and wore a pair of black jeans, Calvin Klein label, a pair of short mid-heeled boots, the name Leboutin embossed on the red-soled undersides, and a black cashmere sweater over a pale pink camisole. She lay on her side, half in and half out of the water, a long swath of dark hair covering a pale face. Even with autumn weather, the body was swollen and bloated. Waves of noxious miasma rose to Sadie's nose as she checked the girl, her gloved hands prodding her in search of clues. Sadie tipped the body sideways and a sickening gurgle rose from the girl's throat. Sadie fought the urge to vomit.

Stay focused. See the crime. See the details. Nothing else.

The white room in her mind reappeared.

The body had already started to rot. The girl's limbs were loose, rigor mortis gone. It had been more than eighteen hours but otherwise it was hard to tell how long she'd been there. Sadie checked the front pockets but there was no wallet, no I.D. The young woman wasn't dressed like a hiker, which dimmed the possibility of a hiker gone missing. Her boots, though low-heeled, were not hiking gear. Her clothing was all neatly zipped, and her camisole still tucked into the waist of her jeans, which suggested that she hadn't been raped. Rapist-murderers, Sadie knew, were not known for tidying the body afterwards. In fact, this girl looked like she had just stepped off a runway. Her clothes were too nice for the area where she'd been found. Her hair—though matted—was free of debris.

Sadie sat back on her heels, frowning. *The girl wasn't running through the woods when she died,* she thought. *She was brought here.*

Turning back to the body, Sadie lifted her gaze to the young woman's face, finding herself staring into a pair of milky-blue eyes, unsettlingly open. The skin on the corpse's forehead was flayed, her temple crushed on the side nearest the ground, skull visible.

Blunt force trauma. Sadie's stomach roiled.

"Jordan," she called. "Take a couple photos of her face."

"You got it."

The camera flashed and Sadie forced her rioting thoughts back under a tight layer of control. *This wasn't an accident. This was murder!*

"Think I've got it, Sadie," Jordan said. "Anything else?"

"Take a look through the trees. We'll come back tomorrow and do a detailed search, but I want to document it all, in case the wind picks up."

"I'll forward you the photos our guys took." Ben spoke and the light wobbled. "We didn't move anything."

"Thanks," Sadie said. "The photos would be great."

For a few more minutes she checked for clues around the body. She took samples of the soil and bagged stray fibers. Some seemed to be brownish-gold hairs from an animal, though Sadie wasn't sure what kind. And with night falling, it was difficult even to be sure of the colour. A scraggly bush near the young woman's feet had several long strands of blonde hair. Sadie bagged those too. Finished with her inspection, she looked up to find Jordan circling the area around the small lake, Ben waited, floodlight in place, watching her work. A thousand dancing insects swirled in the beam of light, but he didn't move.

"I've got what I need," Sadie said, squinting up at him. "We should bag the body, get it sent to Lethbridge."

Ben nodded and the light bounced again. "Andy! Jess! We're ready to go over here."

A few minutes later and the girl was wrapped in a body bag, the stretcher, with its obscene white bulk, bouncing along the trail as the EMTs carried it toward the waiting ambulance. Indian Springs lay silent and still. No ripples marred its surface, only the muddied footprints and body-sized imprint near the edge of the pond even hinted that there'd been anything amiss at all. Sadie leaned down to gather her evidence bags. In the near-darkness, the reflection of the surface was gone. And in that moment, she saw it.

Sadie gasped.

Jordan turned. "What is it?"

"There's hoof prints in the water," she said. "Not just any hoofed animal. These are from horse shoes."

She felt rather than saw Ben walk to her side. "Where?" he said grimly.

"Get down low," Sadie said, and both Ben and Jordan crouched next to her. She pointed out into the water. "See that? You can't see them if it's bright outside, but now you can."

She grinned. There, beneath the surface, were several clear hoof marks. The ones by the shore—the ones that she'd *assumed* to be human footprints, worn by the elements—could have been hooves too.

Ben whistled. "Well, I'll be damned."

"I'll take a few long-exposures," Jordan said, his voice rising in excitement. "When we're out tomorrow, I'll bring in a reflector, see if I can block the sunshine so I can take them in daylight too."

"Perfect," Sadie said.

While Jordan set up the shots, she stood slowly and stretched her back, her mind rushing in excitement. They might not know the name of their victim. They might not know how she died, but they knew *how* she got there. And that was the start.

Her smile wobbled. Jim would have been proud.

* * *

Sadie drove back to Waterton in silence, the only hint of the tumultuous emotions under her calm exterior a single line that incised the space between her brows. The last of twilight's haze had bled away, black night in its place.

"It just doesn't make sense," Jordan said.

"Hmmm?" Sadie blinked, resurfacing from her thoughts. "What's that?"

"Our perp. It just doesn't make sense to me. I mean, why would he drop the girl's body way out there?"

Sadie chewed her lip. While she'd hoped the body had been a simple case of someone wandering off and dying—tragic but explainable—the wounds were *anything* but accidental. They had another murder to deal with, and for Jordan Wyatt, this would be his first homicide.

"I… I don't know yet," she answered truthfully. "I suspect it's because it's out of the way."

"But she was by a lake. I mean… why not leave her in the woods or something?"

"That's a good point. But I'm not the killer. I don't *know* what he or she was thinking."

Jordan's brows rose. "You think it might be a woman?"

Sadie shrugged. "Could be." Through the windshield, yellow light bounced over the road's graveled surface, catching in the dusty haze left by the ambulance. On one side, the wire fence of the Buffalo Paddock blocked the police cruiser from dark shapes that waited, ghost-like, on the prairie. "I just don't have enough info to make that part of my picture yet."

"Your picture?"

Sadie smiled sadly. She remembered, years earlier, Jim Flagstone trying to describe his mental process for solving a case. Now *she* was in the role of lead investigator, Jordan the wet-behind-the-ears rookie. What kind of advice did she need to share? How could she teach him in real time?

"Yeah, my picture," she said. "It's a mental thing I do for crimes."

The crossroad to the highway neared and Sadie slowed the car, heading south toward the town of Waterton.

"How's the picture thing work?" he asked.

"Start big. Focus on the details, then build the missing parts of the picture."

"Alright," Jordan said. "So we wait for the autopsy results and start investigating the crime scene more carefully tomorrow."

"I don't think Indian Springs was the kill site," Sadie said. "I think it's the secondary. That's my gut talking, but… I'm going to check it all tomorrow."

"Of course."

"You can't assume someone's *not* guilty. You've got to keep yourself open to the idea that *anyone* could have done it. And just go where the clues lead."

"Huh. That's cool."

"Thanks."

Jordan cleared his throat. "I, uh… appreciate you telling me this. I do. I don't want to mess up."

Sadie laughed tiredly. "You're doing fine, Jordan. And you'll come up with your own way of figuring things out as we go along. That picture approach works for me. Doesn't mean it'll work for you."

"What do you mean?"

"I mean, you have to learn by doing it. Just try…" She frowned as Jim's face came to mind. "Just try not to *assume* that you know who's guilty or not."

"But isn't that what we do? Figure it out? Find the clues."

"Yeah, but you have to separate yourself and your bias from the situation. You have to take your emotion out."

"Okay…?"

"Look. All I'm saying is that people do things for their own reasons. You go into a situation expecting someone to act one way—the way *you* would act in that situation—then you're already in trouble. People are unpredictable. They've got their own motives for what they do. If you're not careful, they can turn on you in an instant."

She turned off the highway and headed back into the embrace of the mountains. Vaulting peaks rose on each side, the lake an oily mirror. They were almost at the townsite when Jordan spoke again. His voice was low, hesitant.

"That's what Jim did, isn't it?"

Sadie flinched and the car shimmied. She tightened her grip.

"What do you mean?"

"When Susan killed Jim, he was standing there in her house, in her kitchen. He figured she was safe and then... she wasn't."

"Yeah," Sadie said. "That's about it."

Neither spoke for the rest of the ride.

CHAPTER THREE

The dream started with a memory. Not today, or yesterday, not even this life…

Lou stood in a crowded street that stank of unwashed bodies. "Out of the way!" a man shouted. "Or I'll send your slutty ass up there with the rest of 'em!"

"I apologize, citoyen," Lou said, ducking her head. "So very sorry."

The man spat on her rather than answer, but Lou dared not raise her eyes. It would be death to draw attention to herself and she needed to find Rich.

There was a blare of trumpet and Lou's heart began to pound, her fear growing. Someone in the crowd began to sing. Movement caught her eyes and she forced herself to look. A stone's throw away, a group of men and women walked onto a platform decorated with tri-colour ribbons. Some came quietly, others sobbed.

Lou's eyes widened in terror. The wood beneath the prisoners' feet was stained black with blood—

Lou screamed herself awake, heart pounding. The bedroom returned with a snap. The sharp copper of spilled blood had been replaced by the cool scent of trees and water wafting in the second-floor window. She was in bed, alone. Rich safe in New York.

She rolled over and squinted at the clock. *1:11 a.m.*

It was hours before dawn, far too early to get up, but Lou knew she wouldn't sleep again tonight. The urge to hold Rich, to talk to him face to face rose again, and she took a slow breath, blowing it out. Even on New York time, it was too late to call. Lou knew she'd just worry him. For a few more minutes she lay still, trying to calm her mind. The wind whistled past the window and the curtains swirled. In the dream, she'd been looking for Rich. Lou frowned. *That MEANS something.* Another gust pushed impatiently past the curtains.

Shivering, Lou swung her legs out of bed and walked to the window. She put her hand on the pull, then froze.

A figure stood at the end of her driveway. He held a gun in his hand.

* * *

Jordan was just finishing up the preliminary report, Sadie at her computer working through a backlog of emails regarding "Jane Does" when the call came in. Phone in hand, Liz popped her head into the office.

"Emergency call. Lou Newman says that guy she saw earlier tonight is outside her house again."

Jordan looked up. "Earlier tonight?"

"I sent Oscar by when she called. He patrolled the block for half an hour, but didn't see anything," Liz said. "Lou thinks it's the same guy. Says he has a handgun."

"Damnit!" Sadie snapped. "Let's move."

She surged into action so quickly Jordan almost dropped the papers he was holding. A few minutes ago, they'd been counting the minutes to 1:30 a.m. when they officially got off shift, now his heart was pumping. While Liz relayed details, Sadie grabbed her gun, and holstered it. Her jacket was next. Jordan scrambled to follow. Tonight had already been stressful. It was about to get worse.

Sadie had her jacket half-on and she tugged at the sleeve as she sprinted out the door to the police cruiser. Jordan slid into the passenger seat as the car's engine flared to life.

"You think this is serious?" he said.

Sadie squealed the tires as she pulled away from the stonework police station. "That body came from somewhere, didn't it?"

"Shit. Yeah, it did."

"We need to be ready." Her eyes flicked to him. "And, uh… you should buckle up."

With a grimace, Jordan pulled the belt across his hips. "Right. Sorry."

The police cruiser careened down silent streets, past the movie theatre and the scorched lot where the Whitewater Lodge had once stood, past the school and down Evergreen Avenue toward Lou's cabin: Whispering Aspens. Halfway down the first street after the turn off, a herd of big horn sheep, spooked by something in the trees on the east side of the road, bolted in front of them. Sadie slammed on the brakes, sending Jordan lurching against the seatbelt. The animals moved slowly away from them.

"Move it!" she barked.

Fifteen endless seconds later the herd was off the road and into the trees. Sadie *still* hadn't turned on the siren, nor the lights. She hadn't honked. Jordan knew she was trying to catch the guy, unawares. That worried him.

As the last sheep moved away, she hit the gas and the engine roared, pushing Jordan back against the seat. They sped past dark-windowed cabins and empty yards. Lou's house came into view and with that, Sadie hit the lights, but not the sirens. The darkness flashed to lurid, pulsing life.

Sadie brought the cruiser to a stop at the end of the empty driveway. "You take this side of the house," she said. "I'll take the other."

"Got it." Jordan pulled out his handgun. "Meet you round the back."

She nodded as she disappeared around the side of the house.

Heart pounding, Jordan did a slow sweep of the driveway and the back entrance which led to the kitchen. Behind him, the lights flashed red and blue, making the leaves seem to jump and dance. He crossed the driveway. The bushes were thinner than they'd been in the summer, but there was plenty of foliage to obscure anything hidden in the thickets.

Red... blue... red... blue...

Jordan squinted into the darkness. There was *something* in the shadows. But what? From his position, it was a large shape in the thicket of trees. Jordan took two more steps. It certainly didn't *look* like a person, but you could never tell. It was better to be safe than sorry. He looked down at his belt, unlatching the Mag flashlight. He looked up again.

The shape was gone.

With sweaty hands, he shone the light across the trees that filled in the hollow between the two cabins, pausing on the spot where *something* had stood a moment earlier. He moved the flashlight back the other direction, catching a blur of black.

"STOP!" Jordan bellowed, the volume of his own voice surprising him. "This is the POLICE! Freeze!"

The shadow bolted behind the neighbouring house as Jordan made chase.

"POLICE!" he roared. "Put your hands up!"

The figure disappeared. Jordan sprinted after him, flashlight bouncing. He heard the police car's engine roar and the sirens shriek to life. Sadie was coming. The person ahead of him had a good head-start, but Jordan was wiry and pulsing with adrenaline.

"STOP!" he bellowed.

The prowler wove between two houses, heading back toward Evergreen Avenue. Jordan careened around the corner only to run headlong into something large and furry. The bighorn sheep were on the move again. Startled, they milled around him, slamming into his side, and nearly knocking the gun from his hand. The flashlight tumbled to his feet.

"Move!" he shouted. "MOVE!"

Confused, the sheep struggled to escape, but there were at least fifteen in the area between the buildings and when one moved, another took its place.

"Get out of the WAY!"

The animals finally scattered, but when Jordan looked up, the trees were empty.

"Fuck!"

He did a sweep of the area behind the houses, then came around the other side. The street was empty, the prowler gone. Bighorn sheep moved through the shadows, finding new spots to bed down for the night.

"Goddamnit!" Jordan snapped.

"You okay, Jordan?" a voice called.

He jerked in surprise. Sadie had parked the car on the street and was coming into the darkness, her gun held out in front of her.

"I'm fine," he said. "The asshole got away though." He flicked the safety back onto his pistol and slid it back into his holster. "Stupid goddamned sheep. Wanted to SHOOT them for blocking my way."

Sadie giggled. The sound was so *unlike* the woman he knew that he stared at her.

"What's so funny?" Jordan frowned. "I literally got t-boned by a ram."

Her laughter grew.

"I'd have the guy now if it wasn't for the stupid sheep—" He made an angry sound. "And I've got to put *that* in my report."

Sadie was laughing so hard her breath came in pants.

"Seriously *what*?!" Jordan snapped.

"I—I'm sorry," she said through a bout of giggles. "It sounds funny."

"Interference by sheep does *not* look good on a report."

"Oh, God." Sadie covered her mouth, but laughter pushed past her lips.

Suddenly Jordan found himself smiling.

"Okay, so it sounds a *little* funny." He shook his head. "But I tried."

Sadie slapped him on the shoulder. "It's fine. You did good, kid. Real good." Her words unsettled him in their familiarity. This was the kind of thing Jim used to say. "Now let's head back," she said. "We should check with Lou, get her report."

"You got it."

And this time, when he got into the cruiser beside her, Jordan remembered to do up his seatbelt.

* * *

It was barely dawn when Lou tried to call Rich. With the unnerving dream and then the prowler who Sadie and Jordan had assured her "wouldn't likely return," Lou needed to hear Rich's voice, to assure herself he was okay. He had a two-hour head-start on the day by being in New York, so she figured it was safe to call him when the sun broke over the mountains. Today, however, he didn't answer.

Anxious, Louise took a shower and dressed, then put on coffee. She picked up the phone and dialed again. She just wanted to hear his voice, to make sure everything was okay, but Rich's phone rang and rang. She hung up the moment it went to message.

Lou puttered around the house, her eyes on the clock. She cooked eggs and toast, ate, then did the breakfast dishes, and finally made herself a thermos of coffee so strong there was a layer of grounds on the bottom. She sent a silent plea out to the universe as she picked up the black rotary phone and dialed a third time.

No answer.

Frustrated, Lou locked up and headed to work. Tuesday was one of Mila's days off, but Brendan had already arrived, and the neon "open" sign was shining. The teen looked up from stocking shelves as she came through the front door.

"Good morning, Lou. You're in early."

"Morning," she said through a yawn.

"You okay?"

"Yeah. Doing fine."

He frowned. "You sure?"

"Yeah. Why?"

Brendan shrugged. "You just look a little sick. Or… worried maybe."

"Not sick. Just tired." She shook her head. "I was up half the night."

"Oh?"

"Someone was messing around in my yard last night." She shook her head. "Called the police, but they didn't find the guy."

"Shit. Think it was someone passing through town?"

Tourists were the lifeblood of Waterton, and everyone appreciated them for the money they brought. But transients were another truth of the small community, people looking for a place to lay low.

"Someone making trouble?" Brendan wondered. "Someone… *dangerous*?"

Lou smiled. At nineteen, Brendan was searching for more adventure than a tiny town in the Rockies could provide.

"I doubt it," she said. "More likely just someone looking to see if there was anything they could steal." She gave a weary laugh. "My beater's not worth the trouble."

Brendan grinned. "Hey, now. I called dibs on that truck when you sell it."

"Your dad would never let me hear the end of it. It's not worth the trouble. You'd have to repair it once a week."

"Which I'm learning from you."

"Yes, but—"

"Your truck's vintage, Lou. Old vehicle like that? It's got good bones."

"It does," she laughed. "But it's not for sale… At least not for now."

"But when you *do* sell…"

"You'll be the first person I call."

"Like *soon*?"

Lou grinned. "I don't—"

"Like in the next year? The next two years?"

Lou laughed. "I haven't decided, Brendan. I'm in no rush."

"But I am."

"I can tell." Lou took two steps toward the newly-replaced door to the shop, then turned back around. "You know, this reminds me of a story I read once. There was a young man who was studying martial arts. Every day he would practice. Hours and hours, he would hone his craft under the supervision of his teacher." Lou winked. "His very *wise* teacher, I might add."

Brendan laughed.

"Over time," Lou said, "the young man grew frustrated. He *wanted* to understand, but every day it seemed like there was something new to learn." She paused, eyes twinkling.

"So what did he do?" Brendan said.

"He went to his teacher and asked: 'How long will it take me to master martial arts?' The teacher said: 'Ten years.' And the young man was *not* happy with that answer."

"Ten years is a long time."

"The young man asked: 'What if I try very hard?' And to that, his teacher said: 'If you try very, very hard… you'll master it in twenty years.'"

Brendan's face rippled in confusion. "But… what does that even mean?"

Lou laughed. "Think on it, Brendan. You'll get it." She stepped through the doorway to the shop, grinning. "Just don't think *too* hard. Okay?"

"Got it." He laughed and picked up two more cans, adding them to the row on the shelf. "You need any help in the back today?"

"Not right now, thanks."

Lou closed the door behind her, breathing in the scents of engine oil, gasoline, and dirt, the unique combination that was 'home' every bit as the scent of Waterton. She let out a slow breath, her smile bleeding from her face. The story she'd told had been for her. As anxious as she was, she needed to be patient for Rich's return. Rushing would only make it worse.

* * *

Constables Black Plume and Wyatt were back out at Indian Springs by mid-afternoon.

It had been 24 hours since the body had been called in, but with no I.D. and no missing person, they were at a dead end. The autopsy would need to establish more than just the cause of death. If the girl had any identifying marks, tattoos or birthmarks, they might help identify her, but the coroner's report wasn't back yet. They photographed the scene a second time under the glare of midday. There were no new clues, other than a few more of the blonde hairs which looked far less human and far more equine in the light of day. The hoof prints were nearly gone, and Sadie was glad they'd photographed them the night before.

Finished, they drove back to Waterton. Sadie hoped that her carefully-worded request to the coroner's office had been heeded. Delays meant missing time. Missing time meant difficulty solving a case.

As Sadie and Jordan came through the door of the police station, Liz surged to her feet. "Your results are here!"

"Already?" Sadie said.

"Uh-huh. They just faxed them in."

"Well, thank God for small miracles." Sadie took the printed pages from Liz's outstretched hand and walked into the office. "Thanks, Liz."

"No worries."

Sadie fumbled for the light switch, her eyes caught on the details: *Caucasian woman, 5'6," 128 lbs., blue eyes, brown hair. Aged 25 to 35. Blood type: B positive. No identifying marks or tattoos.* Sadie swore under her breath. *Fingerprints and teeth impressions have been uploaded to the Missing Persons Registry.* Her eyes skimmed further into the report: *Blunt force trauma to right temporal lobe resulting in death. Massive sub-cranial bleeding. Likely did not regain consciousness after the blow....*

"What's the report say?" Jordan asked.

"Crushed skull killed her."

"Any other signs of trauma?"

"Hold on…" Sadie scanned through the description, forcing the image of the girl's body away and replacing it with cold hard words. She found her answer in the second-from-last paragraph: *Neck is fractured between C6 and C7 though spinal cord was not severed. No sign of sexual assault. No defensive wounds or skin or fibers under the nail beds.* Sadie looked up. "Not raped. Looks to be a clean kill. One blow to the head, neck broken, and immediate death." She frowned. "No identifying marks either though."

"So we've got a Jane Doe."

"For now."

Sadie passed the faxed autopsy results to Jordan and walked up to the cork billboard. She lifted the printed photograph of the crime scene, the body in the center of the frame, darkness on either side. *Jane Doe.* She pushed pins into the corners and stepped back. One picture. A simple cause of death. It felt like so impossibly little to go on.

Who are you? she wondered. *And why were you in Waterton?*

* * *

Seven hours under the hood of a car hadn't removed the unsettled feeling Lou had carried in her chest since the nightmare. All day she'd been certain that *something* was coming. She just wasn't sure what. But one thing was clear: It involved Rich. By the time 4:00 p.m. rolled around, she was mentally and physically exhausted. Brendan was sweeping the floor when Lou walked to the front door. She closed and locked it, then put up the "closed" sign.

Brendan turned in surprise. "You're not staying open until five?"

This was Lou's usual pattern in the winter months, but tonight that extra hour of work felt impossible to conquer.

"Not today," she said. "You head off once you've cashed out." She smiled tiredly. "Just leave the time sheet as it is. My exhaustion's not your issue."

"You sure?"

"Yeah, I'm—" Her words were overtaken with a wide yawn that left her blinking tears from her eyes. "I'm wiped. Head home, Brendan." She smiled. "Seriously."

"Alright then." He nodded and began to cash out the till as Lou finished the last few end-of-day items. Finished, Brendan grabbed his coat and headed for the door. "Feel better, Lou. I'll see you tomorrow."

"G'night."

Less than ten minutes after she closed the garage, she was home again. Yawning, she headed to the phone. The dream of the guillotine was a warning. Of what, Lou had no idea, but she *needed* to talk to Rich. She waited as the last number lazily clicked through the rotary dial.

"C'mon, Rich," she whispered. "Answer this time."

It rang and rang before going to message.

"You've reached Rich Evans. I can't answer the phone right now, but if you leave your name and number, I'll get back to you as soon as possible."

Lou's shaking fingers tightened around the handset as the tone beeped down its countdown, then squealed in her ear.

"Hi, Rich? It's me, Lou. I…" She cleared her throat. "There's nothing wrong. I mean, *there is,* but—" She laughed. In her tiredness, the words wouldn't come out right. "I just really need to talk to you, so if you could call me back, that'd be great."

She hung the phone back up and stared at it. Where *was* he? That twinging fear that she'd been fighting all day surged, lodging in the centre of her chest, but her physical exhaustion was its equal. Lou stumbled to the cupboard and pulled out a water-scoured glass. Outside, the afternoon sun was unnaturally bright. Lou turned to the fridge, pouring herself a glass of milk to drink rather than eating supper, then headed upstairs with the unsteady gait of a zombie. She knew she *should* try to stay awake until at least seven, but keeping her eyelids open was torture. She dropped her jeans and shirt next to the bed and crawled under the covers.

Sleep came over her in a crashing wave, dragging her to the bottom of exhaustion. Images flashed in her mind: *Talking to Brendan in the shop... changing the oil in Margaret's car... Fixing the air filters on Audrika's van... Rich, standing on the New York street, phone in hand... Buildings burning... Bodies falling from the sky... Crowds surging around a raised dais... Heads in a basket... Pigs eating clotted blood... Rich standing beneath the blade... The executioner reaching out—*

Lou woke with a start.

She lay in her darkened bedroom, but in her sleep-drugged state, Lou had no idea what time it was. Bits of dreams caught and tangled her thoughts, pulling at her as she struggled to awaken. There'd been something she was supposed to warn Rich about. Her hand slid over to find his side of the bed empty, cold.

Rich is in New York. He's getting the resident application finished so he can come home.

Lou turned her head and glanced at the clock. *9:02 p.m.* She rolled back and closed her eyes. *That's right,* she thought. *I came home early.* Lou relaxed back into the embrace of the sheets, her body going slack. The wind was barely a whisper outside the eaves, the wind a comforting rustle, Waterton quiet and calm. She was almost asleep when another noise broke through her thoughts. It was a sound only Lou, who'd grown up in this house, would recognize: an oily squeak that came from someone stepping on the riser halfway down the flight of stairs outside her bedroom. It shocked her awake.

Someone was *inside* the house.

CHAPTER FOUR

Halfway through the night shift Sadie and Jordan were starting to make headway with Jane Doe. Though there was still no official I.D. on the body, the time of death, based on bacterial counts in the blood and body temperature, had been set as Saturday, October 13th, 2001, approximately two days prior to the discovery of the body on Monday afternoon. This gave a specific window for her disappearance. Sadie printed more than fifty pages of notes from the coroner while Jordan uploaded their new information into the Missing Persons database. Jane Doe matched several physical descriptions, but none of the listings had provided fingerprints as of yet.

"That's it for now." Jordan hit 'send,' sat back in the chair, and rubbed his neck. "All sent off. Now we wait and see if any match up."

Sadie pushed another pin into the board. "Hopefully she's got a prior."

"Dressed like that?" he said. "Doubt it."

"Then let's hope someone's reported her missing."

"I'm sure she's got a family somewhere."

"I do too. But that doesn't mean they've noticed she's gone," Sadie said. "Not everyone keeps in touch, and if she was on vacation, well... No one may even know she's gone yet."

"But there's got to be some way of identifying her."

"Not unless it's been called in."

Jordan chewed the corner of his nail as Sadie pinned an aerial map of Waterton park to the board, Indian Springs marked along its northern side. Next to it, she placed a photograph: the muddy shore and the hoof prints under the water.

Jordan's eyebrows rose and he leaned forward. "What if we use something *other* than fingerprints? Like… like another kind of print."

Sadie turned. "What do you mean?"

"How about teeth impressions? Someone might have something like that, right? A dentist or someone. You never know."

"Yeah… yeah, that'd work." Sadie put the final pin in the map and stepped back. "I'll go through all the missing persons lists, starting with Alberta and spreading out from there, you start checking for other records. All we need is one thing to match. One clue. The teeth are a good idea, Jordan."

He grinned and dropped his chin. "Thanks."

* * *

There was one phone in Lou's cabin. *One.* And it was hung in the hallway next to the kitchen. The prowler on the stairs was between her and it.

The stair's riser squeaked as he took another step. Lou jerked upright. The bed springs groaned, but she had no choice with someone in the house! Heart pounding, she scanned the room. She needed a weapon. But what?! Barring picking up a lamp, she had *nothing* with which to defend herself.

She heard another squeak, louder now. The person was nearing the top of the stairs.

Barefoot, Lou bolted to the door. With shaking hands, she

turned the lock, then pulled the skeleton key out and backed away from the door. The footsteps on the stairs paused for a second, as if someone had heard the 'click'. Like many of the cabins in Waterton, Whispering Aspens had been built in the 1920s. The hardware was ancient, but the wood of the doors was old. It wouldn't hold up if someone was determined to get in… but it would slow them down.

Louise took panicked breaths as she searched for an escape. Only one door separated her from the intruder. The footsteps sped into a jog as the prowler neared the top of the stairs. Lou's fingers tightened around the key as she turned in a circle, her gaze catching on the shimmer of glass. *The window!* She slapped the key on the dresser, then jerked up the sash.

The footsteps reached the second-floor landing and walked slowly toward the bedroom. Lou leaned out over the windowsill. Directly below her there was a small ledge, and then a drop of more than fifteen feet, ending in bushes. If she held onto the window-sill and hung over the edge, Lou figured she could make it down enough that she'd be slowed before she hit the Caraganas. Yes, she'd be hurt. She might even break her ankle, but she'd have a chance!

The floor squeaked again, directly outside the bedroom door and Lou scrambled backwards, bumping against the ledge of the open window. The door handle turned and caught—stopped by the lock. Lou swung her right leg out the window and hoisted herself into a straddle. The door knob turned. Lou had one leg in, one leg out the window when the door handle jiggled again, louder. She shifted her weight to jump.

"Lou…? Are you in there?"

Lou let out a sobbing breath, her terror flip-flopping into joy. "Rich?!"

* * *

Jordan had just come back from the coffee machine in the front of the police station when Sadie spoke.

"Something came through the fax a minute ago," she said, not looking up from the papers in her hand. "Mind checking it?"

"Sure thing." Jordan set Sadie's coffee on the corner of her desk and headed to the recalcitrant fax machine. It had spewed out several sheets in the last minutes, sent—strangely enough—from a number in the States. He squinted at the papers.

"We've got ourselves a match!" he shouted.

Sadie looked up. "A what?"

"A match to our Jane Doe!" Jordan laughed. "The teeth impressions came back with an I.D."

Sadie scrambled out of her chair and came to peer at the papers in his hands. "Who is it?"

"Hold on…" He ran his thumb down the page, scanning for details. "Young woman from New York," he said. "Family's been looking for her for about three weeks. A private investigator uploaded her dental records a week and a half ago."

"Name!" Sadie snapped.

Jordan's thumb reached the bottom of the first page. He flicked to the next. A grainy image of a New York driver's license photograph appeared. No question, it was the same girl they'd found. "Miss Gabrielle Rice. She's from New York. Lives in Manhattan."

Sadie made a hissing sound and Jordan looked up. Her mouth was a slash, black brows knit together.

"Should I recognize the name?" Jordan asked.

"No, but look at this." She pointed to the bottom of the fax. There was a line of notes, nearly illegible from the machine's copying, but one sentence stood out. *May be in the company of her ex-fiancé…*

Jordan's eyes widened. "Richard Evans."

* * *

Louise swung her leg back inside, laughing as she stumbled to the bedroom door.

"Rich?!" she called, grabbing the handle of the door. "My God! What're you—"

The handle turned and stopped, locked.

"Lou? You okay in there?"

Tears filled Lou's eyes. This wasn't a dream. Rich was here!

"Yes," she said, "I'm here. Just hold on." She spun around, searching for the key. She'd had it in her hand a moment ago. Where had she put it?

"Honey? Why's the door locked?" She could hear the laughter in Rich's voice.

"I didn't know who was coming up the stairs."

"I was trying to surprise you."

"Surprised is an understatement."

The door jiggled again. "Can I come in now?"

"Hold on. I… I must have set the key down somewhere when I was trying to get out the window."

"You were going *out* the window?"

"Yeah," she said. "You scared the living daylights out of me."

Frustration waged war with her joy as Lou scanned the room.

"Shit, Lou. I'm so sorry, baby."

"It's fine. I just—" Her eyes alit on the key on the top of the dresser. "There it is!" she laughed. A moment later she whipped the door open.

Rich stood on the other side. Lou drew in details like she was dying of thirst and he was a stream of cold water. He wore a wrinkled suit, his tie tugged half-off. His blond hair was shorter than she was used to, his cheeks clean-shaven. He'd lost a few pounds since he'd left, but otherwise he was still Rich. *Her Rich.*

He gave her a crooked grin, hooking his thumbs in his belt loops. "So am I allowed to come in now?" he teased. "Or is there a magic word I ought to—"

With a shriek, Lou launched herself into his arms. His lips found hers and her mouth opened in return. Rich tasted like spearmint gum, and his hands were warm where they ran into her hair, cupping the back of her head. The kiss dragged on, seconds dragging into a minute, then more. Rich's hands combed through the length of her hair before moving down to stroke her back. His palms slid under the curve of her bottom and gravity shifted. Lou squeaked, breaking the kiss, as he picked her up. With her legs wrapped around his waist, they were eye to eye.

"Mind if we move this to the bed?" Rich panted.

"That would be amazing."

In seconds they were through the door. Keyed up from the minutes before, every nerve in Lou's body felt raw. Her heart rattled against her ribs, skin on fire as Rich kissed her again and again.

She tightened her grip around his shoulders. *Rich was home!* Their lips slanted together, his hand moving into her hair and against her waist. He shuffled toward the bed, only breaking the kiss to move his mouth down her neck, tasting her skin. Rich leaned over. Unbalanced, Lou released her legs' grip on his waist, tumbling to the rumpled covers with a peal of laughter.

"You've no idea how long I've waited for this," he growled. "Every night, thinking of you sleeping alone… me, wishing I was here."

"I missed you."

"Not as much as I did."

"Oh, I wouldn't be so sure," she said, sliding off her tank and panties before tossing them aside. "This bed is pretty cold without you here."

Rich grabbed the back of his collar and pulled his shirt over his head, sending a button flying off into a far corner.

"That's not going to be a problem anymore."

Their eyes met as Rich crawled onto the bed, intent on her. She could barely breathe, caught in the riptide of emotions.

"Love you," he whispered. "Love you so much, Lou."

"Love you too."

There was a near-frenzy to Rich's motions, an intensity to his lovemaking that reminded her of the year they'd found one another. Then, that aspect of his personality had worried her, but tonight she welcomed him home with body and soul, finding comfort in his need.

In the moment before all words disappeared, one thought came into her mind: *This was how love was supposed to feel...*

* * *

Night shift over, Sadie drove her two-tone Buick home in the watery predawn gloom. The mountain range rose around her like a broken bowl that blocked the town from the rest of the world. On the eastern side of that bowl the mountains dropped down to a narrow valley where a ribbon of road threaded its way between the peaks. This causeway was the sole connection between Waterton and all the life which transpired beyond.

Here and there, Sadie thought. *Them and us.*

She followed the faint glimmer of pink clouds in the sky down to the silvery entrance road, then frowned. A sliver of asphalt connected Waterton and the world. Nothing more. That detail felt important this morning regarding the murder of Gabrielle Rice.

A single question begged to be answered: Why had she been in Waterton?

Sadie popped the car into park and stepped out onto the red shale driveway. Gritty-eyed, she lifted her hands above her head as she slowly stretched, back popping, before she dropped her hands and headed up the walkway. *There's got to be a reason,* an inner voice said. A voice that, in her exhaustion, sounded suspiciously like Jim Flagstone. *A reason she was found alone. Dead.* The thoughts nipped at her heels as she slid the key into the lock and stepped into the shadowy cabin. If Rich Evans was around, she'd go talk to *him,* find out what business his ex might have here in Alberta, but Rich was in New York and had been for weeks.

So why *had* Gabrielle Rice been in Waterton park?

Exhausted, Sadie toed off her shoes and stumbled to the bathroom. She dropped her clothes where they fell, grateful that she and Jordan were flipping back to days tomorrow morning. Too many nights in a row screwed with your biological clock. A minute later, she crawled between icy sheets.

Why...? her mind whispered. *Why Waterton?* Over and over again, the question rose, a spark in the darkness of her mind. A sleepless ten minutes passed as Sadie tossed and turned. There had to be a link. Some reason Gabrielle Rice had been out there. Perhaps her family knew what that reason was, but with the time difference between Alberta and New York and the lateness of the hour, Sadie hadn't been able to call to ask them. She'd left a message at the precinct in New York. By now someone had likely contacted the family, tearing away the hope that their 'missing' daughter might come home.

"It's shit like this that makes me hate my job," Ben had said to her that night.

"Well, someone's got to do it. Right?"

"Guess so... People can do some pretty fucked up stuff."

With a sigh, Sadie rolled to the cool side of the mattress and pulled the blankets higher, caught between exhaustion and nerves. It was full dawn. Birds chirped at the windows on the other side of the black-out curtains; cars passed on the street. Still her mind would not rest. Sadie punched the pillow and flopped back against it.

Just go to sleep! Long minutes passed. She could sense a connection between the details of what they'd found, but couldn't quite make the pieces fit. And until it did, her mind would not shut off.

Her eyes closed and the crime scene returned. The girl's body, her fractured skull and broken neck, the undamaged nails, the neatly pressed clothing and red-soled boots. Next came the lake at Indian Springs, the churned mud around the body, the hoof prints under the water. Sadie's mind shuffled through them like a film strip, her fatigue growing into a hum … until Ben's words returned:

"We're deep in grizzly territory here… they'll feed on anything they can find, dead or alive. If those hunters hadn't called, well, I doubt there'd be anything to find come spring."

Sadie's eyes opened. "That's it!" she gasped.

She already *knew* that the killer had carried in the body from the kill site on a horse, but she'd ignored one obvious fact that held that all together. The killer hadn't just dumped her there; he'd *planned* for Gabrielle's body to disposed of by bears.

There were only so many people who knew the area well enough to understand the migratory movement of grizzlies.

* * *

It was early morning, just past dawn. Lou lay in the dim half-light of the bedroom, her hand splayed across Rich's chest. He was asleep and dreaming, but not peacefully. His eyes flickered behind closed lids; he groaned. Lou lifted her head, watching him as the nightmare took hold.

"Shhh…" Lou whispered. She pressed her fingers against his skin, her mind catching on the thread of his thoughts. A second passed… two… and an image appeared. *The streets of New York… Rich walking through the crowds… His eyes lifting… The Twin Towers aflame while bodies fell to—*

Lou jerked her hand back. Her elbow smacked Rich's chest and the image dissolved like smoke.

Rich groaned and blinked himself awake.

"Lou?"

"Sorry," she said. "Didn't mean to bump you."

"It's fine." He tucked the pillow under his neck, rolling closer. He yawned. "Everything okay? Was I snoring?"

"Everything's good," she said, forcing the waver from her voice. "You were having a nightmare." It was on her tongue to tell him she'd *seen* what he'd been dreaming, but she bit it back. "Seemed like a bad one."

"Huh. Can't remember it." He trailed his fingers along her arm. "Sorry for waking you."

"You didn't. I wasn't asleep."

"Something wrong?"

Lou snuggled closer, setting her chin on his chest. "Nothing wrong exactly, just something… *off*."

Outside the window, a sparrow began to trill.

"Off how?" Rich asked. "I'm home. Things are good."

"It's nothing with you," she said with more certainty than she felt. "But something. Just… something. I can feel it coming."

"You want to tell me about it?"

"Not really."

He gave her a lopsided grin. "You want to tell me something

else?" His finger ran over her shoulders. "A story maybe?"

Lou wrapped her arms around him, feeling her calm return. With Rich in the circle of her arms, the anxieties of moments before disappeared. She was settled. *Happy.*

"Yeah," she said. "I'll tell you a story. Anything in particular you want to hear about?"

He smiled sleepily. "Tell me about our future, Lou…"

* * *

The switch from nights to days wreaked havoc on Jordan's sleep habits. He was already on his third cup of coffee and still yawning when Sadie walked in the door on Wednesday morning. She looked up in surprise, her coat half-on, half off.

"You're here early," she said. "Something happen?"

"Nah," he said. "Fell asleep the second I got home but woke up weirdly early and couldn't get back to sleep." Jordan smothered a yawn. "Kept thinking about the Rice case. Decided if I was awake, I might as well come on in."

Sadie chuckled as she settled in behind her desk. "You can't turn the investigation off either, huh?"

"Nope."

"Any breakthroughs this morning?"

"Not really. Though Liz gave me a bunch of messages when I arrived." He ran his hand over the top of his hair, leaving it standing on end. "Gabrielle Rice's father called in this morning. He wants us to contact him, says he already has a private investigator looking into his daughter's disappear—" Jordan frowned. "Her death."

"Investigator, hmmm? Anyone we know?"

"Nope. Some P.I. from New York, it seems. Rice says the guy's been looking for his daughter for the last two weeks."

Sadie rolled her eyes. "Looks like he didn't find her."

"Nope." Jordan tossed the notes onto Sadie's lap, talking as she glanced through them. "I figure we should probably start interviewing people around town. If Gabrielle died in Waterton park, it's a fair guess she was staying nearby. And if she was staying nearby, she might have talked to someone here. We could see if anyone remembers her."

"Agreed, but I want to check something else out first." Sadie nodded to the map on the billboard.

"We going back to the crime scene?"

"Nope. But you're close." Sadie pointed to the irregular shape of Indian Springs. Her finger slid north into forest reserve which stretched along the park. "Here's where the guys who saw the body claimed they were hunting," she said. Her finger moved one last time to a straight-edged tract of ranchland. "And *this* is right next door to it."

Jordan squinted at the map. "Who owns that land?"

"The Durnerins," she said. "They're ranchers, yes. But they're outfitters too. A bunch of hunters are staying at the ranch right now. All of those men and women have access to horses and each and every one of them would be able to get to Indian Springs if they needed to."

"Sounds like we've got some interviews to do."

* * *

Sadie was fighting to keep her temper under control and had been for an hour. She *knew* if she yelled, she'd regret it, but Russell Durnerin was making it difficult to stay calm. The man sat at the farmhouse's wide kitchen table, his arms crossed on his barrel chest, pug-faced and impudent.

"I told you," he growled. "I had nothin' to do with the girl's death."

"We never said you did," Sadie said tightly. "We're just looking for leads." He rolled his eyes and Sadie gritted her teeth. "Mr. Durnerin, we're just trying to get a sense of who was around."

"You go talk to those boys that found her," Russell snarled. "*They* was the ones out there. Not me."

"We know that," Jordan said patiently. "Constable Grayden already interviewed the hunters."

"So interview 'em again!"

"Mr. Durnerin," Sadie said, "we just need a list of your guests. There's no reason *not* to give it to us."

"Says you." The rancher's pale eyes narrowed until they seemed to disappear into the lines of a sun-browned face. Russell Durnerin might be fifty, but he looked older.

Meaner, too, Sadie thought.

"I told you," he repeated, "ain't got no list."

"But surely you keep track of the people staying with you," Jordan said cautiously. "If they're paying guests—"

"They are," he snapped.

"Then you must have *some* information," Sadie said.

He glared and turned back to Jordan, dismissing her. "So what's your interest in my hunters anyhow?"

"Until we find the murderer, sir, there's always a chance he could strike again. Now I'm not worried about you and the ranch-hands as much as I am the other people visiting the ranch." Jordan paused and Sadie held her breath. "Your daughter, Shawna, helps you run the place, doesn't she Mr. Durnerin?"

Russell's arms dropped to his side as if catching himself from a fall.

"Yes." He frowned. "You think she's in some kinda danger?"

Sadie caught Jordan's eyes. She needed him to play this out, to hint at a threat without outright *saying* there was one. He gave a barely perceptible nod.

"I can't say either way, sir," Jordan said. "It's far too early on. But we need to talk to the people staying here: the hunters and your ranch-hands... Shawna too, for that matter."

Russell's gaze flicked to Sadie. "Fine," he said. "But make it quick. Don't want everyone gettin' riled up over nothin'."

Sadie bit the inside of her cheeks to keep from cheering.

"Of course not, Mr. Durnerin. We'll just get the facts."

The hunters were easy interviews. Two were a married couple from Montreal who'd come out to Alberta for a wilderness adventure. They'd been either with a trail guide or at the ranch for the last week. The next two were a pair of big game hunters: brothers. One had been tracking bighorn sheep through the forest reserve to the far north of the park—nowhere near Indian Springs—at the time Gabrielle died; the other had been at the ranch with a twisted ankle. Durnerin himself vouched for this. The last hunter was an elderly man from Tennessee who came up to the ranch like clockwork each autumn. He'd been more than happy to share his entire adventures with Sadie and Jordan. It seemed unlikely that the seventy-year-old had anything to do with Gabby's death.

Next came the ranch-hands. The men ranged in age from twenty to fifty, all of them full time employees of the Durnerin ranch. They came to the kitchen one by one, cautiously answering Sadie and Jordan's questions, their hands clasped in front of them as if reciting answers in grade school.

"Didn't even know that someone had died," one said.

"Heard from them boys in Hill Spring they found a body," another offered.

"I heard someone killed her, then dumped for the bears," a third said.

Everyone had their own spin on what had happened, but one question kept recurring:

"You think the killer's still around?"

The last person Sadie and Jordan interviewed was Shawna Durnerin. She'd been working in the pasture when they'd first arrived and her father had sent a ranch-hand to fetch her. As the cowboy left the kitchen, the door reopened and a young woman with a freckled nose and a ponytail of long, caramel-coloured hair came through the door, a wiry black-haired young man at her side. The two of them were laughing but the sound faded away as they saw the two officers.

Jordan stood and offered his hand.

"Ms. Durnerin," he said. "Could we talk to you for a few minutes? We're investigating a homicide."

"If we could just ask you a couple questions." Sadie nodded to the chair across from her. "It won't take long."

"Okay…" Shawna glanced at the young man at her side, then back at Sadie.

"Your friend can stay," Jordan said. He took a seat and the black-haired man did too. "He might have some thoughts on this."

"You from the area?" Sadie asked.

The young man gave Sadie a cocky grin. "You might say that."

Shawna giggled as Sadie and Jordan exchanged confused glances. "Are you a ranch-hand?" Sadie asked. "If you are, we'll need to ask you—"

"Not a ranch-hand. Leastways not *here*," he said.

Jordan frowned. "But you *are* from around here?"

"Uh-huh. My parents have a place near Leavitt, but I'm working for my great-uncle right now. He's got a place near Twin Butte."

Sadie scooted her chair forward. "And who would your great-uncle be?"

The young man waited for several seconds before answering. "Levi Thompson." He lifted his chin. "The name's Bryce, Bryce Calhoun."

CHAPTER FIVE

The sun was setting behind the mountains when Jordan and Sadie drove away from the Durnerin ranch.

"Bryce Calhoun is a goddamned liar!" Sadie snarled.

"Didn't make much of an impression, did he?" Jordan said.

She revved the engine, spraying gravel as she headed toward the highway.

"He might as well have just said '*fuck you both.*' Would've saved us a lot of time."

"And how would *that* have gone over, huh, Sadie?"

"The guy's an asshole. Seriously, Jordan, I think it's in the genes."

"Might be. But do you think he's involved in the murder?"

"I don't know, or... I don't know *yet*. Not enough pieces on the board." Sadie's frown deepened. "He's Shawna's alibi and she's his, the two of them running errands in Cardston on Saturday night, then out on the Thompson ranch on Sunday. Trouble is, neither one of them trusts us because we took down Colt, so I don't know how much either of those alibis are worth. I *think* Shawna Durnerin's telling the truth but..."

Up ahead, the turn off for Waterton appeared and Sadie slowed.

"But what?" Jordan asked.

"But we've got to keep *both* of them on the list of suspects.

They're good riders, for one. He's working at the Thompson ranch. She runs the Durnerin place. Either one could've made it to that lake if they'd wanted to."

"And each would have had someone to help, too."

Sadie glanced over. "You think Shawna would help Bryce if he asked her to move a body?"

"Uh-huh. And vice versa... though I don't think it was a woman who killed Gabrielle Rice." Jordan drummed his fingers on the passenger-side door. "Bryce has access to the lake from Levi's place. He's familiar with all the trails, and we *know* he can handle horses." His fingers paused. "Yeah. We need to confirm the alibi if we want either of them off the list."

Sadie nodded. "If Bryce and Shawna Durnerin really were out in Cardston the night Gabrielle Rice was killed, someone else *must've* seen them, right?"

"You'd think so."

The police cruiser reached the top of Knight's Hill, the lights of the hamlet twinkling in the distance. "Then until we get someone to vouch, we keep *both* of them on the list."

* * *

Lou stared at the document in her hands and grinned. Here it was, the proof she'd been looking for. The solid *future* that had always felt so elusive.

Rich's arm slid over her shoulder. "You doing okay?"

"Yeah. It... it just doesn't feel real yet."

"We're going to have to fix that."

Lou blushed and put the document back into the envelope.

The clerk at the Registry handed Rich a receipt. "Here you go," she said. "You have three months from today to be married. Whether you decide to do it at City Hall, or in a church, you'll need to bring that registration along with you." The woman smiled. "And if you wait more than three months, well, you get to come see me again and get a new registration."

"Don't think so," Rich said. "Three months gives us lots of time." He squeezed Lou's shoulder. "Unless you're having second thoughts?"

"Not a chance." Lou grinned. She'd been expecting to be panicked but felt totally calm. *This is good,* she thought. *Really good.* "You ready to go home?" she asked.

"Yeah. Let's head out."

Rich pushed open the door and the two of them walked out into the fall sunshine. Unlike Waterton, which had been blustery and cool when they'd driven away this morning, Lethbridge was caught up in the delirious heat of late autumn. If not for the cool wind that poked under Lou's shirt, she would have assumed it to be late-August. The coulees were rippled lines of yellow velvet draped over the hollowed bowl of the riverbottom. With the sun setting, they glowed gold and lapis, the colours so brilliant it hurt the eyes.

Lou reached for the truck's handle, then stopped. "You want to drive back?" A gusty west wind blasted her hair, sending a black cloud swirling around her face. "Test out your driving skills again?"

Rich laughed and joined her on the driver's side. "You trust me after a month of New York subways and cab rides?"

"Of course I do."

"Then I'd love to." He cupped her face between his hands. The swirling strands retreated with the brush of his fingers and she found she could see again. "I missed driving when I was in New York." Rich leaned in and brushed his lips against hers. "But I missed *you* more."

Lou closed her eyes as their lips met. "I missed you too."

* * *

Jordan had another restless night, and when Thursday morning rolled around, he found himself dozing at his desk. Sadie offered to get coffee from Hunter's. It was twice as strong and a hundred times better than the office's coffee. Ten minutes later, she came back through the front door looking bright and happy. The bounce in her steps made Jordan feel exhausted.

Liz was at the filing cabinet and she grinned as Sadie arrived. "You're looking chipper, Sadie. Something happen?"

"While I was grabbing coffee?" she laughed. "No. Just relieved to be back on mornings again."

"Mornings, huh?"

"Uh-huh."

Liz smirked. "You sure there's nothing else going on…?"

"Nope. Just feeling good today."

"Nobody feels *that* good without a reason. Just saying. You sure it's not about some good looking rancher you just happened to interview yester—"

"Get your mind out of the gutter, Liz. Bryce Calhoun's not even *close* to my type."

"So you say."

"I say it 'cause it's the truth. I don't trust him."

"Mm-hmmm… sure." Liz's laughter rose.

Sadie headed into the back office and set a steaming cup of coffee in front of Jordan.

"Thanks," he muttered.

She sat down across from him, smiling at him over the top of her cup.

"Drink up. It'll help."

He grumbled a half-hearted reply and took a sip.

"I was thinking about the case last night," she said.

Jordan fought the urge to groan. He could barely *think,* never mind pull apart the mind of a killer.

"Yeah?" he said. "What's that?"

"The initial exam showed that Gabrielle Rice died of blunt force trauma to the skull, but the report showed it was the hemorrhage that actually killed her. And there's more."

Jordan frowned. "More?"

"Details that weren't in the original report."

"Like the broken neck?"

"Not that. Like what *else* was going on with Ms. Rice," Sadie said. "The examiner in Lethbridge was concerned by her blood results and called in an expert from Calgary to analyze them."

Jordan took another sip of coffee, relieved to feel the caffeine hit his bloodstream. "And?"

Sadie grabbed a pile of papers from the corner of her desk and flipped open the folder. "And that *second* report came in late last night."

"What's in it?"

Sadie slid the papers toward him, and Jordan scanned them. Details popped into focus. *Blunt force trauma. Broken neck. Hemorrhage to the right temporal lobe. Loss of consciousness would have been instantaneous, death within minutes.*

"But… we knew how she died already."

"Keep going," Sadie said.

Jordan glanced up. "What?"

"Look on the last page. Toxicology. That's the good stuff."

Jordan flipped through the pages—eight in total—while Sadie chattered. Her voice was animated, hands swooping through the air like birds.

"Something just wasn't sitting right with me," she said. "I knew there was something off, but I couldn't put a finger on it…"

Jordan reached *Toxicology* and skimmed until he reached the bottom.

"Blood work shows evidence of drug use. Levels suggest a sudden stop to regular medication. Residual amounts of anti-psychotics—"

"Whoa!" Jordan said. "She was on anti-psychotics?"

"Uh-huh. Or she *was* at some point prior to her murder."

"You think it's related to her death?"

The question hung in the air, a hint of *something*, though Jordan didn't know what. They had a body in the wrong country. A family trying to find her, and evidence of serious medication use. He set the folder down and stared at it. Things were starting to fall into place. He didn't know *how* they'd come together, but there were details taking shape.

"Related? Yeah, definitely," Sadie said. "I mean, who just walks away from their life?"

She reached for another folder and fingered it open. "Her parents have been searching everywhere for her for weeks. She disappeared a couple days after 9/11. Family told the investigating officers—" she scanned down the page, "—that she might have had a 'mental breakdown.'"

Sadie handed Jordan the folder.

"So she disappears a week after the World Trade Center is destroyed," she said, "and a month later her body is found here, one country and three thousand miles away."

"Shit. So what do we do next?"

Sadie's smile faded, and Jordan had the sudden feeling he'd let her down.

"What do *you* want to do next?" she asked. "This is your case as much as mine, Jordan."

He nervously fingered the file. "Well, we already talked to the ranchers, so I… I guess we keep looking for clues as to why Gabrielle was here, and who knew that."

"Bingo," Sadie said. "We start a list. Once we have that, we just need to decide who to talk to first. I'll see if—"

Jordan sat up. "I know who!"

"You do?"

"We take Rich Evans in for questioning."

Sadie frowned. "But Rich Evans isn't in town."

"He is," Jordan said, excitement growing. "I was talking with Mila down at Lou's Garage last night when I was gassing up my truck. She said Rich came home late Tuesday night. Snuck in on Lou, scared her half to death."

Sadie's eyes widened. "He did?"

"Uh-huh."

Sadie grabbed her coat off the back of the chair, sliding her arms into it. "Time to go."

"Go?"

"If Rich Evans is back in town, I want to know *why*." She glanced back over her shoulder half a second before she stepped through the door. "And if he doesn't know Gabrielle Rice was here, then we're going to have to tell him."

Jordan nodded and grabbed his coat. For the first time in two days he felt completely awake.

* * *

Rich was caught in a nightmare. His gaze skittered around the kitchen. The faded plaid dish towels hung on the oven door, the brightly-printed curtains above the sink. Sunshine bounced on the melamine counter. None of *that* felt real.

"Dead," Rich repeated. "Gabby's... *dead?*"

Lou slid her chair closer and reached out for his hand. Rich took a shuddering breath. What was happening? Ever since Sadie had knocked on the door—asking if she and Jordan could "ask Rich a couple questions"—his entire life had turned upside down. He and Lou were *supposed* to be planning a wedding. Not this!

"Yes," Constable Black Plume said. "Ms. Rice has been missing for the last three weeks. Her body was found on Monday afternoon."

Rich shook his head. "But I... I don't understand," he said. "Gabrielle lives in New York. She shouldn't be here. She—"

"When did you last talk to Ms. Rice?" Sadie asked.

"I..." He frowned. "I'm not sure."

"Try to remember," Jordan said.

"Um... It was sometime after the World Trade Center was attacked." Rich looked up. "Yeah. After that."

"You talked to Gabrielle when you were in New York?" Lou said.

"I... yeah. I did."

Lou's brows pulled together. "But... but why?"

Rich winced. "It was chaos after the planes hit. Everyone was calling everyone. I called my parents first, let them know I was okay. Then Stu. A few other friends and then my phone rang and..." Rich flinched. "It was Gabby's number, so I answered."

Louise stared at him. She hadn't let go of Rich's hand, but her fingers felt wooden.

"She called you?" she said.

"Yes. She called and we spoke. Gabby seemed fine."

Constable Wyatt cleared his throat. "While you were there," he said, "did you just talk to Ms. Rice on the phone, or did you actually see her face to face?"

"Uh... both. It wasn't *just* me," Rich rushed to add. "Gabby and

Stu and I all got together. The three of us had dinner. We were freaked out about what had happened with the World Trade Center."

Constable Black Plume nodded as she made notes. "So you saw Ms. Rice in New York," she said. "You and Ms. Rice and Mr. Callaghan met together for dinner." She looked up. "At a restaurant?"

"Yes. That's right."

"Could that be confirmed with receipts?"

Rich frowned. "I… Yeah. I suppose so."

Constable Black Plume made another note. "And do you remember the very last time you saw Ms. Rice?" she asked. "What day that was?"

Rich felt the room close in. "I… don't remember," he lied.

"Can you make a guess? Estimate?"

"Uh… no."

"Mr. Evans," Jordan said. "I'm sure you realize that for now, this discussion is all voluntary, but if you *refuse* to answer us, then we will be forced to bring you in for questioning."

"Am I being accused of a crime?!"

"Not currently, no," Sadie said. "Do you have reason *not* to answer?"

"Of course not," Rich snapped. "I just don't know what's going on here. When I last saw Gabby, she was fine!"

"And when was that?" Constable Black Plume asked. "You still haven't said."

"I told you, I don't remember."

Jordan leaned in. "Well, let's start with the basics: Do you remember if you talked to her here in Waterton, or in New York?"

"New York, of course." Rich turned from one officer to the other in confusion. "You can't *seriously* think I had anything to do with her death. Do you?"

"We're just getting information," Sadie said. "That's all."

Jordan pulled the written statement closer, scanning through the details.

"Mr. Evans, what day did you return to Canada?"

A look—as quick as the wind—moved from Jordan to Sadie, then back again, but it left Rich's heart pounding.

"What day?" Rich repeated.

"Yes," Sadie said. "You came back to Canada, but no one—including Lou—knew you were back. So tell me, what day did you *actually* arrive." She paused. "Keep in mind that all of this, every detail, *will* be checked."

Rich swallowed hard. He glanced at Lou, sitting at his side. Her hand hadn't moved, but her expression was tight, eyes staring at the table.

"I, uh…" He coughed. "I came back to Canada a week ago."

Jordan gasped, but Rich barely noticed. His focus was on Lou's face, and the disappointment he saw there. Her expression shimmered.

"Why?" she whispered.

Rich gave her a half-sad smile. 'I was trying to surprise you, sweetheart."

"Where *were* you, Rich? What were you doing?"

"I was getting my business in order."

Lou shook her head. "But *what* business?"

"I closed a few accounts when I was in New York, liquidated some assets. When I got to Canada, I transferred my cash funds and retirement savings over to a Canadian bank. For my 401Ks, I had to visit Calgary, and then later Lethbridge to switch them into RRSPs. I met with a couple different financial advisors at Nesbitt Burns, twice in Calgary, once in Lethbridge. All those meetings took time." He turned back to the officers at the table. "I wasn't anywhere near Waterton. I give you my word."

Constable Black Plume gave him a long, hard look.

"Your word is one thing, Mr. Evans, but can you *prove* it?"

* * *

Thursday and Friday, Jordan and Sadie dove into the meat of their investigation. With Rich Evans' phone and credit card records requested, they expanded out into the community. Though small, Waterton was the nearest town to where Gabrielle Rice's body had been found. There was a good chance that she'd been there at some point. Everyone needed gas. Everyone needed to eat. And if she *had* been in town, then there was a good chance that she'd talked to someone while she was there.

"I think we should divide up the task," Sadie announced.

"Divide it up how?" Jordan said.

"You and I both go out and chat with the locals."

"Alone?"

"Exactly. I want to catch them unawares. The news hasn't spread yet, but it's going to... and fast."

While working with Constable Flagstone, two years before, Sadie'd had the unpleasant experience of having the entire town stonewall them, refusing to answer any questions. She did *not* intend for that to happen again.

"I drew up a list of people who might have seen Gabrielle if she was in the area." She handed Jordan a list and a photo. "A picture too, in case they didn't catch her name."

"So I ask if they've seen her?"

"Not *just* if they've seen her." Sadie sighed.

Being able to suss out information was a skill, like every other part of police work. It just took time to learn it. She'd had to over-come a quick temper, when she'd first started interviewing people. Jim had taught her that.

"Find out what they noticed. Make sure you get all of it. Don't tell them that we have a body, or that we're investigating a homicide. Not yet, anyhow. Just… leave that part out."

"But what if they ask what's going on?"

"Say that we're checking into things, and that the investigation is ongoing, so you can't give any details."

Jordan nodded. "Okay…"

"Let them talk." Sadie pointed to the first name on the list. "Mrs. Decker here? She's going to talk your ear off no matter what."

"Yeah, but not her husband."

"True," Sadie laughed. "Fred can be pretty quiet. But if you get them together, you might just get Elaine talking *for* her husband, and then Fred's going to correct her. I guarantee it."

Jordan smiled. "Yeah, he would. Wouldn't he?"

"Uh-huh. Go with your gut. You've got good instincts, Jordan."

"Thanks, Sadie."

"Meet you back here in a couple hours, okay?" She grabbed her coat. "Lunch is on me if you can get Levi to talk without swearing."

Jordan groaned. "Wait… I've got Levi Thompson on my list?!"

"Well, yeah. I mean, I certainly wasn't going to take him." Sadie laughed.

"But that's not fair!"

"Totally fair," she said. "If I took Levi, he wouldn't tell me a thing. You, on the other hand, might just be able to soften him up a bit."

He gave her a dirty look. "Thanks… I think."

She winked. "Anytime, rook."

Sadie headed out the door with a wave, smiling as the bells jangled behind her. This was her favourite part of an investigation: the early times, when every possibility was still open, every avenue a potential answer. She headed down Main Street with a spring in her step, glancing into shop windows as she went. Several of the stores were already closed for the season, with hand-lettered "back next spring" posters on the doors. These, Sadie knew, were the out-of-town owners, the people who came for the summer months, then retired for the rest of the year. She didn't need them. Gabrielle had been alive a week ago. No, she needed the locals, the tight fist of townies who made up the heart of Waterton. These people were the year-round folks. For them, the small mountain town was home. Many of them kept their stores open for a few hours each day. Every sale at this time of year meant more money in the bank to carry the business owners to spring. These were the ones who'd been around when Gabrielle had been murdered. These were the ones she didn't trust.

Don't be like that, Sadie, she could imagine Jim saying. *You know these folks. They're a good bunch.*

Sadie's smile faltered. It had been Jim's love of people that had gotten him killed and Sadie had no intention of making the same mistake.

Sadie knew she was still considered an outsider. Things people *should* have told her—like the mess with Borderline Industries, and the leases that had nearly destroyed many townspeople's finances back in '99—were kept under a veil of privacy. No one spoke of their troubles to anyone outside that inner sanctum. Sadie had been in Waterton for almost five years, but the townsfolk had never accepted her as one of their own. If Jim had still been alive, she would have asked him to get them into one of the informal "coffee meetings" the locals held, but Sadie didn't have the same connections. Jordan, however, had grown up in Mountain View. *Maybe,* she thought, *he could be able to get into one of Hunter's meetings.*

Sadie pushed open the door to Fine and Fancy and stepped inside. The scent of potpourri filled the air. "End of Season Sale" posters hung from the ceiling and flute music, interspersed with wind chimes, echoed from the sound system.

"Mrs. Kulkarni…?" she called.

No one answered.

Sadie headed to the back of the store. A narrow stair headed up to the second floor where Audrika and her husband lived. A rollicking beat from a distant radio blasted upstairs, overshadowing the flutes and chimes. Sadie cupped her hand around her mouth. "Mrs. Kulkarni!" she shouted. "You up there? It's Constable Black Plume!"

The radio dropped by half. "One moment, dear!" a woman's cheery voice called. "I'll be right down."

Sadie wandered back to the main section of the store, glancing at the racks. They were nearly empty. Fine and Fancy, like the other businesses, was winding down. Sadie frowned. Still, it seemed strange to leave the door unlocked and not have someone here.

A flash of bright purple drew Sadie's attention to the arched doorway to where Audrika Kulkarni, in a velour track suit and full makeup and hair-sprayed updo, now stood.

"Thank you for waiting," she panted. "What can I do for you?"

"I wanted to talk to you about someone who might have come into your shop but, before I do—" Sadie thumbed toward the door. "Did you know that your door was wide open?"

"Mmm… yes, I knew." Audrika perched herself on the stool behind the counter. "What of it?"

"You left the shop with no one here. Anyone could walk in off the street."

"Hardly," Audrika dryly. "It's Waterton after all. And being that it's the middle of October, there's hardly a soul around."

"But your till is right there. If someone wanted to steal from—"

"Constable Black Plume," Audrika interrupted. "Are you here to lecture me about how I run my business?"

"Not at all, I just…" Sadie forced herself to relax her shoulders. If Mrs. Kulkarni wanted to be robbed, so be it. That *wasn't* why she was here. "I just noticed it was open," Sadie said. "And since you weren't down in the shop, it threw me for a minute, being a police officer and all."

"Of course," Audrika laughed. "And I do appreciate the concern, dear. But there was no one around and I was only upstairs a moment." She tapped the counter with her manicured nails. "Now, what did you want to ask me?"

Sadie pulled the photograph from her pocket and laid it on the counter. "Do you recognize this woman, Mrs. Kulkarni?"

Audrika lifted the photo and peered at it with the sharp-eyed gaze of a magpie.

"Why that's Gabby!"

Sadie blinked. "You… you know her?"

"Of course I do. She comes in here *all* the time."

"She does?" Sadie scrambled for her notepad and pen. "When exactly?"

"On and off, quite regularly."

"Yes, but *when*, Mrs. Kulkarni."

"Several times in the last few weeks." She tipped her head to the side. "I actually thought it might be Gabby swinging by today."

"To confirm, you're quite *certain* she's the woman from the picture?"

"Well, yes. I know Gabby quite well." Audrika twirled a curl of black hair around one finger. "Gabby is *always* so well dressed, you know! Gorgeous clothing. So fashionable! I'm on the petite side, myself," she said patting a curvy hip. "Certain clothes don't do me justice, but Gabby can pull off *anything*."

"What was she coming here for?"

Audrika's fingers paused. "*Was*…? Did something happen to—?"

"You said she came into your store, that you remember her being here. I assume she purchased something when she was here?"

"Hmmm… yes, I suppose she did." Audrika pouted, then her expression brightened. "It must have been camping gear of something like that."

"Do you *remember* she bought camping gear, or is that a guess, Mrs. Kulkarni?"

"Well, I can't remember *exactly* what she came in for—this was a week or more ago—but I imagine it must have been for hiking and camping."

"Why do you think that?"

"She certainly wasn't dressed for camping, and what *else* could she have been doing in town this time of year?"

"I don't know. I was hoping you could help with that."

Audrika shrugged. "No idea. We only talked fashion. Oh, Gabby. She really does have a style that—"

"Do you recall the last time you saw Miss Rice around town?"

"Hmmm… let's see now…" Audrika made a purring noise. "It wasn't *this* week; I'd begun to think she'd left town. But…" She frowned. "Maybe Saturday? Sunday?" Her face broke into a wide smile. "Oh! Now I remember! It was last Saturday. Definitely."

Sadie waited, her pen poised over the page. "And you know this because?"

"I was wearing my dangling emerald earrings that day. Gabby

complimented me on them; said she had just such a pair at home. She'd gotten *hers* from Tiffany's," Audrika said breathlessly. "Mine came from the Sears catalogue, of course, but I *certainly* didn't say that to her."

"I… still don't understand how you know that was on Saturday."

"Because on Friday I went to Pincher Creek to do banking with Mirran, and left Vasur to run the store. Saturday I was in, and I'd dressed to match the weather. It was *beautiful* that day. Spring like. I wore a lovely green dress, hence the earrings." She preened. "And on Sunday, Vasur and I were emptying the stock room. I remember that I made a point of wearing stud earrings that day. I did *not* want something to catch on any of the boxes." Audrika leaned forward, fluttering her lashes. "I don't know if you've ever caught an earring on something, Constable Black Plume, but I certainly *have* and it is *not* something I'd like to do again."

"One more question: Do you happen to know where Gabrielle was staying?"

"Not sure," Audrika said, "but someone else will know."

"I'll ask around then." Sadie tucked her pen and pad into her pocket and stepped back from the counter. "Thanks for the help, Mrs. Kulkarni."

"No problem at all."

Sadie was almost to the door when Mrs. Kulkarni spoke again. "Constable Black Plume, is… is Gabrielle alright?"

"I can't really talk about it right now," Sadie said. "There's an open case involving her."

"A what?!" Mrs. Kulkarni was off the stool in a flutter of velour limbs in a heartbeat. She practically sprinted across the store. The stilettos didn't slow her. "What's happened to Gabby?!" she cried. "She's not in any trouble, is she?"

"Mrs. Kulkarni, I'm sorry, but I really cannot talk about this with you."

Audrika put her hand to her mouth. "She's... she's not *hurt*, is she?"

"Mrs. Kulkarni, please, I—".

"Oh dear God! Something *has* happened to her! Is she hurt? Is she in jail? What?!"

Sadie backed her way out of the store. "I'm sorry, I really can't—"

"But you know something! I can *see* that you do! Please, Constable Black Plume, I must know what happened! Gabby and I are friends!"

"I'm sorry," Sadie said, and turned away.

Behind her the door locked. When she looked through the glass, Audrika was back at the till, phone in hand, already dialing.

Sadie's shoulders slumped.

So much for keeping the investigation under wraps.

* * *

Jordan started at Lou's Garage.

Louise Newman had been a friend for much of his life and the mechanic often had a sense of what was going on in the community long before anyone else did. When they'd interviewed Rich the previous night, she'd barely said a word. And though Jordan knew Lou didn't know Gabrielle Rice except by name, she *might* have an idea of the comings and goings of the other people in the park. She might even know which B&B owners had out-of-town guests.

He came into Lou's Garage and glanced around. Mila was behind the counter, magazine in hand.

"Hey, Jordan," she said, winking. "What's up?"

"Is Lou in back today?"

"Not today, no." Mila shook her head. "She and Rich ran to Lethbridge to pick up some car parts. Don't expect 'em back until night-fall." She set the magazine down. "You having car trouble?"

"No. Just need to talk to her." He reached for the door handle, then turned back. "Actually, Mila. Can I ask you a couple questions while I'm here?"

She grinned. "Sure. What do you need?" Jordan laid the picture onto the counter and Mila turned it around so she could see it. "Who's this?" she asked.

"I… It's uh… I can't, um…"

Mila winked. "Let me guess. Official police business?"

"Uh… yeah. Sorry. I'm trying to figure out what people know about her."

Mila scanned the picture. "I honestly haven't seen her before. She's pretty." Mila handed the photo back. "Don't you think?"

"I guess so."

"Not your type?"

"No. I mean I wouldn't— I don't—"

"So what is your type, hmmm?"

"I… I don't…"

Mila tipped her head back and began to laugh. Jordan chuckled nervously.

"So you want me to tell Lou you came 'round to ask about that girl?" she said.

"No, that's okay. I actually wanted to talk to her about something else."

"Something *else*, huh?" Mila tipped her head to the side and grinned. "Well, you are just *full* of secrets, Constable Wyatt."

Jordan gave a nervous laugh and stepped back from the counter, face burning. He had the feeling that Mila was toying with him and he didn't know *why*.

"It's nothing, Mila, really. I just…" Jordan folded the picture and tucked it into his pocket. "I'll catch Lou another time." He waved. "See you, 'round."

She grinned as she picked up the magazine. "See ya!"

In seconds, Jordan was on the street once more. He wondered where he should go next. Frowning, he pulled the list from his pocket and scanned it. Levi Thompson's name was in the top spot.

"Not a chance," he grumbled. Jordan needed to get a few things straight before he walked into the lion's den. His fingers dropped down the list of names, settling on a woman he knew well. "Margaret," he sighed. "Yeah. I could talk to her."

Margaret Lu was a Waterton staple, the unofficial 'grandma' to many teens who worked there in the summers. Margaret and her family had moved to the park in the sixties and though her siblings had long since moved away, Margaret had never left. She ran a t-shirt shop on Main Street, where Jordan had worked for two summers when he was in high school.

As expected, the shop was open, and Margaret was puttering around at the front of the store, rearranging a display that had been in position so long the fabric underneath held shadows of the items previously above them. An electronic bell buzzed as Jordan came through the door and Mrs. Lu glanced up.

"Jordan!" she said, coming forward, hands outstretched. "What brings you in today?"

"Just a bit of police business." Jordan gave her a quick hug. He was glad Sadie wasn't here. She'd be reminding him to keep his personal and professional lives separate, but Jordan wasn't sure *how*. "You doing alright these days, Mrs. Lu?"

"Oh… just getting old," she said with a laugh. "But the alternative isn't particularly appealing."

He smiled. "Well, you look the same to me."

"Your eyes must be as bad as mine then. Now what's this business you want to talk about?"

"I have a picture here I want you to take a look at," he said, reaching into his pocket. "It's—"

"Is this about Gabrielle?"

Jordan paused. "You *know* about Ms. Rice?"

"Audrika just called. She's all in a titter. Wanted to know what was going on with her." Margaret's eyes widened. "Gabrielle's not in any trouble, is she? Audrika was terribly worried."

Jordan flinched. "I'm sorry, I—I can't say right now."

"Oh dear."

"You have to understand, there's an active investigation. If I could tell you something, I *would*, Mrs. Lu, but…"

She patted his arm.

"There, there," she said. "No worries. You do your job. Now, what did you need to ask me about Gabrielle?"

Jordan handed her the photograph. "Well, first off, can you confirm that this *is* Gabrielle Rice?"

Margaret adjusted her glasses and peered at the photograph. "Yes, that's her." She looked up, frowning. "She's in trouble, isn't she?"

"I… Sorry."

Mrs. Lu handed back the photograph. "Yes, she came into my store a number of times."

"Do you remember why?"

"She was looking to buy a few specialty items." Margaret laughed. "I couldn't help her, but I advised her to check with the sporting goods stores in Lethbridge."

"Specialty items?"

Margaret nodded. "Yes. She wanted some hunting equipment. Rope, knives, a bone saw, if I remember right. Few things like that."

A frisson of ice ran the length of Jordan's spine. "She told you she wanted a *bone saw*?"

"Mm-hmmm," Margaret said cheerily. "But I don't carry equipment like that."

"Why in the world would she want a bone saw?"

"I asked her the same thing," Margaret said. "Gabrielle said she wanted to process deer meat. Had a bunch of questions about butchering."

"She came here to hunt?"

"I assume so, but I didn't ask."

Jordan scribbled a note. "But why *not*, Mrs. Lu? Didn't that seem strange to you?"

"It's not my place to ask, Jordan."

"But she asked for a bone saw, ma'am. That's odd by anyone's standards."

The elderly woman crossed her arms on her chest, a gesture Jordan knew well. *Annoyed.* "It might be odd, yes, but plenty of big game hunters come from the States. I heard that there are several staying out at the Durnerin Ranch right now. Who am I to ask why people buy what they buy?"

Jordan scribbled another note: *Check if Gabrielle had animal tags for hunting.* He looked up.

"You didn't have the knives she needed, but did she purchase anything?"

Margaret's expression warmed. "Oh yes, Gabrielle bought several magazines. A few t-shirts, too."

"Cash or credit?"

"Cash, always cash." She sighed. "She had money alright, but the poor girl seemed a quite *lonely*, to tell you the truth."

"Oh?"

"She came in every couple days for a while. She'd stand around and chat. Seemed like she was looking for a reason to be here. She asked about the different people in the town, wanted to know who lived here over the winter, who moved away, and which cabins were owned by who."

Jordan's fingers tightened on the pen. "Mrs. Lu, you don't happen to remember if she asked about Rich Evans, do you?"

Mrs. Lu laughed. "Why yes, she did, now that you say it! Seemed quite interested in him, which was funny because I told her he wasn't in town at all. He was back in the States, getting his immigration papers in order, since he and Louise were engaged and all."

"Do you remember how she took that news?"

The old woman's expression cooled. "She didn't take the news well, Jordan. Not well at all."

CHAPTER SIX

Friday night, Sadie and Jordan sat in the Watering Hole, a pitcher of beer between them. They were off work, but like so many things around town, the hours between work and play bled together, and tonight was no different.

"A bone saw," Sadie said with a shake of her head. "That's messed up."

"Unless she really *was* here to hunt."

"Girl like her? A socialite? I really doubt it."

"You sure? Lots of those rich types hunt. Makes 'em feel alive."

Sadie side-eyed him. "Alive…?"

"Hey, I'm serious here!"

She rolled her eyes.

Jordan tipped his beer toward her. "What if Gabrielle Rice had a whole apartment full of trophies?"

Sadie snorted. "Doubtful, but even if she did, she doesn't seem the type to clean and quarter a deer." She refilled her glass, pausing to top up Jordan's. "Most hunters hire a butcher."

"True enough."

For a few seconds the two sat in companionable silence, each of them filtering through the events of the day. Sadie stared down into her glass.

"There's something that's bugging me though," she said.

"What's that?"

"Why didn't anyone *know* Gabrielle Rice was here in town? I mean, if she was going into the shops, her purchases would be easy enough to track."

"Margaret says she paid for everything in cash. No credit card trail to follow."

"Fair enough, but she was chatting with the ladies. People *knew* she was here in Waterton. Why didn't her parents know that too?"

"Maybe they did and just didn't say."

"No. They were definitely in the dark. Police in New York said they were the ones that filed the first report."

"Maybe they had a falling out," Jordan said.

"Nope. Her father called the station twice yesterday. Guy was *really* worked up. Wanted me to send him a copy of our report once its finished. Yelled at me about our investigation taking too long."

Jordan grinned. "And how'd that conversation go?"

"I was polite," she said, "but I'm not letting anyone tell me who to send my reports to, grieving father or not." Sadie shook her head. "Now if the NYPD ask me, well... obviously that's a different matter."

"Obviously."

Sadie lifted her glass of beer but didn't drink. She drew lines in the frosted edge of the glass, frowning down at it.

"We have a sad young socialite wandering around a little Canadian town, befriending the local ladies and asking them how to purchase butcher's equipment." Her finger wiped a bead of moisture away and she looked up. "If we hadn't just found Gabrielle Rice's body, I'd almost wonder if *she* was the killer."

"Bone saw? Yeah, that's one for the books." Jordan chuckled. "So what next?"

"I left a message with the Pincher Creek RCMP yesterday. I want to know if there are people on their watch list; troublemakers, out-casts… you know the type. If they're living in the area, they could get to Waterton with a body. We should make sure they all check out."

"You heard back yet?"

"Not yet, Ben was off the last couple days, but I left a message for him to call me once he was on shift."

Jordan chuckled. "Ben, huh? First names. When'd that happen?" Sadie shot him a dark look. "Sorry," he said. "I… Yeah. That wasn't funny." Jordan cleared his throat. "So what next?"

"I already called the Durnerin ranch. Talked with Shawna again. She swears up and down that she and Bryce were in Cardston on Saturday night."

"Anyone to corroborate that?"

"Not yet. If they really *were* in Cardston the night Gabrielle was murdered, they weren't noticed." Sadie gave a weary sigh. "But that's only the start of our trouble. We've got a fire storm coming."

"We do?"

"I just got a call from the Lethbridge Herald. They've picked up the news, wanted me to give them a statement about our investigation."

"Shit. That didn't take long to get out."

"Nope." She sighed and set down her glass with a *thunk*. "Gabrielle Rice's murder is going to be all over the news tomorrow."

* * *

Louise was tired, but she hadn't slept. Instead, she puttered around the upstairs as night fell over the hamlet of Waterton. Rich was on the phone in the main floor kitchen, talking to Stu in New

York. She could feel Rich's anxiety. There'd been a message waiting on his phone from Constable Black Plume. She wanted to interview him again. She also wanted to talk to him about his movements during the week leading up to Gabby's death.

The whole thing left Lou uneasy. Sadie's message had bothered Rich enough that when they'd walked in the door, he'd immediately gone to the phone to call New York.

"Just making sure I've got my bases covered," he said.

"I'll give you space," Lou said. "Give me a shout when you're off the phone."

That had been an hour ago. She could still hear Rich's voice rising and falling in hushed tones. His worry rose up the stairs, strangling her. Stu Callaghan was Rich's friend first, but he was also his lawyer and had gotten him out of more than one bind in the last three years. She wondered if that going to happen with this too.

Louise changed the sheets on the bed, and shoved them into the hamper, then headed to the bathroom, wiping down the mirror and the sink, changing the towels on the rack. Gabrielle's presence was a worry without a clear name. As Sadie'd pointed out, Rich had been in Alberta when his ex was here. He'd been staying in Calgary and Lethbridge, but both were within driving distance of Waterton. The decision to lie about his whereabouts even to Louise made him seem guilty even if he wasn't.

Lou and Gabrielle had never met, but she knew enough about the situation to understand that her relationship with Rich had ended badly. She had shown up in Waterton unannounced the year that Rich had taken over the management of the Whitewater Lodge. It appeared she'd done it again... only this time Gabby had ended up dead. That alone was enough to upset Lou. But there were too many other bits and pieces in movement too. Nervous energy bubbled under Lou's skin as she worked. She moved to the tub, scrubbing it until her arms ached. Finished, she opened the door again.

Rich's voice drifted up the risers. "…but you and I both know she had issues!" There was a pause. "Stu, it was *never* like that! I mean, you told me…"

Lou closed the door. She didn't want to know. Not yet. Maybe not ever. She knew Rich, trusted him. But why hadn't he told her he was coming back? It made everything so much worse... Fighting anxiety, Lou stripped off her sweaty clothes. Her gaze lifted and caught. There, across her left breast, was the twisted shape of a bullet wound, beside it—crossing her sternum—the long line of the scalpel which had opened her chest. Someone, Lou had been told, had massaged her heart back to life. A human hand inside her. She touched the raised skin, only now starting to fade, and shivered. That scar marked the line between *there* and *here*... life and death. She'd stayed. She'd chosen this life. The chaos which she loved and feared had become her home.

"Rich…" she whispered. As much as any mark she carried, he was a scar that no one save Lou herself knew. In the last three years, he'd become part of who she was, what she carried on her skin and in her heart. His scar, his love, a weight that bound her body and soul.

With a sad smile, she turned on the faucet and climbed into the shower, scouring herself under the hot water. Her tension ebbed as she dried off. When she opened the door and stepped into the hallway, the house was quiet. She knew Rich was still downstairs, but his voice was almost inaudible. Whatever he and Stu were talking about had shifted into another range of discussion.

It is what it is, she thought as she headed to bed. *Worrying wouldn't change anything.* She pulled back the covers and climbed into the cool embrace of fresh sheets. Her eyes fluttered closed. She took slow breaths as the tension eased from her body. There'd been a time in her life when Lou had been able to stand on the outside, looking in and guiding without being tangled in the drama of the lives of those she loved. That moment had passed. It left her both happier and sadder than before.

That was the thing about life: You couldn't truly love if you didn't allow yourself to be hurt. Lou's love for Rich was a raw nerve, so good she couldn't stop the rush of elation when he pushed for them to marry, but so painful she couldn't stand it when he was in danger.

The wind outside the windows rose and an image flickered behind Lou's closed lids: her mother, waiting for her in the in-between.

"You need to make sure you walk the right path, sweetheart," Yuki said.

Lou frowned. "Which path is that?"

"Whatever one you choose."

And with that thought, Lou finally slept.

* * *

Rich had a headache pulsing in his temple. Everything he'd wanted seemed poised to disappear, and he had no one to blame but himself.

"You need to get those records," Stu said fiercely. "Track the places you went, Rich. Use receipts if you have them, so you—"

"I didn't keep my receipts," Rich snapped, then lowered his voice. Lou was upstairs. He didn't want to upset her if he didn't have to. "I was getting my finances in order."

"You must have gone somewhere to do that, right?"

"Yeah. Had a bunch of bank meetings."

"Then get documentation of that."

"Like what?" Rich whispered. "I talked to a financial advisor. I didn't *buy* anything."

"But I bet that there were documents of your meeting. You had to have talked to a receptionist. Right?"

Rich ran a hand through his hair. "Yeah, I guess."

"Then call those people up. Ask for them to send a fax of their meeting lists to me. I'll start a file."

Rich dropped his free hand to his side, his heart thudding heaving in his chest.

"Stu, there's something else I need to tell you."

There was a long pause. "My God, Rich. Did you actually—"

"No! Hell no! How could you even *think* that?!"

Stu gave a shaky laugh. "It was your tone, man. You just… you sounded scared."

"I got to be honest, I am."

"Rich, what's going on?"

"I… I need to tell you something, as my lawyer."

"Got it."

Rich winced. "I… talked to Gabby when I was back in Alberta."

"Shit, man! Have you told the police this?"

"No. I mean, I didn't *know* she was here too. I thought she was back in New York. Her number was the same, and we argued and…" Rich rubbed his hand over his mouth, the panic he'd only barely kept at bay, bright and terrible. "I—I talked to her last Friday—three days before they found her body. She… sounded messed up. She was raging at me. Screaming. Incoherent. Totally out of control and… I hung up on her."

"Right."

"What does 'right' mean?!" Rich snapped. "I'm telling you because I need your help here."

"I get that, man, but if you talked to her, that's going to be an issue."

The floor shifted under Rich and he caught himself against the wall. "But why?"

"Because they've almost *certainly* called for your phone records already."

"Do you think they're going to go after me?"

Stu let out a whistling sound that echoed like the wind outside the cabin.

"I don't know *what* they're going to do, Rich. But I know it already looks bad. And if you were the last one who talked to her before she died, then it's even worse."

"How bad?"

"If I was a prosecutor, you'd be the one I'd go after."

"So what do I do?"

"Go to the police. Tell them you talked to Gabrielle on Saturday. Just say you forgot in the shock of the moment. Trust me, buddy, you *want* to be the one to tell them, not wait for them to find out on their own. Do *not* get caught in a lie."

Rich was about to answer when a shrill scream echoed from upstairs.

* * *

The dream that was not a dream, started like a memory...

Lou stood in a muddy street under the glare of midday sun. The stink of unwashed bodies filled her nostrils, cheering crowds a cacophony in her ears. An elbow slammed into her side.

"Out of the way!" a man snarled at her. "Or I'll send your slutty ass up there with the rest of 'em!"

"I apologize, citoyen. So very sorry."

The man spat at her as Lou stumbled out of his way. The group of sans-culottes heckled the crowd as they passed through it, punching those who did not retreat fast enough. Louise wanted to run, but she forced herself to stay, scanning the wagons heaped with the dead.

She needed to know if Rich was among them.

Someone in the crowd began to sing the Marseillaise and Lou's terror grew. She lifted her gaze as a group of men and women were led onto a decorated platform. Some of the prisoners ascended the stairs quietly, others sobbed. The wood they walked on was sticky black with spilled blood, pigs wallowing in the mud near it.

A woman was dragged forward screaming, but Lou barely noticed her. She searched the faces of the other prisoners. Would he be among them? She had to know. The guards forced the woman into position and the woman's cries rose into screams.

The blade whistled down, ending in a wet thud, and her head tumbled into the basket. She landed face up, her dark hair a tangle obscuring a bloody face. Lou's gaze dropped, searching.

The dead woman caught Lou's eyes. She blinked—

"Lou! LOU! Wake up!"

With a shriek, Lou surged out of sleep. She flailed in panic. The heel of her hand hit something soft, and someone yelped.

"No!" she sobbed. "NO!"

The hands released her, Rich's voice—Rich...?—appearing her mind.

"It's okay, baby," he said. "It's just a nightmare, Lou. You're safe. You're just having a bad dream."

The light on the end table flicked on and the Parisian street rippled, replaced by her bedroom. Confused, Lou struggled upright. Rich sat on the side of the bed. He had one hand to his jaw, the other held out as if afraid to touch her.

"Lou, honey," he said. "It's okay. You're safe."

"W—what happened?"

"I heard you scream," he said, slowly lowering his hand.

"I—I had a dream. A *terrible* dream."

Sobs ripped through her and she slumped forward, wrapping her arms around her knees.

"Shhh… don't cry. It's okay." Rich's hand brushed her shoulder. "You're alright. It was just a nightmare. You're safe now." His arm encircled her, gently at first, then tighter. He pulled her into his lap and she let herself be held like a child. "Relax, baby. Breathe."

Lou cried harder. This wasn't a nightmare, it was a warning. Threads of it tethered her to Rich, hinting at trouble about to unfold. The coppery smell of blood hung in the air. That too, terrified her.

"I—I was trying to find you," she said, hiccupping, "but I couldn't. There were too many."

"Too many *what*?"

"Too many bodies."

His hand on her back stopped moving. She could still feel it there, atop her back, but the steady movement was gone.

"Bodies?"

"Dead. Piles of them… Heads in a basket. It was like the dream I had when you were in New York," she said, "but worse."

"Nothing happened to me in New York." He gave her a wary smile. "I wasn't at the Twin Towers. I was down on the street. You saw it coming, but I was safe."

Lou's hand fumbled until she found his fingers. "But you're not safe now, Rich."

"Why?"

"I don't know. But there's something happening."

She felt Rich's fingers tighten. His eyes hadn't left her face.

"Is this to do with Gabby? With them finding her body in the lake?"

"I… I think so," she whispered, tears filling her eyes. "Something bad is coming. I don't know when and I don't know what, but *something* is on its way."

She wiped tears away with the side of her hand.

"When you were in New York," Lou said, "something started. Something dark… dangerous. And it's not *over* yet."

Rich looked down at their hands. Lou could feel his thoughts drifting, moving into uncertain territory. He turned her hand over and his thumb brushed the ring. He took a slow breath, looked up.

"I need to tell you something, Lou."

"What?"

"I… I saw Gabby more than once when I was in New York. When Constables Black Plume and Wyatt were here, I said we all went out for dinner. That's true, but…" His fingers tightened. "That's not the *only* time I saw her."

A stab of pain ran through the scar over Lou's heart. "When else?"

"In New York, after Stu, Gabby and I had dinner, we split up. I went back to the hotel. Gabby and Stu went their separate ways. I wasn't even thinking about her. She'd seemed fine that night. Happy. Maybe even a little manic," Rich said, shaking his head. "Stu remembered that too… how she'd been a little bit wild at the restaurant, laughing and talking a bit too loud."

"Too loud," Lou repeated. "What do you mean?"

"Gabby was always a little… high strung. But that day was worse. I figured it was because of what happened with the Twin Towers. I didn't really think about it… at least not until what happened later."

Lou winced. "So you went out, just you and her?"

"No! We only had dinner that one night, and Stu was there too.

We all met up at a restaurant in Manhattan, close to where I was staying. We ate together. Laughed, talk, drank a bit too much."

Lou's fingers were limp in Rich's hand. She couldn't move. Didn't dare.

"What happened after that? You said you saw her again."

"That night I headed back to the hotel. Stu grabbed a cab. Gabby headed out to have a cigarette."

"And then…?"

"I thought she'd gone her own way, but when I was coming into the hotel's lobby, someone came up behind me. It…"

"Was Gabrielle," Lou finished.

Rich nodded.

"What then?"

Rich's face rippled in pain. Lou knew it hurt him to be asked, but she needed to know. She had to hear him say the words. If there was a betrayal, truth was better.

"Gabby came in after me. I… I was a little angry with her." He flinched. "I yelled a bit."

"In your room?"

"No!" Rich moved so quickly Lou jerked in surprise. His hands came up to her shoulders. "Christ, no! Not in my room. That's *not* what happened!"

"Then what?"

"Gabby followed me into the lobby. She tried to kiss me. I shoved her off, and we… we… had words." Rich shook his head. "The people at the desk saw it all. Fuck! It looks so *bad*, Lou."

"What did you say to her? Try to remember everything."

"I told her about you," he said. "I said I was going home to Waterton and she shouted something about New York being my home. I told her she'd *never* been home to me like you are, and she started screaming. Hitting my chest with her fists." Rich's eyes glittered, like he was trying to hold back tears. "One of the people at the front desk threated to call security. I said 'go for it.' I was just so fucking angry with her."

Lou nodded. "Does Stu know what's happened?"

"He does now." Rich laughed bitterly. "That's what we talked about tonight. We talked about a lot of things."

"Ah…"

Rich rubbed his hands up and down her arms.

"Look, I'm sorry I didn't tell you before. I should have, but it didn't seem to matter. I was coming home. I was getting the immigration in order." He smiled sadly. "I just wanted to surprise you. You believe me, right?"

"I believe you, but… we aren't done with this yet. There's something happening, Rich. It's starting up, not ending." She shivered.

Rich's hands rose from her arms to cup her chin. "What's coming?" he said. "What's—?"

The moment he touched her face, the dream's vision flashed, as if drawn from his hands. *Lou stood in the mud-churned street. On the platform, the guillotine's blade was hoisted upward, dripping, a man's voice calling out the condemned: "Arman de Cazotte, Emilie Desmoulins, Henri Lavoisier, Georges Corday," he shouted. "These men and women have been found guilty of treason against the rightful government of France, and as punishment, have been sentenced to death."* Lou gasped as the image retracted.

"Lou…?" Rich's arms tightened. "Are you alright, sweetie? You look a little woozy."

"Feeling a bit lightheaded. Let's go to bed."

"Are you sure? Are you sick or—"

"Please, Rich. I'm exhausted and I just…" She lay back against the pillows. "I just want to sleep."

"Okay then, but you tell me if you start feeling worse."

"Of course."

Lou felt Rich lift the covers on his side of the bed and crawl in beside her. She rolled toward him, his arms wrapping her. "Love you, Rich," she said. "So much."

"Love you too, baby. And I'm so sorry for all of this."

"It's alright. We'll get through it."

She closed her eyes. She and Rich were together. They were getting married. She'd chosen him… so why did it suddenly feel so tenuous?

* * *

When Jordan arrived on Saturday morning, Sadie was already in the office, pinning items to the billboard. Two newspaper clippings now joined the other items. One was a smaller, mid-section piece from the Lethbridge Herald. It included a single black and white photograph of Gabrielle Rice. The other clipping—a front-page spread from the Calgary Sun—took up a much larger space. Several colour photographs of the crime scene and details on Gabrielle's wealthy New York family were included in the comments. Jordan scowled as he scanned the contents.

NYC SOCIALITE FOUND DEAD IN WATERTON PARK

by Delia Rosings, October 16, 2001

Two local hunters made a grisly discovery Monday afternoon, in the wooded area just inside the border of Waterton Park, AB. A woman's mutilated body—

"What the hell?!" Jordan said.

"Got to the mutilated part, huh?" Sadie said. "That's the least of it. Keep reading."

—was found, face down in a bog. She was later identified as Miss

Gabrielle Rice, a New York socialite, who had been reported missing in mid-September by her parents. Anonymous sources say Miss Rice's parents—

"Anonymous sources?" Jordan said. "What anonymous sources? Her body was found less than a week ago."

"Keep reading," Sadie said in a sing-song voice.

—believed she'd had a mental breakdown due to the traumatic events of September 11th as she went missing soon afterwards. These same sources note that Miss Rice was involved in a romantic relationship with Mr. Richard Evans, of Waterton Park, who was found "Not Guilty" during the arson trial stemming from the burning of the Whitewater Lodge in 1999.

Local police have deemed Miss Rice's death 'suspicious' and have opened a homicide investigation. Sources have noted that given the discovery of Miss Rice's body in the park, Mr. Evans' residence in the area, and their stormy past relationship, Mr. Evans is a prime suspect. He is currently being investigated by local police for his part in her disappearance and murder.

"What the HELL!" Jordan barked. "They can't just publish shit like that!"

"Can and did," Sadie said. "Rosings always uses the whole 'anonymous sources' angle. Easy to take it back later."

"But it's just not *true*! Evans' isn't charged with anything…" He frowned. "Not *yet* at least."

"Ah… but that's how she gets away with it. If we go after her for the piece, she'll just ask us for our side of things." Sadie shook her head. "Better to forget about it. Delia's not worth the trouble." Sadie gave a harsh laugh. "But the cat's out of the bag now, Jordan. Other people will be asking questions."

"You think Rosings *does* have a source?"

"Don't know. Don't care."

"I don't know how you can be *okay* about this."

"Believe me, I'm not." Sadie grabbed her jacket off the chair. "But there's nothing we can do about it for now, so I'm focusing on what we can." She headed for the door. "I'll catch up with you in a bit."

"Wait. Where are you going?"

"Heading over to Hunter's Coffee Shop."

"For?"

"In theory it's to get coffee," she said, "but it's actually to get a little of the gossip."

"Ah… Talking to locals." Jordan himself had come to several of the unofficial coffee meetings over the last couple years. He'd taken Jim's empty place on the outside of the group, but it had never sat right with him, and eventually he'd stopped coming. There was a line that extended through the locals: *us* and *them*. Jim had been firmly on the inside. Sadie out. And Jordan wasn't quite sure where he fit with all of that.

"You want me to come along with you?" he asked.

Sadie paused in the doorway. "Uh… sure, I guess."

Jordan grabbed his coat. "I need some coffee anyhow."

"Still trying to get used to the switch to morning shift?"

"Just trying to stay conscious."

Sadie laughed. "That's half the battle."

CHAPTER SEVEN

Sadie and Jordan walked down Main Street under a canopy of yellow-leaved trees. Light fractured and bounced through the branches, spots of colour dancing on the ground. On days like this, it was easy to forget that winter was on its way.

Jordan pushed open the door to Hunter's Coffee Shop and stepped inside. The red leatherette booths were full. Chrome gleamed on the edges of tables, and on the metal dishware that flashed through the narrow window of the back kitchen. A familiar figure approached.

"Sadie, Jordan," Hunter said. "You guys here for some coffee to go?" He was already reaching for two china mugs—Hunter's 'to go' was simply a promise to return them—when Sadie spoke.

Not today, Hunter," she said. "I think we'll be staying here, if that's alright with you?"

"Of course, of course!" He pointed over his shoulder. "Lots of booths open. You staying for breakfast?"

"Just coffee," Jordan said, nodding toward the back of the restaurant where several tables had been pulled together. The central core of the Waterton community surrounded it, deep in conversation. "You mind if we join?"

Hunter stared at him for just a second too long.

"Not at all," he said, "but it's a little busy back there this morning. I'm happy to get you a booth or—"

"We'd like to sit with the community members," Sadie interrupted.

Jordan winced at the sharpness of her tone. That was *not* going to help.

Hunter's smile tightened. "I, um… I suppose you can." He stepped back. "Just… let me, uh…" He headed to the back tables.

Sadie elbowed Jordan. "Go!" she hissed.

"What?"

"He's going to warn them. Go!"

"Shit! Right."

Jordan scrambled to follow Sadie as she strode toward the group of tables at the back. Hunter was saying something in hushed tones to Audrika when the two of them came up behind him. Levi rapped his knuckles on the table. Hunter spun back around.

"There you are," he said. "I was just seeing if there was room or if—"

"I'll take this chair next to Levi," Sadie said.

Jordan moved two steps down to an open spot between Ronald and Grant, sitting down a moment later. The group of locals stared at him in confusion.

"Good to see you everyone," he said. "Been a while since we talked."

Levi's gaze flicked from Jordan to Sadie, then back again.

Us… them… us…

"Thought you weren't interested in the coffee meetings, Jordan?" Levi said. "You stopped coming last winter."

"Well, I, uh…" He cleared his throat. "I got kind of busy."

Hunter set a coffee in front of him. "Cream?"

"Yeah, thanks."

Hunter dropped several creamers down on the red check print cloth and moved down the aisle, refilling cups. If there had been chatter before they'd arrived, it was gone now. Sadie took a sip of coffee, sitting silent. Jordan fiddled with the cream, adding two, two and a half, two and three quarters—

"Might as well order a glass o' milk if you're gonna do that to it," Levi snorted.

"Right," Jordan said with a nervous laugh.

Now that he was here, he didn't know how to begin. *What did they know?* He couldn't just *say* that.

"So, uh… how's the ranch going?" he finally asked.

Levi coughed. "How d'you think?" He gestured to his sling. "Busted my arm, so I'm not *at* the ranch."

"Right. Sorry." Jordan winced. "Should've remembered. We talked to Bryce a few—"

"Heard you raked him over the coals for something he had nothin' to do with."

Sadie glared. "We only asked him where he'd been from Saturday to Monday."

Levi rolled his eyes.

"So, uh…" Jordan took a swallow of too-creamy coffee. "Everything good out at the ranch? Bryce has it all in hand?"

"I assume it's fine. Bryce is a farm boy. He knows what he's doing."

Hunter stepped between, dropping another cream in front of Jordan with a smirk.

Jordan cleared his throat. "I, uh… I'm sorry about your arm, Levi."

"Don't need your pity, boy."

"I didn't mean—"

"It's just part o' growin' old," Levi snapped, then turned away, muttering: "Fool boy runnin' off at the mouth."

Jordan cringed. *This* was why he'd stopped coming.

Sadie put down her mug. "Alright, everyone. I'm sure you're all wondering why we're here." Around the table, eyes shifted warily. "Obviously, it's not *just* the coffee. We're investigating a homicide."

A buzz of excited voices followed her announcement. Jordan wasn't sure how he'd expected everyone to react. It had been in the papers, after all. But the panic was palpable.

When the voices lowered, Sadie continued.

"As you know, Jordan and I have been going around town, trying to pin down the movements of Miss Rice. Specifically, we're trying to figure out what she was doing on Saturday last week."

"Was this that girl from New York?" a voice at the back of the room asked. Jordan turned and stared, but he couldn't tell who'd said it.

"I can't give you any details," Sadie said calmly. "But I'm sure many of you have already read today's papers. Yes, Miss Rice's death is—"

"Death?!" the voice at the back cried.

"Oh my heavens," Audrika gasped. "I don't get the Lethbridge paper. I… I never—"

Her voice broke and she burst into tears.

"I'm sorry, Audrika." Jordan reached out and patted her hand. "I didn't know you two were close."

"I can't— I just don't understand— I—" Audrika turned on Sadie, hands in fists. "Why didn't you tell me?" she choked. "I *asked* you if something was wrong with Gabby!"

"I couldn't tell you because we weren't certain of the details," Sadie said. "But seeing as the papers are now running the story, I want to make sure everyone has had a chance to share their information." The buzz of chatter rose, and Sadie lifted her hand to stop them. "We don't have a lot to go on right now. The more you can tell us about Miss Rice, the better we can—"

"But we don't *know* anything!" a woman snapped.

Jordan turned. Was that Margaret or Mila? He couldn't tell.

"You might think you don't know anything," Sadie said, "but there are plenty of times that the few things that you *do* remember are the key to unravelling something important."

"I already talked to you," Audrika said. "That's all I know."

"I talked to Jordan too!" a woman said.

Jordan lifted his eyes at his name, catching sight of Mrs. Lu.

Other voices interrupted. "I never knew the girl…"

"She wasn't a local. How would I know her?"

"Just a seasonal visitor—"

"—can't imagine *we* had anything to do with this—"

"—murderer was probably someone who came from outside the park."

"Wait a minute," Sadie said, but the voices rose in volume, rushing over top of her words. "Wait! Can I talk?"

"—you need to do your job! Protect the town—"

"Don't want danger here—"

Sadie pushed back from the table. "Listen, please! I need to—"

"—the hunters probably did it," someone said, "then called it in."

"Trying to foist the blame on US!"

"—can't think *we'd* have anything to do with this!"

"I don't know why we're even being asked!"

"—reminds me of when you and Jim thought I was involved in the Whitewater fire!"

Sadie surged to her feet.

"SILENCE!" she bellowed.

Audrika gasped, and Margaret Lu stared from behind thick glasses.

"Now I *do* want to hear what you all have to say," Sadie continued, "but I also need you to understand that it's an investigation. This *isn't* just me sharing news."

Hunter stepped forward, his face stern. "What's that mean?"

"It means," Jordan said, "that this is a homicide investigation and we need people to answer a few questions. We will be doing interviews, starting with—"

"But we had nothing to do with this!" a man shouted.

Sadie turned. "Nothing to do with *what*?"

There was a pause… then Grant spoke. "With whatever's going on."

"But I haven't *said* what's going on," Sadie snapped. "Jordan and I are just here to start taking names and information. Who saw Gabrielle Rice in town? Who talked to her? *When* did you talk to her? And what did she…?"

Her voice faded as the group of locals suddenly rose and moved as one. It was like watching a herd of elk switch directions mid-gallop. People scattered.

"Wait!" Sadie shouted. "Where are you going?"

Jordan stood. His hands clenched and unclenched as he watched them disappear out the front door, dismissing he and Sadie without a word. Hunter alone stood next to the table. He wordlessly filled Jordan's cup, then Sadie's.

"What the hell was that?" Sadie asked.

Hunter shook his head. "That was the end of the coffee meeting. Go on now." He dropped three creamers in front of Jordan. "Remember to bring the cups back when you're done," he added, then walked away.

* * *

Audrika had only just reopened her shop after the interrupted coffee meeting, when the bells tinkled over the door. She looked up from the tangled pile of bear bells to see a middle-aged man wearing gray slacks, a light jacket and a golf shirt waiting in the doorway. A warm smile curled the edges of Audrika's mouth. The man was attractive in a neutral sort of way, but more than that, he bore a metropolitan air that intrigued her.

"Why hello there!" she said, smiling brightly. "Beautiful morning, isn't it?"

He glanced sideways as if surprised to discover she was talking to him. Finding no one, he smiled.

"It is," he said, "almost feels like summer out there."

Audrika's gaze flitted over him as he approached the counter, noting the salt-and-pepper in his brown hair and the smile lines that fanned out from his eyes.

"What can I do for you?" she asked. "Are you looking for clothing? Souvenirs?"

"Well… I'm honestly not sure."

"Then why not start with *why* you're here in Waterton." She pushed the pile of bear bells to the side and leaned onto the counter, smiling. "Are you here to hike?" Her eyes flicked to the expensive leather shoes and tailored suit. "Or perhaps to drive through and see the sights?"

"Unfortunately, no." He laughed. "I'm here for a job, actually."

Audrika's eyebrows rose. "A job? How fascinating. We don't get many *new* people in town."

"Not in town. I do contract work."

"Contracts for…?"

"Businessmen who like me to handle things for them." Audrika opened her mouth to ask more, but he spoke before she could. "This must be all very boring to you. I'm sorry," he said, nodding toward the bear bells. "You're obviously busy."

Audrika gave a tinkling laugh. "Oh, don't be. My goodness, I've been searching for things to keep me occupied all morning."

"You sure?"

"Of course. Now, what are you looking for?"

A wry smile tugged the corners of his mouth.

"Why don't you show me what you've got?"

"Perfect." She came around the edge of the counter. "Come on," she said, waving him forward. "I'll give you the grand tour." He laughed and she laughed too, and a moment later, Audrika launched into her sales pitch. "Over here we have our summer and autumn clothing," she said. "All of that's fifty percent off. And over here, we have our hats and gloves. Same deal, though the sheepskin gloves are different prices than the wool mitts, just so you're not surprised. They're handmade, you know. And next to the mittens are our t-shirts…"

For ten long minutes, Audrika walked through the store, talking and pointing, bringing one item up and then another, holding it before him. To each the stranger smiled and nodded, letting her complete her spiel, but he didn't pick up a thing. Eventually they arrived back at the front desk. Audrika wilted. As nice as he was—*and he was nice!*—nothing had piqued his interest.

"Well, then," she said, dusting her hands off on the velour of her jacket. "That's about it." Her smile faded as she stepped back behind the counter and pulled the bear bells back toward her. They jingled as she grabbed the first tangled cord.

"Is it bad if I admit something?" the man said quietly.

"Admit what?"

"When I came in, I *was* looking for a pair of gloves, but then you started talking and I... I just didn't want you to stop." He smiled, showing wide even teeth and dimples in his cheeks. Audrika's heart flip-flopped. She wasn't sure how she'd overlooked it when he first stepped in, but he wasn't just passingly attractive, he had a distinct presence. The intrigue was enough to leave her breathless.

"You did?"

"I know that sounds foolish."

"Oh my!" The room felt too warm all of a sudden. Audrika shook her head and stepped out from behind the counter again. "Not foolish at all," she said, beaming. "But let's find those gloves for you." She fluttered her lashes. "Follow me, Mr...?"

"Farrel." He held out his hand. "But please call me Tom. All my friends do."

Audrika put her hand in his.

"Tom," she purred. "Well, it's very good to meet you." She let go of his hand with reluctance. "I'm Audrika Kulkarni."

Then she spun on her heel and bustled toward the bin of gloves. He was quick on her heels, and Audrika noted how quiet his tread was. *Not like Vasur*, she thought, *who was always stomping about.* She was so close to a sale, and if she could steer him toward the sheepskin gloves, it'd be a good one. And if Tom wanted a bit of distraction, well, she could give that too. There was no harm in flirting, was there?

"Now then," Audrika said, picking up the most expensive gloves. "These are the warmest. They're a little more expensive, but *definitely* worth the price."

He took the gloves from her waiting hand, his fingers brushing hers. "Money's not an object. I'm much more interested in quality."

"Quality in gloves?"

He looked up and flashed her a smile so bright Audrika's breath caught.

"In *everything*," he said, then turned back to the gloves. "Mmm… yes, these are very nice, but…"

"But?"

"I should probably look at the others, too." He winked. "If you'd be willing to show them again. I admit I was a little distracted before."

A rush of heat rose from Audrika's chest to her neck.

"I—I… of course, Tom," she said, picking up the next pair. "Well, these are also very nice, if you prefer regular leather," she said. "And these too, though I don't think they're your style…"

As she went through the various choices, she and Tom chatted. He asked about her business and her family (though Audrika left her answers vague in Vasur's regard), then went on to comment on the beauty of Waterton's location and how exciting it must be to live in a place where so many people visited.

"You're right," Audrika said, "Waterton *is* lovely in the spring and summer, but come winter it gets awfully boring. There are less than a hundred of us that live here year-round."

"Really? That few?"

"Mm-hmmm. It's nice for the first month or so. Everyone needs a break after the rush of the summer months, but after a time it… it can be quite isolating too."

Tom's hand brushed hers. "I'm so very sorry."

She looked up and her breath caught. He was only a hands-breadth away.

"Sorry for…?"

"For *you,* Audrika. I can only think that being alone must be quite difficult for someone as vivacious as you are." He dropped his hand to his side and Audrika had the sudden, inappropriate urge to lean in. She forced it down. "I imagine Waterton must get lonely at times," Tom said.

"I… yes," she said. "I guess it does."

"There must be very few tourists once the summer is over."

"That's true, but there *are* a few."

"Really?"

"Oh yes, there's always someone coming through town. Especially in the fall," she said. "And you never can tell where they're from. Waterton draws a diverse crowd."

"Really?" he laughed. "From where?"

"There was a couple from Germany who came into the shop last week, and a young man from Ireland, backpacking to the coast. Oh! And a woman from New York."

"New York?"

"Yes, New York." Audrika leaned closer. "Very sad story, though." She dropped her voice. "The poor girl was murdered. It was all over the papers today."

Tom's face blanched. "Murdered? That's horrible."

"I know. It's *awful* to imagine someone doing something like that. I mean, I'm here day in and day out. What if that kind of person walked into my store?"

"Dear God." Tom clutched her hand. "*Please* promise me you'll be careful, Audrika." He looked down and released her fingers as if only noticing what he'd done. "Just… be *careful.* Please."

"Oh, I will. I promise."

For a long time, she and Tom spoke. He seemed fascinated by the town and the slower pace that kept Waterton separate from the rest of the world. There was no internet and cell phones rarely got reception. Even cable television was limited to a few channels. Audrika spoke about those who lived in the hamlet year-round and the visitors who came through while Tom listened. Three separate times he prodded the conversation back toward Gabrielle Rice, something Audrika found somewhat distressing, but Tom was very good at waiting out her stilted answers and even offered her a silk handkerchief from his pocket when tears overcame her. A full half-hour had passed since he'd walked through the door. Neither noticed. Audrika preened under Tom's quiet commentary and gentle compliments. He was, Audrika decided as he finally stepped back, the most attractive men she'd ever met.

Tom glanced at his wristwatch and frowned. "While I would dearly love to stay and talk further," he said with a sigh, "I really *should* be going."

"So soon?"

"If I could just purchase these first," he said, holding up the most expensive pair of gloves she'd shown him. "I have wasted *far* too much of your time, Audrika."

"Not wasted," she said, plucking the gloves from his waiting hands and walking behind the till. "Never that."

He waited as she typed the cost into the till, then handed her a crisp American fifty. "I hope it's no issue to pay with American currency?"

"None at all, as long as you don't mind the rate," she said, ringing it through.

"I trust you."

"Thank you." Audrika blushed as the drawer popped open with a ping. "And there's your change, Tom."

"Thank you," he said. "You've been incredibly helpful."

"Come back anytime."

"Oh, I suspect I will."

She giggled as he took the bag and held it up for her.

"Never know when I might need the hat to match the gloves," he said, and with one last smile, he headed out of Fine and Fancy.

Audrika wandered to the window, watching him walk up the street toward Hunter's Coffee Shop. Waterton had its share of boring people, but Tom Farrel intrigued her. He'd been flirting with her—she was certain of that—but that wasn't the *only* thing that had piqued her interest. It was the way Tom kept bringing the conversation back around to Gabrielle Rice. There was something *more* going on there and she wondered what it was. Audrika's eyes narrowed and she returned to the counter with quick, determined steps. She grabbed the phone and dialed, pulling off one clip-on earring with one hand while lifting the handset with the other.

The phone rang once, Margaret's voice appearing a moment later. "Hello?"

"Margaret, dear, it's Audrika."

"Yes?"

Audrika stood on tiptoe, but Tom Farrel had disappeared into one of the shops down the street. "I just met the most interesting fellow."

"Oh…?"

"A man doing a little work in town. His name's Tom Farrel." Audrika dropped her voice even though she was alone in the store. "He seemed mighty interested in what everyone in town was up to, especially in regard to Gabby…"

* * *

Lou woke to the smell of bacon. She sighed and rolled over, groping blindly toward the empty side of the bed. The rumpled covers were cold and crisp. Rich had been up for some time.

She sat up, her stomach roiling uneasily. For someone who'd gone to sleep relatively early, she felt like she'd had only half a night's sleep. The nightmare from the day before lingered. It had been one thing to have the premonition when Rich was in New York. It was quite another to have a dream like that when he was safe in Waterton.

She dressed quickly and headed downstairs. The table was set for breakfast, two settings side by side. Lou grinned as she saw it. A frying pan sat half-off the burner, dry toast—gone cold—in the toaster. Louise did a slow turn of the empty kitchen.

"Rich?"

"Over here!"

Lou turned back the other way, heading into the living room to discover him standing next to the couch, a folded newspaper in hand.

"I was wondering where you'd gotten to," she said. "Thought maybe you'd…" Her words faded as she saw the expression on his face. "What's wrong?"

Rich looked up and the snap of his emotions—sharp and angry—hit her straight in the chest.

"They've got my name in the paper." He handed her the pages. "The Lethbridge and Calgary papers are both running stories on Gabby's death," he said. "The Sun has my name *and* picture in it. Fuck!"

Lou looked up, wide-eyed. "*Your name*? But why?"

"Because bullshit makes good news. People."

Lou felt a wave a nausea rise inside her and she stumbled to a seat on the couch, the paper limp in her hands.

"My God…" she whispered.

"It's not just that either. I talked with Stu this morning, and the NYPD there have been looking into my whereabouts while I was in New York."

"But… I don't understand. None of this makes any sense."

Rich paced the room, a caged bear.

"Doesn't matter if you understand, and it sure as hell doesn't need to make sense. They need someone to go after, and I'm the one they've got." He paused in front of her. "Christ, Lou. This is bad!"

She nodded.

"I'm so sorry," he said.

"For what?"

"For this mess. For coming home, but not coming back to Waterton, for—" He ran his hands into his hair. "Jesus, FUCK! I just need things to settle down for a while!"

Lou came forward to wrap her arms around his waist. "Can I tell you a story?"

He laughed bitterly. "A story?"

"Yes. It might help."

Rich dropped his chin down onto her shoulder, his body softening in the circle of her arms.

"Sure," he said. "A story'd be great."

Lou rubbed his back as she let her thoughts draw out, catching on the many tales she had. Which one would hold the key? Which had the right message? After a few seconds, an image appeared: a churning river and a man standing on one side. Lou smiled.

"There was a young man who was traveling along a road when he came to a wide river. He walked one direction and then the other, searching for a bridge or a shallow area where he could pass."

"Let me guess," Rich said. "There *wasn't* one."

Lou smirked. "Is this my story or yours?"

"Yours, of course." He brushed a stray hair away from her face. "You were saying?"

"The young man walked along the riverside, growing more annoyed by the minute. There *should* be a way over. He was certain of it. But he could not find it."

Rich chuckled.

"Eventually, something moving along the far banks of the river caught his attention. He wasn't certain what it was at first. He stepped right up to the edge of the river and squinted. The shadow grew larger. The young man shaded his eyes, trying to see the other side."

"What was it?"

"It was the silhouette of a man… A Buddhist monk. But not just *any* monk, a very famous teacher, one the young man had heard of many times."

Lou looked up. Rich waited on her every word. His posture had lost the frustration of moments earlier.

"And…? he said.

"At just that moment, the monk across the river looked up and smiled. Seeing him, the young man shouted: 'Wise one! Tell me, how do I get to the other side of the river?' The teacher looked at the banks on which he stood, and then the river that divided them. He answered: 'You do not need to. For you are *already* on the other side.'"

A line appeared between Rich's brows. "But… that doesn't make sense."

Lou shrugged. "It's just a story."

"But the young man asked how to get to the other side."

"Uh-huh."

"And the monk said he was already there."

Louise tipped her head to the side, smiling up at him.

"Yup."

"I…" Rich scowled. "I can't just change my perspective on this. I'm mad as hell this is happening. I don't know what your story's supposed to—"

Lou put her forefinger on the center of his lips, stopping him.

"You don't *have to* change your perspective, Rich."

"But the young man isn't on the right side."

"He doesn't *think* he is, but perhaps he is…" She shrugged. "Who's to say?"

Rich stared at her for a long moment.

"I'm serious!" Lou laughed.

Rich smirked. "Not sure your story works in this situation." He pulled Lou into a bear hug. "But thanks for trying."

"If it helps. I'm on this side of the river with you too."

Rich's arms around her tightened. "That does."

* * *

Constable Black Plume stared down at the newspaper in her hand. *Anonymous sources have said that Miss Rice died of blunt force trauma to the head, compounded by a broken neck. Without medical treatment, there was no chance for survival…* Her fingers tightened, crumpling the paper, and she dropped it on the desk.

"Goddamnit!"

Jordan glanced up. "Everything okay?"

Sadie kicked her booted feet up onto the corner of the desk.

"Fine," she grumbled. "Just wondering where the newspapers have been getting their information."

Jordan picked up the paper. "Delia Rosings again, huh? She's just digging up dirt. You can't take her writing seriously."

"I wouldn't if it wasn't for the part about the broken neck. No one *knew* about that except for the coroner."

"Huh. Weird." Jordan frowned and looked down again, reading. "So it is."

"We've got someone leaking information. I want to know who."

"It could just be a guess."

"It's *not* a guess."

Jordan went back to reading while Sadie pulled out her list of questions and transcribed details. She'd gotten little information so far. The town was swarming with reporters, much like it had been after the Whitewater fire and when she'd arrived at the police station this morning, she'd had to avoid a bevy of reporters asking for her comments. Sadie didn't *know* who'd talked, but she had an inkling it was someone closely connected to the case.

Jordan flicked the newspaper over, reading the final paragraph. "Weird," he said. "It really *does* sound like someone talked. I mean… this part here about Gabrielle and Rich Evans. No one knew that bit either."

"Oh-ho, people in town most certainly did."

"But who'd say that to a reporter?"

Sadie rolled her eyes. "Anyone who has a beef with Rich. Anyone who likes to gossip."

"That's a lot of people."

"Yup."

Sadie stopped writing as her gaze flicked to the open door. At the front desk sat Liz, typing away at an ancient computer, the radio next to her playing a country song. Liz was trustworthy, but she wasn't the only person who could have come into the back office. Sadie's eyes drifted back to the billboard behind her. All the images and details spread across it, a map for whoever came in. She wondered who'd been cleaning the police station at night. Sadie pulled out her notebook, transferring the scribbled notation from her interview with Audrika Kulkarni over to a computer document. She'd just reached the detail about Gabrielle complimenting Audrika's earrings when Liz popped her head around the edge of the door frame.

"Sorry to bother you," she said. "But Mr. Evans is here to see you."

"Rich Evans?" Sadie repeated.

"Uh-huh. Says he remembered something he'd like to add to his official report." Liz dropped her voice. "You want me to bring him back to you, or do you want to talk out front?"

"Let's bring him back," Sadie said. "Don't need any extra details getting out into the press. We've got our hands full already."

"Sounds good; I'll send him in then."

Liz disappeared and Jordan shot Sadie a concerned look. "What do you think it's about?" he asked.

"No idea, but we're about to find out." She pushed out from her desk and stood, straightening her jacket in a single smooth movement. Jordan brushed the items he'd been working on into a pile and pushed it aside. He scanned the desk, then flipped the newspaper article face down just as Rich walked into the room. Rich's shirt was misbuttoned, and though his hair was combed, he was unshaved.

"Mr. Evans." Sadie offered her hand. "Good to see you again. What can we do for you?"

"I, uh… I thought of a few things that I want to add to my report." Rich's gaze skittered up to the board to where a colour image of Gabrielle, face down in the mud, hung. He paled. "I—I need to tell you a few things about Gabby."

"Alright then. Let me get a pad." Sadie nodded to the open chair. "Have a seat."

Jordan shot her a questioning look, then turned to Rich.

"Mr. Evans," he said. "I need to remind you that anything you say can and will be used against you in a court of law. Do you understand that?"

"Of course. I just want to clear a few things up."

"Do you want your lawyer to be present?" Sadie asked.

"No. I'm fine, I just..." He shook his head. "I remembered something I'd forgotten when we spoke earlier. I was really shaken up about Gabby's death. I... I wasn't thinking straight." His eyes pleaded with them. "I want to make sure you have *all* the information."

"Alright then," Sadie said. "What did you remember?"

"Friday afternoon," he said. "That's when I last talked to Gabrielle."

Sadie stared. "But I thought you told us that you hadn't seen Gabrielle after you left New York earlier that week."

"I hadn't seen her... I *spoke* to her. And it wasn't face-to-face," Rich said. "We talked by phone." He reached into his pocket and fished out a folded piece of paper. "Here," he said. "I wrote down all the details I could remember about those days. Every place I went, the financial advisors I met with. The bank meetings in Calgary and in Lethbridge."

He held it out to Sadie, who passed it to Jordan. On it were a list of calls, meetings, and times. Some of the places were business, others were the Nesbitt Burns offices with appointments noted: *Papers signed by financial advisor... Arranged for transfer of 401K into Canadian accounts... Called regarding marriage license...*

"I've been trying to remember everything I did the last couple days," Rich continued. "I wrote it down to make it clear. Not *all* the things on that list have receipts attached to them, but many of them were by appointment, and several at banks. You could check for those appointments. Most of my calls could be corroborated too, even the ones from the hotel."

"Let's talk about your conversation with Miss Rice."

"The one on Friday, or before?" Rich asked.

Jordan shot Sadie another look. "You spoke to her *more than once* after leaving New York?"

"A few times. Yeah." Rich pointed to the list Jordan held. "I tried to remember them as best as I could, but I'm sure they're all in the records."

Sadie scribbled details down, then looked back up. "Did you call Miss Rice the first time, or did she call you?"

"She called me. She's *always* the person who calls."

"Was," Jordan said quietly.

Rich looked up. "Was what?"

"She *was* the one who called. She won't be calling you anymore."

Rich's face crumpled. For a few seconds it seemed like he might get up and walk out, but he remained. Sadie shot Jordan a dark look.

"What did you two talk about when she called the first time?" she asked.

"The first time she called, it was to ask if I wanted to meet her for dinner. And… and to apologize."

"Apologize for what?" Sadie asked.

"We'd had a fight. It…" Rich sat up straighter. "It was at the hotel in New York, in the lobby. Gabrielle showed up and went after me, accusing me of stringing her along. Of being a bastard. She tried to kiss me and I stopped her. I—I pushed her away."

"Did anyone witness this?" Jordan asked.

Rich nodded. "Yes. The woman at the desk called security. Gabby was out of control."

Sadie scribbled a frantic note. *Check for hotel lobby cameras*

ASAP!

"And after that she called you?"

"Yes," Rich said. "It was Monday, I think. I hadn't been answering my phone for a few days. I was finally coming home to Waterton and I'd been traveling. My phone wasn't charged. But when I reached Calgary and checked into the hotel—" Sadie made another note: *Check hotel registrations.* "—there were a number of messages from Gabby, begging me for forgiveness. Saying she'd drunk too much. I…." Rich winced. "I deleted them all."

"And after that," Jordan said. "She called you?"

"Yes. She phoned me several times. I finally answered."

Sadie's pen hovered over the page. "And…?"

"And she apologized for the outburst at the hotel. She wanted to get together some time to talk things over. 'Grab dinner some night,' but I said I couldn't."

"Why?" Sadie asked.

"Well, first off, because I wasn't *in* New York."

"But neither was she," Jordan said.

"But I thought she was." Rich leaned forward. "I didn't *know* she was in Alberta. I swear it."

"Would you swear that under oath?" Jordan asked.

"Do I need to?"

"You might," Sadie said. "Did you tell her you were back in Alberta?"

"No. I—" Rich clenched and unclenched his hands. "I said 'no' to dinner on principle. I didn't want to see her again, not after the scene she'd pulled in New York."

"At the hotel."

Rich nodded. "But it was more than that. Gabrielle… was angry at Lou."

"Louise Newman?"

"Yes. The night of the fight, I told Gabby that Louise and I were getting married."

Sadie jotted another note. *Check if Lou Newman ever met Gabrielle Rice.*

"She didn't take it well?" she asked.

Rich gave a grating laugh. "That would be an understatement. And when we spoke that first time—after I returned to Canada, that is—I was pretty leery about having anything to do with her at all."

Jordan nodded. "So that first call happened on Monday. Is that right?"

"Yes, at least I think it happened on Monday." Rich frowned. "I'm eighty percent sure of that date."

"We'll check the phone records." She nodded. "And you mentioned you talked to her again after that."

"Yes," Rich said. "She… She phoned me three or four times."

"When?" she asked.

"They were just at random moments. One was late at night, another midday. Gabby calling with no explanation. Once she started raging at me for leaving her… and another time when she called, she was crying. On Friday, we argued… loudly." Rich took a slow breath and let it out again. "I was tired of her calling me. I said I would change my phone number if she didn't stop."

Jordan moved his chair closer. "Did you say anything else to her?"

Rich frowned. "'Anything else' meaning what?"

"Did you warn her?" Jordan said. "Say anything that could be considered threatening?"

"No! Never! I just… I needed her to leave me alone. I know it sounds bad, but I just needed her out of my life."

"And then…?" Sadie said.

"And that's all," Rich said. "I just wanted to tell you up front. I'll go under oath if you need me too, and the phone records will back me up." He pointed to the detailed list, still clutched in Jordan's hand. "All of what I told you is true. I wanted to make sure I told you everything up front."

"Alright then," Sadie said. "Anything else you want to tell us?"

"No. That's it," Rich said.

"Jordan?" she asked. "Anything else from you?"

"Not for now, but don't go too far, Mr. Evans." He stood and both Sadie and Rich followed suit. "We might call you in again as we start laying out events. We appreciate you talking to us up front."

"No problem," Rich said. He looked from Jordan to Sadie. "Can I go now?"

"Of course you can," she said. "We'll be in touch."

In less than a minute, he was out the door, leaving Sadie and Jordan alone in the office. She stared down at the page of notes, scribbled in a messy hand.

"Jesus, that was quite a thing to see," she said. "Guy's putting the noose around his own neck."

"What do you mean?"

"He just made himself look a hell of a lot more guilty, Jordan."

"Uh… I don't know about that." He tipped his head to the side. "I thought maybe he was trying to clear things up."

"But why?"

"Maybe he's being honest."

She gave a hard laugh. "Honest… or he's trying to throw us off."

"Do you think he's involved somehow?"

"Maybe… maybe not. I just don't know."

"But this is Rich Evans, Sadie. He's gonna marry Lou in a couple months. The guy's practically a local. You can't *really* think he killed that ex-girlfriend of his, no matter *how* crazy she was acting."

Sadie's gaze lifted to the photograph of Gabrielle Rice, but she didn't see the dead girl. Instead, she saw Jim Flagstone laying in a pool of his own blood on Susan Varley's kitchen floor. Sue and Jim had been friends for years and she'd killed him all the same.

Sadie shook her head to force the memory away.

"I don't know *what* I think anymore."

CHAPTER EIGHT

Rich had been desperate to get back to Waterton when he was stuck in New York. Now everything had changed. Where there had been calm in the mountain's embrace, he felt trapped. Gabrielle's murder hovered just on the side of his day-to-day life, taunting him with its proximity. As Constables Black Plume and Wyatt had warned, he wasn't to leave the area, so there was nothing for Rich to do except carry on. And once he'd gathered all the documents that Stu told him to locate, he found himself with time on his hands.

Returning to Lou's Garage seemed the obvious step.

He swung by the garage around noon but Lou was nowhere to be seen. Brendan Miles sat at the counter, a stubby pencil behind one ear, a book of crossword puzzles in front of him.

The teen looked up.

"Hey, Rich. I heard you were back in town!"

"How've you been, Brendan?"

"Good enough," he said. "The garage has been a little slow."

"That's not necessarily bad."

"Guess not." Brendan laughed and pulled the pencil from behind his ear, printing in a word. "You here to see Lou?"

"Yeah. Thought I might give her a hand in the shop."

"Well, go on back." Brendan grinned. "And hey! It's good to have you back again."

"Thanks," Rich said. "But I'm sure you got along just fine without me here."

"We did okay, I guess, but Lou wasn't herself without you."

"Good thing I'm back then," Rich said, smiling. He passed aisles of canned goods and chocolate bars, finally reaching the back entrance to the shop. His heart tightened as he remembered Lou on the floor, bleeding, but he pushed the dark thought aside, filling in the gap with other memories: like the summer they'd rebuilt his car, and the two years since then, working side by side in the shop.

He knocked on the door.

"It's unlocked!" Lou called.

Rich opened the door and waited for his eyes to adjust to the darkness. A tireless truck was propped up on jacks; Lou, on her back, half under it. A splash of light traced along the outlines of her silhouette, spreading like a pool of sunshine from under the vehicle.

Rich grinned. "You need some help around here?"

"Rich!" Lou laughed, rolling out from under the vehicle. "Didn't you have to talk to Stu again?"

"I did. All finished now." Rich walked to the truck and crouched next to Louise. "What are you working on?"

"Replacing the muffler today." She sat up and wiped her face, leaving a trail of grease along one cheek. she said. "Thing's being a nuisance. The entire undercarriage is worn through."

Rich blurred the mark away with his thumb. "You want some help with that?"

"You still have the skills, city boy?"

Rich snorted. "I dunno. Only way to find out. Willing to take a risk on me?"

"Oh, Rich… you're *never* a risk." Lou gave him a half-sad smile.

"Good. 'Cause you're not getting rid of me."

"Then I'd better put you to work. Overalls are on the wall. Grab a pair. You can take a turn under the truck; my back is aching."

Rich frowned and took her hand. "You can't go pushing yourself, Lou."

Her smile dimmed, but she didn't pull away.

"I'm fine," she said. "Just too long on the backboard. You can't go *worrying* about me all the time. I'm fine."

"Fair enough." He laughed and leaned in to catch her in a kiss. He pulled back. "Love you, Lou. You know that, right?"

"I do. Now go grab those overalls." She stood slowly, stretching her back. "I need a break."

"Got it."

Rich pulled the coveralls over his jeans and buttoned-down shirt, revelling at the feel of the heavy cotton washed into softness. The coveralls smelled of soap and motor oil, and doing up the clasps reminded him of a summer where he'd spent every spare minute with Lou, imagining a future together. That had been the summer of the fire, the year he'd been charged with arson. He'd survived that, hadn't he?

"What're you thinking about?" Lou asked softly and Rich jerked, surprised he hadn't heard her walk up behind him. "You look sad."

"Not sad, exactly," he said. "Just thinking about the summer we fixed my car."

She grinned. "That was a lot of fun."

"It was."

"This is good way to reminisce then. I've been working on this beater for more than a week."

"That bad, huh?" Rich laughed.

"Uh-huh."

In minutes, he was under the truck, staring up at the undercarriage. Lou was right. The entire underside was riddled with rust. If this had been *his* vehicle, he would have taken it to the dump. There were more holes in some places than metal, and he could see into the interior cab in a couple places.

"Jesus," he snorted. "You weren't kidding about rusted out."

Lou took a seat beside his knees. "Pretty awful, huh?" She laughed and nudged him with her toe. "What do you need?"

"Hmmm…" Rich scanned the underside. "Quarter-inch ratchet." He held out his hand and the tool appeared in his fingers. "Thanks."

"No problem."

For a time, they carried back and forth like this, as Rich removed the old muffler and adjusted the structure that held it in place. When he was fighting with a particularly tight bolt, he heard Lou clear her throat.

"Rich, I don't mean to pry, but… if there's anything that you want to talk about, you know you can tell me, right?"

He reached out for her. "I know, Lou… I *promise* I know, and if there was anything to say… anything I'd done, I'd say it."

Lou put her palm against his; held it there. "I know that. I… I trust you."

"Thank you. That means a lot." He squeezed her fingers and let go. With the old muffler taken down, Rich shoved it to the side and pushed himself out from under the vehicle. He sat up.

"There you go," he said, passing her the rusted-out shell of the old muffler.

"You want me to take a turn, or do you want back under again?"

"I'm actually good," Rich said, "but do you mind if I lift the truck up a bit more? I was having a hard time getting my elbows under me."

Lou giggled. "You know, I had plenty of room."

"Yeah, well, I'm not five foot two." Grinning, he reached for the metal handle of the jack, pumping it up and down. "When I'm working, I need to be able to—"

A metallic scream cut Rich off. The jack flew sideways, truck crashing down onto the backboard. The second jack teetered, then slipped.

"Move!" Lou screamed.

Rich rolled out of the way. A heartbeat later, the truck's second tireless wheel well came down hard on the cement, the third and fourth following in quick succession. The tireless truck was flat on the floor, covering the very spot where Rich had been lying minutes earlier. The backboard was pinched underneath.

Rich stared at it, gasping. "Oh my God. I… I could have been, —" The word caught in his throat and he turned, staring at Lou in shock. "You could have been under there. Either one of us could have been dead."

Lou came forward slowly, as if afraid the truck itself would come to pieces. She stared at the lifts, scattered on the floor. "This isn't right," she whispered. "Not right. I put those up myself. I *know* I did."

Rich stared at her. "Someone messed with them."

"And all four went," she said, staring up at him in horror. "That's no accident that's—"

"Someone trying to kill you."

Lou nodded.

"We need to call the police," Rich said.

Lou crouched down next to the jack. She leaned in, but didn't touch it.

"There are scrapes along the side, where the teeth are supposed to hold. Someone filed them down."

"Who?"

She shook her head. "I've no idea. Whenever I leave for the night, I make a point to check the locks."

"Was the lock ever open on the garage when you came in?"

Lou shook her head. "No."

"How about in the morning. Did you ever find the door left open?"

"No."

Rich crouched down next to her, rubbing her back.

"Who has keys, Lou? Who could get in here and mess with your equipment?"

She frowned and chewed her lip.

"Just me, you, Brendan and Mila."

* * *

Audrika leaned on the counter of the police station.

"And why *can't* I get his personal information?"

Constable Black Plume stared.

"Because you're *not* a police officer. You can't just go snooping around in other people's business. This Mr…"

"Farrel," Audrika said. "Tom Farrel." She smiled coyly. "He *told* me he was from New York. I want to know if he was telling the truth or not."

"Mrs. Kulkarni, *please.* Mr. Farrel's privacy is protected in the same way *your privacy* is protected." Sadie paused. "He didn't do anything concerning, did he?"

"Oh no. Not at all!" Audrika laughed. "Perfect gentleman!"

"Good."

"But he *was* very vague about who he was working for, and I… thought you might be able to help me uncover who that was. You know, a little favour for one of the girls."

Sadie took a slow breath and let it out. She could almost *hear* Jim laughing at her.

"While I appreciate you checking with me, I need to remind you that you do not have access to any records, no matter how vague Mr. Farrel might have been about his work experience."

Audrika's smile evaporated.

"Margaret told me you wouldn't help," she said. "I *thought* she might be wrong about you."

Behind the counter, Sadie heard Liz stifle a giggle.

"Look, Mrs. Kulkarni," Sadie said. "It's just a matter of privacy and legality. I appreciate that you are interested in this friend of yours, but I really *cannot* help."

The phone rang, Liz answering a second later.

"Is Constable Wyatt around?" Audrika asked. "Perhaps he'd be able to—"

"No, he's not. And Constable Wyatt would tell you the same thing. This man's personal information *isn't* your business."

"No need to be so rude about it. You could have just said!"

"I did say, Mrs. Kulkarni, and you didn't—"

"Sadie?" Liz interrupted.

"Fine!" Audrika said. "I'll be on my way."

"If you have any *actual* concerns," Sadie said. "Then I'd—"

"Constable Black Plume," Liz said, voice sharp, "this is *important.*"

"—be happy to reply to those."

"Never mind!" Audrika said. "I've got things to do." She turned from the counter, stomping away.

Liz cleared her throat. "Constable Black Plume?"

"What?!" Sadie spun around to find Liz waiting. The receptionist's face was ashen.

"Louise Newman is on the phone," she said.

"Why?"

"She says someone tried to murder her."

* * *

Hunter heard the racket as soon as he climbed out of his truck. The dogs were baying in panic.

"Levi!" he gasped, jogging up the sidewalk toward the house. He fumbled for his keys, nearly dropped them, then looked up.

A stranger waited on his front porch.

Hunter put on a false smile and continued up the sidewalk. "Hi there. What can I do for you?"

"Are you Mr. Slate?"

"That's me."

"I just want to talk a minute, if you have time." The stranger nodded toward the door. The dogs were howling like banshees on the other side. "Sorry I upset your dogs. I swear I only rang once."

"It's fine. They're just wound up. Now what can I help you with?"

"I was wondering if I could talk to you about a young woman who might have been in town the last few weeks."

Hunter's false smile rippled into genuine confusion.

"Sorry, who?"

The stranger reached into his inside pocket, pulling out a front-page clipping from the newspaper. "This girl here," he said. A pale young woman with dark hair, smiled into the camera. In the grainy background some kind of party of social event was taking place. "Miss Gabrielle Rice."

"Face is familiar, but I don't know her. Why d'you ask?"

The stranger laughed. "I… Well, if I'm honest, one of the other people in town said that you know pretty much everyone. You own the coffee shop, right?"

"Yes, I do."

"And this girl here." He tapped the paper. "She might have come in sometime."

"Is this an investigation?"

"In a way, yes."

Hunter stared at him. Something wasn't adding up.

"Could I see your badge, please?"

The man chuckled. "Oh… when I said 'investigation' I *didn't* mean I was with the police. I'm investigating, yes, on my own."

"Why?"

"I work privately."

"So you're a private investigator, then?"

"Well, yes. That's one of my roles, though I prefer to think of myself as a businessman."

"Meaning?" Hunter said.

"I'd prefer not to say."

"And I'd prefer if I knew what *exactly* you did."

The man's smile faded.

"Given my business, I'm not at liberty to say."

Behind the man, the curtains flickered. Levi was inside, watching. If Levi's arm wasn't broken, Hunter knew he'd be holding a gun. Even now, it was a possibility.

"You know," Hunter said, "you're making me feel mighty uneasy here."

Inside, the howls grew louder.

"It's a simple question," the stranger said. "Did you see this woman or not?"

Hunter nodded. "Yes, I did. She came in a few times over the last couple weeks. Nice girl. Quiet."

"Did she sit with anyone? Talk to anybody?"

"I'll tell you the exact same thing I told the police," Hunter said. "She sat alone. She didn't talk to anyone except the waitresses who served her. She seemed… *sad*. Now excuse me, but I need to see to my dogs."

The man stepped out of Hunter's way. "Appreciate the help."

Hunter snorted. The man walked away and Hunter heard the door unlock from the inside, Levi's face appearing in the crack a moment later.

"He gone?"

Hunter nodded. "He is."

* * *

Sadie spent most of an hour checking the back room of Lou's garage. She tagged the broken jacks as evidence and searched for clues. One of the windows had marks along the side with the latch; Sadie photographed that too. As far as she could tell, someone had used a thin blade to push up the latch, crawled inside, and then filed down the teeth on the jack so that they failed. Sadie swore under her breath. *When it rained, it poured.* This was the second of two investigations. But she *needed* her attention on the homicide.

This could have been one too, she imagined Jim saying.

Sadie flinched, and looked up from the report she'd transcribed from Lou and Rich's description.

"You should replace the windows," she said. "Perhaps install a security system. Do you have one back at your house?"

"No," Lou said. "Though the windows there were replaced about five years ago. Double paned. Locking."

"Good. But think about a security system too," Sadie said. "That's always a deterrent."

"Do you think someone is targeting Lou?" Rich said, sliding his arm over Lou's shoulders. "Is she in some kind of danger?"

"I hope not. But given this and the guy we chased away from the cabin, it's probably—"

Rich's eyebrows rose. "What guy?"

Constable Black Plume looked from Rich to Lou and then back again.

"I'm sorry. I assumed…"

"I forgot to tell you," Lou said. "There was someone hanging around the house one night. I called the police, and they checked it out. They weren't able to catch the guy."

"Why the hell not?!"

"We *did* follow the suspect, Mr. Evans," Sadie said. "But he got away. I'm taking this crime…" she said, gesturing to the jacks, "completely seriously. And yes, there is a good chance that they're related. I just can't say how." Rich scowled as she put the report aside. "Now, while I'm here," she said. "Could I ask you a few questions, Louise?"

"Sure. About what?"

"I've been asking everyone about Miss Gabrielle Rice." Sadie turned to Rich. "If you could give us a few minutes, please?"

With Rich gone, Sadie ran through her questions. Louise looked at the photograph, but admitted that she'd never even seen—never mind met—Gabrielle before.

"Do you remember anyone in particular coming into your store the last couple weeks?" Sadie asked.

"Not really," Lou said. "There were lots of people around because September and October have been warm."

"Any in particular you remember?"

"No. Sorry," Lou said. She frowned. "I… I know you're just doing your job, Sadie, but I *know* Rich didn't do anything wrong."

Sadie sighed.

"You can't actually think he was involved, can you?" Lou said. "I mean, this is Rich. Not some… some…"

"Local with a dark past?" Sadie said. "Someone like Colton or Susan. Someone sitting there in plain sight, but dangerous all the same."

"That's not fair!"

"It is, Louise. And you'd check *every* lead if you were in my shoes."

Sadie grabbed her papers and walked away. Lou wrapped her arms around herself, fighting the urge to cry. The dream image flashed in her mind—bodies in the cart, heads in the basket—and she shuddered.

"What does it mean?" she whispered.

In the hard light of day, she had no answers.

* * *

Brendan Miles was just cashing out the till at Lou's Garage when a flash of colour drew his attention to the window. He stopped counting in the middle of a pile of ten-dollar bills and looked up.

A large red van, with the smiling face of a blonde woman splashed across one side, had just stopped across from the garage. Video crew members carrying gear and cameras stepped out onto the sidewalk.

"What in the world…?"

"What's up, Brendan?" Lou asked.

"It… It looks like someone's filming the garage."

He heard Lou walk up behind him.

"Damnit," she muttered. Lou set the broom and dustpan aside and flicked the 'open' to 'closed'.

"What's going on?" Brendan asked.

"It's just the tabloids."

"For?"

Lou turned to look at him.

"You haven't heard?"

She walked over to the window where the newspapers sat. She grabbed the one with the front-page headline "*NYC SOCIALITE FOUND DEAD IN WATERTON PARK*" and carried it to the counter.

"This," Lou said. "A young woman was found on the far eastern side of the park, she—" Brendan gasped. "Brendan?" Lou said. "Are you alright?"

"I—I know her." His face was aghast, his eyes so wide she could see a ring of white around the irises.

"You do?"

"Yes, I mean… sort of, I… I think I need to go home now, Lou. I'm not feeling well."

"Wait! What aren't you telling me?"

"I'm sorry, but I've got to go."

Seconds later, he was out the door and jogging down the street, the uncounted till sitting open on the counter, piles of bills on either side. With shaking hands, Louise reached for the phone, dialing by memory. The landline rang once… twice… and clicked through.

"Waterton Police Force, how may I help you?"

"Liz, this is Louise Newman. Can I talk to Sadie or Jordan, please?"

"Sure, Lou. What do you need?"

Lou watched out the window as Delia Rosings and her crew took position.

"I think I've got a lead in the Gabrielle Rice case."

* * *

Sadie sat in the Pincher Creek RCMP detachment office, fighting the urge to fidget. She'd already waited fifteen minutes past her scheduled meeting with Constable Ben Grayden but—according to the smiling secretary—he'd been held up with a phone meeting. She picked at the sharp crease, ironed into the front of her slacks. *On the phone, hmmm?* That was *exactly* what she wanted to talk to him about.

Sadie had already spoken with the coroner and the doctor who'd signed off on the autopsy for Gabrielle Rice. Both assured Sadie they hadn't spoken to anyone. She believed them. There was the possibility of someone *else* on the floor who might have seen them bring the body in. That could and did happen with alarming regularity, but Gabrielle Rice's autopsy had taken place late at night. Few nurses or porters would have been on shift at the Lethbridge Regional Hospital by the time the body arrived near midnight. And *that* left another, more likely source to the leak.

Constable Ben Grayden.

As much as Sadie hated the idea, the news had gotten out, and that was making her life hell. It also bothered her. For a split-second, Jim's voice echoed in her mind: *I grew up with Ben. He's a good guy, Sadie! He'd never do that.* She cringed. For a moment the pain was on the surface again. Her face tightened as the memory hit—the smoky kitchen, a C-shaped blood smear across the yellow linoleum floor, the dark puddle beneath the body, footprints heading to the door. A tide of anguish rose, then fell, like a wave, and Sadie smoothed her expression.

It was done. Jim was gone. No use crying over it. She'd done enough of that to last a lifetime.

Outside the office, a bustle of activity drew Sadie's attention. Though she couldn't actually *see* Ben, she wondered if he was there.

She stretched her back and sat up straighter, composing herself. Ben's grinning face appeared in the distance, half a head through the others. She watched him surreptitiously through the doorway. Attractive in a raw-boned sort of way. The secretary leaned in to say something and gestured to the phone. He turned toward the office, his gaze catching on Sadie, and he grinned and waved. Sadie waved awkwardly back, fighting the urge to smile.

She needed to be professional. He was a colleague after all, and he'd understand why she was concerned about the news getting out. She needed to bring this issue up tactfully. Trouble was, 'tact' was not her strong suit.

"Sadie!" Ben said as he strode through the door. "Maggie told me you were waiting. What're you doing here?"

"We have a meeting. It was supposed to start at…" Her gaze flicked to the clock. "Two."

His dark brows shot up. "Oh shit! Right." He threw himself into the chair across from her, loose limbs making him seem even taller. "I totally forgot."

"I thought you were on an important call."

He grinned. "Nah! That's just Beck covering for me. I'm sorry for wasting your time though. Not my plan." He leaned forward. 'Hey! Can I make it up to you?"

"I… It's fine, Ben."

"No, really. Let me buy you lunch." He glanced at his watch. "I missed mine."

"You don't have to, I mean…" She waved her hand, then let it fall to her side. *Bring it UP,* her mind screamed. "Aren't you busy?"

"Not anymore. Got the worst of things dealt with." He shook his head. "Farm truck side-swiped a car full of kids out by Standoff."

Sadie felt her stomach drop. She'd grown up on the Reserve. She likely knew the kids. "Was… was anyone hurt?"

"Luckily, no. But it was a damned close thing. Driver of the truck gave me a bit of a hassle though." He nodded toward the open door. "Tried to pin it on the teens. He said they were weaving back and forth across the line and hit his truck while he was trying to pass 'em. 'Stunting' he called it. But I could smell his breath the moment I sat him down in the cruiser to take his statement."

"D.U.I.?"

Ben nodded. "Uh-huh. But the kids were fine." He smiled. "I made sure of it."

Blushing, Sadie looked away. Why in the world was he so darned *earnest* all the time? It made it hard to be annoyed at him. And she *was* annoyed, wasn't she?

"So can I buy you lunch?" he asked.

"I…"

"Hey, no pressure," Ben said. "It's only if you want to, Sadie."

"I do but—"

"I probably shouldn't have said it like that. I'm not *making* you go. It's not a date. I mean—" His brows pulled together, the confident officer gone. "Unless you want… er… I mean, there's no pressure. I just thought— I mean— I— I—" He groaned and leaned back in his chair, staring at the ceiling. "Shit. I really screwed that one up, didn't I?"

Sadie laughed. "You always this smooth, Ben?"

He grinned and Sadie's heart flipflopped.

"No," he said. "I'm usually better, but… I've been wondering if you'd call."

"You have?"

"Well, yeah. Hoping."

Sadie smiled and looked back down at the crease in her pants.

The questions could wait. After all, she *was* supposed to be on her lunch break. She looked back up. "I'd like to go for lunch." She paused. "As long as you don't mind us talking shop at the same time."

Ben was out of his chair in half a second. "It's a deal!"

CHAPTER NINE

Lunch was a small diner which reminded Sadie a bit of Hunter's coffee shop. Where Hunter's shop featured the original 1950s style of red vinyl and chrome, this restaurant had embraced its rural roots. The floors were rustic wood, the plaster walls a cheerful yellow, and a blackboard with hand-written specials announced the menu.

"You ever been here before?" Ben asked.

Sadie turned to find him watching. The urge to look away caught her, but she forced herself to hold his gaze.

"I've been to *Pincher* before, but not the cafe." She laughed. "I grew up on the side of the Reserve that's closer to Cardston. Those are my stomping grounds."

"Aha! So *that's* why we never crossed paths in high school."

Sadie snorted. "I would have been in junior high when you were graduating. Don't think my parents would have appreciated me hanging out with boys that old."

"But we never met when you joined the Waterton dispatch either."

"They're two different jurisdictions."

Ben grinned. "Hey now! I know plenty of people from the park. Maybe Jim just liked keeping you to himself."

He laughed, and Sadie tried to, but the mention of Jim had dampened her mood, and the sound that came out of her was forced. She wondered if there would be a time she wouldn't think of him, if Jim would slowly fade away and disappear like the great-grandmother she'd lost before she reached kindergarten.

"You mind if we grab a table by the window?" Ben asked. "It's nothing particular, I'm just…"

"On shift? Keeping it on the up and up? Avoiding the malicious chatter of the town gossips?" Sadie teased.

"Uh… yeah." He laughed. "Sorry."

"Totally fine. No offense, but I'm here for the food."

"Then we're in the right place, 'cause it's second-to-none." Ben headed to the table and pulled out her chair, stepping out of her way and taking his place on the other side before she could protest. "You want to get business out of the way first?" he asked.

"Probably should. I need to ask who you've talked to."

"Talked to?"

"About the Gabrielle Rice case." She paused. "About *my case*. Details have gotten into the news somehow."

Ben's brows tugged together, but he didn't pull back. She'd been waiting for it. *Watching for it.* Instead, he leaned closer. "Is this about that Calgary Sun report this morning?"

"Uh-huh."

"Jesus, Sadie, I thought that *you* were the one who told the reporter those details."

She blinked. "Hell no!"

"Then who?"

"That's what I wanted to talk to you about. We've got a leak."

Ben frowned. "A leak, like… an informant?"

"Call it what you want, the story is out and I didn't tell anyone."

"Neither did I."

"I wanted to check with you," she said. "Get your thoughts on it."

"Right." Ben's expression grew stern. "It's got to be someone with access, right?"

"With those details? Yeah."

Ben grabbed one of the photocopied menus out of the holder with one hand, a pen from his breast pocket with the other. He folded the paper in half and made a few notes along one side, before looking up.

"Have you asked around the hospital? Checked with the nurses?"

"I have," she said, watching as Ben wrote. His handwriting was unexpectedly curving, childish even. "Doesn't seem likely though," Sadie added. "The one shift checks out."

"Porters? Volunteers?"

"They didn't have any porters coming on or off shift that night, and those that were there were mainly in the ER."

"Huh." Ben tapped the pen on the table for several seconds. "How about the other doctors who were on-shift in the ward?"

"Checked that too. No go."

"Mortuary attendant?"

"They were short-staffed that night," Sadie said. "Guy wasn't even on shift."

"Crap." He scribbled another note.

"I know," Sadie said. "It doesn't make sense. But someone *knew* what those reports said."

Ben tore the piece of paper off the menu, folding it away.

"Let's think about this reasonably. It's got to be someone connected to the case. Someone close. Someone who knows what's in those files."

"Yeah," she said, "but that means it's got to be someone in the Pincher Creek Dispatch."

He looked up. "Or someone in Waterton."

Sadie stared at him. She suddenly didn't feel so hungry anymore. Once he'd said it, she couldn't deny the chances.

"That's a possibility, too."

* * *

The Durnerin and Thompson ranches shared a border along one side, Waterton Park the other. On the far southwestern side of the ranch where Shawna Durnerin rode today, the division between civilization and the wild was narrow; she kneed her horse into a trot, keeping her eyes on the trees. She carried a rifle in her saddle's holster. The foothills where she'd spent her morning moving cattle from one pasture to the other was good grazing, but grizzlies lived in this borderland too, and they were readying for the winter.

Her gaze moved across the pasture and docile cattle that dotted the landscape, reaching the border to the next ranch. She squinted. A dark smudge moved across the horizon: a truck moving fast on a gravel road. Shawna's face brightened as it neared. She wasn't the *only* person working on a Saturday. She swung one leg over the horse's side, dropped deftly to the ground, and left the gun behind.

The cattle milled as the dust cloud grew nearer. Shawna grinned and jogged forward; the truck rounded the last turn, the back-end of the pick-up shimmying. Her smile wavered. *Dad would kill her if Bryce hurt one of their cattle.* Before the thought even finished, the vehicle came to a sliding stop and the engine cut out. Dust swirled past like fog. Shawna coughed as Bryce emerged from the driver's side, slamming the door behind him.

"Goddamnit, Shawna!" he roared. "We need to talk!"

Shawna's smile disappeared in an instant.

"W—what…?"

Bryce stormed forward grabbing Shawna by the upper arms.

"The police! What did you tell the POLICE?!"

* * *

Events had shifted into high gear the moment Sadie returned from her meeting with Ben. Lou's tip had changed *everything* and Jordan was struggling to keep up!

He shifted uneasily at the Miles' kitchen table, his gaze moving from Constable Black Plume to Arnette and Murray. The couple sat on either side of their son, Brendan, their shoulders forming a protective barrier against Sadie.

"—and I don't care *why* you didn't come forward as soon as you knew she'd gone missing," Constable Black Plume snapped. "But you know it *now*. You've got to make a statement."

"What if I don't want to?" Murray argued. "What then?"

Jordan flinched. He hated this part of the job.

"If you don't *want* to, then I'll call you in for questioning and make it official," Sadie said. "You are *more* than welcome to bring your lawyer too." She cast her steely gaze toward Brendan. "You can explain to *him* why you were so upset when I showed up today."

"Because you're the police!" Arnette cried.

"Which *shouldn't* be an issue if you haven't done anything wrong."

"Likely story!" Murray crossed his arms on his chest. Quiet and bookish, Murray *never* lost his temper, but it looked like he might today.

"Well, if that's your approach," Sadie said, "then—"

"Wait," Jordan said. Sadie shot him an angry look, but he ignored it and scooted his chair closer to the table. "Brendan," he said. "I was wondering if I could ask you something."

Brendan gave him a wary look. "What?"

"Nothing hard," Jordan said. "Just a question. And if you *don't* feel comfortable with that question, just don't answer it, okay?" He ignored the hiss of Sadie's breath. "My question is why you didn't come *tell us* if you noticed that Miss Rice wasn't around?"

Brendan stared at the table, silent.

"You obviously knew her," Jordan continued. "Seems to me you probably knew her relatively well." He smiled. "Right, Brendan?"

There were several long seconds of silence.

"I didn't know her *that* well," Brendan said.

"But you *did* know her?"

"I'd seen her around is all."

"When, Brendan?" Jordan forced a laugh he hoped sounded genuine. "'Cause right now I feel like I'm putting a puzzle together with the lights off. I don't know what way is up." His gaze caught the boy's and held. "When did you *last* see Miss Rice?"

"I, um…" Brendan's gaze skittered to his father and back. "Maybe a week ago?"

Sadie began to scribble into her notepad; Jordan didn't break eye contact. He could feel that there was more, but knew if he spooked the kid, they'd get nothing. "Any chance you can remember the day?" Jordan asked.

"Uh… I dunno. Can't remember."

"Were you working at Lou's garage when you saw her?" Jordan said. "Did she come in for gas?"

"No. It was—" The boy's eyes widened. "No."

"Brendan, you don't *have* to tell me. You really don't." Jordan leaned forward and put his elbows on the table. He smiled. "But I've got to tell you, this girl had a *family*." He nodded to Murray and Arnette. "She had a mom and dad, just like you've got. And Gabby's parents are heartbroken. They called the station, y'know. I spoke to her father." He shook his head. "It was rough, man. So anything you could tell me, *anything at all*, might help. Are you *sure* there's nothing else you remember?"

Brendan's gaze flicked to his father. This time it stayed there. "Dad?"

Jordan turned in surprise. Murray's eyes swam with tears, his cheeks blotchy.

"Mr. Miles?"

Murray pulled a handkerchief from his pocket and blew his nose loudly before folding it closed and tucking it back in his pocket. He looked, Jordan would think later, *shaken.*

"We *all* knew the girl," Murray said, "but not personally. Nothing like that. She—" He cleared his throat. "She rented one of our cabins a while back."

Jordan gasped.

"Did you know her name?" Sadie asked.

Murray scowled. "Of course."

"And you didn't come forward?" Sadie said.

Jordan tensed, but Murray just looked deflated. "I honestly didn't *know* she'd disappeared. Not until…" He pulled the handkerchief and wiped at his eyes. "Not until I saw that in the paper the other day."

"Why not tell us once you knew?" Jordan said.

"I was going to, I just kind of… didn't."

"Why not?" Sadie said. "If you *knew* she was dead, then you certainly knew the risk at not telling."

Arnette was the one who answered.

"'Cause that cabin was already rented. The money was direct transfer. Privately arranged."

"From where?" Jordan asked.

"Don't know," Arnette said, "and never cared. As long as the cabin was rented—and the money was coming in every three days—I didn't see the point in changing it."

Jordan touched Sadie's elbow and she looked over. *Do NOT say it!* he silently pleaded. *You bring up embezzlement, we've lost their trust.*

"Given the… new details," Jordan said. "Sadie and I will need to see that cabin."

"Let me call the station and get the search warrant set up first," Sadie added. "We want to do this by the book."

"Are… are we in trouble?" Brendan said.

"Let's just look at the cabin first," Jordan replied. "Who knows what's in there."

* * *

Vasur Kulkarni was in Fine and Fancy when the door opened, and a middle-aged man walked in. He wore a sharply pressed gray suit with a pale gray golf shirt underneath. His salt and pepper hair was close-cropped and neat, jaw clean-shaven.

The stranger approached the counter slowly, his gaze moving through the store as if looking for someone.

"How can I help you, sir?" Vasur asked.

"I am actually here to talk to someone." The man smiled. "I assume you're *Mr.* Kulkarni?"

"Yes, that's me." Vasur wondered what Audrika had done this time. His wife was the love of his life, but she was notorious for finding her way into trouble. "What can I do for you?"

"I was wondering if I could ask you a few questions. The name is Tom, by the way. Tom Farrel."

"Ah… Mr. Farrel. Good to meet you," Vasur said mildly. Audrika had spent most of last evening talking about Mr. Farrel, the "delightful New York investigator" she'd befriended. It irritated Vasur that the man had returned to the store. "What did you want to ask me about?"

"About your wife, actually."

Vasur paused. "My... wife?"

"Nothing about *Audrika,* directly, just about who she—"

"If this is about Miss Rice, my wife didn't even know the girl. She sold Gabrielle a few things and—"

"That's not why I'm here."

"Oh?" Vasur frowned. "Well, um... perhaps you'd like to talk to Audrika herself."

"No. I've already talked to her." Mr. Farrel moved toward the counter so quickly, Vasur stepped back without meaning to. The man that had, minutes before, seemed so innocuous—so irritating—was now closer than he needed to be. "This time," Mr. Farrel said in a low voice, "I want to talk to *you.*"

"About what?"

"Who *else* has your wife been talking to?"

Vasur snorted. "If you've met my wife, Mr. Farrel, I'm certain you realize that Audrika's chatter means no harm. Everyone in Waterton knew about Miss Rice."

"I'm not talking about Miss Rice."

"You're not?"

The investigator shook his head. "No."

Vasur crossed and uncrossed his arms. Mr. Farrel's expression held an intensity he found difficult to bear. "Then if it's not about Miss Rice," he said, "what is it?"

"A few of my associates have noted that there've been some... inquiries."

"Into what?"

"Into *me*, oddly enough."

"Look, I don't know anything about that. And I'm certain Audrika would never—"

"Stop."

Vasur's mouth snapped shut like a trap. He wanted this conversation over, wanted this man out of his shop. Mr. Farrel's gaze—hard and unflinching—never left his face.

"I am telling you," Mr. Farrel said, "so that you know that *I know*. I'm telling you that I am highly protective—of my privacy. Understood?"

"Yes, sir."

"Good. And I would appreciate it if you'd make sure that your wife, as well meaning as she is, is aware of that."

Vasur swallowed with a dry throat. "I—I understand."

The expression on Mr. Farrel's face rippled like a light switch, calm replacing his anger. "I knew you would. That's why I came to *you*, Vasur. Not to Audrika." He winked. "I didn't want to upset her. Not when I'm *certain* she means well." He stepped back from the till. "Do we have an understanding?"

Vasur nodded.

"Good. I'm glad." And with that the investigator walked away, giving a cheery wave as he headed out the door.

* * *

"I didn't tell the police anything," Shawna gasped. "I swear, I never—"

Bryce's fingers tightened "Then WHY are the police snooping around Cardston now!"

"I don't know. Maybe they're just—"

"Who did you TALK to?!" He shook her the way a dog might

shake a rabbit. "WHO?"

"Bryce, stop!" she cried, teeth chattering. "I—I don't—" Shawna gasped as he shoved her away. Bryce's hands were in fists, his stance wide. She'd seen him break horses, and it struck her that *this* was the same pose he took. "P—please," she gasped. "I swear, I didn't talk to anyone. I haven't talked to the police since the day they came by the ranch."

"One of the Thompson boys who live in town called me up, said that the police was going 'round and askin' people if anyone'd seen us on Saturday."

Tears rolled down Shawna's cheeks. "So…?"

"You KNOW I can't have the police snooping into things!" Bryce stepped forward and she flinched. "You're damned lucky one of the people who got asked was a friend o' mine."

"But the police have no idea you—"

"And *that's* how it's gonna stay!"

Before she could answer, Bryce strode back to his truck and drove away.

* * *

Hunter stared at Lou, his face caught in an expression of shock.

"Brendan," he repeated. "As in Brendan Miles who works the front of your store?"

Sitting here in his bright kitchen, the claim made no more sense than if Young Brendan had walked in the house with a gun and demanded all his money.

"That's the one," Lou said. "I didn't want to cause him any trouble, but I clearly had to do something." She pulled out a chair and sat down. "I feel awful, but given the last couple years…" Her words faded off, the ghosts of friends alive between them.

"Well, then. That *is* a problem." Hunter sat down next to Louise.

"Why you didn't just ask him about it? He's your employee, after all."

"I tried to, Hunter. *I did.* But he took off on me before I left." She shook her head. "This all happened before noon. Brendan wasn't even supposed to be off until five. Left me to run the garage alone."

"You could've called," Hunter said. "I'd have swung by and covered for a few—"

A voice interrupted from the kitchen doorway.

"Looks like you just caused a whole mess lot more trouble for that Miles' boy."

Both Louise and Hunter turned to find Levi hobbling forward in short, halting steps.

"Trouble?" Lou said.

"That's right. Trouble."

Hunter's chest ached to see Levi's slow progress to the table. The man had always seemed inexplicably *young* despite his advanced age. *No longer.* In the days since Levi had come to Waterton, Hunter had seen the change. Winter would be hard for his friend, and Hunter *hoped* he'd be able to convince him to stay, even after the cast was off.

"Waterton's been full of trouble the last few years," Levi said as he reached the table and sat shakily down. "And it always seems to circle back to people meddling in our business."

"I *had* to tell the police," Lou said. "There was no other choice about it."

The old man shot her a dark look. "There's *always* a choice."

"A girl was *killed,* Levi. If Brendan was involved—"

"He weren't involved."

"But he might *know* something. It certainly *seemed* like he did."

Levi rolled his eyes and turned to stare at the dogs, asleep by the back door. An uneasy silence filled the kitchen.

Hunter cleared his throat, then spoke to Lou.

"You did what you thought you should do. You were worried for Brendan. That's all. You know, I'd probably have done the exact same thing, if he'd been working in the coffee shop and had taken off on me."

"There's something else," Lou said.

"What?"

"They've been asking Rich about the case. Jordan and Sadie came by a couple days ago."

Hunter patted her hand. "I'm certain this will all blow over. They're just asking him to get information. They're talking to the rest of the locals too. Besides, Rich wasn't even *in Canada* when that girl was killed."

"He, uh…" Lou opened her mouth, closed it again. Tears glittered along her lashes. Hunter's eyes widened. The fear that he'd first felt when she'd said the name "Brendan Miles" rushed to fill his chest.

"Oh, Lordy," he said. "Rich *was* around when the girl was killed?"

Lou nodded, wiping tears away with the back of her hand.

"Christ, Lou. Not good."

"It gets worse," she said, her throat bobbing. "He was in Lethbridge and Calgary. Easy driving distance from the park." She let out a teary gasp. "God! You should have *seen* how Sadie looked at Rich when she talked to him. She practically accused him right then and there."

"Was he charged?"

"Not yet but…" The first tears rolled down her cheeks. "But I feel it coming."

Hunter swallowed down the question of *how* she knew that. For as long as he'd known Louise Newman, she' d had feelings, intuitions of things to come. Like how she'd often call the moment he reached for the phone or how she *sensed* the things he was thinking. This was one of the things about Louise he didn't *want* to know.

"So if he wasn't home with you," Levi said, "and he weren't back in the States where he was *supposed* to be, why *was* Evans skulking around Waterton?" One of the dogs whined in his sleep and Levi paused before adding: "I ain't no police officer, but that sounds mighty strange to me."

"It's not strange at all," Lou said. "He just wanted to surprise me."

"Surprise?" Levi snorted. "Shoulda brought ya flowers. They're less trouble."

Louise swore under her breath.

"Relax, hon," Hunter said. "If you just let things settle down, I'm sure—"

"No!" She stood and the chair squealed across the floor. The dogs in the corners woke in a rush, skittering nails sliding across the linoleum as they jumped to alertness. "I can't relax! And I can't just let things settle down. Rich is here in Waterton because of me. He *stayed* because of me. And now I've got to help him."

She stomped to the door, grabbing her coat from the hook and sliding on one arm.

"You ever figure out who your prowler was?" Levi asked.

Louise paused with her arm halfway up the sleeve. She turned back to eye him warily. "What do you mean: *my prowler*?"

"That guy that was hanging around Whispering Aspens looking in the windows," Levi said. "You ever figure out who that was?"

Lou shot Hunter a concerned look. "I told you that in *confidence*, Hunter."

"I was worried about you," Hunter said. "Levi and me, we live here in town too. If there's someone hanging 'round, causing trouble, then we've *all* got to deal with it."

"Does everyone at the coffee meetings know too?"

Hunter studiously avoided her gaze. Levi chuckled.

With a swear, Lou shoved her other arm through the second sleeve.

"I can't tell you two anything," she said. "You're worse than a sewing circle."

Levi hooted happily, drawing the attention of Duke, the youngest of Hunter's dogs.

"It's not funny," she snapped.

"I find it mighty humorous myself," Levi said. He scratched behind the dog's ears with his good hand. "You been tryin' to keep secrets in the town you grew up in. You should know it'll all come out in the end."

"Levi…" she warned.

"Oh, Lou, you *know* he's just teasing," Hunter said. "People in town want to help. That's the truth."

Lou put her hand on the door handle and three dogs bounded to her side, barking.

"Just *ask* me if I want the help next time. Alright?"

And with that she headed into the night, slamming the door behind her.

Hunter turned and frowned. "You shouldn't needle her, Levi."

"Oh, she gives as good as she takes."

"True enough…" Hunter stared at the closed door. "Brendan Miles in a panic," he mused. "Wonder what *that* was about?"

Levi shrugged. "Don't know. Don't care." And he went back to petting the dog at his side.

* * *

When Audrika arrived to relieve Vasur from his shift, her husband's stern expression was still firmly in place.

"What's up with *you* today, Vasur?" she said. "You look like you're about to blow a gasket."

"You should stay away from that man."

Her feet slowed. "What man?"

"Mr. Tom Farrel. He came in here today. He wasn't happy."

Audrika tipped her head. "No? Why not, dear?"

"He was angry at you."

Laughter, bright and happy bubbled from Audrika's chest.

Vasur grabbed her wrist. "I'm not kidding! He was here. He *warned* me!"

Audrika jerked her hand back. "I think you must be overreacting. What could Mr. Farrel possibly say about me?"

"That you're digging into things about him that he doesn't like."

"I'm not doing anything!"

"Don't lie to me. He *knows*, Audrika. You can't go putting your nose where it doesn't belong."

"I haven't done a thing."

Vasur glared.

"Honestly," she laughed. "I haven't!"

"Au-dri-ka…"

Audrika flipped a raven's wing of hair over her shoulder, grinning.

"Oh, pish," she said. "You're just jealous my sweetheart."

"No, my love, I'm not." He frowned. "That man is dangerous."

* * *

The warrant was on its way.

Sadie's knee bounced nervously, hands tight around a half-full cup of coffee, as she waited at the Miles' kitchen table. Arnette and Murray puttered around—washing dishes—apparently at ease under Jordan's newfound rapport. Brendan, it seemed, now wanted to make a statement.

"You can ask for a lawyer if you want," Jordan repeated. "There's nothing wrong with that, Brendan. We can wait."

"But I honestly didn't *do anything*." The young man gave him a pleading look. "I just want to make things straight. Do the right thing."

Now you do, Sadie thought.

The walkie-talkie on her belt buzzed and she stood, heading out of the kitchen to the foyer, four sets of eyes watching her.

"Constable Black Plume here," she said.

"Sadie, it's Liz. I've got that warrant for you. Brian headed over with it a few minutes ago."

"Then what's taking so long?"

"I don't know. He *said* he was going directly there. But maybe he—"

"Get hold of him! There's only so long we can ask them to wait."

"Alright then. I'll check." The walkie-talkie crackled and Sadie drummed her fingers on her pantleg. In the kitchen, Jordan and Brendan spoke in low voices. There was another crackle and Liz's voice returned. "Not sure what's up. Brian's not answering now. He *should* be there by—" The sound of a doorbell interrupted. "—now."

Arnette Miles, her face peaked and angry, brushed past Sadie on her way to the door.

"Hold on a sec', Liz," Sadie said.

The door swung open to reveal Brian, paper in hand.

"Mrs. Miles," he said, "are Constables Black Plume and Wyatt here?"

"They are."

"Can I see them?"

"Don't think I can stop you." Arnette swung the door wide. Her gaze caught on Sadie's and fury—sharp and hot—passed between them. "Come on inside," she grumbled. "Everyone *else* is."

Sadie pressed the relay button. "Hey, Liz. Brian's here now. I've got to go." She snapped the walkie-talkie back into her belt, and headed to the door, taking the warrant from Brian's hand.

"Sorry for the delay," he said. "There was a herd of bighorn on the road by the school. Wouldn't move. Had to go around the other way."

"No worries." Sadie gave a small nod. "Thanks."

"You guys need anything else?"

"If you don't mind securing a perimetre around the cabin, Jordan and I can check inside to check the interior."

"You got it." He nodded. "I'll grab the tape and start securing the scene."

"Thanks, Brian."

She turned to find Murray and Brendan waiting. Waterton might be small. Things *might* work on a different schedule than a big city, but in a pinch, she could still get things done where murder was concerned.

"Mr. Miles, Mrs. Miles, I have a warrant," she said. "It gives Constable Wyatt and myself the legal right to search your properties. I'd like to start with the cabin being rented by Miss Gabrielle Rice."

* * *

Audrika waited until Vasur had left the shop before the coy smile slid from her face. She rubbed her sweaty palms along the side of her track suit and walked to the front of the store, flipping the 'open' sign to 'closed'. She leaned against the plate glass, her gaze moving from one end of Main Street to the other, heart pounding. Tom Farrel *knew* she'd searched his files. But how?!

Certain no one was on the street, Audrika retreated behind the till and picked up the phone, dialing her sister-in-law by memory.

"Hello?"

"Mirran," Audrika interrupted. "It's Audrika. I need to talk. It's *important.*"

"What's wrong, dear? You sound—"

Audrika's voice dropped, though there was no one to hear. "Someone noticed the information search you did for me."

There was a long pause before her sister-in-law replied.

"What do you mean by 'noticed'?"

"The investigator, Tom Farrel, came into the store today. He scared Vasur."

"Scared him? How?"

"No idea. But he said something. And he *knew* that I'd looked into his background. He might know about you locating those old Borderline accounts." Her voice sharpened. "Who did you tell?!"

"I didn't tell anyone! I just ran through the information through our online system."

"You didn't happen to use my *name* while you did it?!"

"I…" Mirran's breath whistled through the phone. "Well, yes, I did, Audrika."

"Why?!"

"I *had* to!"

"Why couldn't you use your own name?"

"Because I'm not one of the leaseholders listed in those Borderline files. Only people whose name appears on leases or documentation can access any data for shareholders or—"

"But Mr. Farrel *knows* someone was searching for information on him. He told Vasur it was me!"

"I—I don't know how he could know that. The system is secure.

It shouldn't be possible to—"

"Shouldn't be, but it is!"

"Are you *certain* he knows we were looking into his background?"

"Would I be talking to you otherwise?" Audrika snapped.

"You're right. Shall I delete the information for you? Scrub the file?"

Audrika cringed. There was so *much* information there and she'd only begun to uncover it. The bank accounts were what she wanted, but they were the hardest to get into. She needed time to go through all the data, to find the clues that would give her access.

"Audrika?" Mirran said. "Are you still there?"

"I am."

"What do you want me to do? I can pull it up now. Give me twenty minutes and I'll have deleted all the inquiries into—"

"Wait!" she cried.

"For what, dear?"

Audrika's fingers tightened around the phone. "Let me drive into Pincher. You print off what you have *then* you can delete the information. I'll go through it by hand later."

"Even the accounts information?"

"Especially that! There's money there, right?"

Mirran's voice dropped. "Well, yes. Quite a bit. I told you that."

"I want it."

"But you'll need to show you've got signing rights for the Borderline corporation to access those funds, Audrika. Get me identification of one of the shareholders and I should be able to—"

"I need some time. Print me the documents first."

"You'll have to pay for the paper. There's more than two hundred pages of—"

"Fine."

"Good. Then I'll see you this afternoon."

"You'll see me sooner than that," Audrika said. And without a word of goodbye, she hung up the phone. Mr. Farrel might be a charmer, but Audrika *knew* someone with a secret when she met them. Tom Farrel had many. She'd bet her life on that.

* * *

The rental cabin was three lots down from the Miles's house, so they walked. Brian had arrived and was already stringing yellow 'crime scene: do not cross' tape through the trees.

Murray pulled out a large ring with a mess of keys.

"Sorry," he said as he flicked back and forth. "I'm not sure which is the spare."

Jordan chuckled. "No worries, sir. As long as we get in."

Sadie pursed her lips as the key flicking continued. *We could always break down the door.*

"Ah! There it is," Murray said with a laugh. He removed an aging iron skeleton key. "Here you go, Constable Black Plume."

"Thanks." She slid the key into the lock. "You sure this is the one?"

"Pretty sure."

Sadie's fingers tensed as she turned the key. The lock was stiff and her hands slipped and slid beneath the latex gloves. "Come on…" The lock began to move, tumblers clicking, before it froze again. "Come on… almost there." She twisted harder. For a moment, nothing happened, and then the key shifted with an audible *click*. The heavy wooden door of the cabin swung inward. "Looks like that was the right—"

Her throat caught on the sickening stench of rot.

"What the hell is *that?*" Murray said. "Smells like something died in there."

A knowing look passed between Jordan and Sadie.

"Just stay outside, sir," she said. "We'll let you know what we've found once we've gone through the house."

"You sure? I want to help if—"

"Stay where you are, Mr. Miles," Jordan said, holding up his hand. "We've got this under control."

Sadie cupped her hand to her mouth, shouting: "Brian! We're going inside now. Murray's waiting here. Can you come 'round?"

His answer echoed from the side of the house.

"Got it! I'll be right there. Just finishing this up."

Sadie turned back to Murray. "Stay here," she said sharply. "This is a crime scene. We can't contaminate evidence."

"But it smells like—"

"We'll be right back, Murray," Jordan said. "Just relax."

He swung the door closed, separating the two officers from the man waiting on the front step.

"Thanks," Sadie said. "Murray's getting on my last nerve today."

"Don't know what's up with him." Jordan said. "He seem weird to you?"

"A bit. But then, it's Murray." She smirked. "Weird is relative."

"Fair enough." Jordan laughed, then gagged. "Jesus. What *is* that?"

"Only one way to find out."

Sadie walked forward with slow, steady steps, her ears and eyes attuned to the smallest of details. The entranceway—though benign enough—was cluttered with coats and several pairs of shoes. At least two of them didn't seem to have a pair. Sadie carefully stepped around the scattered footwear, heading toward the inner rooms. She glanced up. The lights in the hallway were on.

"You didn't turn on the lights when we came in, did you?" Sadie said.

"Nope. Just walked in. You?"

"Not me."

She pulled out her notepad. "I'll make a note: Lights in hallway on when we came in."

"I'm going to document the entrance," Jordan said, lifting the camera to his eye. "Tell me if you see something."

"Got it," Sadie said, walking forward. "Shout if there's anything you need tagged."

"Uh-huh. Thanks."

The flash of the camera began like a lightning storm, filling the hallway as Sadie headed away from Jordan. Nearing the end of the corridor, the light grew dim. The faint sound of a television rose. Sadie paused. The scent of death was stronger here and it had the copper-penny undertone of blood. The memory of Jim lying dead on Susan's kitchen floor flashed and disappeared into the darkness of her mind, making the skin on the back of her neck crawl.

She took a shaky breath. "Just a step at a time," she whispered. "There's nothing in here."

It only *felt* like there was.

Sadie scanned the hallway. Barring a few scuffs along the edges—the results of an overzealous vacuum cleaner—there was nothing noteworthy in the main section of the hall. Her gaze lifted. A darkened doorway waited for her on the left, an open stairwell leading to the second floor directly in front of her, a third entrance visible further down the hall. Her feet slowed as she neared the shadowy entrance and she swallowed hard.

Behind her, the flashes stopped. "You find something?" Jordan called.

"Not yet, but it smells worse here."

"On my way."

Sadie took a single step toward the darkness. The fug of decay rose, filling the air, pressing down on her. Nausea rose and she coughed. Through the doorway, she could see the dim outlines of furniture, but little else.

There's something inside.

She jerked at the unexpected memory of Jim's voice. A second later, a hand brushed her elbow and she squeaked in surprise.

"Jesus!" she snapped. "Don't *do* that, Jordan!"

"Sorry. You looked worried." He squinted into the shadows. "What do you see in there?"

"Nothing yet." She touched the flashlight on her belt. "I'm going to turn on the lights, but I… I want to check the light-plates first."

"Check 'em for what?"

She caught Jordan's eyes.

"For blood. There's something in that room. Can't you smell it?"

"I figured it was rotten food or something."

Her jaw tightened until her teeth hurt. "That's not rotten food. That's something dead."

"You think there's—?" Behind them—at the far end of the hall-way—the door swung open. Jordan spun. "Murray!" he bellowed. "You can't just walk IN here! This is a crime scene, for Chrissake!" Murray said something inaudible and Jordan stormed down the hall. "I'm not kidding! Get out or I'll have to arrest you! Brian! Get over here!"

Sadie waited. At the end of the hall she could hear an argument unfolding, voices rising. For thirty seconds she waited… a minute…

She stepped into the darkness.

The room was solid black, shadows full of unknowable terror. Her fingers fumbled for her flashlight's release and she swore under her breath. That feeling was back. The one that hinted at something *else*. She could imagine what Jim would tell her if he was here: *Take it easy now. Just look at each item like a puzzle piece. Nothing else. Figure it out later.* Sadie knew this, but right now her calm had fled.

The flashlight would not come free!

"Come on, you bitch!" She fought until the edge of her nail finally caught the snap. It flicked open on the holster and she pulled the torch free. With a shaky breath, she clicked it on and lifted it to shine into the room.

A crimson image flashed across her eyes.

With a cry, Sadie stumbled backward, her legs moving on their own volition. Her heart was in her throat, ears ringing. She caught her foot on the carpet edge leading to the hallway, almost going to her knees. Somewhere—impossibly far away—she could hear two men arguing. She couldn't understand their words, not with the horror filling her mind.

"Jordan! JORDAN! Get *down* here! We've got another body!"

CHAPTER TEN

Jordan stared, slack-jawed, into the living room. Blood flecked the walls. A red-black stain marred the carpet, spreading outward. In the center of this stain near the fireplace, a glistening black shape huddled low, a butcher's choice of blades and a bone saw beside it. The television hummed, but there was another sound too. *Buzzing.* Sadie swung her flashlight over the body and the skin shivered and crawled. The sound made sense.

The body was covered in a pulsing layer of flies.

"What the hell?" He swallowed bile. "What *is* that?"

"A body. Not sure what *kind* of body though." Sadie took two halting steps into the room. "Photograph the light switch, then turn it on," she said. "I need some light. Gotta figure out what we're dealing with here."

"Is… is it a *person*?"

"I don't KNOW, Jordan. I need some goddamned light!"

Her tone jerked Jordan out of his panic.

"Got it," he said. "Hold on."

Jordan lifted the camera to his eye. What advice had Sadie given him the day of Jim's murder? *Document. Detail. Think later.* He focused on the light switch, forcing his panicked thoughts away. Having a camera in his hands calmed him. He didn't need to think *beyond* it. At least not as long as the shutter was clicking. Things were easier when he saw them through the viewfinder. He pressed the button again and the camera flashed. He did it a second time. A third, fourth, fifth...

Jordan looked up. "Done."

"Good. Turn the lights on."

He flicked on the light with a gloved finger. Colour, deep and pungent, saturated the room. The scene had looked bad in the flare of a flashlight. *It was worse.*

"Fuck," Jordan said. The room was destroyed. A disassembled car-jack lay next to the fireplace. He frowned seeing it. *Hadn't Lou said something about having trouble with the jacks at her garage?* Next to it were a pile of knives, dissection tools, and a single bone saw—the stuff of nightmares. His stomach rolled.

"Not a person," Sadie said. "Well, that's a relief."

"It's not?"

"Nope."

Jordan stepped up next to her. "What kind of body is it?"

"Hold on." She crept forward, eyeing the carcass on which a miasma of fat-bellied flies buzzed and circled. "An animal of some kind. Elk maybe."

Jordan followed Sadie's footsteps. An armchair was flipped sideways, food wrappers and empty soda cans littered the floor; bathroom towels were pressed to the carpet next to the body in a failed attempt to mop up the blood.

"What a fucking mess," he muttered.

The den was in ruins. Once the cozy centre of a home, the room had become a slaughterhouse. Jordan's stomach roiled and he paused, breathing in through his nose and out through his mouth.

"Disgusting."

"It's a deer," Sadie said in a flat voice. "It's been chopped up. Legs severed. Head removed."

Jordan lifted the camera and hit the button with numb fingers. Light flashed.

"Whoever butchered it made a hell of a mess."

"Yeah, but they tried *not* to." Sadie nodded toward the corpse. A large yellow tarp had been spread underneath the carcass, but it could not contain the sheer volume of blood. "The tarp was a precaution, but the blood spread."

"You can't slaughter a deer in a house." Jordan said. "Jesus, you can't do it in a *barn* without hanging an animal up to drain first."

Sadie turned. "You wouldn't *know* that if you'd grown up in the big city."

"You think Gabrielle Rice did this?"

"Don't know. But this *is* her rental after all."

Jordan's jaw tightened. "She told Mrs. Lu she wanted a bone saw."

"Looks like she got one."

Sadie and Jordan moved through the room, documenting the bizarre dismemberment of the deer. The air hummed, flies swirling near their faces and hands. When they fluttered away from the animal's haunches, Jordan gagged. The flesh was white with maggots.

He turned, caught himself against the chair's armrest, and dry-heaved.

"You head out," Sadie said. "I'll tag a few more things."

"You sure?"

"Yeah, but you find anything else fucked up, you call me. I'll come."

Jordan nodded. "Same with you. I'll come back."

She forced a smile. "I know you will."

Jordan headed back into the hallway. The main corridor broke the cabin in two. Stairs headed up from the centre to the second floor, while a few steps down, a doorway awaited. It led to the kitchen. Stepping into the semi-darkness, the stench of rot caught him off guard. Heart pounding, Jordan swung his flashlight through the room, but nothing appeared out of the ordinary. Nonetheless, he photographed the switch from all angles before he turned on the lights. His stomach tightened, then eased. There was nothing dead in here, though the smell was nearly as rank as in the living room.

A pile of unwashed dishes filled the sink; garbage tumbled out of the can and across the floor. On the counters, several bags of groceries sat, some items—like a swollen container of whole milk—sitting out as if someone had wandered away a moment ago. The ripe smell came from the rotting food. He forced himself to focus on the task at hand.

Document, he thought. *Figure it out later.* Right now, there were too many missing pieces.

He focused on the counter near the fridge, then moved to the kitchen table. It heaved under a layer of crusted plates, soda cans, and garbage. The viewfinder moved across the wooden surface, capturing images as he went: a half-empty bag of chips, milk-scudded coffee mugs, moldy pears, an open bag of bread—green on one end—and a piece of paper, covered in tiny handwriting. Jordan lowered the camera. He leaned closer and frowned. The paper was dove grey parchment with a thin line of gold along one side. It had been folded at some point, but lay creased open, a pen on the counter next to it.

The words on its surface jumped to life:

—and you think you can just pretend it never happened, but you can't just walk away from me. I WON'T LET YOU! We had something! You felt the same until you moved. I know if you'll just let me

*show you what you mean to me, I know you'll understand. This isn't
a GAME to me, Rich! I—*

"Jesus," he gasped. "This is a letter to Rich Evans."

"What's that?"

Jordan turned to discover Sadie in the doorway. Her tan face
was unnaturally pale, cheeks pinched. She carried the evidence kit
half-open, a pile of bagged items poking out from the top.

"I found a letter," he said, "on the table. I think Gabrielle wrote
it."

"Letter, hmmm." Sadie set down the kit and came forward.

"You find anything else in the den?"

"There was a purse next to the couch. Gabby's I.D. was in it, and
a few other things. No keys though."

Jordan narrowed his eyes. "No keys for the cabin?"

"Nope. None for the car either." Sadie pulled out a fresh plastic
evidence bag, scribbling a note on it in black marker. "There was
a contract for a rental car in the purse. She rented it in Calgary a
couple weeks ago."

"You think that's when she flew to Canada?"

"Uh-huh, but the car's nowhere to be found. Keys neither." Sadie
rubbed her fingers to release the bag's seal and shook it open with a
pop. "Now, what's that letter say?"

"I only read the first part." Jordan picked up the camera and took
two more photographs, documenting the exact angle of it on the
table, the haphazard way it had been dropped, the pen uncapped,
the green fur that crawled across the skin of a nearby pear. "There.
Got it now. You can bag it."

Sadie picked up the handwritten note and placed it into an
evidence bag. In moving it, a second paper—twinned behind the
first—fell to the floor.

Sadie crouched to pick it up. "There's more."

"The second half?"

"Looks to be. Hold on a sec." Jordan waited as she read through it, her expression growing concerned. She looked back up. "This is fucked up."

"What does it say?" Jordan asked.

Sadie pointed at a single, unsteady line of text. "She threatened to go after Rich if he didn't take her back. She said…" Sadie squinted. "If he didn't give her another chance, she was going to destroy his life the same way that Rich destroyed hers."

Jordan frowned. "Did Rich Evans destroy her life somehow?"

Sadie tucked the second piece of paper into the evidence bag and looked up. "I don't know if he did. I honestly don't know *any-thing* about this woman, but I think we've got to get Evans in and talk to him again."

"Agreed." Jordan nodded to the doorway. "You find anything else?"

"Not really. The bedroom's a mess. Clothes everywhere. Gar-bage." Her eyes flicked to the doorway and she shuddered. "Nothing like the living room though."

"Why'd she threaten Rich in the letter. He told us they were talking. She could have said it then."

"Maybe she did. He said they'd argued and he'd hung up on her. This would fit."

"True, but if she wrote a letter, why didn't she send it?"

"That's only if it *is* her letter. We're going to have to check her handwriting first."

"Agreed, but if it *is* her writing, then we've got another issue to deal with."

Sadie stared at him. "What do you mean?"

Jordan waved at the room, taking in the jumbled array of moldy food and garbage.

"The girl was obviously messed up. This was *her* place; she rented it. She killed a deer—and I'd bet my badge she didn't have a deer tag—brought the thing *inside,* then butchered it. That's weird. No question. But it *still* doesn't explain *why* she was doing it. Why kill the deer? Why butcher it here—in the house? That's not the behaviour of a game hunter, so *why*?"

Sadie stared out at the cluttered kitchen, as if considering the question. "Why indeed…" A few seconds passed and then she spun back, her dark eyes dancing with excitement. "I've got it!"

A thrill of excitement ran the length of Jordan's spine. "What?"

"If it was her. And that's still a big 'if,' mind you, I think Gabrielle Rice might have been *practicing.*"

"Practicing for what?"

Sadie lifted the plastic bag, the handwritten words visible beneath its transparent surface. "I think she was practicing for how to dispose of Rich Evans' body when she killed him."

* * *

Louise didn't realize she was being followed until she was halfway home. It wasn't the silence that had alerted her. Nor was it a noise. Partway home, a worried *twinge* arced in the recesses of her mind.

You should watch yourself, girlie, an old man said. *He's right behind you…*

Lou lifted her head and blinked. The thought that had passed through her consciousness was not her own, and she truly had no idea where it had come from. *What in the world…?* Lou's footsteps kept their steady beat, but her eyes searched the trees that surrounded her. Autumn sunset came early north of the 49th parallel. Long shadows crossed the road, leaving one side of the street painted in buttery yellows, while the other fell into murky purple. Above the gold-painted peaks, the sky was pink. The wind had stilled and—

You need to WATCH OUT! a woman cried.

This time the voice was so crisp that Lou yelped in surprise. She half turned, expecting to discover someone next to her, but she was alone. Lou stumbled and caught herself. In that split-second, she saw the car.

The dark gray sedan had tinted windows and it was trailing along behind her a block away. Lou dropped to one knee, pretending to do up her shoe as she took surreptitious glances behind her. The car slowed to a stop and waited.

No one got out.

After a few more seconds, Lou stood up again. Her heart had begun a frantic pounding in her chest; she walked more briskly now. Her eyes glanced into the golden reflections in the windows on the side of the street. There, reflected by the bright sun, the nondescript sedan started its slow journey once more, pacing her as she carried on up the street. She reached the corner and paused. Going right would take her home to Rich, but since both sides of the street were caught in the mountain's shadow, it meant losing the reflected windows. If she kept going forward, she could see the car, but she was going further away from safety. Left would take her directly toward the woods.

Lou swallowed down her fear and headed right. The reflections ended once she reached the mountains, but she forced herself to keep going. The cabin was three blocks away. *Perhaps*, she thought, *it was just a sightseer. Not someone following her at all.* The shakiness of her limbs left her feeling loose and untethered. She picked up her speed as the road slowly cantered downward. She reached the first crosswalk—two more to go—and stepped out into the street. She glanced over her shoulder as if checking for traffic.

The car was behind her again. Closer.

She fought down terror, her legs picking up speed, taking her halfway down the second street. She looked back again. The car matched her increase in speed and was gaining on her.

Run, girl! GO! A new voice, loud and insistent pulsed in her mind.

Lou reached the second crosswalk. She peeked back. The distance between her and the car had halved. A dark figure sat in the shadowy front seat.

Hurry! a young man shouted. *HE'S COMING FOR YOU!*

The thought unleashed her, and Lou sprinted for home. The cabin appeared—so close—but the car was closer. Lou pushed her legs, forcing them to move despite the weariness of a day's work that made her muscles tremble and jump. She could hear the engine now, but she didn't dare look back, not if it meant losing precious seconds. *Five houses… four houses… three houses…* Behind her, the engine roared.

Lou tore away from the sidewalk, heading between the second and third houses before her own. It was a place where elk and deer bedded down in the wintertime, and Lou'd played here often as a child. It led to the unfenced backyards, and from there to her own property. *A shortcut!*

Brakes screamed as the wheels came to an abrupt stop.

Lou ran.

She heard a door slam and the rustle of someone following her into the underbrush. Lou sprinted behind the second house, narrowly avoiding an upturned wheelbarrow. Ahead of her, she could see the backdoor to the cabin and next to it, the kitchen window.

Rich stood at the sink, doing dishes, his gaze downcast.

RUN GIRL! GET AWAY! YOU NEED TO HURRY!

"Rich!" Lou shouted. "Help!"

At the window, Rich picked up another plate. He hadn't heard.

* * *

With the crime scene at the Miles' cabin secured and the perimetre of the lot marked with yellow tape, Constables Black Plume
and Wyatt emerged from the rental unit. On the far end of the
porch stood Arnette and Murray, deep in hushed conversation. Sadie closed the door behind her and their voices abruptly stopped.

"You want me to talk to them?" Jordan whispered.

"I've got it." She cleared her throat. "Mr. and Mrs. Miles," she
said, walking forward. "Jordan and I were hoping we could talk a
moment."

"Of course." Murray nodded to his wife. "Arnette and I are happy
to help."

"That's great. Is Brendan around?"

A look passed between the Mileses.

"He, um… He's at home," Arnette said. "I had something in the
oven."

Sadie grimaced. *Likely story.*

"That's no problem at all," Jordan said. "I'm certain we can talk to
him again later, if needs be."

"Of course," Murray said. "So are you done in there?"

"We're done for *now*," Sadie said, "but it's a crime scene, so you'll
have to stay out for the next couple days. I want to call in a forensics
team from Lethbridge to make sure we've got everything we need."

Murray and Arnette exchanged a worried look. "Forensics?" Arnette said. "Is there something *in there* that we should know about?"

"The smell when I opened the door," Murray said. "What *was* that?"

Sadie frowned. "Mr. and Mrs. Miles, until we *finish* with the scene, I can't go into detail."

"Constable Black Plume and I understand your concern," Jordan said. "We really do. And there were a number of things that smelled in there." He caught Sadie's eyes. "You were in the *kitchen*, Sadie. Right?"

"Yes. Rotten food," she said. "There was a table full of it. Milk spoiled, vegetables rotten, and… other things too."

"Other things?" Arnette repeated.

"You'll have to deal with the maggots and flies later," Jordan said. "The carpet and, well, everything else in there, it's…" He shook his head. "It's a hell of a mess."

"Maggots?!" Murray said. "Should've known not to trust that girl."

Arnette crossed her arms. "I told you the rental agreement was too good to be true."

Murray glared. "You *always* say that when it's someone you don't know who wants to rent."

"For a reason," she snapped. "A girl like that, with money to burn, offering to pay twice what any other customer would as long as we gave her space."

"So what if we did?" Murray grumbled. "The place was rented and that's more than—"

"Space?" Sadie interrupted. "What does that mean?"

Murray crossed his arms. "Nothing."

Sadie turned to Arnette. "Mrs. Miles?"

"Gabby said she didn't want any phone calls," Arnette said. "Didn't want me coming in to clean up after her. Didn't want *any-one* interfering in her—" She made air quotes. "—'rest and relaxation.' Made us promise not to tell anyone she was here, even if they claimed to know her. Who were we to insist? The bookstore barely breaks even at the best of times. The suites are what keeps us going in the winter."

"But you didn't call it in when she disappeared," Sadie said.

"Why should I?" she said in an irritable voice. "The girl kept odd hours to begin with. And when she stopped showing up to ask for things, I didn't even think about it."

"Why not?" Jordan asked.

Arnette rolled her eyes. "Who am I to ask the comings and goings of some spoiled little rich girl. She said she didn't want to be bothered, so Murray and I didn't bother her."

"But you didn't check on her either," Sadie said.

"No. I didn't. What of it?"

"Well, maybe we should have," Murray grumbled. "We've got a mess to deal with now."

His wife spun on him. "Heavens above! I should have known it would end up like this. I blame *you*, Murray!"

"Me? You're just angry 'cause of the smell! I had nothing to do with that. You're mad—"

"Damn right, I'm mad!"

"No one could have known!"

"I knew!" she snapped. "What'd I say to you: *That girl's trouble*, and she was!"

"But I never knew what she was—"

"I don't think anyone could have known what was going to happen, or what mess she'd leave," Jordan said, interrupting. "But either way, I need to get that key from you."

Murray's chin bobbed. "The key?"

"The key to the cabin, Mr. Miles." Jordan held out his hand. "It's a crime scene, and until the Lethbridge forensics team goes through and checks everything, it needs to be secured."

Arnette stepped toward the two officers.

"Can't you at least tell us what you found first? What was she *doing* in that cabin?"

"No, ma'am, we can't," Sadie said. "But we do need the key."

"Well, okay then…" Murray handed them the key. "But we *will* be able to get in there to clean up at some point, right?"

"You will," Jordan said.

"Should I drive to Pincher and rent a carpet cleaner?" Arnette said. "If the smell has soaked into the carpet and drapes, it'll *all* need to be washed or dry-cleaned."

Sadie swallowed laughter. They'd be pulling out the carpet for sure, maybe even the underfloor. She knew of nothing that would get out that much blood. "Just let the team from Lethbridge do their job first," she said. "It'll take a few days. Wait on everything else. And one more thing… Don't leave town."

"Why not?"

Constable Black Plume stepped closer. "Because you're involved in a homicide investigation," she said grimly. "The murder of Gabrielle Rice might not have happened *here,* Mr. and Mrs. Miles, but it happened, and you were one of the last people to talk to the victim before she died."

Murray Miles stepped back so fast he stumbled.

"But I never hurt anyone. I never—"

"Let us do our investigation," Sadie said. "Then we can talk more." The hint of a smile curled the edges of her mouth. "And in the meantime, think about the last couple weeks. I'd be interested if either of you remember something new."

White-faced and silent, Arnette Miles said nothing.

* * *

The sound of footsteps neared. Lou's heart, riddled with scars, pounded until she was light headed.

Hurry! HURRY! a chorus of voices in her mind chanted.

With the light gone, the area in the shadow of the mountains was in deep twilight. She jarred her leg and gasped, pain radiating from ankle to knee. She took a gulping breath.

"Rich! RICH!" she screamed.

Leg aching, she pushed onward. Behind her, there was a loud crash, and she jerked around in surprise. A dark figure struggled to stand, the wheelbarrow knocked sideways. Lou turned back, her gaze catching on Rich's in the window, his eyes wide and confused. *"Lou…?"*

A second later, the door to the kitchen swung open, porch light coming on as Lou reached the yard.

Rich caught her in his arms as she fell. "What in the—"

"There's someone—" she choked, "chasing me!"

Rich half-carried, half-dragged Lou into the safety of the house, kicking the door closed and locking it behind them.

"Call the police, Lou," he said. "I've got this."

"What're you doing?"

Rich rummaged through the drawer next to the sink and pulled out a knife.

"I'm going to go see who's out there."

"NO!" she screamed. The panic hit and she dissolved into tears. "Please don't! Don't go! There's something WRONG. You'll die if you go out there!"

Rich set the knife on the counter and pulled her into a tight hug, though his eyes stayed on the door.

"Shhh…" he whispered. "It's okay."

Lou found herself being led toward the hallway where the phone hung. She clung to Rich, not even letting go of him when he picked up the handset and dialed. The numbers on the rotary rolled through with lazy clicks. Tears soaked Lou's face and dampened Rich's shirt. His arm around her shoulders never moved.

"This is Rich Evans." Lou heard him say. "I need an officer to come by the house. Someone just attacked Louise."

* * *

The sky above Waterton was black velvet by the time Sadie and Jordan had finished dusting for prints and the last of the evidence bags had been packed into the police cruiser. Brian stood next to a baleful looking Murray, watching them carry evidence from the cabin. An icy wind whistled through the trees, fingers of cold reaching under Jordan's jacket, leaving him shivering. Tonight there'd be frost.

He set the last box into the trunk and stretched his back.

"Lordy, but I wish tomorrow was my day off. I'm exhausted."

Sadie laughed. "Keep wishing, kid."

"Kid? I'm barely two years younger than you."

She rolled her eyes. "Two or twenty?"

"Christ, Sadie. You sound like J—"

The walkie-talkie on Jordan's belt crackled.

"Constable Wyatt," the receptionist's voice interrupted. "Liz here. Reply please."

He pulled the receiver from his belt.

"Constable Wyatt," he said, yawning. "What's up, Liz? Over."

"Just got a call from Rich and Lou. There's trouble at their cabin."

Sadie looked up in surprise.

"What kind of trouble?" Jordan asked.

"Someone chased Louise to the cabin. Scared her good. I know you and Brian are working at the Miles' place right now, but do you have time to respond?"

"Tell them we're on our way," he said.

Sadie threw herself into the driver's seat and slammed the door closed; Jordan followed a moment later. "You good to go?" she asked.

Jordan slid the seat belt across his lap. "Yeah. You?"

He looked up, catching Sadie's eyes. All laughter was gone, her expression fierce. Seeing it, Jordan's chest eased. If Sadie was here, it'd be okay.

"I'm ready."

And with that, Sadie popped the car into reverse, spinning gravel onto the empty street as she backed from the driveway.

* * *

Ben Grayden had been thinking about Sadie Black Plume all day. Long after their lunch meeting had ended, her words had haunted his mind. Tonight, alone in his police cruiser, she was there too. Part of it, Ben knew, was boredom, but another part held something more. As he drove the lonely roads between Pincher and Waterton, alert for traffic violations, her words returned once more.

"We've got a leak," Sadie'd told him.

"A leak, like… an informant?"

"Call it what you want, the story is out and I didn't tell anyone."

"Neither did I."

And that was the part that bothered him. That Sadie *hadn't* told a reporter. That she'd assumed it was Ben who'd shared the details. But hadn't he assumed the same thing…? Frowning, his gaze moved from the road ahead of him—flat on the prairie—over to the eastern edge of the Rocky Mountains where ripples of land sat frozen in undulating waves. The foothills were borderland. Untamed. A few ranches cut into the rugged forests that flowed like skirts along the mountainside, but none had the orderliness of those square domesticated farms that moved out across the plains.

The highway curved around a hilly outcrop before dropping into a small river valley, then rolling back up again. Ben's hands moved by muscle memory. He'd driven this road countless times since joining the force, and the smooth shapes of it were as much a part of him as the hands that gripped the wheel. There were times it felt like he blinked in Pincher Creek, only to find himself at Waterton's gates. Tonight, few cars were on the road, and the hypnotic hum of the engine pulled at him.

Up ahead, the lights of a vehicle appeared on a service road adjoining the highway. He couldn't tell the make or model—he was still too far away and it was dark—but it was on a road that led to one of the nearby ranches that touched the edge of the park. *A pretty area,* Ben thought. *Close enough you could practically walk to the mountains if you wanted to.* At the thought, his hands tightened on the wheel.

Maybe the killer knew that too.

In the last few seconds, the lights of the vehicle had grown, a plume of grey dust rising into the air behind it. Seeing it, the homicide investigation disappeared from Ben's mind.

"Slow down asshole," he muttered.

The lights reached the highway and the vehicle shimmied on the chatter-marks of the graveled road as the driver fought for control. The vehicle swerved across both lanes of the highway, then pulled back again. Ben flicked on the radar. Numbers flashed across the screen as it picked up speed, tail lights receding into the darkness.

79... 84... 97... 105

"And we have a winner," Ben said. He hit the sirens and lights, then pressed the pedal to the floor, Gabrielle Rice and whoever had murdered her a thousand miles from his mind.

* * *

Lou sat at the table for a long time after Constables Black Plume and Wyatt left. She stared down at her hands and the ring that had already—mere months in—worn a hollow into her finger.

"Lou, baby," Rich said quietly. "Are you alright?"

"I… I don't know."

"It's over. The police are going to keep an eye on the house to-night. We'll get a security system set up this week."

"This *isn't* about the guy who chased me."

"It's not?"

Louise shook her head, unable to speak. If she did, then the tears would come and she'd worked so *hard* to hold them back.

"What is it then?" Rich asked.

She felt him slide into the chair beside her, his knee bumping her leg. Hot tears filled her eyes. This was supposed to be their new beginning, but everywhere she looked, danger waited.

"Talk to me, Lou. Tell me what's going on."

"I just feel so… so… raw."

"But if it's not about the guy who chased you, then—"

"It's Gabrielle." The name alone choked her.

Rich's arm slid over her shoulder.

"Hey now. We're okay. Gabby is—*was*—always dramatic. The police saying she'd been staying in town doesn't mean anything oth-er than… she was here."

Lou looked up. "But it *does* mean something, Rich."

"She was out of my life years ago."

"Until September eleventh. And then she was back in it."

"That was just a friend checking on a friend. You would have done the same if it was Hunter or Levi or—"

"Gabby left you a letter at the cabin." Lou's shoulders slumped and the first tears broke over her lashes. "She was angry at you. She wanted revenge."

Rich stared at her. "Sadie never said anything about…"

"No, Sadie didn't say it, but *I know.*"

There was a long moment when Rich didn't speak. Around the room, emotions swirled and spun. Two years ago, Rich would have run from this admission: *Lou's knowing.* Tonight, his fingers tightened around hers.

"Tell me," he said.

"Sadie read a letter. It was from Gabby to you. I could feel it, Rich. Whatever she read upset Sadie. Gabrielle Rice was angry with you. She was… *unhinged.*"

"Shit. So you… you just *felt* all of this?"

"Bits and pieces. Worries, mainly. Things that Sadie was trying to control. It…" She laughed tearily. "It's different than a vision. Reading someone is catching onto their emotions, riding them. I… I could sense Constable Black Plume was worried." Lou looked up at Rich, held his eyes. "Sadie doesn't think she can trust you either."

"She thinks I killed Gabby."

"She isn't sure, but you're the most likely suspect."

CHAPTER ELEVEN

It was nearly midnight before Sadie and Jordan left Lou's cabin. Sadie waved to Brian who sat in an unmarked car, waiting in case the unknown assailant returned. Rich had promised there'd be a security system installed tomorrow.

That part, at least, Sadie believed.

Constable Black Plume wanted to stay on shift and watch the house herself—*to catch the asshole*—but the adrenaline that had kept her going for the last hours of overtime was gone, her body woozy from exhaustion. For now, everything in Waterton seemed calm. Sadie knew this was a lie.

She tapped her fingers against the wheel. "What the hell is going *on* with them?!"

Jordan blinked. "You say something?"

"This isn't a coincidence that Lou got chased tonight. She saw the guy before, the night the body was found. My gut says that matters."

"You think the guy she saw was the same one who killed Gabrielle Rice?"

"Don't *you*?"

"I don't know. I haven't seen enough evidence yet to decide either way."

"Right." She laughed.

"What…?" Jordan asked warily.

"It's nothing."

"No, really… *what*? You laughed at me. Why?"

If Sadie had been rested, she might have refused to answer, but tonight the truth tumbled from her lips.

"You sounded like Jim there," she said. "When we were partners, we… we had a way of working together."

"What way?"

"I'd be going on about my 'gut' and he'd be all reason." A sad smile touched the corners of Sadie's mouth. "But somehow we balanced."

"I'm sorry."

"Don't be." Sadie shook her head. "Jim was a good guy."

"He was."

There was a long silence filled only by the hum of the engine. There was something pressing at Sadie. She could feel it, the same way she could feel the loss of Jim at the edges of her heart, waiting there, the pain of his death ready to cut if she allowed herself to think too much about him.

What's your gut telling you Sadie? she imagined him saying. *Tell me what you're thinking.*

"I'm not saying I *know* what's going on with this Gabrielle Rice case," she said. "I'm just saying there's *something* more than just a murder. The connections are there—Lou and the guy waiting in the dark, and whoever murdered Gabrielle—and while I have lots of pieces, I can't quite see the bigger picture yet." She laughed. "It pisses me off."

"Maybe they're not connected at all."

"Maybe… but a person chasing Lou down the street isn't the first time someone came after her. She called in a prowler before. If that

Rice girl was still alive, I'd almost think it was her."

"Ghost stalker?" Jordan teased.

"I don't believe in ghosts. But there's *someone* stirring up trouble. So who?"

"This time of year, Waterton's almost empty." Jordan smothered a yawn behind his hand. "So who's new in town?"

"Gabrielle for one." She slowed as a deer, spooked from its night-time hiding place, crossed the street in front of her, a spindly fawn whose spots had almost faded, trailing behind. "You think someone was staying at the cabin *with* her?"

"Like… a friend or something?"

"Yeah, a partner. If someone was helping her, they might be our lead. I dusted for prints. We can run those tomorrow." Sadie pressed the gas as the two deer disappeared into the shadows on the far side of the road. "I'd say it's rather lucky Rich *didn't* have a run-in with his ex."

"A partner would explain the missing key and car."

"Then we've got to find the vehicle."

Jordan pulled his notepad from his pocket.

"I'll call in the plates and put in an APB for them when we get back."

"Thanks."

Ahead, the stonework fence that surrounded the Waterton police station appeared and Sadie pulled the car over to the curb.

Jordan tucked the notepad away. "Sadie?"

"Uh-huh."

"I… I want you to know something."

"What's that?"

"Gut or not, I think there's something else going on too," Jordan said. "I just haven't figured it out yet."

She nodded. "We've got to find out who *else* is in town. Because there's someone alive, harassing Waterton residents, and if Gabrielle Rice's death is related, then they're more than just a nuisance. They may be the murderer."

Jordan put his hand on the door, then turned. "You think the guy who chased Lou was the same guy who killed Gabrielle?"

"If the killer wasn't Rich Evans? Yeah, I think that's a good possibility."

* * *

Louise was still half-awake as the first golden bands of light climbed over the mountains. She hadn't been able to sleep after the police had left. Nor had she slept during the long, restless hours at Rich's side. Lying in the darkness, she sifted through the stories she knew so well, but none offered the answer her heart needed. A single thought circled her mind: *Everything that has a beginning has an end. Make your peace with that, and all will be well.*

The words gave her no solace.

Exhausted, she gathered her clothes, dressed in the hallway, and left a note on the fridge.

Rich,

Couldn't sleep so I went into the Garage early.

Love you, Lou

If sleep wouldn't come, she'd take on the one thing she *knew* would settle her nerves: Car maintenance.

Lou unlocked the front door and flicked the switch. Outside the pane glass window, the aging red neon of 'Lou's Garage' flickered once and turned on. Lou smiled. This had always been her job when she helped her father around the garage. How many times had she turned it on in the morning? How many times had she flicked it off at night? Childhood felt close, but impossibly far away. Life was strange that way.

She turned on the pneumatic bell and headed to the back of the garage. If someone came through for gas, she'd hear them.

The destroyed truck was back up on jacks, but Lou had no intention of going underneath. Instead, she took an easy task. Mrs. Kulkarni had brought her aging sedan in for a tune-up and Lou puttered under the hood for half an hour before the bell rang. She headed to the front of the shop, catching sight of the mail truck from Lethbridge. The driver waved as he dropped a pile of newspapers onto the sidewalk, leaving before Lou stepped outside to pick them up. Her gaze dropped to the front page.

MURDERED NYC SOCIALITE TIED TO US DRUG CARTEL

by Delia Rosings, October 21, 2001

The Waterton murder which has dominated the news for the last two weeks has taken a disturbing turn. New details have emerged which link the dead woman, Gabrielle Rice, to a known drug cartel working throughout the US. Gabrielle's father, Edward Rice, a New York businessman, is rumoured to have connections to Tyrone "King" Fischer. Mr. Fischer is part of the same international drug cartel as Darren "Dax" Xavier, a known felon, whose one-time connections to drug running in the Waterton area, dominated headlines in 1999...

Lou's stomach dropped, her hands shaking where they gripped the paper's edge. Gabrielle Rice wasn't *just* a victim. She was also the daughter of a man with connections to the underworld...

* * *

Waterton was winding down for the year, but from the looks of Hunter's Coffee shop, you'd never know it. A group of locals filled the tables along one wall of the cafe. Audrika sat next to Margaret, Murray and Grant and the elderly Mr. Hamamoto, a few chairs down. Levi took a seat that put his back to the wall as he always did, and seemed more interested in arguing with the waitresses than in coffee conversation.

Hunter had just done another round of refills and was switching to a fresh pot when a familiar face appeared in the front window. He frowned. Lou's expression was drawn and tired, purple Cs hollowing the skin under her eyes. She had a newspaper tucked under her arm. The bell jangled merrily as she strode into the coffee shop and headed directly to the group at the back.

Hunter grabbed a full pot of coffee and followed.

"Louise," Audrika said. "What're you doing here this morning?"

"I need to talk to everyone," she said. "I… I saw something in the paper that concerns us all."

Hunter set a cup in front of Lou, filling it without asking.

"You alright, hon?"

"No Hunter. I'm not."

"What is it?" Warden McNealy asked. "This about Rich again?"

"No," Lou said. "But it'll affect him too."

Hunter dropped a handful of creamers in front of Lou.

"What's going on?"

"Today's paper just arrived. Have you read it yet?"

There was a hubbub of answers, but Hunter couldn't follow the different threads.

"Today's article made connections between the troubles Waterton had in 1999 and Miss Rice's death," Lou said. "We need to be careful. Darren Xavier has ties to the Rice family. Who knows what else people in town are mixed up in."

"There are lots of people who've been mixed up in lots of things," Hunter said, "but that doesn't mean—"

"You're not listening to me!" Lou snapped. "This isn't just *any* felon. It's the guy who worked with Colt."

"Colt, you say?" Levi grumbled.

Lou pursed her lips. "Yes. Colt *didn't* work alone. When Sadie and Jim were investigating Borderline, they mentioned Darren Xavier. Colt worked for him. And Gabrielle's father has ties to those people."

Levi scowled and turned away without answering.

Audrika tutted. "Now look. Colton Calhoun was mixed up in a lot of things he shouldn't have been, but that doesn't mean we'll have trouble with those people."

"I wish I could believe that," Lou said, "but it says right here that Gabrielle's father is connected to a man called Tyrone Fischer. He's mafia, it seems. Worse yet, he has ties to Xavier."

"So what?"

"So that connection *matters*. It's dangerous for us, for Waterton."

Levi crossed his arms. "And how do you know all of that, huh?"

"Because I just do! There's trouble brewing here."

"What kind of trouble?" Hunter asked.

"The worst kind. And I don't know *how* this will all play out, but I can tell you one thing: This mess with Gabrielle's murder isn't over yet."

Audrika leaned forward, her dark eyes flashing. "Did something happen to you, Lou?" Audrika said.

Lou's voice returned, lower now: "I was chased on my way home last night." Gasps rose alongside a chatter of concern. "The guy came after me in a car, but I took a short-cut. He *followed me* by foot!"

The rumble of worry grew:

"—trouble again!"

"We need to be careful of outsiders in town—"

"—man came by, asking questions—"

"Are you sure that—?"

"Listen," Lou said, her voice rising above the din. "I need you to *listen!*" The rumble of chatter dropped. "I think we *all* need to be careful," she said. "There's something *else* going on, and I know it sounds crazy, but we're *all* wrapped up in it."

"How, exactly?" Levi growled. "'Cause as far as I can see, it's just one girl dead. An outsider at that, and no trouble to us."

"How can you say that?! It's like you don't care!"

"That's 'cause I don't!"

The roar of voices joined the growing argument. Lou was still speaking, but Hunter could no longer pick her voice from the crowd. He'd just filled up Mrs. Lu's coffee when Audrika put her hand on his arm.

"Has Mr. Farrel talked to *you*, Hunter?" she asked.

He frowned, remembering the man on his porch.

"He did."

"What about?"

"About Miss Rice."

Audrika tipped her head to the side. "He talked to *me* about Miss Rice too, you know."

"Not a surprise," Hunter said. "The man's a private investigator after all."

"Really? Mr. Farrel told *me* he was a businessman."

"He mentioned that to me too." Hunter frowned. "Guy's a bit dodgy, if you ask me."

"Some of the ladies seem to like him."

Hunter snorted. "They would."

Audrika pursed her lips. "Well, I should be going now." She patted Hunter's arm. "Do let me know if Tom comes in here again, would you?"

Hunter blinked. "Tom?"

"Yes," she said with a coy smile. "I'm doing a little investigating of my own."

"Oh, Audrika," Hunter groaned. "I don't know if that's wise."

She laughed. "This from *you*, Hunter? Please save me the platitudes." And with a knowing smile, she headed from the coffee shop into the morning sunshine.

* * *

Rich was in the shower when he heard a door open somewhere deep in the first-floor recesses of Whispering Aspens. He whisked the water away from his face and turned his head as he strained to hear. Lou's note said she was at work, and it was too early for lunch. He waited a second… two… and then—

"Rich?" Lou's voice called. "Are you up there?"

"Yeah! Upstairs."

The tension from seconds earlier was gone. *Starting to freak out over nothing.* Rich spun the four-pronged knob on the shower and the water slowed. Deep in the walls, the pipes moaned and shuddered. It was a sound he knew as well as the creaks in the floor. The sounds of home. He stepped from the tub, grabbing a towel as he did.

Lou's footsteps pattered up the risers and the door handle turned.

"Rich, can we talk a second?"

"Of course," he said with a grin. "I didn't expect you back so…" His expression rippled into concern. "What's wrong?"

She held out the newspaper toward him. "This."

MURDERED NYC SOCIALITE TIED TO U.S. DRUG CARTEL

The cool air from the hallway swirled through the bathroom, making the hairs on Rich's arms rise. "What's this?"

"It's a connection between Gabrielle and Colton."

"But…" A line of worry appeared between Rich's brows. "That's not possible."

"It *is* possible, Rich. And worse yet, I think it might be true." Lou stepped up beside him, pointing at the newspaper which hung limp with moisture in his hands. "Dax Xavier," she said. "He was Colt's drug running partner… his boss."

"So what?"

"So… *everything.*" Lou stared at him. "This matters. This connects her death back to Waterton, and the troubles from two years ago."

"Wait. No. This just doesn't make sense. Why would Gabrielle have any connection to—" He shook the newspaper, finding the line again. "To a drug cartel."

"Because it's her *father* who is connected," Lou said. "Not Gabrielle herself. Mr. Rice has ties to a man named Tyrone Fischer; Fischer is linked to Xavier."

"You mean Tyrone 'King' Fischer? The drug lord?" Rich laughed as he handed her the paper. "No. It's not possible, Lou. Sorry. It's just not. Rice is a businessman."

"Not the good kind."

"You don't know that."

"Yes," she said. "I do. And I know it's hard to hear because Gabby was your friend, but—"

"She wasn't—"

"She was your *fiancée* at one point, but that doesn't mean it's not true. There's been something worrying me about this whole thing from the beginning. I couldn't figure out *what* but it's starting to come together."

"I…. I don't think so. I mean, I *met* Gabby's father. A couple of times, actually."

"And?"

"He didn't seem like the kind of guy to be messed up in drug running." Rich laughed. "Gabby's mother is a socialite; her father does charity work. They throw parties with senators. God! This whole cabin *and* the one next door could fit in their apartment." He flipped the towel over his neck and smiled down at Lou. "You're making something out of nothing."

"I'm not."

"But—"

"What was Mr. Rice's business?" she asked.

"He was a businessman."

"What *kind* of business?"

Rich shifted from foot to foot. The bathroom, warm minutes earlier, was now icy cold. "He…" Rich's brows shot up as he remembered a dinner years before. "He's involved in real estate! Handles a lot of land titles for other people and he has connections."

"Connections?"

"Yeah. He helped me get things set up for my lease. It was taking forever, but as soon as Mr. Rice stepped in, his connections…" Rich's hands rose involuntarily as the truth finally hit him. "Shit."

"It's true," Lou said. "I've felt like there was something *more* happening from the beginning. And now we know what it is." She tossed the newspaper with its soaked edges into the garbage bin. "You need to be *careful* Rich. There's something bad coming."

He pulled Lou into his arms, burrowing his face into her hair.

"It's going to be okay," he said. "We're together, you and me. Everything is going to work out."

"Someone came after me last night. That's *not* okay."

"I—I know. I'm just saying, we've got each other."

"Yes, we do." Her hands rose to his back and she took a shuddering breath. "But you *need* to be careful, Rich. Okay? You need to watch yourself, because if Gabrielle's father is connected to Dax, then—"

A loud knocking from the front door interrupted.

Lou turned. "Who in the world could that be?"

* * *

Days started early at the Durnerin ranch. Shawna and her two younger brothers were up two hours before dawn, the three of them in charge of the endless chores that were day-to-day life on a working ranch. By six they'd eaten breakfast with their father and the ranch-hands who worked in the crew. On weekdays, the younger boys were at school, but today they mucked out the barn, leaving Shawna to deal with the cattle. She loaded the mixer wagon and brought it to the pens, then loaded several bales of hay onto the back of her pick-up, heading out where the herd was pastured.

Her eyes narrowed as she drove along the bumpy gravel road. There'd been a time she wanted to escape the daily grind. No longer. With her mother gone, there weren't enough hands to do all the chores, and with Dawson and Jackson still in high school, that wasn't going to change… at least for the time being.

No. Right now, Shawna's focus was keeping them all afloat. She'd worry about her 'dreams' later.

The Durnerin ranch had survived for five long generations. The only ranch that had existed in the borderland of the Rocky Mountains longer than theirs was the Thompson place next door. Shawna had no intentions of letting it end with her. But that meant planning. Hard work. Days like today that started at five, and didn't end until nightfall.

Two men on horseback appeared on a nearby trail and Shawna slowed the truck, giving them time to cross the road. *The American hunters*, she thought, irritated. But she smiled and waved all the same. Those men and women who came to hunt were part of why the Durnerins had survived. Even with a full herd and no major costs, there were years that the ledger hit the red. Add to that the expense of sick cattle, and the inevitable losses from grizzlies, cougars, and the occasional poacher, and you always had your toes on the line. No matter the difficulty, ranching was in Shawna's blood. She'd ridden almost before she'd walked and during her school days, she'd spent her time in the 4-H club. Today as she headed to the pasture she felt that same surge of joy.

This land is ours.

Mid-morning sunshine had warmed the grassland and cattle moved toward the truck, calling out. She put the truck in park, then pushed the door open with a squeal. Further out the cows milled uneasily. Shawn frowned. October was Grizzly season. Though attacks were relatively rare, they happened.

Nervous, Shawna climbed into the back of the truck and tossed down the first few bales. The herd moved forward, but they didn't come in a straight line. Knots of them circled nervously away from an outcrop of trees near the border between the Durnerin ranch and Waterton park.

"What's out there?" she muttered. Shawna tossed the last bale out of the truck, then stepped up onto the roof of the cab. She squinted toward the treeline. There, just inside the shadows of the trees, a shape huddled. It was smaller than a cow, which meant they'd just lost a calf.

Shawna gritted her teeth. "Goddamnit!"

She climbed back down and headed to the cab of the truck, pulling the rifle case out from under the seat and loading two shells into the barrel. She tossed a handful of shells into her coat pocket and walked toward the trees. The cows moved with bovine patience, stepping past her. Shawna kept her eyes on the shape, watching and ready.

"Should've brought a dog," she muttered.

As she neared the treeline, her steps slowed. She paused, breathing hard, her body reacting before her mind really understood what she was seeing. She lifted the rifle with shaking hands, put the sight to her eye. A man's body lay before her. His neck had been slashed from ear to ear and the congealed blood was black where it spread across his neck and shoulders like a cloak.

Shawna stumbled backwards, adrenaline flooding her limbs.

"Oh my God!"

The body wasn't a calf, but a man, and not just *any* man… It was someone she knew.

Tears flooded Shawna's eyes as she turned and stumbled back to the truck. She grabbed the CB radio and dialed in the number with shaking fingers.

"10-4," a voice responded. "This is Durnerin ranch, who—"

"Dad! You've got to call the police." Shawna took a shuddering breath, her gaze moving back to the trees and the lump that, even now, the cattle avoided.

"Shawna? What's going—?"

"It's Ben Grayden! He's dead!"

CHAPTER TWELVE

Jordan had been waiting for Sadie to speak ever since the call had come into the station. She hadn't yet. Her gaze was fixed on the horizon as they drove the back roads west of Twin Butte, heading into the curve of the mountain's shoulder where the Durnerin ranch was found.

A dusty haze rose off the road, sifting in through the ventilation system and coating the car's interior with a fine layer of grit. Jordan took a breath and choked. They needed rain, but the last precipitation had been the week that Gabrielle Rice had died. Now they had *another* body to deal with. Found, yet again, just inside the confines of Waterton Park, in their jurisdiction.

Only this time, it was Ben.

Jordan took another surreptitious look at Sadie. Her eyes were red, either from the dust or from trying not to cry. The fingers that wrapped the wheel were white-knuckled, a line of muscle in her jaw flicking like the tail of an angry cat.

"What?!" she snapped.

Jordan blinked. "Sorry?"

"You're staring at me. What do you want?"

"I just—" He dropped his eyes. "This is Ben. I can't wrap my head around that."

"Well you'd better fucking try," she said, "'cause we're going to be at the crime scene in a couple minutes." Her mouth tightened, and she added. "Sorry. I… I shouldn't swear. I'm just *tired* of having the killer two steps ahead of us."

"You think it's the same guy?"

Her gaze jumped from the road to him and back again.

"Don't you?"

"I… I don't know yet. Could be a copycat."

"Guess so. Seems a bit too close: Ben Grayden's body being found just a few kilometres from Gabrielle Rice's."

"You think it might have been one of the hunters we spoke to?" He paused for a second too long. "Or Bryce Calhoun. Thompson ranch is just over the hill."

"Everyone's a suspect at this point."

Sadie tapped the brakes. Up ahead, a truck appeared, the back half-full of square bales of hay, a police cruiser marked *'Pincher Creek RCMP'* sitting next to it. Several dozen head of cattle milled around the two vehicles.

"The hunters had access," she said. "The body was found at the ranch they're staying at, but… I don't see the connection to them yet."

"We should watch ourselves then," Jordan said quietly. "Jim didn't see the connection to Susan and look where that got him."

Sadie's cheeks paled.

"Sorry, Sadie. I shouldn't have said—"

"Yes, you should have," she said, slowing as they reached the truck. "You're right about Jim."

"But—"

"It's the goddamned truth. No use pretending it isn't." She popped the cruiser into park. "Now let's get started, Jordan."

Without another word, the two officers stepped out of the car.

* * *

Lou tiptoed down the stairs. Upstairs she could hear Rich opening and closing drawers in the bedroom, things being moved around as he rushed to dress. Lou paused halfway down the stairs and peered through the triangular cut-out that led to the living room and the rarely-used front door of the house. Visitors almost always came in through the back. The appearance of someone at the other door threw her.

A man waited, his shoulder visible through the window. Lou frowned uncertainly. There was something familiar to his stance, but what? The man reached out and the doorbell rang a second time.

"Almost done!" Rich called. "I'll be right down."

Lou jogged the last few stairs to the main floor. For a moment she could remember the night that Hunter's dog had arrived on their step, frightening Rich. Her nerves this morning had the same unsettled feel. She heard the bedroom door open and Rich start down the stairs.

The bell rang a third time.

Forcing a smile, Louise pulled the door open. A middle-aged man with graying hair and a dark jacket stood on the other side.

"Yes?" Lou said.

"Oh, hello," the man said, smiling warmly. "I'm so sorry to bother you, but do you have a minute to talk?"

Rich came up behind her. "Talk about what?"

"About Miss Gabrielle Rice," the man said. He flashed a license of some kind at Lou—far too fast for her to read—then tucked it back into his pocket. "I'm investigating her death."

"I thought the police were doing that," Lou said.

"They are," the man said. "But I've been hired by the family."

"Gabby's family?"

"Yes, exactly." The man extended his hand and grinned. "You're Rich Evans, I take it?"

Lou frowned. She wanted to catch the thread of the stranger's emotions, but every time she reached out her thoughts, they slipped away like water.

"I am," Rich said. "I've got to be honest. I'm a little confused about why *you're* investigating."

The man chuckled. "Can I come in a moment? It'd be easier to explain."

Rich opened his mouth to answer, but Lou interrupted.

"I'm sorry," she lied, "but the house is a mess. I'd rather we just talked here."

The investigator peered over her shoulder into the tidy interior, then back at her.

"Are you sure we couldn't just—?"

"No," she said. "Thanks for understanding. It's good to meet you, Mr...?"

"I'm Tom, Tom Farrel," he said, extending his open hand. "And you are—?"

The moment their palms touched, Lou's body went cold. Words disappeared. Even the front steps and the vast mountains that rose on either side of the lake faded into half-light. There was a rush of icy cold. She couldn't breathe! Lou let go and took a shuddering breath.

Tom stared at her.

"Lou," Rich prompted. "Mr. Farrel asked your name."

"Louise Newman," she said, then crossed her arms. Her hand ached like it had been soaked in ice water.

"Good to meet you." Tom turned back to Rich. "So as I was saying: Miss Rice's father asked me to come assist the police in any way that I could. I'm not part of their investigation, but I'm sharing anything I find with them."

"And have you found anything?"

Tom's smile froze for a split-second, like a movie caught in a loop, then released. "Nothing solid," he said. "Just bits and pieces of gossip. It seems Gabrielle was in Waterton for a couple weeks before her death."

"I thought she was still in New York," Rich said. "Why did she come to Alberta?"

"I honestly don't know," Tom said. "But she did." He looked back at Lou. "Did you happen to meet Miss Rice during her visit?"

Lou shook her head. "No."

"Did she ever come into the Garage where you work?" he asked.

"Not that I recall."

"She was a very beautiful young woman." Tom held out a photograph of Gabrielle. "You certain you don't remember her?"

"No, I don't," Lou said. "But I mainly work in the back of the garage in the shop. I don't see everyone who comes through."

"Ah, yes, I should have known," Tom said. "You're a mechanic. I'd forgotten that." He chuckled. "I've been checking around, you see."

Rich shot Lou a concerned look. "Checking on *what*?"

"On the people in the town. I've been trying to get things settled, figure out where things fit."

Lou put a shaking hand against the door. "Well, I'm sorry we can't help you but—"

"Please! Just a minute longer," Tom pleaded. "I'd like to get a list of what you were up to when Miss Rice was in town."

"With all due respect," Rich said. "You're not part of the police force. We don't have to tell you any—"

"I'm not asking about *you*," Tom said. "You were in New York at the time of Miss Rice's death, isn't that right?" Tom smiled at Lou. "Now, *you* were in Waterton the entire time. Right? You were working late nights, staying in the shop…"

Lou's irritation grew as his words droned on. She pushed it aside, catching onto the thread of escaping calm. She didn't often sway events. She didn't like to. But sometimes it was the most expedient way.

"…and people in town saw Brandon Miles in the front of the shop the day Gabrielle Rice disappeared, but not *you*," Tom said. "You could have been anywhere at all, Louise."

With Herculean effort, Lou forced calm to settle around her like a cloak. She smiled at him intently. *We are done,* she thought. *And YOU are going to leave.* Tom opened his mouth to take a breath and Lou interrupted. "We're finished this conversation," she said, forcing obedience into her words, gentleness in the soothing tone. "I'm not going to talk to you anymore. You're not going to come back here either."

Tom blinked, and Lou started to close the door, but he caught it before it closed.

"I'm sorry, Miss Newman, but I'm not done," he said stiffly. "You never answered my question."

Lou frowned. "We *are* done," she said again, forcing the words deeper, threads of them looping around him. "Although you want to continue, we can't. It reminds me of a story I once heard."

"What story?" Rich murmured.

"A story about a man on a voyage from far across the sea," she said. "When it came time to leave—"

"I don't care about your story," Tom said. "And you're not going to change my decision on this." He stepped closer, and Lou's breath caught. She could see he was angry. Waves of it rose like heat off pavement. "I want to know what you were doing the day Gabrielle Rice disappeared. I've been trying to figure it out for a week!"

"I—I don't—" Lou struggled to form the words. She'd never met anyone immune to her nudging. Even Alistair could be swayed. "I was probably at home—"

"Lies! You weren't anywhere *near* this house!"

The shout roused Rich from his reverie and he stepped between them.

"You will lower your voice or I'll—"

"Or what?!" Tom said. "You're already caught up in this! You're in it deep. Have you told Louise you weren't in New York when Gabrielle died?"

"We are done," Rich snapped. "I've been totally honest with the police and—"

"I don't give a shit about the police! You do *not* want to fuck around with Mr. Rice. He wants answers!"

"But I didn't *do anything* to Gabby!" Rich said. "We were friends! For YEARS we only—"

"I've seen the hotel footage!" Tom said. "You think you can lie about what happ—"

"The police know all about the hotel!" Rich yelled. "I TOLD them!"

"But do they know *why* Gabby attacked you? What you did to that girl?"

Rich's hands rose in fists. "I didn't do anything, now get OUT!"

"You destroyed her," Tom snarled. His eyes flicked to Lou then back to Rich. "She was already a stupid, broken girl and you made it worse!" What could have been mistaken for a smile crossed Tom's face. "Her father *knows* what you did."

"I didn't do *anything!*"

"Rich, please!" Lou turned to Tom. "You need to *leave.*" Her voice rose as she tried to force him away, but there was no emotion to catch onto. Nothing to sway. It felt, she would think afterwards, like Tom Farrel was completely empty inside. A shell. "I'm going to call the police," she said. "You're a private investigator. You don't have any right to be here."

He laughed.

"Go," Lou repeated, even though her voice shook. "Get out."

Tom leaned in, and in that moment, the mask of civility dropped.

"I'm not done." He caught hold of Lou's hand. Waterton disappeared. A shadow pulled down, obscuring all light. Only Lou and Tom remained.

"Let go!" she cried.

His fingers tightened and the darkness bloomed into shapes. It was like being caught in the in-between with her mother, two years earlier. Death hung in the shadows. Snatches of memory floated forward, surrounding Tom—reaching for Louise—as they spread through the air like double-exposed film: image upon image upon image. *A young man, screaming as Tom leaned forward... water, dark with blood... the moon overhead... a city skyline... Tom laughing.*

Lou twisted in his grip and jerked her hand back, resurfacing.

"The boy's head wouldn't sink," she choked. "His body went down right away, but the head... the head kept floating back up."

Tom jerked back in surprise. "What did you say?"

"Th—the head," Lou stammered. "You h—had to fish it back out of the river. It rolled around the bottom of the fishing boat. You kicked it, like a football, then—"

Tom staggered back off the steps. His face was the pale greenish gray of spoiled milk. "Who the hell are you?"

"You killed that boy," Lou said. "You cut up his body. You—"

"Enough!" Tom bellowed. "I don't know who the HELL you talked to, but I'll mess you UP!"

"King sent you after the boy! And not just him," Lou said. "Others too!" The veil of grey had returned. She could see Tom's ghosts, waiting in the shadowlands around him. "They're there now. The people you killed. Watching you. *Waiting for you…*"

"Leave!" Rich shouted.

"You're making a mistake," Tom hissed. He stepped backward. His eyes were slits, hands raised as if ready for attack.

"Go!" Rich barked. "Don't come back!"

Tom turned and walked stiffly down the street. He didn't look back. Lou stared at him, wondering if Tom Farrel was the same person she'd seen on the night-time street. If perhaps he'd been the person who'd chased her. He didn't seem tall enough, but she couldn't be sure. When he disappeared at the end of the street and Louise turned back to Rich.

"What the hell was that?" he said.

"That," she said, "is the thing I've been worried about."

Rich stared out the open door.

"I can't believe that Gabby's father would do anything to me, but…" He let the words hang. Finally, he swung the door closed. "I'm sorry, Lou. I'm sorry we're caught up in any of this."

She wrapped her arms around him. "You need to stay away from him, Rich. He is not normal… He's empty inside. He feels… *wrong.*"

Under her hands, she felt Rich shudder.

* * *

Sadie crouched next to the body. She tightened her gloved hands into fists in a feeble attempt to stop their shaking.

Oh fuck, she thought. *This is bad.*

Ben's face was unmarred, pale eyes staring blindly forward. If she only looked at his face, she could hold it together. But below his chin… Her eyes flicked down and the bile in her throat rose. Ben's neck had been slashed from side to side. A black bib of blood poured down his neck, soaking his shirt. He'd been alive for a short time after his throat was cut. He'd been upright. He'd *tried* to get away.

Oh fuck, fuck, fuck! I can't DEAL with this!

Panic filled Sadie's chest, tearing through her ribs. This was Ben! She could see his face, hear his laugh. She blinked and the moment in the cafe returned. He wasn't a stranger. She knew him. Her fists tightened into rocks, but the palsied shaking of her fingers grew. *Why Ben?!* Jordan was taking photographs, but Sadie couldn't move. Not yet. Not when it was Ben Grayden lying in the long grass.

Hold it together, Sadie. You can do this. You've seen worse.

Sadie's chin bobbed and she turned, searching for the familiar voice before she even realized what she was doing. A cool breeze rippled past her cheek. She shivered. It felt like Jim was standing next to her shoulder. Her eyes peered into the trees, knowing that she was alone. *Jim…?* Indifferent cattle milled around the pasture. Jordan snapped pictures of Ben's corpse. A little beyond that, Shawna Durnerin sat white-faced in the cab of the truck, staring out at the mountain range. She looked like she'd seen a ghost.

Sadie felt like she'd heard one.

You've got to figure this out, Jim's voice interrupted. *Walk away from this… Ignore it, and someone else dies. You know that.*

Sadie hissed. She knew for a fact it *wasn't* Jim Flagstone that she was hearing. The idea was goddamned crazy! This was her head, messing with her. She'd been carrying the weight of his death for two years, and right now her thoughts were a jumble. She took a slow breath and blew it out again. Took another.

Stay out of my goddamned head, Jim! she thought angrily. *I can handle this.* She could imagine his rumbling laughter.

Sadie put her hands against her knees and pushed herself upright. She scanned the scene.

"Look for clues," she muttered. "Got to find this bastard."

That's my girl.

Sadie flinched. If this kept up, she'd need to talk to someone about hearing voices, but she had no idea who would believe her. With her panic receding, she found herself tugged back into the clarity of police work. She walked through the crime scene, making mental notes. There was a splash of blood that drew a jagged half-circle around the body. *Arterial spray.* Ben had been alive for at least a short time after his throat had been slashed. She crouched next to it. Around her the grass was down-trodden by cattle, but she could also see that a few small shrubs had been crushed by a car or truck turning around. Sadie looked up, forcing herself to see the distance between the turn-around, and the body.

"Ben was brought here to be killed."

Once the idea arrived, she couldn't put aside the idea. And it made sense. Ben's throat *had* to have been cut at the scene, otherwise he'd have bled to death long before he arrived, leaving plenty of evidence wherever that had been. That's *not* what had happened. The footprints she'd found led from the end of the road over to the trees. He'd been butchered on site. Whoever had killed him *knew* what they were doing. And they hadn't botched the wound either. It was ear to ear, the way a hunter would slice the throat of a deer. Ben bled out in a matter of minutes. His killer *knew* this would happen.

Sadie looked down at the broken twigs and grass. She walked back to the road, then frowned.

"Why would you get in someone's car, Ben?" she whispered.

"I'm done with the body," Jordan said.

Sadie turned. "What's that?"

"I've got all the photos I need," he said. "I'm going to look through the trees. You ready to check Ben? Uh… the body I mean? It's all yours."

"Got it."

Sadie came back around the other side of the corpse—a position which left Ben's face hidden—and squatted down once more.

"Alright," she muttered. "It's okay. I'm okay."

She waited for the panic she'd felt before to return, but it had faded into the buzzing of a mosquito. Faint, but annoying. She took a slow breath. *Just see the details,* she thought. *Look for patterns later.* She snapped the wrists of each latex glove, then patted down the body, checking for clues. There were no wounds on his back that she could see, nor any bruising around his neck. Reaching Ben's arms, she checked his wrists. No ligature marks.

"Not tied up then," she muttered. "Maybe the guy had a gun on him."

Done with Ben's back, she moved to his jacket. She lifted back the open front, seeing just how far the black cape of blood had spread. She blinked. The holster was there, but Ben's gun was gone. She moved onto his pockets. Ben's I.D. was missing too. As she worked, the calm inside her spread. Sadie went through his jacket, putting items into evidence bags. Finally, she reached the breast pocket of his shirt. Sadie moved around in front of the body. Ben's eyes stared forward, pleading with her, but she didn't meet his gaze. Instead she tipped him back so she could reach into his shirt. The gaping black mouth under his chin yawned. The cut was so deep she could see the back of his trachea. With a shudder, she reached into his inside breast pocket.

A piece of paper brushed her gloved fingers.

Sadie jerked in surprise, almost losing her grip on Ben's shoulder. She grunted as she tipped the body back a second time. Her fingers dug through the pocket, finally catching on the edge of the paper. She carefully pulled it out.

It was a piece of beige paper with a print pattern along one edge that Sadie found oddly familiar. She frowned, staring at it. She *knew* those small flowers, the line of twined vines. A memory of the lunch meeting with Ben surfaced.

"It's part of the restaurant's menu," she said. She ran one latex-clad finger along the edge, then flipped it open.

A message was written inside:

LRH Nurses
Porters / Staff / Shift change
Pincher or Waterton police
Data collection? Who'd have access? Parents?

Underneath it was a new note, scribbled in pencil rather than pen. It simply read:

Call Sadie.

She took a shaky breath and folded the paper closed, then put it in the plastic bag. Her gaze rose. Out near the highway, a plume of dust appeared as the ambulance trundled slowly up the gravel road. She sealed the bag and stood.

No calling me now, she thought, and walked back to the police car, leaving the remains of Ben Grayden behind.

* * *

Lou backed away from the door. The emotion that had built

since the investigator's arrival had yet to dissipate. It roiled around her, a storm about to break.

"You saw a head?" Rich said.

"Yes."

"Like… an actual head? You saw it *here*?"

"No… not here." The room felt ten degrees too cold and Lou crossed her arms. "It was a memory, I think. Or maybe a flash of something." She frowned. "Not another life. Not a dream… but *real*."

"Shit."

"That man carries darkness around him. There's… something there." She shuddered.

"A sociopath?"

"Maybe. It feels like all his human emotions have been pushed aside," she said. "He brings danger."

"What kind of danger? And to who?"

"Everything… everyone. I can't describe it other than he's got ghosts. *Real* ones. I heard them when I was chased home, but I didn't know what I was hearing. I need to talk to Sadie and Jordan about him, but I don't know what to say."

"Say he yelled at you. That's true."

"I guess."

Rich pulled Lou into a hug, resting his chin on the top of her head. "Are you okay?"

"I am now. I want to get out of here… go for a walk or something." She snuggled closer. "Feel like a drive?"

"With you? Always." He stepped back. "I'll finish getting dressed. I'll be back down in a second."

Lou puttered around the kitchen for fifteen minutes. She was at the sink, rinsing dishes, when the phone rang. She dried her hands on a dishtowel, heading to the phone.

"Hello?"

There was a staticky crackle. "Is this Louise Newman?" a man's cultured voice asked.

"Yes, this is Lou. Who is—?"

"How DARE you *refuse* to talk to Mr. Farrel?"

Lou jerked like she'd been slapped. "I'm sorry. Who is—?"

"I need to *know* what happened to my daughter!" The sound of strangled breathing echoed through the earpiece.

"Mr. Rice? I'm sorry, I—"

"My daughter's gone, Miss Newman! Do you understand that?! She's DEAD and no one can bring her back to me!"

"I—I'm sorry."

"I need to know what happened to Gabby! I need her killer brought to justice…"

His words rolled on and on, rage and pain tangling together. A footfall interrupted and she turned. Rich trotted down the stairs, his hair combed back, face calm. Lou covered the receiver.

"Rich! You need to come here."

He frowned. "Who's on the phone?"

"Gabby's father."

Under her fingers, the muffled shouts continued: "…and I've been trying to find out what happened! She cut us out of her life. Just up and disappeared! You can't imagine what it's like to lose a child! The pain at not knowing what happened!"

Lou put the handset to her ear. "I'm sorry, sir, but the private investigator you sent was—"

"How DARE you say you're sorry when you refused to help him!"

Lou flinched. "I—I'm sorry. It must be awful—"

"Give me the phone," Rich said.

"Don't apologize to ME!" Mr. Rice bellowed. "You're the one who destroyed Gabby and Rich's relationship!"

"Me? What do you mean?" Lou stared at Rich. He waited, hand outstretched. Gabby's father's voice roared over top of her thoughts, drowning everything else out.

"The phone, Lou," Rich repeated. "Give me the phone."

"I—I'm sorry, Mr. Rice. I have to go."

"Don't you DARE hang up on me! Gabby is DEAD because of you! If you—"

"Rich is here," Lou said. "I can't talk anymore."

"—hang up this phone and I warn you, I'll—"

With shaking hands, Louise passed the receiver to Rich. She swallowed convulsively. Edward Rice blamed her for Gabby's death. The anger came from the other side of the continent, but it was a palpable force drowning her.

"Mr. Rice," Rich said. "I need you to calm down. I can explain—"

A man's furious roar came through the phone. Lou stepped back, the pounding of her heart so fast she felt faint.

"Sir, you need to calm down," Rich said. "I know you're upset but—"

Another bellow of pain. The words were incoherent, but the emotion was clear. Lou's eyes filled with tears. The man's fury-filled anguish tore through her.

"You don't understand sir. It… It wasn't like that…" Rich's gaze flicked to Lou and then back. "No! She had nothing to do with our break-up… I understand but—" His mouth pursed. "No. No! That's *not* what happened, I—" There was another lengthy pause. "Mr. Rice, if you'll just listen to me, I—"

Rich suddenly looked down at the receiver. He frowned as he

put it back to his ear. "Hello?" He tapped the cradle. "Mr. Rice?"

The sound of a telephone's hum echoed from the earpiece. Rich stared down at it for a few seconds longs as if it contained an answer to a question. With a heavy sigh, he replaced it and looked up.

"He blames me."

"For what?"

He gave a one-shouldered shrug.

"For leading her on when I left New York in 1999 and came here."

There was a long moment when the question was caught in her throat. Lou's gaze slid down to the ring on her hand. "Did you lead her on?"

Rich sighed. "Not on purpose, but I didn't make a clean break either." He cleared his throat. "I just kind of walked away from my life and picked up here."

Lou nodded. She remembered that summer, the sparks that had flared into flame the moment they'd met. She felt the intensity of the attraction even now, years later. Rich pulled Lou into his arms and she sighed. She was his and he was hers. That fact wouldn't change, no matter what.

Lou forced herself to say the words: "Do you need to go back to New York and talk to Gabby's father? Do you need to make it right?"

Pain crossed Rich's face. "Do you *want* me to go talk to Gabby's father?"

"No. God no!" She let out a pained laugh. "I want you to stay here in Waterton with me, but…"

"But *what,* Lou? What is it?"

She pressed herself closer, looking up into his eyes, blue and bright and earnest.

"Having you stay in Waterton is what *I want*. What do *you* want to do, Rich? You have choices too."

He leaned in until his mouth was almost on hers.

"I want to marry you, I want to start our life here, to live and breathe and not always be looking behind me when I walk down the street."

She looped her hands around the back of his neck and pulled him down to meet her lips. "Then stay here, love…"

CHAPTER THIRTEEN

The kiss was the push both Rich and Lou needed. The day had been a tangle of emotion, but that tension had finally broken. Lou moaned. Rich pulled her closer and stepped back one step... two... until he leaned against the kitchen counter.

"I love you," he whispered. "Love you so much, Lou."

"Love you too."

He pulled back, holding her gaze. "I would have gone back to New York if you'd asked me to. You know that right?"

"I don't want you to go anywhere," she whispered. "Stay with me."

"Always." He leaned in, catching her lips again.

Lou's mind was abuzz, her body weak. She pushed her hands under his shirt, her fingers shaking where she touched him. *Could she have let him go,* she wondered, *sent him to face Gabby's father?*

Her throat ached as she broke the kiss and tugged Rich's shirt up over his head. They shed their outer clothes, their bodies burning despite the coolness of the kitchen. Lou's mouth moved to Rich's throat and she reached for the waistband of his boxers.

"We should go upstairs," Rich chuckled.

"Mm-hmmm..." She nipped the edge of his jaw. "But I'm a little busy right now."

"Lou…" Rich groaned.

"Uh-huh?"

"Baby, please."

"Please, what?"

"Not here…" With a growl, he lifted her up, walking them to the stairs.

Lou squeaked and looked up. "We going somewhere?"

Rich dropped his chin and kissed her again, hard.

"There are windows in the kitchen," he chuckled, the rumble of laughter moving from his chest to hers. "I want some privacy. And a bed."

She laughed as he jogged up the stairs. She wrapped her arms over his shoulders as they reached the landing. "Your legs are going to be sore from carrying me."

"Don't care," he said, kicking the bedroom door closed behind them. "Need a bed."

With the curtains closed, the room was swathed in velvet half-light. Rich tumbled Lou onto the bed and she pulled him down on top of her. Rich's mouth moved over Lou's skin. A second later, his fingers found the edge of her panties and slid them down while she wriggled out of her bra.

You need to choose the right path… Lou had struggled for so long to figure out what her mother had meant, but now she knew: She wanted this life… this man.

In the dim light of the bedroom, Rich moved over top of her. Lou clung to his shoulders, her body humming with emotion. Rich Evans had been the most unsettling force in her life, but he'd also been the most joyful. He'd broken down walls she'd spent a lifetime building. As their passion grew, tears of happiness filled her eyes.

"Love you!" she gasped.

"Love you too," Rich gasped. He slumped against her, his face pressed into the sheet of her black hair, then rolled sideways, "That," he panted, "was a good idea."

"Yeah, it was."

Rich pulled her into the crook of his arm. With her ear pressed up against his ribs, she could hear his heartbeat. It was a sound she knew. The sound that had marked her almost-death years before. Rich had been the tether. The line that ran between them had grown stronger in the time since.

What am I waiting for?

Like that, she knew what she wanted.

"Rich?"

He lifted his head. "Yeah?"

"I want to go to Lethbridge today."

"Uh, okay?" He ran his fingers over her shoulder, brushing away her hair. "Any reason?"

Lou rolled onto her side and put her hand against his chest. She smiled. Two years ago, she'd been terrified of the thought of sharing her life—*herself*—of being open and honest. Today she couldn't think of any place she'd rather be.

"I want to marry you, Rich," she said with a smile. "And I want to do it *today*."

* * *

Audrika Kulkarni was on a mission.

She spent her day sitting at the front counter, reading page after page of fine print as the connections came together. Encountering the name "D. Xavier" would have meant nothing to her a week ago, but after Lou's panicked warning, Audrika knew *exactly* who he was. The chain linking Borderline to Tom Farrel grew shorter with each page.

Late in the afternoon, Vasur popped his head in to ask if she was coming up for dinner.

"I'm going to stay here," she said. "I'm feeling a bit off tonight."

"Can I take over the store for you? Let you lie down for a bit?"

"Oh, no, I'm fine, Vasur." Audrika swept the papers she'd being working on into a messy pile.

Vasur glanced at them and frowned. "Audrika, you're not—"

"I'm just doing a bit of inventory," she lied. "Almost done. You go on up and make a sandwich for yourself. Isn't there a hockey game on tonight?"

"There is, but if you're not feeling well, I can—"

"I'm fine. I just overate when Mirran and I met for lunch today," she said, patting his arm. "You head on upstairs. I'll stay here."

"Okay, but shout if you need me."

"I will, dear." She gave him a peck on the cheek. "Off you go."

* * *

Around the tiled floor of Lethbridge's city hall, knots of people milled. Businessmen and farmers, Hutterites and university students alike paid bills, argued over fees, and—in the case of Rich and Louise—got married.

Rich took a deep breath and tucked the marriage license into his pocket. A line from an old Stevie Wonder song—"Signed, Sealed, Delivered"—ran through his head. He couldn't keep the grin from his face.

"Wow," Lou said with a giggle. "That was... fast."

"I know, right?"

"I feel good. Different, but..." She laughed and twirled in a circle. "I feel like I'm where I'm supposed to be. Here, with you."

"Me too." He held out his hand: "Ready to go, wife?"

Lou giggled and slid her fingers into his. "Absolutely... *husband*."

"I like how that sounds, you know."

The two of them headed out the doors. *Married.* It still didn't feel real. Rich pulled her in for the hundredth kiss that day just as a gust of wind sent Lou's hair swirling.

He looked up at the sky. "Looks like the weather's starting to change."

"It's Lethbridge. Wait five minutes and that'll happen."

"So what now?" Rich said. "You want to grab dinner before we head home? O'shos maybe?"

"Excuse me?" Lou laughed. "It's our wedding day. We might have eloped, but I still want a wedding night."

A bright grin broke across his face. "Hotel?"

She nodded. "How about that fancy one Stu stayed at when you were on trial? The one with the pool and the courtyard inside it. I always wanted to stay there."

"The Lodge?"

"Yeah, that's the one." Lou slid her arms up his chest and looped her wrists around his neck. "I want late night room service and pay-per-view and…" she pulled him in until his lips were just above hers. "I *don't* want to sleep."

"You got it."

* * *

With Vasur out of the way, Audrika got back to work. Between customers, she organized the data from Mirran, reading through the details until nightfall. They provided a fascinating view into the dark forces that had once controlled Waterton.

Tom Farrel wasn't *just* a businessman. He, Dax Xavier, Edward Rice, and a variety of other individuals were listed as shareholders in the now-defunct Borderline. Through a complex network of documentation and legalities, the business was foreclosed, but much of the cash remained. Various withdrawals and deposits had been done for years through "designated trustees," and that, Audrika thought gleefully, was her way in. All she needed was proof that she worked for one of them. Mirran would smooth out the rest.

But as the streetlamps came on outside the windows, Audrika's plan hit a snag. She needed legal identification of one of the shareholders. She chewed the end of a pen. Tom was the most likely target, but he'd been unexpectedly elusive.

Sometime later, the door jangled and Audrika jerked. She gathered the papers scattered across the counter in one efficient movement, tucking them back into the box between one heartbeat and the next.

"Audrika, dear?"

Margaret waited just inside the doorway. "Margaret! How are you?"

"Fine. I saw the lights on and got worried." She glanced at the watch on her wrist. "It's almost ten."

"Oh, goodness! It is?"

"Yes, dear." Margaret bustled to the counter. "Is everything alright? Are you fighting with Vasur?"

"Oh no, not at all." She shoved the last few papers into the box, hoping none had been misplaced. Vasur was already suspicious and she couldn't have him discovering her subterfuge. "But now that you mention it, Margaret, I was wondering if you could keep something for me."

"Of course. What?"

Audrika put the lid on the box and shoved it toward her.

"If you could just set this aside for me…" She glanced behind her to the stairs where the familiar strains of Hockey Night in Canada rang out. "Vasur gets so irritated by the clutter. I'm going to tidy up but…" She laughed. "You know me."

Margaret glanced down at the box. "So you just need me to store it?"

"For a few days, if you don't mind."

Margaret smiled. "Of course not! Why would I?"

* * *

The following morning, Audrika and a handful of Waterton locals were back at Hunter's Coffee Shop for one of their unofficial coffee meetings. After this yesterday's drama, Audrika had expected Lou to show up again, but the mechanic hadn't appeared. Mr. Farrel, however, the focus of Audrika's attention, was having lunch at the front of the café and she watched him with narrowed eyes. Mirran's research had given her *much* to consider.

What was Mr. Farrel up to? she wondered.

As people left the coffee meeting to reopen their shops, she lingered. First, because she'd always believed that a cup of tea always tasted better when someone else had brewed it. Secondly, because after yesterday's investigation into Mr. Farrel's ties to Borderline, she had come up with a plan. And for this particular plan, Audrika *needed* someone to help her.

Audrika scanned the thinning crowd as they gathered their items from the tables and headed off to enjoy the rest of their day. Her gaze paused on a woman's wrinkled face. Margaret was Audrika's friend and had been for years, but she had no mind for intrigue. She was too honest by half.

Margaret stood from the table.

"You heading off?" Audrika asked her.

"Yes. I've got to get back to the shop." Margaret blinked. "Should I have brought your box back? Do you—"

"No, no," Audrika interrupted. "I'll get it later." She dropped her voice. "And please *don't* go mentioning it to anyone"

Margaret frowned. "Alright...?"

"Vasur and all that," Audrika said, waving her hand. "I'll pick it up from you later."

Margaret smiled. "Okay then." She waved on her way out the door. "Bye now!"

Audrika took another sip of tea, watching as Grant headed out the door into the gusty autumn wind.

"I should get going too," a man said loudly. "I'm expecting a call from my daughter this afternoon."

Ron could barely hear, Audrika thought. She couldn't tell him or she'd have to use a megaphone to explain.

"And I should head back to the bookstore," Murray answered.

Audrika watched as Ron, Arnette, and Murray stood from the table, still deep in conversation. Murray glanced around warily. The man was as jumpy as a newborn deer these days. He'd spent at least ten minutes telling the group about the team of 'cleaners' who'd gone through the cabin yesterday, and the stink that had been strong enough that Grant had warned him about attracting bears.

No, Murray was much too wrapped up in his own troubles right now. But there had to be someone else she could trust.

Her gaze moved down the line of townspeople. Sam Barton, the Park Superintendent, sat at the end, dipping a half-eaten donut in his coffee. His shirt was pressed, hair combed childishly back. Audrika rolled her eyes. *It was no good to tell Sam*, she thought. *He'd just go right to the police; and they'd have her arrested.* No, Audrika knew she needed someone who'd see the *benefit* of the drama. Who—like her—would be willing to exploit it... She took another sip, watching friends and neighbours over the rim of the cup.

Who, she wondered, *would see the opportunity in her plan?*

The coffee group had thinned since fall had arrived. Only a few of Waterton's inner circle remained at the tables, finishing cups of coffee and plates of pie. She set back her cup and turned the other way. She jerked in surprise.

Levi Thompson stared back at her. "You look like yer up to no good."

"Whatever can you *mean*, Levi?"

"Measuring the group up. Watchin' 'em leave, one by one. Don't go tryin' to lie to me about it. Yer *up* to somethin'... and it ain't no good."

"Hardly!" Audrika laughed. Levi's advanced age hadn't dulled him in the least. And while he wasn't her *first* choice to be lookout, she knew his distrust of the police. If she got him involved, he'd say nothing, of that she was sure. Audrika pushed her cup aside and gave Levi a warm smile. "But now that you mention it," she said. "I do have a little something on my mind."

Levi rolled his eyes. "You don't say."

"Be *nice*, Levi," she tutted. "And maybe I'll tell you about it."

He made a noise that could have been a snort or a laugh

Audrika scooted her chair closer. "If I *do* tell you," she said. "I'd need to know you won't share it with anyone else."

"I ain't promising you nothin'. I don't know what'n the world you're even talking about."

Audrika's smile tightened. "I figured something out. Something that might be... *useful*."

"Useful?"

"To people in Waterton." She tipped her head to the side. "But I can't possibly tell anyone until I *know* that it won't be blabbed all around. And until I have proof. I have my reputation to preserve, you know."

"Your reputation, hmmm?" Levi smirked. "Sounds like you're lookin' for a reason to spill the beans."

"Oh no. It's not like that at all."

"No?"

"I… I've found a few things, but… I need some help to prove some of the things I've found."

"Why's that?"

"Because it's something that might be… a useful bit of information in the right hands." She leaned in, heart pounding. This was the best part… the subterfuge. "The town of Waterton could benefit from it."

"How?"

"Well, I'd have to explain what I *found* for it to make sense."

"Then git. I'm listening."

Audrika pouted. "But you never promised…"

"Yes, yes, woman. I'll keep your damned secret for Chrissake!"

"Good," she said, "because this is an *opportunity*, Levi, but it's one that has a bit of risk." Audrika narrowed her eyes, all pretense of coyness gone. "You cannot go to the police. You can't go off and talk. Understood? Not even to Hunter."

"Fine," he grumbled. "Now spit it out."

"The investigator," she whispered, nodding to the front of the shop where Tom was finishing up the last of his lunch. "Have you met him?"

"Who's that?"

"Mr. Farrel," Audrika huffed. "Right there. The one who's been going around asking everyone questions. I said, have you met him?"

Levi turned and squinted. As the two of them watched, Tom stood, dropped several bills on the table and headed out the door. "No," Levi said as the door closed behind him. "But Hunter did."

"But you *know* who he is, right?"

"I do."

"Well, I've been doing a little checking on my own. Records and that."

Levi narrowed his eyes. "How?"

"Well, I'm friends with Elaine, for one. And whenever she can't get the computer at the hotel to work, I give her a hand. I couldn't help but notice who her guests were. She had the booking page open on the desktop after all."

"You snooped."

"I simply read." Audrika slid her chair even closer. "The investigator who Hunter met is staying at her hotel, and his name is Tom Farrel. I might have… looked up the scan of his I.D. and credit cards. Poked around a bit."

"And what'd you find out?"

"Tom Farrel is not *just* an investigator. He works for Mr. Edward Rice, the father of poor Gabrielle."

"Who's that?"

"That young woman who was killed out at Indian Springs. Mr. Farrel is here on Mr. Rice's bidding."

"So what if he is?"

"Goodness, Levi!" Audrika hissed. "*Think* what Louise told us yesterday. There's a daisy-chain of people between Mr. Farrel and Gabrielle's father and that chain goes all the way to Dax Xavier, the man who set up Colton's Borderline scheme."

Levi scowled at the mention of Colt's name.

"A lot of people lost money with Borderline," she said. "And I've always wondered if we could get that money back. From the looks of the files, it's still there."

"So what if it is?" Levi growled.

"That's money people in Waterton *lost.* Now, if I can find the right information, I should be able to get into the account and the money could be transferred—"

"I never lost any money to Borderline."

Audrika narrowed her eyes. "Well, Colt was your relative, after all, I wouldn't expect he'd—"

"I had *nothin'* to do with his mess!"

"No," she said. "But lots of other people *did.* I never had a lease with Borderline, but I had a few... personal loans, so to speak." She smiled coyly. "Now, can I ask for your help, or not?"

Levi leaned back, his white brows dropping low over his eyes. "Help with *what,* exactly? All you've given me is gossip. I hardly think—"

"Goodness! I thought it was obvious. I'm going to break into Mr. Farrel's room."

"You're *what*?!"

Levi's squawk caught the attention of a few customers and Audrika shushed him before continuing. "I need some documents. That's all!"

"But I thought you said you'd found—"

"I found *links,* but nothing I can use to get into the files. Mr. Farrel doesn't keep anything in the car he rents," she said matter-of-factly. "I already watched him. He never goes to the trunk, and if he keeps things with him, that means they'd have to be in the briefcase he carries." She nodded. "I need into the room."

"I'm not helping you break in."

Audrika smirked. "I've got a key."

"How in the world did you manage that?"

"Oh, Elaine's half-blind," she laughed. "I just 'borrowed' the master she has hanging in the office."

"Why're you telling me this?"

Audrika leaned closer, smiling. "Because I need someone to watch the door, Levi. I wouldn't want Mr. Farrel to *find* me snooping in his room."

Levi crossed his arms. "That man—the investigator—ain't gonna take lightly to being crossed. You should go to the police."

"And *what*?! Tell *them* to find that contact information? Admit that I was wrapped up in the Borderline mess from the beginning? If the police get those accounts, *none of us* will get that money!"

"You don't even know that there's money *left* in that account. For all you know, this is a wild goose chase."

"It's there! My sister-in-law looked!"

"So tell the po—"

"I can't tell them without admitting I knew that Borderline was a front. But if I can get a few names and phone numbers, I'll be able to access the account."

Levi glared at her.

"My sister-in-law works at the Bank of Montreal," she said. "She can get me in, so long as I have those things. I had signing privileges before Colton died. I… I should still be able to get into the accounts once I have the names and numbers." She let out a little huff of air, her shoulders dipping. "Please, Levi. I… I could use the help. I'm sure I can do it, but I'd like someone watching my back."

"No."

"What?!"

"You're a fool," he said. "I'm not getting involved in this."

She grabbed her handbag off the back of the chair and stood, her hip bumping the table. "Fine," she said. "I'll go do it myself."

"Do *what* exactly?"

She brushed past him. "Get back my investments. Get Hunter's back too." She shot him an angry look. "Some friend *you* are." And with the sharp clicks of high-heeled steps, she exited the restaurant.

Levi watched her for a long time after she'd gone, and then, with a resigned sigh, he put his good arm on the table and pushed himself upright. The broken arm shifted and he winced. He *knew* he should try to stop Audrika from making a fool of herself, but the tiredness he'd been feeling for weeks had settled around him like an early frost. Instead, he lifted his cowboy hat from the table, crushed it onto his head, then headed out the door.

If Audrika wanted to play the fool, he thought as he walked slowly back to the house, *who was he to stop her?*

* * *

Rich and Lou lingered in the Lodge's restaurant, eating a late lunch after checking out of the hotel. As they emerged from the glass-fronted foyer, they were met by an angry wind. Icy knives cut through their coats and under their collars, leaving them shivering.

Rich wrapped his arm around Lou's shoulders as they walked to the car.

"Colder than yesterday," he muttered. "Should have brought my heavy coat."

"Winter's coming," Lou said, blowing on her hands. "There'll be snow in the mountains tonight."

Rich glanced up at the sky. Overhead, the clouds had tightened into a solid blanket, blocking out the morning sunshine. A gusty breeze, ripe with the scent of feces, reached them and Rich coughed.

"Christ! What *is* that?"

"That," Louise said as they reached the silver sportscar, "is the smell of money."

He unlocked the passenger side door, then headed around to the driver's side.

"Money?" he said as he climbed in. "Smells more like a latrine."

"You're not far off. The wind's blowing from the north. That's where the cattle yards are."

"Disgusting."

"It's Lethbridge, and the temperature's dropping." She shrugged. "Those two things go hand in hand. Once we get past Magrath, it'll be gone."

"Good. Then let's head home."

Lou caught hold of his fingers. "Home. I like when you say that."

* * *

Audrika Kulkarni knew a business opportunity when she saw it and Mr. Farrel's connection to the now-defunct Borderline Industries was just such a moment. She had every intention of seizing it! The money was there… all she needed was a few details from Farrel's ID to get it back.

She pranced up Main Street in the midday sunshine, her quilted handbag tucked under her arm. Yellow leaves swirled in the wind, tossing a shower of gold coins down on her head. She shook them from her hair, then paused at the side entrance to the hotel parking lot. Audrika looked left, then right. All alone. She stepped through the narrow entranceway and into the inner courtyard parking lot. The gray car she'd come to recognize was nowhere to be seen.

"Perfect!" Audrika breathed.

The hotel where Mr. Farrel was staying was located next to the marina and Audrika had spoken to the owner, Elaine Decker, more than once about her guest. *"He's very quiet,"* Elaine had told her. *"Keeps to himself mainly."* Audrika had purred her way through two cups of tea before getting Elaine to provide the information she needed. *"The girls go in to clean around one,"* Elaine said. *"He tends to be out about then. Goes for a drive or takes a walk on the beach most days. Comes back after they're done."*

Audrika checked her watch. *1:25p.m.* The chambermaids would be gone by now. If she was careful, she could be in and out of the room before anyone was the wiser. *If Levi had come along, she would have felt better, but—* She shoved the thought from her mind as her steps moved faster.

"Nothing to it but to do it," she muttered. How many times had Levi told her that in their years as friends? Today was yet another chance—another opportunity—one she intended to take, with or without his help!

The pounding of her heart increased as she headed to the side entrance of the hotel. There was no one to be seen, and as she unlocked the side-access, she found the hallway empty. Mr. Farrel was staying in room 22. Audrika climbed the stairs to the second floor and tiptoed along the hallway, checking the numbers. His was the last at the end of a long corridor and she paused before the door, glancing both ways. Somewhere, at a distance, the sound of a vacuum roared. The chambermaids were still at work.

Audrika knocked lightly.

No answer.

She knocked louder, peeking both ways in case anyone was nearby. The hallway lay empty, so Audrika pulled the master-key from her pocket and unlocked the door.

She pushed it open. "Hello…?"

No reply.

She stepped inside and closed the door behind her. The room was spotless, the bed made with a keen eye to hospital corners. *Elaine had good staff,* she thought as she headed to the dresser. *The girls weren't lazy, even in the off season.* It left her feeling piqued, but for reasons she couldn't quite understand. Audrika and Vasur were the only staff at Fine and Fancy these days.

She pulled the first drawer open.

Layers of neatly-folded clothing met her gaze, and Audrika was careful not to wrinkle them as she checked underneath. Finished, she closed the first drawer and moved onto the second. It was full of boxer briefs—again, folded—socks in rows of pairs, and a line of silk pocket squares. She ran her finger along the edge of one, her lips pursing. Vasur could barely be bothered to dress up for their anniversary, never mind on a day to day basis. With a sigh, she closed that drawer, moved onto the bottom.

It too was clear of any clues.

The closet didn't contain anything important. Nor did she find the briefcase in the bathroom or the small closet. She put her hands on her hips, irritation sharpening her features.

"Where would you keep it?" she muttered. "Where would you *hide* something in a room this small?" Her eyes lit on the sharp creases of the bedspread and her plucked eyebrows rose. "The bed," she gasped. "Of course!"

Audrika bustled over to the nearby side of the bed and crouched next to it. She lifted the bedspread. It was solid black as far as she could see, but she reached underneath, swiping blindly. Deep in the shadows, her nail brushed something solid. She let out a huff of irritation (missing the sound of the door softly opening) and crawled around the far side of the bed. She reached under again, fishing in the darkness, hoping against hope. If she had a broom or a cane, she could—

"Mrs. Kulkarni…?"

She squeaked in surprise, jerking back so quickly she banged her forehead on the nearby end table. She placed her hand on her forehead as she looked up. Her heart sank.

"Mr. Farrel," she said with a tittering laugh. "I… was hoping to run into you," she lied. "Thank goodness you've arrived." She climbed from the floor, forcing her brightest smile.

Tom stood between her and the door, watching her in apparent confusion.

"What're you doing here?"

"I thought I'd lost an earring," she said. "But it doesn't look like it's here."

"You thought you'd lost an earring in *my room?*"

"Well, uh… yes." Audrika brushed off her slacks as she stalled for time. "Or at least I… I *thought* it was this room. Elaine and I—the owner that is—we are friends and she showed me some of the refurbished rooms." Audrika nodded. *Yes!* Elaine had done that last winter. "But when I got home, I discovered I was missing one of my favourite pearl earrings." She clasped her hands in front of her, preening coquettishly. "But today when I came by, I thought I'd check."

"Someone let you inside?" he said quietly.

"Oh no," she laughed. "I, uh… I came in the side entrance. A guest was leaving, and then, well, I saw the side door was open and I came in." She nodded. "Yes, and once I was in the hallway, I just thought I'd check the door. It wasn't locked." She shrugged. "One of the cleaning ladies must have forgotten."

"Oh."

Mr. Farrel's expression was flat, neutral. He didn't look angry, and that gave Audrika hope. She took a step toward the door.

"So I looked around a bit," she said, dipping her chin and smiling up at him. That always worked with Vasur. "And it turns out it wasn't here after all. I'm so very sorry for intruding on you, Tom. I'll get out of your way."

She moved to go past him, but Tom abruptly matched her and, like a dance step, both were suddenly over at the side, her path blocked.

"So sorry," she said with a nervous laugh. "I'll just—"

She stepped the other direction.

So did Tom.

"—I should go," she finished lamely.

Long seconds passed. "Mrs. Kulkarni," he said in a velvet voice. "Is that the *real* reason you came here?"

"Y—yes."

"Are you certain there wasn't another reason?" He smiled, but it wasn't like the other smiles they'd shared. "Perhaps a... *personal* one?"

"Personal?" she repeated. "I—I don't know what you mean."

There was another long moment. Audrika glanced over Tom's shoulder. When he'd come in, he'd shut the door behind him. When she looked back up, Tom was half a step closer.

"I really should go," she said.

"I thought maybe you came by because..." He shook his head. "No. It's too silly."

Audrika frowned. "What?"

"I thought maybe you felt... the same connection."

"C—connection?" The panic Audrika had been feeling seconds earlier faded. Mr. Farrel was close, closer than they'd ever stood before. And he was smiling warmly at her.

He brushed a strand of hair away from her cheek. "I find you very *attractive*."

"You do?"

He nodded.

"Well, I... I don't know what to say, I mean I'm married. I... I..."

Her words disappeared as he reached out again.

"Oh, Audrika." Tom's index finger trailed along the side of her jaw. "I'd never expect you to betray your husband."

She made a soft sound in the back of her throat as Tom's hand slid into her hair.

"It's just a disappointment," he said.

Audrika sighed.

"I've thought of this moment for so long," Tom murmured. His fingers brushed the back of her neck and she shivered. "You're so very beautiful… so vibrant…" His other hand reached up to cup her chin. "So lovely and full of life…" He leaned in and Audrika's lashes fluttered closed. Her lips parted for the kiss. "So very…"

In a lightning-fast motion, Tom wrenched her neck 180 degrees, cracking it like a piece of firewood snapped over a knee. Audrika didn't gasp. She couldn't; her spine had been severed. She hung limp—extended neck trapped between his palms—as he lowered her body slowly to the floor.

"So very, *very* foolish," he whispered.

CHAPTER FOURTEEN

Tom let go of the body and Audrika's head flopped to the side. Her dead eyes stared, unseeing, under the bed. At this angle, the briefcase she'd been searching for—the one that contained the documents connecting Edward Rice to Tyrone 'King' Fischer, to Darren Xavier, to Colton Calhoun, and even to Audrika herself—was just barely visible. All the documentation, all the evidence she'd needed, was safely ensconced in its interior.

She didn't need it anymore.

Tom's feet passed next to Audrika's face. A moment later he came out of the bathroom with a facecloth and wiped the room down, inch by inch. He did the doorknobs twice. Finished, he crouched by the body and checked her clothing. He pocketed the master key for later.

Content that his room was clean, Tom opened the door to the hallway, and peered out. The corridor was empty. He walked to the side entrance and looked down from the second-floor window. On the ground level, his car was visible, but there were other people in the lot. He walked to the other end of the hallway. The interior stairwell, servicing the far side of the hotel, was empty. Tom smiled. The hotel had no security system. He'd made certain of this detail.

Five minutes later, Audrika Kulkarni's body was arranged, quite artistically, at the bottom of the stairwell. He wiped his fingerprints clear of the master key and placed it back in her pocket. A moment later he was back in his room.

He glanced at his watch. 1:58 p.m. He'd been in the hotel for approximately fifteen minutes.

It was time to be seen elsewhere.

* * *

Rich drove past stubbled fields, scattered with bales of hay, the car shuddering under the onslaught of wind. He wished they'd driven into Lethbridge in the truck, but it'd been bright and warm when they'd left. Now it took all his focus to stay in his lane.

As they passed the airport and moved out on the open prairie, Lou spoke.

"You're pretty quiet."

"The wind's making driving a chore." He smiled. "You got a story for me?"

"Mmm… maybe. What kind of story do you want?"

"I don't know. Maybe something about—" The wind gusted and the car jerked; Rich's fingers tightened on the wheel. "—your life, or your family. Honestly, *anything* at all is fine, Lou. Just talk."

"Okay but that's pretty broad." Lou giggled. "What're you interested in?"

"I'm pretty interested in *you*."

"Well, that's good," Lou said. "From my life or family, hmmm? Let's see…" She leaned closer, her hand brushing his arm. "How about both?"

"Sounds good." The car shuddered, but this time Rich was ready.

Lou stared out the window, quiet for ten seconds, twenty… and then he felt her posture change. She sat up taller and he smiled. She'd found the story. He could tell.

"Once," Lou said, "when I was five or six, my family and I were hiking deep in the back woods of Waterton. It was late spring after a long, hard winter, and runoff was high."

"Runoff?"

"The water coming down from the mountains; the snow-melt that comes each spring. That year in particular, there was a lot, and the streams were swollen, the banks crumbling."

Outside the car, the wind howled, but Rich's imagination transformed it into the rush of water. He could imagine Louise, young and black haired, her parents, who Rich only knew from photographs, on either side.

"Mom, Dad and I were hiking the Tamarack trail, camping along the way. We'd planned well, and the weather was good on the first day, but as we made camp that night, the wind and rain began..."

Rich glanced up at the sky. Outside the car's window, dark clouds rose over the mountains, anvil-like. There'd almost certainly be rain in Waterton by now, possibly snow at higher elevations. But inside, they were safe and warm. Lou's voice ran over Rich with the persistence and comfort of a steady rain. It felt like the nights they were in bed together, the house creaking around them.

On the windshield, the first drops of water dotted the glass.

"All through the night, the rain came down. Sheets pelted the tent walls, soaking the fly and dripping on us. I remember lying in the darkness, shivering. There was a roar—water in the creek—growing louder each hour. It felt as if the heavens themselves had opened up." Lou laughed. "My mother was so worried. She'd grown up on the prairies. The mountains and their tempers worried her."

Rich squeezed Lou's knee. "I've felt like that on occasion."

"And now?"

"Now I know there are plenty of reasons to stay."

Lou leaned her head against Rich's shoulder. "By morning the clouds had dropped down, blocking out the sun and filtering the light. We packed our camp, ate a cold breakfast, and started walking. *Still* the rain came. We were cold, wet. But there was no other way to go home except through it…"

Outside, the wind finally dropped. A moment later, the rain began in earnest. Rich flicked on the windshield wipers.

"It was so *cold* as we walked. Everything was wet, all of us soaked to the bone. My father had taken the sleeping bags in his pack, but even with that, the water weight bogged us down. I remember the exhaustion of that hike. How desperate I was to get home."

"Christ. That sounds awful," Rich said.

"It was," she said, "but it was memorable too."

"I bet you—" Rich's voice caught as the car shimmied. "Shit!"

"You okay?"

"Yeah… fine." He eased off the gas, his whole body attuned to the vehicle's motions as the water on the highway's surface caught the edge of the tires. At this speed, hydroplaning was a serious concern. Rich wanted off the road. He squinted into the distance. He *knew* the ridge of mountains that marked Waterton were ahead, but with the sluice of rain, he couldn't see anything except mist. "Just need to slow down a bit," he said through gritted teeth. "Road conditions are getting worse."

"You want me to stop talking?"

"No. It's good. Go on." He nodded to the windows. "The rain?"

"We were nearing a portion of the trail that cut through a narrow mountain pass when we discovered that the trail was gone."

"Gone?" Rich remembered another story Lou had told him, years before, of three boys lost in the woods.

"Not 'gone' as in disappeared," she explained. "But broken away.

Damaged. The snowmelt had created a creek where there shouldn't have *been* one, and it had dug a channel right through the trail."

"But how?"

"The rush of water blasted away the soil. It happens sometimes in the spring, and it happened *then*."

The windshield wipers' drone continued as the rain fell harder. Rich's fingers tightened on the wheel, frowning as he imagined himself, Lou, and the child he sometimes daydreamed about caught in the mountains, a raging creek blocking their way.

"What did your father do?"

"He tried to find a way around the watershed," Lou said. "He climbed up the slope as far as he could go, but the incline was too steep. There was no way across. He did the same down below the trail. No way to get across that way either."

"Shit."

"Pretty sure that's almost *exactly* what my father said when he saw it. We couldn't go back the way we'd come. It was more than twice the distance, and there was every reason to believe that it would be blocked too. We couldn't go forward. The stream was in our way. And the rain just... kept... coming."

Lou paused as the rain on the roof hummed like static. Rich glanced over. She had her lower lip caught between her teeth and she was frowning out at the storm.

"You okay?" Rich asked.

She blinked, then looked up at him. "Yeah. Just... thinking about how things can change."

Rich nodded, remembering the moment two years before when he'd believed he'd lost her. "So what happened? How'd you get through?"

After twenty minutes of swearing, Dad decided that the only

way was to go across."

"*Through* the flooded creek?"

"Uh-huh. It… was probably as much because of his temper as anything. My mother was upset and cold. She kept saying she'd *known* we shouldn't come. Dad was swearing. Mom hated that. It was just a bad situation all around."

"Glad I wasn't there." Rich laughed.

"We were trapped. No way forward or back. We *had* to do something. Dad tightened up his boots and grabbed the first pack. There were a few large boulders scattered in the stream—too far apart to walk on easily and dangerously slippery—but still slightly above the water's surface. My father used them as stepping stones. He crossed the raging water, step by step, and tossed the pack on the other side. Then he came back. He took my mother's pack and crossed. Then mine. Each time, he balanced on those rocks. Each time, he came back to us."

Lou's fingers against Rich's arm had gone still. "When all the packs were moved, my father came back to us. My mother was sobbing. I remember that. She was so strong with most things, but she… she wasn't then. Mom took my father's hand, and he led her over those rocks. I stood at the edge of that creek and I called for her: 'Mama! Mama come back!' but she kept walking. Step by step, following my father."

Rich's hand found Lou's, pressing tight. His brows knit together, imagining that moment, Louise just a child, alone on the far side, her parents on the other.

"Dad came back for me." She sighed. "It was such a relief. He'd always been so strong, and he seemed to be then too. Looking back on it, I know how tired he must have been. He'd carried all our equipment. He couldn't carry me. I was too big and the rocks were slippery, the water still rising. But Dad took my hand and led me forward, one stone after the other. 'Don't let go of me, he said. 'Watch your feet, not the water. Everything will be alright, Louise.' And we started to cross…"

Outside, the afternoon sky darkened to deep purple, the lights of the car slanting through silver lines of rain. The hair on the back of Rich's head stood on end, tension thick around them. He wanted to turn on the heat, but that would mean letting go of Lou's hand and interrupting the flow of her story. He waited, chilled and wary, as her voice carried on.

"Stepping across the first few stones was fine. I was too focused on not slipping to worry about the raging water. Dad would take a step, then I would follow. One by one by one." Lou's voice dropped in volume. "I… I don't know what made me look away from the stones, and out at the creek, but, I did, I—"

She stopped speaking. Long seconds passed, filled only with the sound of the rain and Lou's breathing, laboured like she'd been running.

"You *what*, Lou?"

"I looked up, and… I froze."

"Shit."

"I—I couldn't go on. I stood there. *Trapped.* Dad had a hold of my hand, but we were on two different rocks. 'Come ON, Louise!' he shouted at me. 'You need to take another step!' But… But I just couldn't." Her voice broke. "I couldn't make my feet move. Not after I saw the water. The drop down the mountain. The death at the bottom. I could… *imagine* it, Rich. See it, almost. And it terrified me."

"Jesus."

"My father tugged at my hand, trying to get me to take the next step, but all it did was unsettle me. I… I started to slide, and I

dropped down to my knees on the rock, letting go of his hand—"
Lou's voice caught. "I remember Mama screaming, the sound just
barely audible over the sound of the water. And then my father was
there. He'd stepped right into the stream, right into this torrent,
ripping the mountainside apart, and he—" She wiped a tear away.
"He lifted me into his arms. The water shuddered and raged, nearly
taking both of us down, but he held on and carried me to the other
side."

"Christ! You would have drowned if he'd fallen."

"Yes," she said with a teary laugh. "And maybe in some other life
we did. But in this one, he made it all the way across, and put me
into my mother's waiting arms. Then he fell down onto the banks."

Rich tapped the brakes again, slowing further. Lou's fingers were
tight around his and he stroked her knuckles with the pad of his
thumb. "He saved you."

"He did, but he could just as easily have died doing it. I... expected him to yell at me when he finally sat back up. The three of us
were soaked, the water raging a stone's throw away. I *knew* I'd done
wrong by freezing up, and I expected he'd yell at me for it. Instead,
he put his hands on my shoulders. I remember looking into his face,
white with terror. 'Don't you ever do that again,' he told me. And
then, before I could answer, he grabbed the biggest of the back-
packs, and pulled it on. My mother took hers, and helped me with
mine, and we walked the rest of the way home."

"Wow. That's crazy. I'm so glad you were okay."

Lou nodded. For a long time they drove in silence. Rich turned
up the heat and the defrost, easing the chill from his bones. They
passed through the town of Cardston, and the rolling foothills began. The mountains belatedly appeared, sentinels in the misty air,
bulky and indifferent. As they neared the entrance gate, Lou spoke.

"Years later, after my mother died, Dad took sick." She cleared her throat, though her words still sounded thick with tears. "The… the doctors discovered that at some point—years earlier—my father had had a heart attack. It had damaged his heart muscles. Weakened him." Lou took a shaking breath. "It happened that day in the creek."

"Oh Lou, sweetie," Rich said, as he slowed the car and turned left, taking them into the embrace of the mountains. "I'm so sorry, but you don't *know* that it was because of you."

"No, Rich. I do," she said. "And I— I can accept it. I just wish…" She shook her head. "I wish I could fix things. I wish I could have taken that next step. I—" She let go of his hand and pressed her fingers to her mouth, breathing hard. "I've never told anyone that story, you know."

"I'm glad you told me."

Ahead of them, Waterton appeared through a flash of red then blue. Rich frowned. There was an ambulance at the Emerald Bay Lodge, its lights flashing through the fog that hugged the town.

Lou cleared her throat and wiped away tears. "There's an ambulance," she sniffed. "Something's wrong."

Rich nodded, the raging creek alive in his mind. "Wonder what happened while we were gone."

* * *

With Constable Black Plume busy getting Elaine Decker's statement, Constable Wyatt was tasked with talking to another witness: Tom Farrel. Jordan waited until the man calmed down to start his official statement. Tom had been hyperventilating when he and Sadie had arrived. As his breathing returned to normal, Jordan sat down beside him in the front lounge of the Lodge and pulled out a pen.

"Mr. Farrel…?"

No answer.

Tom's hands hung limp on his knees, his mouth slack as he stared down at the floor. Unease filled Jordan's chest. The man was clearly shaken. But there wasn't any time to be wasted. If Audrika's fall *hadn't* been accidental, then they might have a serial killer on their hands. If it had, well, they still needed to know what had happened.

"Mr. Farrel? Tom." Jordan cleared his throat. "I know today's events have been a shock, but I need to ask you a few more questions." He waited. The man was almost *too* quiet. Jordan cleared his throat again. "Mr. Farrel, I need you to understand that anything you say to me in this statement can be used against you in a court of law."

Tom's chin bobbed, and he looked up, revealing bloodshot eyes. "Am I in trouble or something?"

Jordan shook his head. "Oh no. Not at all, Mr. Farrel. But this is an official report and given Audrika's death, I am treating it seriously. When we're done here, I'll need you to you sign it. Verify what you've said to me."

"Of course." Tom wiped his hand over his face and gave a quick nod. "I—I want to help out."

"Thank you. It's appreciated." Jordan flipped over to the notes he'd taken since they arrived. "You and Mrs. Lu discovered the body at what time?"

"I… It was two forty-five, maybe closer to three." He shook his head. "I… I didn't check the time. Sorry. I probably should have, but when we walked in and saw her—" He made a choking sound.

"It's fine," Jordan said. "We'll check with the police station for the time of the call." He looked down at his notes. "It says here that you'd been at Mrs. Lu's shop after lunch. Is that right?"

"Yes."

"Did you go directly there from lunch?"

"What?"

"Did you go anywhere between Hunter's Coffee Shop and Mrs. Lu's shop?"

"No. I window-shopped for a few minutes, then came into Margaret's store."

Jordan nodded as he wrote down the details. "What were you doing in Mrs. Lu's shop?"

"I was buying shirts, trinkets, little—" He waved his hand. "Memorabilia."

Jordan made a note. "Why?"

"Why *what*?"

"Why were you buying things?"

"I'm done with my investigation. I'll be heading back to New York this week. It sounds silly, but I wanted to bring a few things home with me."

"You were in Mrs. Lu's shop for quite some time after lunch," Jordan said. "What took so long?"

Mr. Farrel shrugged. "We got to talking. I… didn't think it was all that long, but Mrs. Lu showed me around her store and we got chatting about Waterton and its history." He laughed. "Just about bought her out of stock."

"Ah… that happens," Jordan said. He made another note. "Is that when you came back to the Emerald Bay Lodge?"

"Yes. When I was done shopping, I found I had more bags than I could carry and Mrs. Lu offered to take a couple."

Constable Wyatt eyed him. Mr. Farrel was a muscular man. It seemed strange that Mrs. Lu had even offered.

"So you came back to the hotel," Jordan said. "Which door did you use?"

"We came in the front entrance."

Jordan nodded. He'd already been told as much by the proprietor, Elaine Decker.

"And your room is on what floor?"

"The second floor," he said. "At the end of the hall. And as we walked toward the stairwell, I… noticed there was someone on the floor."

"But how could you see that?" Jordan said. "There's a door on the stairwell."

"Yes, but I could see through the glass. It looked, at first, like a pile of clothes one of the cleaning ladies had dropped. But something about it caught my eye…" Tom had his hands clasped on his knee and he stared off into the distance. The story made sense, but the way he was saying it felt odd. *Like it was rehearsed*, Jordan thought. *Like this was a movie and he was describing what he saw onscreen.* "It was the colour," Tom continued. "I turned and stepped closer, and it was at that moment that Mrs. Lu screamed that it was Audrika."

"You knew her?" Jordan asked.

"Not well."

"But you *had* met Mrs. Kulkarni before."

"Yes. I'd made some purchases in Fine and Fancy."

"You *did* know her name though."

"I— Waterton is a small town," Tom said. "I've tried to get to know most everyone the last while. Yes, I knew who Audrika—Mrs. Kulkarni—was. She's hard to miss."

Jordan nodded and wrote down the answer. "What did you do when Margaret saw that it was Mrs. Kulkarni at the bottom of the stairs?"

"I dropped my things and opened the door to check on her."

"And what did you find?"

Tom frowned. "She was dead. I checked for a pulse, couldn't find one. Mrs. Lu was screaming, so I left her and ran back to the front desk and told Elaine to call the ambulance."

"You didn't attempt CPR?"

"I…" His voice faltered. "She had no pulse."

"But you didn't know how long she'd—"

"No. I didn't attempt CPR. Neither did Margaret, and she was the one who'd actually found her."

Jordan stared at him for a long moment, then nodded, and made the note into the report. Finished, he looked up again. "Do you recall how long it took for the ambulance to arrive?"

"I don't know. Ten minutes. Maybe more."

"I suspect it was closer to half an hour," Jordan said, "given that the EMTs came from Pincher Creek. Elaine Decker called us after the ambulance. We were here at around the fifteen-minute mark."

"If you already knew that, then *why* are you asking me?"

"Because you didn't attempt to revive her during those fifteen minutes. I'm just… a little confused about that decision."

Tom's eyes narrowed. "She was already dead."

"Already…?"

"When I— When *Margaret* found her in the stairwell, she had no pulse."

"But Elaine Decker said that she wasn't certain if Audrika was dead or not." Jordan flipped the page over, pointing to his notes. "There was no sign of a wound. No blood. Even Margaret said she couldn't tell if her friend was unconscious or, in fact, deceased. You checked the body. The other bystanders didn't."

"Yes."

"Then obviously, Audrika *might* have been unconscious—at least at first. Why not give her mouth-to-mouth while you were waiting for the police and ambulance?"

"I didn't think of it."

Constable Wyatt's pen paused on the page. "Why not?"

"I don't know," Tom growled. "I just didn't." Mr. Farrel's calm facade had slipped away and he sat, hands white-knuckled on the armrests of the chair.

"Alright then," Constable Wyatt said. "What *did* you do?"

"I did what I thought was right. I had Mrs. Decker call for help. I… didn't think of doing more."

Jordan wrote the words down. "Mrs. Lu said that while you were waiting for the police and ambulance to arrive, you picked up the things that had fallen from the bags you'd been carrying and you carried them up to your room."

"I did."

"That seems very sensible."

Tom shot Jordan a dark look. "So?"

"I'm just saying, you seemed pretty upset when we arrived," Jordan said. "It's just interesting that you could be so thoughtful prior to that." He tapped his pen, not breaking eye contact. "And yet so anxious you *didn't* think of doing CPR when you found an unresponsive acquaintance of yours lying in the stairwell."

A line of muscle flickered under the skin of Mr. Farrel's jaw.

Jordan looked back at his notes. "When the ambulance arrived, you seemed rather upset."

"I was."

"Are you feeling better now?"

"I am. I'd like to finish this up though. It's been a rough day." Tom's voice was velvet over a blade.

Jordan added the last few notes, then turned the document around and held it out to Tom. Much to his surprise, the man didn't read it—didn't even skim through—he simply found the spot at the bottom and scribbled his name. He held the document back out Jordan.

"May I go now, Constable Wyatt?"

Jordan's brows pulled together. "You seem like you're in a rush, Mr. Farrel. Is something wrong?"

"Not at all."

"You'll tell me if you remember something else. Right?"

"Of course I will."

Tom smiled but it held no warmth at all. He was, Jordan would think later, an entirely different person than he'd appeared to be when they'd sat down in the lounge of the Emerald Bay Lodge.

Jordan didn't trust him.

* * *

Rich drove the car to the Emerald Bay Lodge and pulled over to the side of the road. Lou peered out the window. A knot of townspeople huddled under umbrellas, talking. The locals had come out like this only one other time that she could remember: the night the Whitewater Lodge had burned to the ground. *Misery loves company,* she thought grimly. Something bad had happened while they'd been gone.

"You want to get out and see what's going on?" Rich asked.

"Yeah. Can you wait for me a minute," Lou said, unbuckling.

"Of course. I'll come along too."

Lou forced a smile she didn't feel. The last hour had been a rehashing of dark times and it felt like she'd stumbled right back into that afternoon, decades earlier when she'd been trapped by rising water. All that was missing was her father, white-cheeked and sick, lying on the banks of a swollen creek. She forced the image away as she slammed the car door.

On the far side of the street, Levi and Hunter stood under the awning of a nearby house, the two men deep in conversation. A short distance away, Margaret, Ron, and Grant waited. The elderly woman was bowed almost in half, a plaid handkerchief pressed to her eyes as she sobbed. The image sent a sliver of ice through Lou's chest.

"Margaret," she whispered. Lou turned to Rich. "I have the worst feeling about this."

Rich nodded.

Hand in hand, they jogged across the street to Margaret's side. Rain plastered Lou's hair to her head, trickling down her neck to her back.

"Margaret?" The old woman didn't move or look up. "Margaret," Lou said again, "are you alright?"

Mrs. Lu's chin bobbed and she looked up. Her eyes were bloodshot. She shook her head: *No*.

"What happened?" Lou asked. A wave of sobs overcame Margaret and Lou looked to Grant and Ron. "Grant? Levi? What's going on?"

Grant pointed. With a feeling of dread, Lou turned, following the line of his finger across the street to where Elaine Decker stood, deep in conversation with Constable Black Plume. Behind them, two EMTs carried out a stretcher, a body strapped to it. A bright flash of colour caught Lou's eyes. *Is that…?* As she watched, one of the EMTs zippered the body bag closed. The realization hit Lou like a lightning strike.

"Audrika, no!" Lou cried. Behind her, Margaret's sobs grew in intensity.

Rich slid his arm over Lou's shoulders. "It's okay."

Lou shook her head. Death had come yet again to Waterton and even with her warning, Louise hadn't been able to stop it.

* * *

Sadie was alone at her computer station, trying to make sense of the inchoate notes and snippets of information. It was enough to overwhelm. A single light flooded piles of statements, waiting to be typed. She could hear Liz tapping away at her own computer now, but there was more to be done. Snapshots of both Ben's murder scene, and Audrika, dead at the bottom of a flight stairs lay in an untidy mess. At least that death seemed to make sense. Audrika, in her high heels, appeared to have slipped. All evidence suggested a quick, dramatic death. But something about it worried her.

What's your gut telling you, Sadie?

She jerked in surprise as Jim's voice, as clear as if he was standing next to her, echoed through her mind. She glanced warily behind her. Finding the room empty, as she knew she would, her eyes filled with tears and she blinked them angrily away. *Been awake for too goddamned long,* she thought. *That's the problem.* Imagining that Jim was here wouldn't help. With a sigh, she stood and carried the photographs from Ben's murder scene to the billboard. She pinned a picture of the body next to the image of Gabrielle Rice and frowned. Two bodies. Both found in distant locales, both located just inside Waterton park.

You're missing one person though.

With a hiss, Sadie spun on her heel. The room was empty. But there was a scent now, a faint whiff of what she recognized as Jim's particular brand of aftershave: sandalwood with a hint of amber. Sadie lifted a shaking hand and tucked a strand of hair back behind her ear. She blinked away the last dregs of exhaustion. There was no one here in the room. She knew it; she could see it. *But it felt like there was.* Fear rose alongside her heartbeat.

"I don't have *time* to go crazy," she whispered.

She'd seen people destroyed by grief—her mother, after her brother's death was one—and it was easy to get lost in that well of anguish. She had a murderer to catch. Three people had died—two of them homicides—and if she didn't keep her head together then—

It's actually three homicides.

Sadie flinched. "Stop it, Jim!" she hissed.

The keystrokes stopped. "What's that?" Liz called from the other room.

"Nothing," Sadie said, then cleared her throat. "Just thinking aloud. Sorry about that."

"Alrighty then. Call if you need me."

Liz's typing returned.

Sadie took one more look at the pile of papers on her desk. She walked over and picked up an image of Audrika Kulkarni with her neck twisted at a horrifying angle. After a long moment, Sadie walked back to the board. Her logical mind said it was an accident, but her gut said otherwise.

With a grim smile, she pinned the photo in place.

"Fine," she said. "Audrika makes three."

CHAPTER FIFTEEN

Jordan had just returned from his break, joining Sadie in the office, when there was a knock at the door. Liz peered around the edge of the doorframe.

"Guys, we've got a Mr…" She glanced at a hand-written note. "Tom Farrel out front. He'd like to talk to you."

Jordan glanced at Sadie. "He's that investigator guy from New York. The one I interviewed when you were getting Margaret's statement."

"What do you think he wants?"

"Not sure." Jordan said. "But I told him to come by if he remembered anything else. Could be that."

"Huh."

They headed out of the office to find Mr. Farrel waiting. *He looked calmer than when they'd spoken,* Jordan thought. His hair was combed back from his forehead, his suit neat and buttoned. On the counter next to him was a packing box with black printing on top.

Tom looked up. "Ah, Constables Black Plume and Wyatt, I'm so glad you're here."

Irritation rankled under Jordan's calm exterior. Something bugged him about Tom Farrel, and he wasn't sure what.

"I brought you my investigative notes." Tom pushed the box forward.

Sadie caught Jordan's gaze for a split-second. "Notes?"

"Yes," Tom said. "I came to Waterton to find Gabrielle Rice. To locate her, if possible, but with her death my task is done."

"I don't understand," Jordan said. "You've been interviewing everyone in town. I thought you wanted to figure out who the killer was."

"Oh no," he said. "I'll leave that in your capable hands."

"Then why *were* you interviewing the townspeople?" Sadie asked.

"Honestly? To find out if Rich Evans killed Gabrielle Rice."

Jordan's eyes widened. Rich was high on the list of suspects.

"And what did you find?" Sadie said.

"Not much," Tom said. "After talking to everyone, I think it's fairly certain Rich Evans wasn't involved."

Sadie's eyes narrowed. "Why're you telling us this?"

"Because I want to help." Tom pushed the filing box across the counter. "I'm heading out of town. When I came into Canada, I told Customs I was here for a week or two—to find Gabrielle. It's been almost three." He shrugged. "Mr. Rice wants me back in New York. I'm supposed to give him my final report."

Jordan frowned. "But…"

"But what?" Tom said.

"But *you* were the one of the two people who found Audrika Kulkarni. Constable Black Plume and I are still investigating her death."

"It was Mrs. Lu who actually saw the body. I told you, I thought it was a pile of clothes."

"But you were there."

Tom's eyebrows rose. "Yes, but… I was under the impression it was an accident."

"It likely was," Sadie said, "but we can't be certain. The investigation isn't complete."

"Do you need me to stay in Canada a little longer?" Tom asked. "If you could contact the Canadian consulate, I'm certain you could get things arranged. I'll need an extension on my work permit. You'll have to drive to Edmonton and arrange that." He gave a short laugh. "I spoke to them this morning, actually. They seemed… less than helpful regarding my request."

Jordan sighed. Tom *seemed* like he wanted to help, and Audrika's death didn't seem like murder. She was wearing heels and she'd fallen. Case closed.

"Do you have your flights booked?" Sadie asked.

"I do, but I can always change them. Mr. Rice is footing the bill."

Jordan forced a smile he didn't feel. Mr. Rice was already a thorn in his side. Keeping his private investigator here in Canada without any evidence to implicate him as anything other than a bystander would only make things worse. "Mr. Farrel," Jordan said, "if you could just wait here a moment. I need to check something with our files. Don't leave, alright?"

"Of course."

Jordan shot Sadie a knowing look and she followed him into the office, closing the door behind her.

"You need him to stay?" she said.

"I don't know. I don't think we can keep him. There's nothing to suggest that he had anything to do with Audrika's death."

"True, but we still have two other bodies. Tom Farrel was here in town at the time." Sadie nodded to the billboard. "There's a possibility the killer was him."

"Shit! I wish everything wasn't happening so fast."

"Me too," Sadie said. "But if we don't have evidence to charge Farrel, we aren't going to convince any judge to let us hold him."

"So what do we do?"

"We let him go."

Jordan swore under his breath.

"Relax," she said. "We know his employer. We know he came to Canada legally, and he's following the rules to a 'T'. If we need him again, we know where to find him." She turned, glancing back at the images that cluttered the billboard, now full of competing evidence. "But for now, we let him go."

"Alright, let's tell him." He reached for the door handle.

"Hold up."

Jordan turned. "What?"

"You were getting papers, right?" Sadie pulled open the drawer of a nearby cabinet and grabbed several pieces of photocopied paper. "Let's make it worth his while."

Jordan laughed as she handed him the pages. "Bystander summary? But we already have Tom's statement."

"We do. And now he's going to give us another." Sadie winked. "Maybe he forgot something."

"You're terrible."

"No. Just covering my bases."

Jordan smirked as Sadie pulled open the door. Mr. Farrel still waited at the counter. He perked up as they neared.

"Everything alright?" he asked.

"There you go, Mr. Farrel," Jordan said, pushing the papers across the desk toward him. "If you could fill these forms in before you leave, that'd be great."

Tom wilted. "No problem," he said. "And this here." He nodded to the box, still on the counter. "If you don't want it, I'll drop it off to be shred—"

"No, no." Sadie tapped the box. "I'd like to take a look through."

"Alright then. I wish you both luck with this case. I thought it was Rich Evans, but…" he shrugged. "I just couldn't make the pieces fit."

He smiled and Jordan's hands clenched into fists. "Don't forget the forms," he said. "You'll need to fill those out."

"Of course," Tom said. "I'll bring them back this afternoon." He stepped back from the counter. "Please let me know if there's anything else I can do to help."

"Will do," Sadie said.

Jordan said nothing, just watched him as he walked out the door, letting it bang shut behind him.

"Asshole."

Sadie laughed. "You okay?"

"That guy rubs me the wrong way."

"Me too," she said. "Now we just need to figure this mess out."

Jordan rolled his eyes. "With all our spare time."

* * *

Lou stood at the stove, the spatula held over the frying pan, sizzling meat forgotten. "Sadie told you *what*?"

"Told me that Mr. Farrel had been investigating me. He apparently handed over a box of stuff to the police yesterday."

"What kind of stuff?"

"Detailed summaries of my comings and goings, receipts showing my whereabouts." He frowned. "There were even photographs."

Lou dropped the spatula and it splattered in the pan. "Photos."

"Yeah."

Lou pushed the still-hot frying pan off the burner and flicked it off. "That guy was following you?!"

"From what Sadie gathered from the photos, it seems like it, yeah."

"This worries me, Rich."

Rich stepped up and laced his hands around her waist. "It's not so bad though."

Lou looked up. "Why's that?"

"Farrel's on his way out of town." He shrugged. "That's what I heard anyhow."

"I…" Lou frowned. "Well, that's good, I guess."

"It is." Rich's arms tightened. "Sadie told me that he didn't think I'd had anything to do with Gabrielle's death."

"Farrel *told* the police that?"

"Apparently so."

"Huh. After that confrontation with him, I didn't know *what* he might say."

"Like I told Sadie and Jordan: I've got nothing to hide."

"I know." Lou smiled and buried her face against his chest. "I'm glad this is finally ending. It's been an awful few weeks."

"It has been, but you and I are strong."

"We are."

"I meant those vows." His lips brushed hers, hands sliding into her hair. "There's nothing that'll get between—" Knocking interrupted and Rich turned to glare at the door.

"You were saying?" Lou giggled.

Rich touched the tip of her nose. "We will be finishing *this,* later."

"Promise?"

Rich leaned closer. "Absolutely. I just wish—"

The knocking returned, louder and more insistent. "We'd better let Hunter and Levi in," Lou said.

"I suppose." With a sigh, Rich headed for the door. The knocking grew louder. "Coming!" Rich shouted. "Just hold on a minute." He swung the door open to find Hunter and Levi on the other side, Hunter's hand lifted to knock yet again.

"Wasn't sure you could hear me." Hunter said with a wink.

"Knocking was certainly loud enough."

"Yeah, well. I needed to be loud." Hunter gave Lou a quick hug. "Thought you two might be… busy."

"Hunter *stop.*" Lou laughed. "You're worse than Dad was."

He took his place at the table, pulling back the chair so that Levi—arm in sling—could join him.

"Nah," Hunter said, "I'm only trying to carry that torch."

"I'm not sixteen, you know," Lou said.

"But not too old for a guiding hand."

Lou rolled her eyes. "And when's that going to end, hmmm? Like if I were married," she said, "would that make a difference?"

"I suppose it would, though I'll never stop thinking of you as that little black-haired girl I met, balancing on a bucket next to that sink to fill a…"

Hunter's words trailed off, eyes widening.

A heartbeat passed. Another. The question hung in the kitchen between the four of them, waiting to be answered.

Suddenly Levi hooted. "You sly dog, Evans! Didn't think you had it in you."

Levi's laughter released the rest of them. Hunter laughed and rushed to Louise, pulling her into a bear hug.

"When?" he said in a thick voice. "And why wasn't I told about this?"

Lou grinned. "I'm telling you *now.*"

"Yes, but when?" Hunter let go of Lou and turned to Rich. Rich held out his hand, but the older man threw his arms around him.

Lou's chest tightened at the sight. Hunter was as close to blood family as she had left and it felt good to see her past and future knit together.

"Thanks, Hunter." Rich's eyes met Lou's over Hunter's shoulder and Rich grinned. "Got to say, I'm pretty happy about it."

"I'll bet you are," Levi snorted.

Hunter let go of Rich and stepped back. He wiped tears from his wrinkled cheeks. "I'm happy to hear about it too." He gave Lou a baleful look. "Though I would've liked to have been there."

"If we'd done something traditional," she said, "you would have been." Lou reached out and Rich took her hand. "It was spur of the moment."

"It's my fault," Rich said. "I was the one in a rush."

Levi's hoots grew louder.

"Well, I'm sorry I didn't see it, but I'm happy for you," Hunter said. He smiled, though his eyes were shining. "I've been waiting for this, you know?"

Lou's throat ached as she nodded. "I know."

* * *

The Watering Hole was almost empty, the early evening sky beyond the smudged windows growing dark. A scattering of locals sat in pockets around the dim room while a skeleton crew of serving staff did double-duty both behind and in front of the bar. Out in the dark, an icy cloud hunched over the town, never really breaking into rain, never really fading. The chill in the air hinted there'd be snow by morning.

At the table in the corner, Sadie Black Plume sifted through a pile of papers. On top lay a news article from this morning's paper, Ben Grayden smiling up at her from a grainy photograph.

WATERTON KILLER STRIKES AGAIN!

by Delia Rosings, October 23, 2001

A shocking turn of events in a small town that has had its share of infamy. The body of Constable Ben Grayden, an officer investigating the Gabrielle Rice murder case, was found just inside the park on Sunday morning. A local rancher discovered the mutilated body a short distance from Indian Springs, the location of the Gabrielle Rice murder. Grayden's throat had been slashed from ear to ear, though it appears he was alive at the time of—

"Who the hell is your anonymous source?!"

Sadie shoved the newspaper article aside. There was no way the reporter could have known those details! Annoyed, she turned her attention to another item in her pile: the coroner's report on Audrika's death. She frowned as she read it. *Some small bruises and contusions around the face and neck. Head twisted at an acute angle, consistent with a fall...*

Sadie knew she ought to be focused on the two homicide cases, but Audrika Kulkarni's untimely death had undone her focus. Audrika was a local, fiercely protective of the town. Like Ben Grayden, her death felt personal. Sadie's gaze fell on the last line:

Death likely accidental.

She threw the report down on the table with a grimace. *So that was it,* she thought. There was nothing to do about it now.

Unless it wasn't an accident.

Sadie jerked at the sound of Jim's voice. She waited, heart pounding, for it to return, but it was gone as quickly as it had arrived. The rain on the roof tapped. The bartender whistled under his breath as he polished glasses. Nothing else. Sadie took a slow breath and blew it out again.

Just overtired, she thought. *My mind's playing tricks on me.*

She picked the papers up once more. *Neck broken,* the document announced. *Spinal cord severed between vertebrae C1 and C2. Breathing would have stopped, and death would have been almost immediate.*

She frowned. *At least it had been fast.*

A split-second later, another voice—*a different voice*—answered: *Fast or just efficient?* Jim said. *What's your gut tell you, huh?*

She flinched. "Stop," she whispered.

"Stop what?"

Sadie turned to see Jordan approaching the table. His coat was shiny with water, and droplets splattered to the floor as he shook it off, then hung it over the back of the chair at her side.

"You were saying something?"

"I… It's nothing," she said. "Just talking things through."

"Yeah," he said. "I do that too, sometimes."

Sadie slid the papers aside. "You want something to drink?"

"What're you having?"

"Coke."

He wrinkled his nose. "Think I'll pass on that." He twisted in the chair, waving toward the bar. "Whatever's on tap!" he called. Jordan turned back. "Which case is this?"

"It's not a case," she said, then frowned. "Not yet, anyhow."

"Ah… Audrika's fall."

"You still think that's what happened?"

"You don't?"

Sadie frowned. "I… I do. At least most the time."

The server appeared, a glass of beer in hand. "Thanks man." Jordan picked up his glass, waiting until he'd left before continuing. "What do you mean 'most of the time'?"

Sadie didn't speak. Her gaze rested on the glass of coke and the dark liquid it held. How many times had she sat here with Jim? How many times had she argued what her gut knew? So why was she holding back today?

"Sadie?" Jordan said. "You okay?"

She shook her head. "I'm a little tired these days. *Over tired*, really."

"You sick?"

"No, I just…" Sadie frowned. There was no way of explaining her fear: that Jim's death had broken her and she was slowly losing her mind.

"Just what?" Jordan asked.

"I, uh… Nothing."

"C'mon Sadie. This is me. You can tell me."

She sighed. "Fine. My mind's playing tricks on me."

Jordan frowned. "What kind of tricks?"

"I keep feeling like I can hear…" She scowled.

"Hear what?"

"Hear… Jim."

"Jim. As in Jim Flagstone?"

"Yes, Jim." She let the statement sit. Jordan took a sip of his beer, watching her over the surface. He didn't *look* upset, but that meant very little. She knew that a comment like that—even one in joking—could result in being put on leave. *Jordan must think I'm nuts.*

No, Jim said. *He doesn't.*

She closed her eyes, fighting for control. She didn't *want* to hear this. Didn't want Jim interrupting her every moment.

"You know," Jordan said quietly. "I sometimes feel him around."

Sadie's lashes flared wide, the bar snapping back into focus. "Y—you do?"

"Yeah. Not like, *literally* there, but it's more like… like an echo."

The hair rose on Sadie's arms. "An echo."

"Yeah. Like he's still around, giving me hints as I go through. Sometimes I'm rushing and I can imagine him giving me hell."

Sadie picked up her glass and stared into it. She needed something to hold onto.

"Do you imagine it or d'you actually *hear it*, Jordan?"

"I don't hear it." He laughed. "Jesus. I'm not crazy."

Sadie forced herself to laugh along with him.

"Yeah, right."

"It just *feels* like Jim's around." He took another sip. "When my grandma died, it felt like that too. My mom couldn't sleep, and sometimes at night, I swear I heard Gran shuffling around. It… it was weird, but when I talked to Lou, she told me—"

"You talked to Lou Newman about it?" Sadie's voice cracked and she took another sip of coke to cover it.

"Yeah, I did. A few weeks after Gran died, I went to talk to her about the dreams I kept having. Lou helped me move past it. It didn't stop those feelings I was having, but it sure made me feel better." Jordan set the glass down and squeezed her shoulder, before dropping his hand back. "You're going to be okay, you know that Sadie? You're tough. You'll be fine."

Sadie tried to answer, but her throat was on fire and all she got out was a cough. She could feel Jim again, standing just out of sight behind them. She knew, if she turned, he'd be there in the darkness of the Watering Hole. The idea terrified her.

I don't believe in ghosts! she thought.

Jim laughed. *Yeah, well, we believe in you.*

Sadie groaned and pressed her fingers to her temples. "I think it's the last couple weeks… all the deaths. They're messing with my head. First Gabrielle, then Ben, and now Audrika."

"But Audrika's death was an accident."

"My gut says… maybe not." Tears filled her eyes. "But is that my gut, or just me being messed up because my partner died two years ago?" She grabbed a damp napkin and wiped angrily at her cheeks. "It's fucked up."

"It's not, Sadie."

She glared at him.

"Go and talk to Lou," Jordan said gently. "It'll help."

"Maybe…" She stood from the table. "And maybe not."

A moment later Sadie was headed out the door. Outside the bar, the wind howled, the first flecks of sleet dotting the windows. Autumn was dying, winter on its way.

CHAPTER SIXTEEN

The first meeting of Waterton's coffee crowd after Audrika's death was a somber affair. Wednesday morning, Margaret Lu sat with a bevy of friends and neighbours, the group of them buttressing her from the loss of her dearest confidante.

"I couldn't believe it when I saw her there," she whispered. "It didn't seem real… It still doesn't."

"Vasur wants the police to check into the investigator fellow," Grant said. "Was absolutely up in arms about it."

Margaret shook her head. "But it couldn't be Mr. Farrel. He was talking with me when Audrika fell." Murmurs of concern rose around her. "Besides, it's too late to talk to him," she said. "He's already gone."

Hunter had been refilling coffee pots, but he looked up in surprise. "He's gone?"

"Yes. Elaine told me he booked out of the hotel yesterday. He's apparently gone back to New York. Poor Audrika…" Tears began to roll slowly down Margaret's cheeks. "I just wish I could have gotten there a few minutes earlier. If Mr. Farrel hadn't been in the store with me. Perhaps I could have."

"Here," Levi grumbled as he shoved a pile of napkins toward her. "No use worrying about it now."

"Thank you." She dabbed at her eyes, her glasses fogging with the moisture. "It's all such a shock."

"Agreed," Arnette said. "You never expect—"

The bells on the door jangled and her voice stopped.

Constable Black Plume stood in the doorway, the bright fall sunshine making one side of her black hair sheen blue. She strode forward, no hint of a smile on her lips.

"Good morning, everyone. Could we talk a moment?"

An uneasy hush fell over the group, conversations abruptly ended.

Hunter stepped forward. "Coffee, Sadie?"

"Not today," Sadie said. "I'm here to talk about the ongoing investigation into the Gabrielle Rice homicide and the gossip that's begun to impede the case." She pulled out a chair and sat down. Around her, the group stared at their coffee mugs, the tabletop, the patrons around them. No one met Sadie's eyes. She pursed her lips. "While I appreciate that all of you have your own reasons for not getting involved." Sadie shot a dark look at Arnette and Murray. "I need each of you to know that Constable Wyatt and I will be investigating all three of the recent homicides—"

"Three?" Hunter said.

Sadie nodded. "Yes. Although there's not a great deal of evidence, I'm still considering the possibility that Audrika's death may not have been accidental."

Margaret shrieked. Sudden chatter rose into a roar as the townsfolk burst into rushed discussion.

Sadie's voice carried on over top of them: "My job is to find out the truth… period. I hope all of you will be forthcoming—specifically with *me*—rather than the news."

"What d'you mean?" Grant asked.

"Someone outside the police force is sharing information," Sadie said. "Making things public that shouldn't be known." She paused. "I'm guessing it's a local."

The rumble of voices rose.

"Now, I don't *know* who that person is, but I will be looking for them too," she said, standing from the table. "If that's *you*, and you'd like to avoid prosecution for obstruction of justice, I'd suggest you come talk to me or to Constable Wyatt as soon as you can." She gave the group a hard smile. "This isn't a joke, and it isn't a game. The leak is a danger to all of us."

Voices interrupted, people shouting on top of each other to be heard:

"—how can we know who it is?!"

"I've never told anyone anything! It couldn't—"

"I just can't believe you'd think we were involved!"

"—all this trouble in town! Need to stay together!"

Outside the snowy window, a movement caught Sadie's attention. A news van had pulled up to the curb. On its side a full colour picture of Delia Rosings beamed out at them, blonde-haired, blue eyed and smiling.

Sadie gritted her teeth.

"My advice is to keep your mouth shut," she said. "Don't spread rumours." She pointed over her shoulder as the camera crew clambered out onto the sidewalk. "I promise the more that gets out into the news, the longer it'll take for us to solve these murders." And with that, Sadie spun on her heel and stalked toward the front door.

It pushed open in front of her.

"Officer? Could I talk to you?" Delia said. "I'm doing an exposé on the town and—"

"We put out an official report to the news outlets," Sadie snapped.

"Do your research before you go bothering me." She pushed past her and onto the street.

"Well, I never!" Delia gasped. She made a beeline toward the table at the back of Hunter's coffee shop. "Excuse me!" she called. "If I could just ask a few questions…"

The townsfolk scattered.

* * *

Lou yawned and flicked the long braid of hair over her shoulder. Her eyes were gritty, limbs filled with lead. Inventory had never been her favourite task at the garage, but today the minutes were ticking by at a glacial pace. She glanced up at the clock and groaned.

Barely noon.

Clipboard in hand, Lou moved to the next row. *Finish this one up and I'll head home for a nap,* she thought. *Rich and Mila can cover the garage without me.* She'd made it through the first section of dried goods when the first customer of the day arrived.

Lou peeked out from behind the shelves. "Margaret," she said with a laugh. "What brings you by?"

The old woman had a banker's box tucked under her arm and she set it on the counter.

"I wanted to leave something with you. I… I'm not sure who else to give it to." She pushed it forward. "Could you store this for a while?"

"Sure. What is it?"

"It's some papers of Audrika's. I took a peek at them this morning; it looks like business stuff from Mirran."

"Mirran?"

"Vasur's sister who works in Pincher. Audrika gave me the box and asked me to keep care of it, but then she slipped on the stairs and—" Margaret's voice broke. "I just can't keep it anymore."

"If it's Audrika's box, shouldn't it go back to Vasur?" Lou said.

"I… I don't think it *should*."

Lou frowned. "But why?"

"Audrika gave it to me. She didn't *want* Vasur to have it. She sometimes made—" Margaret winced, "—poor investments. Please understand. Audrika and Vasur fought about money sometimes, but they were mostly happy, Lou. They were." She nodded. "Keep the box. Please."

"It *needs* to go back to Vasur," Lou said gently.

Margaret stepped back from the counter. "Fine. But you bring it over. I can't face him right now." She wiped tears from her cheeks. "I'm sorry, Lou. I just can't." A moment later, she was out the door, bells jingling happily.

Lou's shoulders slumped. *Inventory first, then I'll return Audrika's box, and THEN I'll take a nap.* Bone-tired, she turned back to the shelves and began to count.

* * *

Tom Farrel's return to New York was purposefully eventful.

At the small Lethbridge airport, he made a point of arguing with the clerk about the airport surcharge as he returned the vehicle he'd rented. His sharp tone reduced the woman at the counter to a stammering mess.

With a swear, he threw down his credit card.

"Goddamned *robbery* is what that is!" he barked.

"I—I'm sorry, sir."

"I doubt it. Hurry up! I don't want to be late, too."

"Of course, sir," she said, taking the credit card off the counter as she rushed to comply.

Around the small, brown-tiled airport, people stared. Tom knew they were watching him. He *wanted* them to.

On board the small twin-engine that took Tom to Calgary, he made a point of interrupting two separate conversations to ask the time, then muttering about the delay. Those people, too, remembered his presence. At the Calgary terminal, he asked for directions to the connecting gate three separate times. All those people were left with impression of a man very determined to make his flight and frustrated by delays… all part of Tom's plan.

On the plane to New York, sitting in first class, he called the stewardess over.

"When will the dinner be served?"

"I'm sorry, sir," she said with a patient smile, "but this flight is a red eye. We don't serve a meal, just snacks or you can order—"

"What the hell?!"

"I'm sorry," she said. "But there is never a meal if the flight is an overnight—"

"But I'm in First Class! Surely you serve a meal for *First Class* patrons."

"No, sir. We don't. But you could order one of our—"

"Fine!"

The stewardess's expression wobbled, and she stepped back.

"I'll go get you the menu."

The minute she was gone, Tom nodded to himself. Yes. She'd remember him. He relaxed into the seat, ticking off the remaining details in his mind. He needed at least one more scene when he was back in New York. That would be easy enough to accomplish if he took a cab.

The stewardess came down the aisle, her gaze wary. She held out the menu to him. "I'm sorry for the misunderstanding," she said. "I talked to my supervisor, and he'd be glad to cover your meal."

Tom glared. "That's the *least* you can do, given how much I paid for this flight."

"Sorry, sir." She stepped back. "I'll give you a moment to decide."

Tom enjoyed the free meal, the extra blankets and pillow he was offered, the night cap he didn't pay for. He slept soundly, content he'd both covered his tracks to Audrika Kulkarni's murder and to any suggestion that he might have stayed in Alberta. When the plane landed at La Guardia early the Thursday morning, he took a cab to his apartment, making a point of talking to both his doorman and to his elderly neighbour, Mrs. Braithwaite, who he met in the elevator heading up to the twelfth floor.

"God, I think I could sleep for a week," Tom said, faking a yawn.

"You need to keep care of yourself, Mr. Farrel," Mrs. Braithwaite said, patting his shoulder.

"Thanks. I'll try."

"You do that," she said, smiling. "Just take a few days to yourself, Tom. Call your parents. Watch T.V. Eat something. You're looking a little thin, dear. The world can manage without you."

"Maybe so, Mrs. Braithwaite."

She nodded. "Yes, it can."

The elevator door pinged as it opened and Tom stepped back, waiting for Mrs. Braithwaite to step out. She waved once as she reached her apartment door. Tom did the same. When her door closed, he unlocked his door, placed his luggage inside, and then—without taking even a cursory glance into the apartment—headed back out into the hallway to the stairwell. He walked down the risers, coming out in the basement, out of sight of the security cameras. From there, he took a circuitous route, keeping himself off the cameras tracking, to reach the service entry, and eventually into the alley.

He pulled out his cell phone and flicked it open. Dialed. It rang once… twice…

"How may I assist?" a neutral voice answered.

"This is Tom," he said quietly. "I'm standing in the alley behind my apartment. I need safe escort to see Mr. Rice. Tinted windows, please."

"On our way."

Fifteen minutes later, Tom was ensconced in the dimmed backseat, a bottle of sparkling water waiting for him in the car's cooler. Half an hour after that, he stood in the lush private office of Edward Rice, in his Manhattan apartment. Edward Rice paced in front of the desk as Tom waited, hands behind his back. Annabelle Rice, curled in a chaise lounge near the window, sobbed quietly into a silk handkerchief. Outside, the Manhattan morning shone bright and clear.

"I hate that goddamned fool!" Edward raged. "He's the one who got Gabby into this mess! I don't give a damn what the police say. I *know* that he was responsible!"

"Be that as it may," Tom said patiently. "It really doesn't look like he was the one who killed her. I checked the credit card information, and it looks like Rich Evans was in Calgary—"

"Fuck the credit cards!" Spittle flew from Ed's mouth, flecking Tom's jacket. "She went to that godforsaken town because *he was there!* She'd never have left if it wasn't for Rich Evans! She never got over him leaving her." Edward stalked forward, stopping in front of Tom. The elder man's cheeks were florid and splotchy. Tom knew better than look away. "My daughter," Mr. Rice said, "is dead. While it may not be *directly* at his hand, it was certainly precipitated by his actions."

Tom waited for him to continue. Mr. Rice did *not* tolerate interruptions. A few seconds passed in silence only broken by Anna's muffled sobs. Rice spun on her.

"Give us some goddamned *silence,* woman! I can hardly think."

"Of course." Annabelle Rice stood wobbly from her seat, and tottered from the room, muttering apologies. When the door closed behind her, Tom spoke.

"What would you like done, sir?" he asked quietly.

"What do you *think,* Tom?" Edward's smile was a rictus of his facial muscles, seething with hatred. "I want him to suffer."

"That's a given, Mr. Rice. Any other requests?"

Ed turned on his heel, stalking toward his desk. He shuffled through the bottom drawers for a moment, then pulled out a video camera.

"I want Rich Evans to *know* it was me."

A smile flicked the corners of Tom's mouth. *This* was the part of the job he enjoyed. This was his forte.

"Understood, Mr. Rice…"

* * *

In a surge of awareness, Lou jerked into being, her mind filled with a thousand details at once. She stood in a muddy street under the glare of midday sun. The putrid stink of feces and unwashed bodies filled her nostrils as the sound of a cheering crowd rose in a cacophony. She was jostled by an elbow to her side.

A man wearing a battered black jacket and a sweat-stained red cap strode forward. "Out of the way!" He snarled in French. "Or I'll send your slutty ass up there with the rest of 'em!"

"I apologize, citoyen," Lou said, stumbling out of the way of the sans-culottes. "So very sorry."

The man spat on Lou's blue striped dress rather than answer, but she dared not raise her eyes. The so-called "sons of the Revolution" were more dangerous than the wolves that had terrified her as a child.

Here, in the teeming square, they heckled the crowd, punching those who did not retreat fast enough. Louise wanted to run, but she didn't dare.

She needed to know.

Someone began to sing the Marseillaise, and several of the people around Lou joined in. The jovial sound was at odds with her terror. With the sans-culottes gone, she lifted her gaze. A stone's throw away, a group of men and women were being led onto a platform gaudily decorated with tri-colour ribbons. Some of the prisoners ascended the stairs quietly. Others sobbed.

Below the platform, gore had turned the street to mud. A pair of fat sows foraged for clotted blood. Beside the pigs was a basket piled high with heads, their blind eyes staring heavenward. On the other side sat a wagon, heaped with bodies and hazed with flies.

Lou's fear grew as a middle-aged man walked forward. He carried a rolled piece of parchment and he held it out, squinting in the sunlight. "Arman de Cazotte," he shouted. "Emilie Desmoulins, Henri Lavoisier, Georges Corday..." The names rolled on and on. Lou's heart was pounding so hard in her ears she could barely hear his final words. "These men and women have been found guilty of treason against the rightful government of France, and as punishment, have been sentenced to death."

Lou pushed through the crowd as the first man was led to the platform, his hands tethered behind him with a hemp rope. She was halfway to the front when he knelt and the blade fell. The crowd cheered. A woman came next. She screamed hysterically as the guards pushed her into position. Her final shriek was cut short by the thud of the blade. Another cheer from the crowd.

Foot by foot, Lou struggled to reach the front row where a group of tricoteuses stood, knitting. Later, they'd count their lines by the heads in the basket. Lou could barely breathe. The blade whistled down into a wet thud and a woman's head tumbled forward. It landed face up, her dark hair a tangle obscuring a bloody face. Her eyes blinked once... twice... and her gaze caught on Lou's. Lou gasped as long-delayed recognition finally hit her.

The dead woman at her feet was Gabrielle Rice—

Screaming, Lou came awake to find Rich crouched on the mattress next to her, hands on her shoulders.

"Lou," he shouted. "You've got to wake up! Lou, baby! It's just a dream!"

With a shriek, Lou threw her arms around Rich's chest, hugging him.

"She came back!" Lou cried.

"Who came back?"

The woman's dead eyes flashed in the darkness of Lou's mind and she shuddered.

"Gabrielle. She came back."

Rich froze. "Did you say *Gabby*?"

"Y—yes. She was in my dream." Tears blurred the room and flooded over Lou's lower lids. "I—I don't know what it *means*, but I'm scared, Rich! Really scared!"

"I know." He pulled Lou tight against him and kissed the side of her hair. "Is this... a warning dream, like before?"

Throat burning, Lou choked on her answer. "Yes."

"Is it something that'll happen soon?" Rich asked.

"I—I think so."

"What do we need to do to be safe?" Rich leaned back so he could see Lou's face, but his hands were warm and steady against her cheeks. "You've had dreams before, Lou. They've given you warnings. Tell me what this means."

"I don't know!" she cried.

"What's the same in it? What image keeps coming back to you?"

"It's the bodies in the street." She wiped a tear away. "There are so many of them."

"What else is the same?"

"It's Paris," Lou said. "But this time…" Her voice faded.

"This time, what?"

"This time Gabby was one of them. She was dead—" Lou choked. "But I saw her. She was staring at me."

"Yes, but that's got to mean something, right?"

Lou nodded. "I—I think so."

"Good." Rich's face was grim but determined. "Then let's figure this out while we've got a chance. We use what we have. We can talk to Murray and the people in town. Someone must have known something. You said there were bodies. We can check the papers for details about Gabrielle, that Pincher Creek police officer who was killed and even Audrika—"

"Audrika? But I thought she fell down the stairs."

"What if she didn't, Lou? What if she was killed too?"

"That's it!" Lou gasped. "Her death is the thing I was missing. That's what I needed to see."

"What do you mean?"

"I have a box she left with Margaret."

"What's in it?"

"I don't know. With everything else going on, I haven't had time to look. But Margaret told me Audrika didn't want Vasur to have it. Maybe *she* knew something about Gabrielle. Maybe they were in business together." Lou chewed her lower lip. "Should we call Sadie and Jordan about this?"

"If we find something, yeah. But for now, let's focus on what we can do."

Louise stood from the bed. "Then I'll go make some coffee and grab that box."

"Thanks." Rich smiled, though the expression looked worn. "We can handle this. We just need to figure out what the warning is about."

Lou took his hand. "I already know: It's about death."

"Do we have time to stop it?"

Lou frowned, her hand reflexively reaching up to brush the scar in the center of her chest.

"There's always a chance to make things right, Rich," she said. "*Always.*"

* * *

Tom moved through his twelfth-floor apartment with a purpose. The suitcases he'd carried in three hours earlier sat untouched by the door where he'd left them. He brushed past them on his way to the bedroom where he grabbed a fresh carry-on from the closet. In it, he laid two sets of clothes and toiletries. He grabbed a coat and gloves; these too went into the bag.

The *other* items he needed would be provided by Mr. Rice's associates.

Finished, Tom reset the programming of the timer lights to a separate-switch randomized setting. He turned on the speaker-system next, adjusting the timer to play a combination of quiet music, muffled footsteps, and the faint sound of television shows during the daytime hours. Done, he returned to the living room and lifted down the framed photograph above the couch. Behind it was a wall safe. From it, he retrieved one of several falsified passports. Tom Farrel—with all his accoutrements that Audrika had uncovered—had returned to the ether where he'd first emerged weeks earlier.

Barry Goldman stood in his place. The same fail-safe security net—extending from basic internet searches done at universities, to paid informants in police stations, to spies in government agencies—that had protected Tom Farrel, would watch out for *Barry*, too. Done, he grabbed one of several wallets, double-checking the match. Inside was fake ID, credit cards, and several hundred dollars in cash.

"Barry Goldman," he said aloud, then more confidently. "Barry, Barry Goldman, New York City." A marionette's grin crossed his face. While he preferred the alias Tom Farrel—which was close enough to Thomas, his real name—not all dead men carried that moniker. Barry would have to do. "Name's Barry," he said one more time, "great to meet you!" then tucked the items away.

Barry Goldman had been reborn.

Finished, Tom showered and shaved, then dressed, emerging from the bathroom with Barry's name and information in his pocket. He rolled the carry-on to the door before making the call. It rang twice and was answered.

"How may I assist you?" the voice asked.

"I need transport to La Guardia." He relayed his apartment's address. "The name is Barry Goldman."

"Understood. We're on our way."

By the following morning, he was in the state of Washington. A young woman met him at the Spokane International airport. Dressed for an office in high heels and a business suit, she stood in the arrivals area, holding a small sign to her chest: *Barry Goldman, NYC*. Seeing that name unsettled him. Tom's feet stumbled for half a second, before he caught his stride and headed toward her. He expected someone to be available here—a contact, that he'd call like he'd done in New York—but the fact that the woman was waiting meant she already knew his schedule and his name. That was worrisome. He *hadn't* called those details in. And yet here she was, blonde haired and smiling in the arrivals lounge.

He came toward her, his rolling carry-on bouncing along the floor.

"Barry Goldman," he announced. "And you are…?"

She smiled. "His assistant."

Tom nodded.

"There's an unmarked car waiting for you along with the items you requested." She tucked the name plate into a black folder and gestured him closer. "But he'd like to talk to you before you leave on your trip," she added. "Face to face."

"He would?"

"Yes." Her smile grew. "It'll only take a minute."

Tom's stomach churned. He had the uneasy feeling that—should Mr. Xavier find Mr. Rice's request too dangerous to fulfil—then Tom would never come back from this 'just a minute' request. But there was no choice about it. Not really.

Tom forced a smile. "Of course, I'd be happy to chat."

"Good." She turned away. "Follow me please."

The walk through the airport dragged into what felt like hours. There was no place to escape, not with Dax waiting. Tom surreptitiously wiped his hands on the side of his jacket. *Well, it was a good run,* he thought grimly.

A few feet from the exit door sat a dark-windowed SUV. The woman at his side slowed her steps and pointed to it.

"There you go," she said cheerfully. "I'll just wait here." She stepped back.

"You're not coming?"

"Oh no. I'm just supposed to make sure you arrived." She smiled, but it didn't make it to her eyes.

"Alright then." On watery legs, Tom walked to the vehicle. He glanced back to find the woman waiting. Her right hand was in her jacket pocket, the smile gone. Seeing it, Tom's blood ran cold. *So this was it.* He pulled the door open. There was no choice, not really.

He climbed into the dim interior.

As the car door closed behind him, the interior lighting rose and he found himself face to face with a man he knew only by reputation: Dax Xavier. Unlike Mr. Rice, with his silk Armani suits and thousand-dollar Italian shoes, this man was an entirely different type of criminal. *One,* Tom thought, *who didn't mind getting his hands dirty.* He wore a black t-shirt, jeans, and a pair of highly polished cowboy boots. No jewelry. But beyond the short shirt sleeves he wore, ran layers of tattooed sleeves. Dax wasn't someone who'd be easily forgotten if you met him, and this didn't appear to worry him. A line of sweat ran down the centre of Tom's spine.

Dax looked up, but he didn't smile. "Hello Barry."

"Hello, sir."

"You seem surprised to see me here."

"I… I am."

The corner of Dax's mouth twitched, as if he found the hesitancy funny. "You've been on my radar for some time. It's good to finally meet you."

He held out his hand and Tom shook it.

"You too, Mr. Xavier."

"Dax please." He let go of Tom's hand and sat back. "All my friends call me Dax."

"Of course."

"Now, let's get down to business." Dax reached over to the seat next to him and pulled up a white manila folder. He flicked it open. "I received a fax from Edward Rice this morning. He asked that I assist you. You're going back to Waterton," Dax said. "That correct?"

"Yes, Mr.— Dax."

Again, the flicker of a smile. "And I understand you'll be removing an obstacle for Mr. Rice?"

"Yes."

"Who would that be?"

Tom *knew* he wasn't to share this information. That was rule number one when he was on a job, but he also knew he'd never leave this vehicle alive unless he did.

"His name is Richard Evans. He's—"

"Oh, I *know* Rich Evans." Dax made an angry sound in the back of his throat. "I'm just surprised he knew Ed at all. What did he do? Screw over a business dealing?"

"Evans knew his daughter. His *late* daughter, that is."

"Ah," Dax said. "That explains it." He glanced down at the dossier for a moment longer, then flicked it closed. "I have the items you requested and a vehicle, licensed and ready, for your use. One of my Canadian associates will take care of the disposal when you're finished." He tossed the dossier at Tom and he scrambled to catch it. "Call when the job's done."

"Thank you, sir."

Tom had just looked down at the dossier—which included the correct insurance forms for the vehicle, the registration and plate information—when Mr. Xavier spoke again.

"Now Barry, there's one *last* thing we need to discuss before you go. You'll be doing a favour for *me* too while you're there."

"Of course, sir." He paused. "A person, I assume?"

Dax smiled, though it was anything but warm. "I'm glad you understand." He reached into an inside pocket, pulling out a photograph with a list of information and details typed neatly underneath. From his position on the other seat, Tom couldn't see anything other than a smudgy female face with long dark hair.

"A few years ago," Dax said, "I oversaw a thriving transportation industry centred around Waterton Lakes. I had several people working for me. Trustworthy people. But the local police caused me no end of trouble."

He held out the piece of paper to Tom and he glanced down at a woman who wore two dark braids and a sharp expression on her face. Tom *knew* her.

"Constable Black Plume," he said, scanning the details typed below: work schedule for the week, home address, phone number.

"Yes," Dax said. "Sadie Black Plume. Her partner, Jim, was killed in the line of duty two years ago, so he's no longer my concern. She, on the other hand, has been a thorn in my side since day one." Laughter, dark and angry, filled the vehicle. "She needs to be removed."

Tom folded the paper in half, then tucked it into his breast pocket.

"Understood, sir."

"Good. And make sure she suffers as you do it."

Tom smirked. "It wouldn't be fun if I didn't."

CHAPTER SEVENTEEN

It was early evening. Outside the windows of Whispering Aspens, the trees bounced and rolled, the last few leaves shaken free under the wind's onslaught. In the empty kitchen, only the light above the stove shone. And in the living room where Louise and Rich sat, two reading lights illuminated the darkness. An oldies radio station hummed. It was a scene of comfort and familiarity, but Lou could barely breathe.

She stared down at the newspaper in her hands. *No. Please, not this.* The woman, whose grainy face looked back at her, was all too familiar. Gabrielle Rice. But this time, a man's image had joined her: Ben Grayden. He was a friend of Jim Flagstone's and Lou had met him more than once. He too, had died at the killer's hands.

"What're you reading?" Rich asked, startling Lou from her thoughts.

"The paper."

"Well, yeah," Rich laughed. "I figured as much. But what? You were frowning."

"They've published another article about Waterton."

"Delia Rosings?"

"Of course."

"Christ," he groaned. "What now?"

Lou shook the edges of the newspaper. "Says here that another body was found on the fringes of the park. There are similarities between the two deaths and a concern that whoever the murderer is, he'll strike again." She looked up. "Waterton may have a serial killer.

"Is this the danger you sensed coming?"

"I think it might be." She sat up straighter, pushing her exhaustion away. "There has to be some way to find out what happened to Gabrielle and Ben. Waterton's small. There has to be clues."

"How?"

"I looked through Audrika's box. It's not investments at all. It's about *Tom Farrel*. Bank records and the like. I need to go through it closer. Maybe there are some clues in there. Something anyhow…"

She let her head fall back against the headrest, lashes fluttering closed. Exhausted, a flicker of images began: Rich and Lou standing in the Lethbridge courthouse, Rich at the table, Sadie and Jordan across from him, Gabrielle smiling up from the front cover of the newspaper, and then glaring at Lou in her dream. The images flickered faster, coming in a blur of *then* and *now*. Rich young and old, her father and Hunter and even Mrs. Parcelle. Her mother, Yuki, alive in this house, then waiting on the other side.

One last image flashed, catching Lou's attention and she gasped as if surfacing from a dive.

"Murray!"

"Murray Miles?"

"Yes, Murray! I need to talk to him." Lou scrambled from the couch, the dregs of sleep fading as she strode into the kitchen.

Rich followed. "Lou?"

She looked up from the coat rack. "Yeah?"

"You're going to talk to him *now*?"

"It won't take long," she said, already sliding her sock feet into her shoes and pulling on her coat. She held out her hand. "Come with me."

* * *

Tom stayed overnight in Spokane. The next day he paid his bill, then headed north to Chewelah and from there to Colville in his newly acquired vehicle. He turned east, passing inside the Colville National Forest. The road bordered the Pend Oreille River, small towns growing amorphously along its banks, then disappearing back into individual houses, lonely and secluded: Tiger, Ione, Metaline, Metaline Falls. He passed them all, and then he was surrounded by forest and nothing else. *There were lots of trails in these woods*, Tom thought as the trees tightened in on either side of the car. *Plenty of places for Dax Xavier to set up shop, bring in product.* He admired the man even though he feared him.

Eventually, Tom reached the Nelway border crossing where, according to Dax, he had several personal connections. Taking this route added a full hour to his drive, but there were people who could "smooth things out" if there was an issue with Tom's ID or vehicle registration. Seeing the Canadian Customs building up ahead, he tapped the brakes and slowed.

The border station was manned by a handful of customs officers at a time. Three cars waited in the entrance lane as he drove up. This was Borderline's new way station, Tom realized. Sitting right there in plain sight. A new thought bubbled up and Tom's smile melted away. *Unless Dax had sent him here so the feds could deal with him.* The first car moved past and the second took its place. Tom inched the vehicle forward. His chest tightened as the anxious feeling rose inside him. He was heading into the lion's den. *If Dax wanted him dead*, he thought, *the man would only need to say the word.*

The second car moved on. Now there was only one person between Tom and possible danger. He glanced in the rearview mirror. A large SUV with Texas plates blocked his way. He no longer had a choice.

The third car headed into the Canadian wilderness. Now it was Tom alone. He tapped the gas, inching forward.

Goddamnit, Ed. You'd better not have sent me into a trap.

* * *

In less than five minutes, Lou and Rich were driving her truck through Waterton's night-time streets, headed toward the Miles' cabin. It was close enough to walk, but the lateness of the hour drew a steely darkness to the town. The skeletal branches of leafless trees reached out, clawing at them. Streetlamps, blocked by pine trees, blotted out any light within a few feet. Between them, long stretches of shadows barred the way.

Lou could see the Miles' cabin. She could also sense Rich's growing anxiety. He'd been chased through the dark his first summer in Waterton. And though Lou knew it *hadn't* been wolves, she still jerked when she heard a dog howl in the distance.

"It's just one of Hunter or Levi's mutts," she said.

Reaching the Miles' house, they parked and walked up the driveway. Lou rang the bell, then turned, staring out at the street. It hadn't been long ago she'd been chased. An uncertain anxiety filled her lungs, making it hard to breathe. She lifted her hand to ring the bell a second time when the door pulled inward.

Brendan Miles stood on the other side, staring at her in confusion.

"Lou, Rich," he said, nodding. "What's up?"

"Brendan," she said. "Are your mom and dad around?"

"Uh... yeah." He stepped back into the house, motioning them inside. "Everything okay?"

"It is," Lou said. "I just need to ask a favour."

Brendan gave her an uneasy smile. "Um… Well, I'll go get Dad then."

He disappeared into the interior of the house, leaving Lou and Rich standing at the entrance. The scent of cooking lingered in the air from dinner. At a distance, a television played some kind of game show, but the laugh track was soon interrupted by the sound of approaching footsteps. Lou forced a smile as Murray came down the hallway, Brendan on his heels.

"Hey, Lou," Murray said. "Brendan said you needed a favour?"

"Yes," she said. "But that's only if it's okay with you, and the police." Murray stopped a little further away than made for comfortable conversation, but Lou didn't comment on it. She smiled. "It's going to sound strange," she said, "but I'd… I'd like to see inside the cabin Miss Rice rented from you."

Murray frowned. "Why?"

"It's to… read it, I suppose. I know that sounds weird, but I need to figure out what she was feeling."

He stared at her for several long seconds. "What *Miss Rice* was feeling?"

"Exactly." Lou smiled, hoping that the anxiousness she could sense from him had to do with the whole investigation into her death and not her request. "Is the cabin still a crime scene?"

"Not anymore," Murray grumbled. "But I'm going to warn you, the place is a hell of a mess. The police even cut out some of the carpet, kept it as evidence."

"Carpet?" Rich repeated.

"Uh-huh." Murray shook his head. "You'll see what I mean when we get there." He reached into his pocket and pulled out a ring full a keys. "I'll let you in, but I'll lock it after you. Just close the door when you leave."

Lou touched his arm. "Thank you, Murray. Truly."

"Of course, Lou. Whatever I can do to help." His gaze flicked to Rich. "I understand they're trying to pin it on you now that they couldn't connect the death to Brendan."

"Er... yeah," Rich said.

"I didn't realize they'd gone after Brendan," Lou said.

"They did. Brendan admitted that he'd misplaced his keys a while back. Turns out Miss Rice had stolen them."

Lou's eyes widened. "She... she had keys to get into my garage?"

"Seems like it."

Lou frowned. "Murray, when I called Sadie, it was because I was concerned. Brendan didn't answer me. He just walked—"

"Forget it," he said. "The whole town's wrapped up in this mess. I was mad until I heard they were going after Rich. Then I figured it was just karma."

"I'm still sorry."

Murray shook his head. "It's fine." He headed outside, leaving Lou and Rich to follow him up the street. His shadow lost detail, blending with the darkness. Reaching the door of the rental cabin, Murray pulled out the key ring, fumbling through until he found the correct one. He slid it into the lock with a sharp click, pulled the door open, and stepped back.

"Go ahead," he said. "Close up when you're done." He tapped the handle. "It'll lock behind you."

Rich gave Lou a worried look. "You're not coming inside?" he said.

Murray's face paled. "Not a chance. I won't go in there unless it's daylight." He retreated off the step. "But close the door after you, alright?" He laughed nervously. "Wouldn't want someone seeing the open door and wandering into… *that.*"

Then before Lou could ask him what he meant, Murray turned and sprinted up the street *away* from the house.

* * *

A scowling man with brush-cut black hair approached Tom's borrowed vehicle, hand on his gun. Seeing him, Tom turned the car off, put his hands onto the steering wheel, waiting with a neutral expression on his face. That was his forte: play indifference. Charm was another gift, but it'd get him nowhere if these were Xavier's men.

"Passport," the custom's officer grunted.

Tom reached onto the seat next to him and lifted it. Each movement was slow and smooth. Everything done with care.

"There you go."

The man flipped it open, his gaze moving from Tom, to the photograph on the passport, and back again.

"How long are you coming into Canada?"

"Just a few days. I'll be—"

"Business or pleasure?"

"Pleasure."

The customs officer handed back his passport. "Have a great day, Mr. Goldman."

Tom blinked. *Do I know him?* "I… yeah. You too." He put his foot on the gas pedal, but the man tapped on the car's side. Tom hit the brakes. "Yes?"

The officer stepped closer. "Just wanted to remind you that the border is open twenty-four hours a day this time of year." He paused. "In case you were wondering about that."

"Thanks," Tom said. "I was."

"Then I'll see you again soon."

"You will." And in seconds, Tom was off again.

On the Canadian side of the crossing he entered a deep border-land of forest reserve. The towns here were even more sparsely populated and signs warned drivers: "Flashing red; snowplow ahead." The difference between the two countries grew with each kilometre. Daylight faded and night fell. He passed through Creston, Cranbrook, Sparwood, and Lundbreck, finally emerging from the gaping teeth of mountain peaks into the smooth ripples of prairie farmland. Reaching Pincher Station—a crossroad, nothing more—he drove south through Pincher Creek. The stars had just appeared in the night sky as he saw the first sign for Waterton.

Perfect, Tom thought. *Done tonight and out of the country before they found the bodies tomorrow.* He'd do Xavier's job first, then Rice's. He'd be back in the States by morning, on a plane back to New York that same day. He'd make a point of being seen. Perhaps check in with Mrs. Braithwaite and see if she needed him to pick up anything for her at the grocery store. As to his illicit foray back to Canada, no one would be the wiser.

Tom chuckled. It was almost too easy.

* * *

The minute Louise stepped into the cabin, her stomach roiled. The stench was overpowering. It held two noxious layers: a caustic haze of bleach so strong it made her eyes water, and under that, the unmistakable odor of rotting flesh.

Lou turned away. "Oh my God! That smell!"

"Christ!" Rich coughed. "What *is* that?"

The urge to vomit hit Lou and she dry heaved. "I don't know but I… I don't know if I can go in."

"We can go back. You don't have to—"

She took his hand. "No," she gasped. "I want to help. I just need a minute." She squeezed her eyes shut, forcing herself to breathe through her mouth. "I'm okay now. We can go in."

"You sure?"

"Yes." She opened her eyes again. The only light came from the streetlamp, half a block up. With her free hand, Lou fumbled for the switch. Her finger caught on it and light flooded the hallway foyer. "Let's take a look."

Rich nodded. "You tell me if you need to leave."

"I will." She gave him a wary smile. "Don't let go of my hand though. Okay?"

He squeezed her fingers. "I never will."

"Good."

Step by step they tiptoed down the hallway. Waves of emotion—old, but not yet faded—echoed around Lou, distracting her from the place where she stood. She was here, yes, but she was *there* too. Gabrielle's face rose in her mind. She was angry! Lou blinked and the image was gone. Throughout the cabin, pain and anger were interwoven so tightly Lou could barely tell where one began and the other petered off.

"Gabrielle was so unhappy," Lou whispered. "It's all pain here. Everywhere. The emotion is fading but not—" She gasped as they reached the doorway, leading to the living room.

"What the hell is that *smell*?" Rich asked.

Lou's fingers tightened into a claw. A double image had appeared in her vision. Gabrielle stood over the hunched form of a deer's corpse, hacking at it with a saw. Lou's knees wobbled.

"She was practicing on game."

"Practicing *what*?" Rich said.

"Cutting them up—" Lou's words caught. She took a breath through her nose and blew it from her mouth, fighting a spiral of nausea. "She killed the deer in the yard." The image flared—bright for a moment—blood splashed red across the plastic tarp, Gabby angrily crying. "*Just need... to take off... the legs...*" Lou staggered and Rich steadied her.

"Then she dragged the body inside," Lou said. "Hacked it up."

"But *why*?"

"To practice," she whispered. "She was practicing so she could kill someone. So she'd know how to cut up the body, dispose of it."

"Jesus fuck!"

Lou's mind was in disarray. "I—I need out of this room," she gasped. "Please." After images of Gabby's fury echoed like waves, pounding into Lou's thoughts. "Let's see the rest."

"Of course."

With Rich's help, she stumbled out of the living room and crossed a hall into a cluttered kitchen. She took several slow breaths.

"You sure you don't want to get out of here?" Rich asked.

"No. It's not as intense in this room. It's still troubling, but... not as fresh."

Hand in hand with Rich, Lou moved around the kitchen, pausing now and then to touch the table, the wall, the sink. Each one carried emotions. Some were intense and sharp. *Gabrielle stood next to the table, paper in hand, sobbing. "How COULD he?!"* Others were faded and tired. *Gabrielle, with her legs tucked under herself as she spoke on the phone.* While the feelings varied, the chaos of what had happened within these walls remained. Gabby was damaged. Her hatred painted everything around her. Lou walked past the table once—wary of what she sensed—then came back a second time.

"Gabby wrote a letter to you here," Lou said. "I think the police must have it. It's why they think *you* might have killed her."

"How do you know that?"

"It's like a record scratch. Like why a basement gives you uneasy feelings. Years and years of fears piling up on each other. Only here, it was one person." With shaking fingers, Lou placed her free hand flat on its surface. She groaned as memories overtook her.

"Lou?!"

"It's okay," she said through clenched teeth. "I—I need to know." She wobbled and Rich caught her. "My God, she was angry with you, Rich."

"About what?"

"About everything."

She reached out for the table. The second her fingers brushed the worn surface, an image flashed in her mind—Lou's own face, photographed—and she jerked back like she'd been shocked. Gabby's hatred was a live wire. Lou remembered the dream: *Gabby's eyes on hers.*

"My God," she gasped. "I don't think Gabby was after you, Rich, she was coming after *me*." Her brows tugged together. "I just don't understand *why*?"

"I…" Rich frowned. "I think I might know."

"What?"

"When we argued when I was in New York, Gabby talked about wanting a new start. She refused to believe that I'd moved on." He shook his head. "But *you* were the one thing she couldn't change."

"She must have figured if I was out of the picture, she could have that life." Lou retreated from the kitchen and down the hall, leaning into Rich. "She wanted to kill me. I can feel it." They reached the foyer and Lou looked up. "Question is, why didn't she? She was ready. She had the tools. She'd already practiced how to get rid of the body."

"What stopped her?"

A frisson of fear ran through Lou's chest, lodging in the scar above her heart. She could feel the answer waiting for her in the darkness.

"Not what, but *who*." Lou swung the door open. Outside the cabin, the town of Waterton was swathed in sooty black. She stepped over the threshold, breathing in the icy air. "Who in town knows everyone's business?" she said. "Who talks to everyone who visits? Who knows all the ins and outs?"

"Hunter?"

"Exactly." Lou nodded. "We need to talk to him."

* * *

Sadie woke in the dark. Her sheets were wrapped tightly around her legs, her arms icy where they'd been uncovered. She reached down to untangle the blankets, then froze.

"What the…?"

The sound of something caught her ears. The *same* something which had woken her seconds earlier. She waited—breath held—as she pinpointed what she'd heard. Somewhere outside on the street, a car's purring engine revved once, then stopped. She waited. A door opened and closed with a quiet click.

Sadie relaxed. *It was probably nothing,* she thought, *just someone coming back late to town or—*

GET OUT OF THE HOUSE, SADIE!

She squeaked in surprise as Jim's voice roared through her mind. Panicked, she fumbled for the light on the bedside table.

Don't turn it on! He's already standing outside, watching the windows. He'll see the light.

The silver bob on the end of the cord bounced against Sadie's palm, cool and solid. Her fingers tightened. Below her bedroom window, footsteps neared.

Go! Get OUT!

Sadie let go of the cord and swung her legs from the bed, creeping silently to the window. There, on the street, half a block away, was a sports car. A shadowy figure stood on her front step. The light from the streetlamps was behind him, but his silhouette showed him to be a man. Sadie's frown deepened. As she watched, he reached into his breast pocket and pulled out a firearm.

Sadie jerked back from the window, spinning into motion. Her gun was in the gun case on the main floor in the gun safe. *Locked.* The key was on the key ring of her jacket pocket… next to the front door where the intruder stood. She'd never have time to get it! Sadie had knives in the kitchen near the back door, but she'd have to turn on the lights to search the drawers. Besides, a knife wasn't going to cut it if he was carrying a gun. She needed time to—

Hurry, Sadie! He's COMING!

With a hiss, Sadie sprinted from her bedroom, taking the stairs down toward the kitchen in a rush of bare feet. She headed straight for the back door. She didn't turn as she heard the tinkling sound of glass breaking in the foyer, nor when she heard the door open and the entrance floor squeak as someone walked inside. She held her breath and twisted the lock with a silent prayer. One squeak from the door's hinge and he'd know where she was. There'd be no escaping then.

The footsteps moved slowly through the house and Sadie held her breath as he passed the entrance to the kitchen. A moment later, he reached the stairwell. She heard the first riser squeak and took her chance, pushing open the back door. Night scents—pine and water and grass—reached her nostrils as she crept onto the porch.

Two years ago, she'd stood here, Colton Calhoun hidden in the shadows of the trees. Tonight, *she* was the one on the run. Barefoot, she tumbled through the bushes, away from the steps, and into the brush-filled divide between the houses. Branches tore at the bare skin of her legs and grabbed her hair, twigs cracked under the calloused soles of her feet. She heard the back door re-open as she jogged through the yard of the neighbouring cabin, now closed for the season. Gunfire popped and she pushed into a full-out sprint.

Her pursuer followed.

For a few seconds, her head-start held, but when she reached the brambles between two cabins, Sadie's ankle twisted and she yelped. The man crashed through the bushes, closing the gap. *Run! Jim roared. Don't stop! RUN!* Ignoring the branches that slashed her, she pushed on, out past the bushes into the open space of an empty yard. Her pursuer was heavier than she was and his progress was slowed by the trees. Sadie knew the terrain. He didn't. Before he'd emerged from the trees, she swung round the other side of her neighbour's cabin and switched back across the street, two houses down from her own.

Her gaze flicked to the license plate of the nearby car she'd heard drive up minutes before. *755-SNA*. She chanted the number under her breath as she ran. "755-SNA… 755-SNA… 755-SNA"

Reaching the far side of the road, her sore ankle rolled on the uneven grass and she came down hard, smacking her chin. Blood flooded her mouth, the pain of her split lip shocking her into stillness. *Get UP! Jim ordered. He's coming!* She struggled to her feet, fell, then clambered back up again. At that moment, something bit through the skin of her shoulder, the sound of gunfire an afterthought. *RUN!* Sadie's mind was a white scream of terror. All thoughts disappeared. She ran, chased by the sound of a car's ignition and wheels that peeled across the pavement as her pursuer came back toward her.

Go into the brush! He can't drive there.

She'd been aiming toward the police station, but she immediately changed directions, moving into the knots of empty cabins which housed the summer tourists. There, empty swing sets creaked on unmowed lawns. The pain of her shoulder pushed to be addressed, but she ignored it, moving deeper into the woods. The sound of water rose as she neared Cameron Creek, and she followed the backyards along it, never coming out into the open, never going onto the street. Eventually, she passed the campground and the small squat cabins that hinted at Waterton's origins. The man was no longer on foot. She heard a car roar as her assailant drove up and down the streets, searching for her.

Out of breath, Sadie stumbled toward the back-alley that led to the police station. Her right arm was numb and when she reached up to touch her shoulder, a stab of pain ricocheted through her body. She wobbled. Sadie could see the station. She had less than fifty meters to go, but her legs were shaking, limbs weak.

Sadie reached the treed yard of the house two lots down. A few more steps had her staggering into the one next door. She was so close she could see Liz moving back and forth in the back office of the police station. Sadie pressed her hand against her side, her lungs burning. The sound of the car had faded. She was almost there... almost safe... when something large and dark surged toward her.

Sadie screamed.

CHAPTER EIGHTEEN

Lou's shaking worsened as she and Rich walked back to the truck. Her body was caught in a storm, the remnants of Gabrielle Rice's damaged life whirling around her. Gabby wasn't *there* anymore, but the echo of her was, her fury a live wire.

"Lou," Rich said, "are you sure you're okay?"

"Yeah," she lied. "But do you mind driving over to Hunter's house? I'm a bit tired." She handed him the keys.

"Of course." The engine started with a roar loud enough neither of them heard the pop of gunfire three streets over. "You can tell me what you saw," he said. "You don't have to deal with this alone."

"I—I will, but… not yet." She squeezed her eyes shut. "It wasn't good."

Rich shifted the truck into drive, ambling up the darkened streets toward Hunter's house. There was another pop in the distance. He turned in surprise.

"Did you hear that?"

Lou's lashes fluttered open. "What's that?"

"A bang. Fireworks, I think. Just a second ago."

"I didn't hear anything. Probably just kids fooling around." She yawned and her eyelids slid closed.

"Probably, I guess. It's just weird this time of year."

Rich frowned as they reached Hunter's cabin. The windows were dark and the rusted orange truck was conspicuously absent from the driveway. No dogs howled at the door. No smoke rose from the chimney.

"Hmmm... doesn't look like he's home," Rich said. "You wait in the truck. I'll double check if anyone's around." He jogged up the steps and rang the bell. A distant scream broke the night. He jerked around, heart pounding, then walked warily back down the steps to the cab.

Lou's chin bobbed as he opened the door. "Any luck?" she asked.

"Neither Hunter nor Levi are there."

"Probably out at the ranch then."

"You up for a drive?" he asked.

"Absolutely."

Rich headed east along Vimy Avenue. It was full dark, the moon hidden by clouds; the mountains hulking shadows leaned in from all sides. Lou slumped lower in the seat.

"You okay?" he asked, but she didn't answer. "Lou...?"

Distracted, Rich slowed rather than stopped, as he reached Windflower Avenue. He was still moving when a silver car peeled out in front of them. Rich slammed his foot on the brake. The tires locked and they slid forward. The silver car swerved—headlights swinging across their faces—before the driver got it back under control. For a split second, Rich caught sight of a man's face behind the wheel, but the vehicle was past them a moment later. It raced alongside the campground as it headed toward the cabins that lined the shore.

"Jesus," Rich gasped. "That was close. You alright?"

"I'm fine." She watched the taillights move down Vimy Avenue, past the old Pattinson place, and then west. "Crazy driver."

"There are assholes everywhere."

Rich eased the vehicle back into motion, heading toward the center of town, and from there, to the exit out of the park. Unseen, the silver car did a U-turn and switched directions, abandoning its pursuit of Sadie Black Plume in order to follow them.

The lights flicked off and Tom Farrel tailed Lou and Rich out of the park.

* * *

Sadie stumbled back as a cougar that was at least seven or more feet long from nose to tip of tail emerged from the bushes next to her. The animal roared. Its voice was a woman's scream blended with a lion's and the sound nearly took Sadie to her knees. She took an uncertain step backward, but the second she moved, the cougar took two steps forward and bared its teeth, hissing. The cat's eyes flashed in the darkness. Cougars were plenty big enough to kill an elk. A human was child's play to them.

She was going to die.

A heartbeat passed as moments from her life, growing up on the Blood Reserve, flashed in her mind. Her parents held hands as they sat around the campfire on a summer evening. Her brother, gone years ago, was there again for just a moment, laughing. Images of her friends at Lethbridge College where Sadie trained to be a police officer appeared. In one flash, she saw her first post in Okotoks, remembered the frustrations of trying to prove herself again and again. Another brought her thoughts back to her arrival in Waterton. She remembered Jim grinning down at her. *"Why you've just come to the prettiest place in all the world."* In the memory, he reached out to shake her hand. *"Welcome aboard, Constable Black Plume..."*

Sadie blinked and the memory ended. The cougar shifted back

and forth, paw to paw, the way a house cat did before attacking a mouse. The back door to the police station was less than twenty feet—and a full lifetime—away. Sadie's legs tensed and she took another step backward.

The cougar roared.

Sadie was out of breath, her limbs shaky. She had a bullet lodged in her shoulder, but the pain faded as fear took hold. She *wasn't* supposed to run from a cougar. Of that, she was sure, but she couldn't remember the rest. The cougar shifted its weight onto the balls of its feet, ready to pounce.

Tears welled in Sadie's eyes. *No! Not now! Not yet!*

* * *

Louise woke as the truck reached the Thompson ranch. "Whoa. We're here already?"

"Yeah," Rich said. "You nodded off for a bit."

She yawned as she took in the prairie scene. The ranch had changed little in the last hundred years of operation, and the same sturdy farmhouse that had greeted Ephraim Thompson's mail-order bride from Nova Scotia, and later Yuki, her husband Lou, and young Hunter Slate, now greeted Lou and Rich. The truck rolled to a stop next to the porch and Rich turned off the engine.

"Porch light is on," Lou said, frowning, "but I don't see any lights on in the house. You think they're hunting?"

"Don't think so." Rich nodded to the barn where an orange truck sat, a faded blue one parked next to it. "Hunter's truck is here and so is Levi's."

"Then they've got to be around here somewhere, right?" Lou undid her seatbelt. "I'll go check the house."

Rich pushed open the door, against the steady onslaught of wind; it howled through the cab, tossing bits of dust into his eyes.

"I'll check the barn."

"Hurry," Lou said. "I'm feeling a little off tonight."

"Off?"

"Something feels *wrong*, Rich."

He nodded. "I'll be careful."

While Lou headed to the porch, Rich jogged toward the barn. With the wind howling over the prairie, neither one heard the silver car arrive, lights turned off. Neither saw it ease its way past the Texas gate or enter the far end of the yard. The door opening and closing was muffled too. And as Lou jogged up the steps to the house, the figure inside the car's cab pulled out a gun and stepped into the darkness.

He made a beeline toward the barn.

Lou knocked on the door, her heart in her throat. Something was happening. She could feel the scattered emotions rising like the unsettled tempest that tore across the prairies. This wasn't *just* Gabby anymore, it was something else too. Danger on its way.

"C'mon, Levi," she muttered. "Answer the goddamned door." She knocked again, louder.

Far inside the house, she heard someone yell. "Hold yer horses!"

"Levi," Lou said with a shaky laugh.

The door swung open. Behind Lou, the strange man disappeared into the barn.

"Lou?" Levi said, gesturing her inside. "What're you doing here?"

"Levi, I need to talk to Hunter."

"He's not around."

"I *saw* his truck in the yard," she said

The old man glared at her.

"Come on, Levi," Lou pleaded. "I'm not here for coffee and a visit. This is important."

His eyes narrowed suspiciously. "Why?"

"Because I need to talk to him about Gab—" Lou stopped. Levi didn't care about outsiders; never had. Never would. "Look," she said, "I'm just… I'm *worried* about what's happening around town and I need to talk to him, alright?!"

"He's out in the paddock with the horses."

"I thought Bryce was keeping care of them for you."

Levi scowled. "Fool boy went and got himself a D.U.I. last Saturday. Didn't tell me about the charges neither. He's in Lethbridge this week, going to trial. Left me high and dry." He lifted the arm in the sling. "I sure as hell can't work the ranch myself. Goddamned useless is what I am these days."

"It'll heal," Lou said gently. "It'll just take time." The old man made an angry sound. "But I need to find Hunter," she said. "Which paddock is it?"

"The western one. But don't bother. He'll be back soon enough."

"How soon? I need to—" Lou glanced backwards. It felt like someone had shouted her name. But it was gone now. *Silent.*

"Need to what?" Levi grumbled.

She turned back, fighting a wave of unease. "Did you hear something?"

"Not a thing. You…" Levi turned his hawklike gaze into the yard. "What in sam hell?!"

Lou's eyes widened as she saw the car they'd nearly collided with an hour earlier, waiting near the barn. A shadowy figure dumped something large and bulky into the trunk.

Levi shoved past Lou. "You there!" he bellowed. "What're you doing on my proper—?"

A gunshot rang through the night, the window next to Lou exploding in a shower of glass. Seconds later, the silver car peeled into the darkness, spraying gravel behind it.

* * *

Rich woke to the rumble of an engine and the steady vibration of wheels on a gravel road. He knew the sound. Recognized it. But it made no sense for him to be here. The floor bounced under him and he rolled to his side, groaning. His head felt like thunder, the pain of his arms—tethered behind his back—an agonizing stab.

He'd felt like this only one time before.

For one confusing moment, Rich was back with Colton Calhoun, pleading for his life. Rich thrashed in panic. He tried to sit up, but only succeeded in banging his forehead on the ceiling, less than half a foot away. The pain in his head surged.

"What the fuck?!" He struggled to see, but the darkness was solid. The engine roared.

I'm in a car.

Rich's confusion faded as memories of the evening returned. He remembered walking into the barn, finding it empty. He recalled hearing someone open the door behind him. He'd turned, and then... *Nothing.*

Rich struggled to free himself. His panic only tightened the knots that held him and eventually he fell back against the floor of the trunk, panting. The car slowed and the road grew bumpier. *Heading onto the back roads.* Realizing it, fear hit him like a splash of ice water. He was in the trunk of a car. The driver was taking him who-knew-where. He struggled to pull back the last minutes before he'd lost consciousness, to catch the thread of his memory, but the only thing he could recall was the sound of the barn door opening. Everything after that was absent, a skip in the record. *Gone.*

Understanding arrived like a light in the darkness.

"Oh my God..." Rich gasped.

Waterton's killer had *him*. And no one else even knew he was gone.

* * *

The cougar's eyes narrowed.

"No," Sadie said. "Not like this." She lifted her chin and took several deep gulps of cold night air.

Stay sharp! a voice said. *You've got to be ready!*

Exhausted, Sadie forced herself to remember what she'd seen before the cougar had appeared. Were there any sticks on the ground? Any yard tools? She thought there'd been a rake, *but where*?! If she had that, she could use the branch as a weapon. Or if she could throw something to distract the cougar for a few seconds, she *might* be able to make it to the back door of the police station.

Her gaze scanned the area around her, belatedly catching on a broken branch. It was smaller than she wanted, but it'd have to do. Eyes never leaving the mountain cat, Sadie reached down and grabbed it. She swung it above her head.

"Go away!" she screamed. "I'm NOT giving up! You're gonna have to fight me!"

The cougar's ears flattened and it hissed. It stepped backward one step, two. Sadie swung the branch wildly, her voice booming. "GET OUT OF HERE!"

The cougar's hackles rose, a golden line across its back and shoulders. Sadie gave one last primal scream and lunged toward the animal. It bounded through the trees, disappearing between one breath and the next. The club fell from Sadie's fingers and she let out a sobbing laugh. She'd done it. The cougar was gone. She was safe.

She took two steps and stumbled, catching herself against a nearby tree. The motion swung her around. Sadie gasped.

Jim Flagstone stood before her.

* * *

Levi had *known* Louise wouldn't find anything in the barn. His eyes might not be good, but the man they'd seen had been loading *something* in the trunk. Levi just didn't know if the 'something' was *dead* or not.

The door to the house swung wide, Lou rushing back inside. Her cheeks were tear-streaked, breath ragged.

"I need to go!" she said. "Call the police, Levi. Tell them to get out here. Rich is in danger!"

Levi put his good hand on the chair's arm and hoisted himself upward.

"If you'll wait a minute, I'll—" She slammed the door, cutting off the rest of his words.

Levi dialed the police first.

"Waterton Police Station. This is Liz. How may I—"

"Less chatter, woman," Levi snapped. "I need Jordan Wyatt out here at the ranch right quick."

There was a pause. "I'm sorry, who is calling?"

"It's Levi Thompson," he growled. "There's trouble at the ranch. You tell that Wyatt boy to get out here. Somebody kidnapped Rich Evans."

"Kidnapped?!"

"Yes!" he snapped. "That's why I'm callin'! Now get me someone on the double!"

"Hold on, Mr. Thompson," Liz said. "I need some information."

"I don't have *time*! I'm trying to catch this guy!"

"Sir, you need to stay right where you are!" Liz said. "I'll send someone out right away, but first I need a description of the—"

Levi hung up the phone.

"Don't got no time for this foolishness. Time's a wasting."

He shuffled to the closet. The interior was full of coats, but he reached up to the shelf above them, fumbling blindly for the cool bite of metal. His fingers wrapped the double-barrel of the shotgun and he pulled it down. Levi grabbed the box of shells next, filling his pockets with them the way he'd done when he was duck hunting with his Pa. Finished, he peeked out the window. Louise rushed from one side of her truck to the other, the woman's panic palpable.

"You ain't got no keys," he muttered.

Outside, a storm was brewing, black clouds pouring over the mountains and spreading across the prairie. Levi grabbed his coat from the hanger, wriggling the one arm on and leaving the other dangling over his shoulder. It annoyed him, but it was too cold to be running around in the dark with only a shirt. *A blanket...* An uneasy emotion rose inside him and he pushed it away. Levi grabbed his cowboy hat; pushed the brim down. He tucked the double-barrel shotgun under his arm, wedged the front door open, and stepped through.

A blast hit him. It was the icy north wind that stole your breath and made your eyes water. *Snow's coming.* He squinted through the yard. Lou stood on the passenger side of her truck, jiggling the handle.

"You headin' off?" he called, his voice disappearing into the wind.

"I can't! Rich has the keys. I'm locked out."

Levi limped to her side. "Just wait," he said. "I'm sure Hunter'll be back before we—"

"I can't wait!" Lou yelled. "Rich is going to die if I don't get to him!"

"What're you going on about? I called the police. Liz said to wait here and she'd send someone—"

"I don't have TIME to explain this to you, Levi!" she cried. "I—I need to find Rich NOW, but I don't know where to go!" She ran her hands into her hair, tightening her fingers into fists.

Levi pointed to the horizon. "There. That's where the car's headed."

Lou followed Levi's gnarled finger toward the far western range of the ranch where it bordered the park. A plume of dust hung in the air like a signal.

"The car!" she gasped. "Quick! I need to catch them!" She grabbed Levi's hand. "Please! I need your truck. Rich is in danger!"

"This ain't smart, Louise."

"There's someone trying to kill Rich! It's the same person who came after me. I… I don't know *how I know* other than to say I dreamed it. I saw it." The storm rumbled, pins and needles of icy rain pinging down on the two of them. Levi frowned. Even if the driver *left* Rich out in the foothills, he'd be dead of exposure come morning. "Please, Levi!" Lou cried. "I'm begging you! I need to—"

"Fine. But you're gonna have to drive it," he said. "My arm's busted."

"Thank you!"

He hobbled toward his 1953 Ford pick-up. Its long bench seat was covered in tattered saddle blankets, a spiderweb of glass on the front windshield on the passenger side. Neither door was locked.

"The key is under the front seat in a mason jar," Levi said.

Lou fished under the seat and pulled it out. The keys jangled as she dropped them into her shaking palm.

Levi set the shotgun onto the center of the seat. Lou's eyes widened. He waited for her to say something about it as he climbed inside and pulled the door closed behind him, but she didn't.

"Buckle up," she said. The engine sputtered, then caught with a roar. "I'm going to try and catch them."

Levi snorted. "Buckle up? This truck ain't got belts. So you go as fast as you want, but you watch yerself."

"Right. Thanks." Lou released the clutch and moved the gear shift into reverse, backing out over the bumping yard. Ahead of her, the porch light broke into a starburst across the damaged window. She slammed it into first and pulled out of the yard, heading out onto the range road that ran past the ranch.

"Can you see the tail lights?" Levi asked.

Lou peered through the lined glass. "No lights. Just dust."

The truck hit a pothole and a stab of pain shot through Levi's arm. He gripped the seat with his good hand.

"The car ain't gone far," he said. "We'll get Rich back for you."

"But what if he's already—"

"Don't go sayin' that," Levi growled. "We'll find 'em. Look there," he said, pointing. Partway up the road, the haze of dust thickened, red tail lights in the gloom. "They're up ahead. I... I know where they're headed."

Lou's gaze flicked over to him. "Where?"

"It's a... a..."

"A *what*, Levi?!"

"It's a range road that passes by Indian Springs." He cleared his throat. "But there's another way. A short cut." He pointed. "You're gonna turn right here."

"But the car—"

"Is gonna be there long before we will. So if we want to catch 'em, we've gotta be smart."

"But—"

"Lookit Lou, I grew up on this ranch and I'm *tellin' you* I know where they're headed. That's the end of the road. But we can get ahead if we hurry." He glared at her. "So, d'you trust me or not, girl?"

Lou's fingers tightened into claws on the wheel. "I… I do."

"Then turn! *Now*!"

Lou lifted her foot from the gas, hitting the brake and shifting gears as they neared the turn off. It looked like something between a gravel road and a twinned mountain path, the ruts exactly the same width as a vehicle's tires. As she turned onto the secondary farm road, the truck lurched and an image flashed across her vision.

Gabrielle Rice sitting on the bench seat next to her.

Lou gasped and the vision was gone. "Here?" she asked. "This road? Is this the right one?"

"Yes. Follow it right on up," Levi said. "You gun 'er and we'll be there before that boy o' yours and whoever's got him arrive. Hurry. Put that pedal down."

"Hold tight!" She slammed her foot down on the gas. The engine's whine rose over the sound of wind, buffeting the windows. It felt, Lou would think later, much like the time when she'd been unconscious and drifting—crossing between here and there. As they neared a crossroads, the dust thickened. The other driver *had* passed this way, and only minutes before. Lou slowed the truck, nearing the 'X' of the two converging roads. Next to her, Levi reached out with his good hand, grabbing hold of the dash as if preparing for a crash. Her gaze flickered to him. Levi's wrinkled face taut with concentration.

Gabrielle.

Lou slammed on the brakes as her body flooded with sudden awareness; the emotion from the dream rolled over her, dragging her into the turbulence she'd been sensing for weeks. The truck sat at the convergence of the two roads.

"What're you waiting for?" Levi bellowed. "Keep driving!"

"Gabby was on this road," Lou gasped. "She was *in this truck.* Here… with *you.*"

Fear and fury rippled across his face. "What're you talking about? I ain't never killed no one. Now you hit the gas or I swear I'll…"

Levi's words faded into a rush of sound and colour. The past was so near, Lou could already see it. *Sense it.* Atop the image of the truck, and Levi, shouting at her side, was another place, another time, drawing Lou away.

Gabrielle Rice was waiting…

CHAPTER NINETEEN

"Start the truck!" Gabrielle screamed, the handgun bouncing dangerously in her hands. "Get driving, or I'll shoot you, old man!"

Levi glared down at his gnarled fingers, tight on the steering wheel. Beyond the window in the darkness sat the rental car, mired in mud. When he'd pulled up to it, he'd thought he was doing a good deed—these days, he wanted to balance the ledger on that account as much as he could—but the woman in the car had pulled a gun on him, demanding his vehicle. When she'd climbed into the driver's seat and seen it was standard, she'd insisted Levi drive.

"I'm not gonna drive you anywhere except the nearest gas station," Levi said. "I'll forget about the gun, if you'll just—"

"Oh, I'm not taking orders from the likes of you!" she spat. "I've got things to do." The gun wavered perilously close to Levi's cheek. "Now drive, damnit!"

Levi started the truck, glancing up and down the road in hopes that he'd see another vehicle, but few people, barring Hunter or his daughters, ever visited, and no headlights lit the darkness. Levi shifted into first, slowly easing the truck to life.

"Stop wasting time," the woman snapped.

He hit the gas and she slid on the seat. Levi bit back an angry smile. "Whatever you want, lady."

For a few minutes they drove in silence. Levi had no idea where the woman was going, but with her waving the gun around like a lunatic, he didn't feel he could ask. Eventually they came up a small rise on the road on the far western edge of the Thompson ranch. The crossroads appeared in the distance. Levi scowled. He'd been hoping to run across one of the Durnerins, but there were no headlights out *here* either.

"There's supposed to be a little lake," the young woman said. "I need to find it."

Levi glanced over at her. "A lake?"

"Yes. A little lake, right near the mountains. There's lots of wildlife there. It's… a good place to hunt."

"No hunting though," Levi said. "It's inside the park."

Her eyebrows shot up. "You know the place?"

"If it's on this road, that'd be Indian Springs."

She laughed manically, the gun's barrel bouncing and Levi winced. "Then you know where it is!"

"Range road up ahead." He nodded. "It leads into Waterton park, but you can only drive halfway."

"Why only half?!"

"It's a trail after that point. You'd have to walk—"

"But I can't! I couldn't carry everything I'd need."

"I mean, you could take a horse, I suppose. I've done that a time or two, but…" He glanced over, frowning. "What're you plannin' to do out there?"

She gave a weird, high-pitched laugh. "I'm taking someone to see it. And *you're* going to *help* me bring them out there." Her eyes widened. "You're a rancher, right?"

He frowned. "Yes."

"We're going to take your horses to do it."

"Oh no. I ain't helping you with nothing."

"Yes, you *are*!" The gun prodded him in the ribs. "Turn the truck around," she snapped. "Take us to Waterton."

"Waterton?"

"I've got someone to pick up."

Levi's blood ran cold. "Who?"

"Louise Newman."

Up ahead, the crossroads grew closer. It was a low dip on a narrow road, high banks on either side. Seeing it, Levi's booted foot hit the gas rather than the brake.

"I've had my eye on her for weeks," the woman said in a singsong voice. "I've got everything I need to make it look like an accident. But I can't walk the whole way. No, no, no! Not to Indian Springs. Not with all my equipment. But *you* and your horses could carry it!"

"Carry *what*?"

"The tools and me and the body." She tipped her head back, giggling. "We'll pick her up in Waterton. Louise will trust *you*. You're an old man. You're a local. She'll come with us if you tell her to!" Her laughter rose into unnerving cackles.

The crossroads neared.

Levi's booted foot jammed the pedal to the floor, pushing the truck to nearly eighty. The woman in the passenger's seat was still laughing when they hit the ditch. Levi slammed forward, smacking his chin and breaking his arm as his body bounced against the steering wheel. His eyelids fluttered open.

Gabrielle Rice slumped against the dash, *dead*, a single pinwheel marking the glass where she'd hit the windshield.

Levi sat up, tasting blood. He panted until the nausea passed, then straightened. With his unbroken hand he opened the door and stepped out onto the empty road, scanning for escape. There were horses here in the paddock. He could use one of them to get the body away from here. Hide it. The car he'd deal with tomorrow. There were lots of empty backroads where vehicles could be left.

He took a step and the grating of bone on bone almost took him to his knees. "Oh Jesus…"

He paused, panting, as scenarios ran through his mind. Call the police, and he'd have to explain what had happened in that truck. It'd be his word against a dead woman, and that wouldn't look good. At best, he'd be charged for reckless driving. At worst, manslaughter. Yes, she'd abducted him, but who'd believe that? Levi wasn't tied up. She was a foot shorter than he was. She had a handgun, but there'd been no struggle. No fight. He groaned and leaned over, panting.

"I done messed up this time."

The indifferent wind roared around him, and with it came a memory of a young man standing in his yard, decades earlier, begging for a second chance. When he lifted his chin, he knew what to do.

Hunter would understand. He'd help, just like Levi had helped him years earlier. No one else needed to know. There'd be no trouble. No fuss.

One foot ahead of the other, his mouth and nose bleeding and his left arm broken, Levi Thompson walked back to the ranch where he'd been born and lived his whole life. He'd more than paid his debt to Yuki, but he had no intention of going to jail for doing it.

* * *

Sadie couldn't breathe. Jim Flagstone, as real as the day she'd last spoken with him, stood before her. His dark hair was combed back away from his smiling face, his uniform sharply pressed, open at the collar.

"You're dead, Jim," she blurted.

He laughed. "Don't hold it against me."

"This… This isn't real."

"You sure? Then what is it?" He winked.

"There's a reasonable explanation," she said. "I'm hurt; bleeding. Adrenaline does crazy things."

"Could be."

"This is a hallucination."

He shrugged. "Six of one, half a dozen of the other."

The wind howled through the trees and Sadie shivered.

"C'mon," Jim said. "You've got to get moving."

"Can't."

"Yes, you can,"

Sadie gave a broken laugh. "Fine. I don't want to."

"Don't be like this."

Sadie took a shuddering breath. "I hate that you died, you know."

Jim's smile faded. "I know."

"I miss you."

"I know that, too."

"Why'd everything have to come apart, Jim?" Her voice broke. "Why'd you have to go and die on me?"

"'Cause sometimes that's just how it goes."

He stepped closer and Sadie realized that she could see *through* him. Past the dark blue of his shirt, the window to their office in the station was visible. She could see someone walking back and forth next to the billboard, phone in hand. *Liz?* What was the receptionist doing in the back office?

"Sadie," Jim said, "you've got to get yourself inside the station."

"But I want to talk to you."

He smiled. "You're always so goddamned stubborn."

"No, that was you." She took a step, and her shoulder roared in pain. She gritted her teeth. "God, I feel like shit."

"That's 'cause you've been shot," Jim said. "You need to get to the door. Get help. There's a line of blood all the way back to the alley. Stay here and that cougar'll smell it and come back."

Sadie's throat ached with unshed tears. "I… I can't."

"You can."

"But I don't *want* to."

Jim stepped nearer. At this distance, the details faded. His dark hair was a canopy of pine branches swirling in the wind, the shadows around his eyes, splotches on a tree trunk. *Was she dreaming all of this?* Sadie wondered. *Maybe she really was crazy.*

"You can't just give up," Jim said. "This town needs you."

"No, Jim. They don't."

"There's trouble out there and no one's going to stop it except you."

Tears rolled down Sadie's cheeks. "I can't keep going. It's… it's too hard."

"Too hard for someone else, but not for Constable Sadie Black Plume."

"Stop! I can't."

Jim reached out and for a moment, Sadie swore she felt his hand on his shoulder.

"You can and you will," he said gently. "You're not alone, Sadie. I promise. Now go. Get walking."

She took a step and stumbled on a hidden root, pain pulsing alongside her jarring footstep.

"Ugh. Just need to rest a minute. My shoulder—"

"Move, Sadie! Or I'm gonna harass you every moment of every day for the rest of your life."

"Bastard." She forced herself onward, picking her way through the underbrush. If she didn't move too much, the gunshot was only an ache, entirely manageable. She just needed to be careful.

"Good," he said. "Now you just keep moving."

She crossed the yard slowly. The back door to the police station was a few feet away, Liz visible in the office window, phone in hand. She carried a file folder under her arm. Sadie frowned. *Liz shouldn't have been in the back office, unless…* Her eyes widened. *My God, that was it! She was the leak!*

"Walk, Sadie."

Sadie stumbled as she reached the back step of the station, but she caught herself against the doorframe.

"You can do it," Jim said. "Just—"

"I know," she snapped. "Stop nagging me!"

Jim's rumbling laughter filled her ears as she turned the knob. She heard the door click and it swung inward, pulled open from the inside.

"Sadie?!" Liz gasped. "My God! You're bleeding!"

Constable Black Plume stepped inside.

"Been shot," she said. "Now give me that."

"Give you *what*?"

"That." Sadie snatched the folder out of Liz's hands. She turned, staring back out the open door into the night. The area beyond the doorway lay empty, the midnight sky dark with clouds. Tears filled Sadie's eyes.

Jim Flagstone's ghost was long gone, if he'd ever really been there at all.

* * *

Rich felt the car slow in the seconds before it stopped. He pulled his legs under him, ready to escape if he could. Footsteps echoed outside.

"Mr. Evans," a man's voice said. "I'm going to let you know that I have a gun pointed at the trunk. If you try anything... *anything at all*. I will be forced to shoot you." There was a long pause. "Understood?"

Rich's heart pounded against the cage of his chest. He waited.

"Alright," the voice said. "I'm opening the trunk now."

There was a click and the roof swung upward, a glaring light blinding Rich before he even had time to move. He struggled to get his feet under him.

"Easy now," the voice said. "I'd be annoyed to have to shoot you in the trunk, but you should know I'm happy to do it if I need."

Rich squinted as the man came into focus. Ice filled his limbs.

"You're Tom Farrel," Rich whispered.

"I am," Tom said genially. "Get out of the trunk."

"This would be easier if I could use my hands," he grumbled.

Tom laughed. "Oh, I have all the time in the world."

Rich slowly shifted himself upright and climbed from the trunk. Tom waited, gun in one hand, a small video camera in the other.

"What's that?" Rich asked.

"A message for you." Tom pressed play and the small screen flashed to life. Gabrielle's father appeared, his face blotchy.

"Rich, at one point I thought of you like a son. I thought that someday, you and Gabby would marry." He stepped closer to the camera. *"And you took that from me! You destroyed my world!"*

Rich looked at Tom. "But I never—"

"Listen to the message," Tom said, lifting the gun.

Rich fell silent as the video continued.

"When Gabby told me she'd met you again in New York, I thought it was one of her games. She'd done it before—lying to us about what

she was up to—but this time seemed genuine. She told us you were together again—"

"That's a lie!"

Tom slammed the gun's barrel against Rich's temple and he saw stars. He staggered sideways, gasping.

"Listen," Tom said darkly. "It's a message, Rich, not a trial, but I told him I'd show it to you. I keep my promises."

"...and when she disappeared, I worried you might have done something to her. But when I got the coroner's report..." Mr. Rice's voice broke. *"I knew. I knew you'd done it! She'd never run off like that, not without a reason."* He leaned forward, his image in the camera shifting in and out of focus. *"And now you're going to pay. Know this. I ordered your death. I ordered it for Gabby. But YOU are the one who caused it."* He tapped a button and the screen flicked to static.

"See?" Tom drawled. "That wasn't so hard." He tossed the camera into the trunk of the car. "Now, let's go."

"What are you going to do to me?"

"Oh, I thought that was obvious." Tom laughed. "I'm going to kill you."

Fear took away Rich's ability to form words.

"If you mean *how* am I going to do it, we're going to walk to the woods," Tom said. "There's a little lake out there. It's where the police found Gabby's body. I'm going to shoot you. Fitting, don't you think?"

"You killed her!" Rich snarled.

"No, actually, I didn't."

"I don't believe you!"

"I don't care." Tom shrugged. "Gabby's father always thought she was an angel, but that girl had enough drama to last a lifetime.

Some of it finally caught up with her."

"You mean *you* caught up with her," Rich spat.

"No, though I was closer than I realized. I'd tracked her to Waterton and was going cabin to cabin the night she disappeared." He chuckled. "I'd been wandering around, trying to see who was staying at the Miles' place. I wonder if I spooked her… because *someone* found her later that night."

Rich's hands tightened. As much as Gabby's erratic behaviour had disturbed him, the thought of her death brought a wave of fury.

"She deserved better."

"A lot of people do. Doesn't change what is." Farrel prodded Rich with the barrel of the gun. "Come on, Richard. You and I are going to walk."

"But if you *know* I didn't kill her, then why are you doing this?"

"It's a job."

"But I'm innocent—"

"They frequently are."

Rich shot a wary look over his shoulder. "They…?"

Tom nodded. "Yes. Mr. Rice and his associate, Mr. Xavier, often employ me to remove problems. This time, the problem is you."

"So you're going to kill me even though you *know* I'm innocent."

"Oh, I don't *know* it," Tom said. "I just suspect it. You could have been the one to smash in her head that night. No one knows." The gun barrel poked him again. "Keep walking. We've got a ways to go."

Rich walked forward, eyes darting from place to place. They were in the foothills somewhere, but he couldn't tell what part. The mountain range that led to Waterton rose in the west, the prairie like an unfolded blanket rippling in the east. He needed to figure out where he was. Rich glanced back over his shoulder again.

"You've killed more than once?" he asked, stalling.

"I've killed more than I even care to remember," he said. "I've killed more than once in the last week." He nodded to the north. "Had a police officer pull me over for speeding. He was… irritating. Couple days later I had to deal with a local whose snooping was getting a little *too* close for comfort."

"So it doesn't matter to you who you kill."

"Not really," Tom said. "It's just part of the job." He laughed. "Thought I might end up killing your girlfriend for a while."

Rich stumbled and Tom jabbed the barrel between his ribs. "I used to watch her, you know. Night after night, checking in, making note of her comings and goings. She was the one person in town who had a connection to Gabrielle Rice." He laughed darkly. "Through *you*, I should say."

"So that's it. I'm dead no matter what I do or say?"

The skin on Rich's back tightened, waiting for the gunshot that would kill him. *Run!* His mind screamed. *Just RUN!* He scanned the hills. The foothills gave as little protection as the prairies. Run here, and Tom could casually aim and shoot him before he got to the top of the hill. *He had to wait until he reached the treeline,* Rich thought. *At least then he'd have a chance to hide.*

"Well, yes, but I can make it better or worse." Tom snorted. "I could shoot out your kneecaps, let you bleed out. Leave you for the animals like I did with Constable Black Plume. Or I could make it clean."

"Clean," Rich muttered. "Right."

They walked for a few more minutes, the trees growing closer. At the bottom of a slope a faint glimmer appeared. Indian Springs, Rich realized, was where they found Gabby's body. The barrel poked him hard in the back and Rich flinched.

I'm sorry, Lou! I wish—

"There's someone following us," Tom growled.

Rich spun. "What?!" He tried to look back behind them, but the gun barrel slammed into his temple.

* * *

Sadie sat in an office chair in a borrowed pair of sweatpants, her shoulder bound tight, bandages covering bloody feet.

"I'm *not* going to the hospital yet," she snapped. "Levi wouldn't call unless he was scared!"

Jordan glowered. "But Sadie, you're in no condition to—"

"Don't 'but Sadie' me, Jordan. I know what I know. Someone's grabbed Rich Evans, and it's up to us to stop them."

Jordan glanced over his shoulder to where Brian sat, talking animatedly with Liz, the receptionist. She was in tears. Sadie had uncovered their leak—and Liz would almost certainly be charged for it—but there appeared to be more to her concerns.

Jordan crouched next to the office chair and dropped his voice.

"Sadie, what happened to you tonight?"

"Other than someone trying to kill me while I slept?"

"Yes."

"I..." She opened her mouth, then closed it again. "I can't talk about it right now."

Jordan's frown deepened. "But you're hurt. You need a doctor to check that shoulder. It's taped up, but—"

The phone jangled and all of the people in the office—Sadie, Jordan, Brian and Liz—all turned at the same time. Brian jumped up. "I'll grab that."

"Fine," Sadie said. "Call me an ambulance if you want, but send it to the Thompson ranch."

"Why there?"

"'Cause we're going there anyhow!"

"No way. I'm going with Brian. You can just stay here and—"

"I'm not staying!" she barked. "So if you want an ambulance, you'll damn well send it out to—"

"Guys, listen!" Brian interrupted. "Hunter just called from Levi's place. Neither Lou nor Levi are there. Looks like there's more trouble!"

Jordan's eyes caught on Sadie. She'd stood from the chair and was slipping shoes on top of her bandaged feet.

"What kind of trouble?" Jordan asked.

"Hunter says he thinks the lot of 'em are headed out toward Indian Springs. No sign of Rich Evans either."

"Then we need to get there," Sadie said. Before Jordan could argue with her, she strode to the police locker and grabbed her handgun and ammunition.

"Brian," Jordan said. "I need you to come along."

Sadie stepped in front of him. "No way! I'm—"

"You come along too," Jordan added. "But I'm gonna drive tonight."

The corner of Sadie's lip twitched in amusement.

"You been waiting to say that for a while, haven't you?"

"A bit."

She laughed. "Fine then. You drive."

As the trio headed out the door, Jordan turned back one more time.

"Liz? Tell that ambulance to get out to the Thompson ranch pronto."

* * *

Lou woke up in the cab of the truck at the crossroads, alone. The vision of Gabrielle was gone, but so was Levi. Confused, she sat up, and stared out at the darkness beyond the shattered window.

"Rich…?"

The sense of panic that had filled her moments before the vision had shifted into urgency. She knew she needed to reach him, but there was only so much time. She popped the truck back into gear, and headed down the gravel road.

"Where *are* you, Levi?"

It made no sense that he'd left her in his truck, but the old man was nowhere to be found. With a broken arm, he obviously couldn't drive, but he should have waited for her to wake up. The truck reached the top of the next hill and Lou slammed on the brakes.

Up ahead, the road ended and a narrow horse-trail began. A silver car was parked next to it. Beyond it, untouched prairie met foothills, swirling grass pulsing like waves on the ocean. A distant line of trees stretched out to the foot of the mountain, their dark humps barely visible in the misty shadows beyond.

"Rich!"

If he'd been taken, then this was where. She'd bet her life on it. Adrenaline thrumming in her veins, Lou scanned the seat next to her. The shotgun was gone.

She got out of the truck and began to run.

* * *

Levi Thompson's broken arm ached as he strode down the night-time trail, his gaze on the two men in the distance. He held the gun in his one good hand, the shells already loaded into the chamber. Levi'd never shot a man before, but he suspected that he might have to do it tonight.

You've done just as bad, a voice whispered in the recesses of his mind. *It was only a blanket the boy asked for, after all.*

Levi shoved the memory away and focused on narrowing the distance between him and the two men that walked ahead. He'd tried to wake Louise when she'd passed out, but she'd been some-where else entirely, her lids flickering as she dreamed. That, too, had worried him. He didn't want *another* death from Yuki's family on his hands.

Finding Rich had been his only choice.

Up ahead, the two figures paused. Levi pushed himself faster, the ache spreading from his side to his shoulder, and eventually to his chest. At one time, a jaunt like this would have hardly winded him, but age was the great leveler, and Levi too would be laid flat before his time was done.

The wind howled, the storm ready to break. Levi knew the cattle would be bedding down, Hunter on the way back to the ranch house once the rain began. He might be there already. Levi hoped the note would be enough to guide him to Indian Springs. He frowned and walked faster. When Levi'd been a young man, his focus had been the ranch he'd inherited. There'd never been any money, and the debts his father had accumulated had taken decades to repay. Levi had worked two jobs his whole life, the ranch becoming his life, his blood.

Tonight, he walked away from it without a second thought.

The shorter of the two figures turned. His arm lifted. It was the only warning Levi got. He dodged sideways at the same moment an explosion rocked the silence of the night. Levi dropped to the ground, gasping as the broken arm shifted in the cast.

"Goddamnit," he snarled. "Too old for this foolishness." He wig-gled until he was a few feet away from the trail. A rock blocked his path, and Levi paused, then shimmied up to it. He laid the rifle on top, peering through the sight.

Two hundred meters ahead, Rich Evans stood, bruised and bat-tered, his arms bound behind him. A man Levi recognized from

Hunter's porch stood beside him, gun in hand. *The investigator. Tom something-or-other.* Levi used his good arm to wiggle the gun into position. He was almost ready when the second gunshot rocked the night. A puff of dust exploded from the rock in front of Levi.

"Well, you're a wiley one, aren't you," Levi muttered. His finger tightened on the trigger. *Aim where he's widest* had been his father's advice when Levi was a boy, hunting deer. *Don't think, just let out your breath, aim and shoot.* A whistling breath emerged from wrinkled lips, and he pressed the trigger. The sound rocked Levi and left his ears ringing.

Ahead on the trail, Tom dropped to a crouch, scuttling to the side. For a second, Rich did nothing.

"Run, you fool!" Levi snarled. "He's gonna kill you otherwise."

Tom moved forward, lifted his gun, and Levi pulled the trigger a second time. Another volley of thunder roared across the valley.

Rich bolted for the trees.

One-handed, Levi reached into his pocket and fished out two more shotgun shells. He was still loading them when the dirt next to his leg exploded, pain tearing through his knee like a knife. Levi howled.

Another explosion hit the rock, knocking the gun out of position.

Levi inched sideways, his torn kneecap leaving a trail of blood on the grass. He fumbled to get the next shell casing into the rifle.

"Come on…" he hissed. "Just need one more shot." His gaze flicked up. Tom was jogging up the trail toward him; Rich was nowhere to be seen.

The wind was a relentless gale, bits of rain snapping against Levi's face and hands. Squinting into the breeze, he wedged the rifle back in place on top of the rock, waiting for another shot. When none came, he lifted himself into position. Tom was headed right toward him, gun in hand. A flash lit the barrel and Levi felt it slam into the cast that covered his broken arm, then bury itself into the flesh. He let out his breath.

Just one more, he thought. *One that counts. One that'll make up for all the others...*

Levi's finger tightened on the trigger as Tom lifted his gun. A third explosion echoed across the prairie at the same time as lightning lit the sky. Tom Farrel fell where he stood, the gun tumbling into the grass at his side.

"That's right," Levi gasped. "You can't— can't—" An arc of pain tightened around his chest, spreading over his shoulder to his arm. He groaned.

Overhead, thunder roared. The quiet patters of rain were replaced by a steady pulse of droplets. They soaked through Levi's jacket, and under his shirt, leaving him shivering. He was cold, wet, his leg on fire. The fingers of his hand tightened into a fist as memories surged.

I know a few things about debts, a woman whispered. *You want to talk about that, Levi?*

"No," he whispered. "I don't want to talk to you..."

A blanket. Isn't that what he asked you for?

"Stop!" Levi cried as another wave of pain crossed his chest, dragging him away. "I—I can't—"

And you told him 'no.'

Levi closed his eyes as the sky broke open and the rain pelted down. He knew he needed to move, but his chest was on fire, the beat of his heart grown unsteady.

"I'm sorry," Levi whispered.

Somewhere in the distance, sirens rose. He tried to lift his head to find them, but even that effort was too much. Levi's thoughts drifted, time shifting between the night on the prairie and other times... other memories. For a moment, Hunter stood before him—a twenty-something young man—in the light of the porch.

"You ever work on a farm, boy?"

"No, sir, but I know hard work."

Lightning flashed again and Hunter was gone; the dark night and the mountain range under a leaden sky in his place. Another flash of lightning lit the sky and he sat in the kitchen with Bryce Calhoun, the boy's dark eyes shifting nervously.

"I need a place to lay low 'til this whole thing with Colton blows over," Bryce said. "Someplace I can say I been workin' this summer."

"Why?"

"Police know Colton had mules moving product, but they don't know who."

Levi scowled. "And why should I protect you, huh?"

"'Cause we're family and family sticks together." A dark smile slid over Bryce's lips. "'Sides," he said. "I could tell them about the poaching if you don't."

Levi's eyes narrowed. "You mess with the bull, boy, you're gonna get the horns."

"I won't mess with you unless you mess with me."

"Fine," Levi snarled. "You can help with the herd, long as you keep out of trouble..."

The boom of thunder dragged Levi to the surface. Sirens expanded alongside the sound of rushing in his ears. There was an ambulance on its way.

"Too late." He groaned as another wave of pain rode through him.

Lightning stretched bony fingers across the sky and in the flash,

Levi found himself in yet another time. It was the hut at Slocan, a place that had haunted his nightmares for decades. He shivered. It was deathly cold inside those walls, but a tiny light flickered in one corner. A wave of longing rode through him. To see the child. To make things right. As if caught by his thoughts, Levi felt himself drawn forward. Other nights he would have resisted the little boy with the dark hair. Tonight, he let himself be dragged.

"I'm sorry, boy," he whispered. "I done you wrong."

The light grew and he found himself staring down at the child. He'd hidden from him for all those years. *It was a prison,* Yuki whispered. *They took children to those camps…*

The boy looked up at him, as if seeing him for the first time.

"Please," he said. "I'm so cold."

"There now," Levi said. "Take it. Be warm."

In his dream, he passed the child the wool blanket. Levi's lips were blue where they brushed the rain-drenched ground, and they moved as if in sleep.

"I'm sorry," he mumbled. Each beat of his heart brought the struggle closer, life slipping away.

Footsteps neared, and then slowed. A hand found his in the dark.

"Levi? That you?" It was Hunter's voice, and Levi struggled to follow the words. "My God, what happened?"

"I'm sorry," Levi choked. "I should've done more… should've done better."

Hunter's fingers tightened around his. "Just relax. You're going to be okay. Just hold on. The ambulance—"

"Listen. Just… listen…"

Hunter turned to glance over his shoulder, his voice broken as he shouted: "Tell them to hurry! Levi's been shot! He's hurt bad!"

"Listen, boy," Levi said. "I… I know now."

"Know what?"

Levi squeezed, though it sapped the last of his strength to do it.

"Things happen. We… we tell ourselves that it ain't our fault but—" He gasped as the claw around his heart tightened. "We all gotta take a stand. We got to do what's *right*… We've got to—"

The black clouds swirling atop the mountains roared and boiled, thunder booming as Ephraim Thompson's last living grandson took his final breath and released it. Hunter crouched over him, sobbing.

The rain came down.

* * *

The sun was rising in the east as Lou and Rich finally stepped out of the Waterton police station into a brisk autumn morning. Faint bands of golden light touched the edges of the mountains, gilding white-crested peaks with a painter's touch, while in the distance, the upper lake remained cloaked into bluish shadows, as yet unwoken. Out on the prairie, one final rumble of thunder echoed, then faded as the storm moved away from Waterton, blowing itself out over the plains.

"It's morning," Lou whispered, lifting her gaze to the sky. "God! What a night."

"One I never want to relive," Rich said.

"Me neither."

She wrapped her arms around Rich's waist as they walked slowly back to Cameron Falls Drive, where the truck was parked. Lou's eyes were red from last night's tears, but her heart was full. Hours ago, she'd watched Hunter follow the stretcher of his oldest friend: Levi Thompson, who'd died killing Rich's would-be murderer. Levi had given his life freely, and—if the emotions Lou felt were any sign—his choice was purposeful. Rich wasn't an outsider any longer. She smiled as the bands of light spread across the sky above Waterton. The storm had passed. They had their new start.

Reaching the truck, Rich pressed a kiss to the side of her head.

"Want me to drive?" he asked.

"Yeah." She smiled up at him. "You still doing okay?"

"I am. Thanks for coming for me last night."

"You'd do the same if it was me out there in the dark." She tightened her grip. "You did before."

"I'll always come for you, Lou… *Always*."

"I know."

Rich's gaze moved to the hamlet of Waterton, huddled against the sleeping bulk of the mountains.

"What're you thinking about?" Lou asked.

He sighed. "That's the second time Levi saved me. I wish he…"

"You wish what?"

Rich shook his head. "I wish he hadn't had to."

Lou slid her arms up his back and smiled. "No one made Levi Thompson do anything in his entire life. He wasn't just tough, he was *immovable*. He was out there last night because he wanted to be, Rich."

"Maybe…"

Lou could sense the trail of Rich's thoughts, spinning back toward last night's events at Indian Springs. The two of them had watched Levi's body be loaded into the back of the truck. They'd seen Hunter, sobbing, crawl into the ambulance after him. They'd waited as Constable Wyatt had walked around Tom Farrel's car, snapping photographs, and Constable Black Plume, dressed—oddly enough—in her off-duty wear, stood next to the police cruiser, arguing with a medical technician trying to check her sling. This morning, threads of each of those thoughts spun around Rich like strings, tethering him to that moment, that fear.

"Hey," Lou whispered. "Come back to me."

He shook his head and looked down. "Sorry. I was just thinking about last night."

"I know."

Lou smiled. She could feel the ebb and flow of things around her and today, the threads of the past were being corrected. Rich, and his uncertainty of place here in Waterton, was part of that. She wasn't certain how each individual line of connection would play out, but she knew things had found clarity. While Levi's death brought grief to her, it also carried *solace*. Lou's mother, Yuki, felt closer than she'd felt in years.

"We're past the worst," Lou said. "We can go forward now."

"I know, I just…" Rich put his hands on her shoulders. "Lou, I… I need to tell you something."

"About?"

"About Gabby. About what happened that night we argued in New York."

Lou's eyes widened. "What?"

"When Gabby followed me back to the hotel, she told me outright that she wanted to get back together. She… she said that she wanted the life we'd started." Rich frowned. "She told me she'd do anything to get that back again."

"And…?"

Rich's blue eyes glittered with unshed tears, his voice growing hoarse.

"And I told her that as long as you were alive, my heart would be yours. That nothing would pull me from you. No one. That my life—" He put his hand on the spot above her heart the same way he had the day she'd lain bleeding on the floor of Lou's Garage. "—was *your life.* And that I'd never willingly let it go. As long as you were living and breathing, I'd be with you." His voice broke. "I… I'm sorry I said that."

"But *why*, Rich? That's beautiful."

He wrapped his arms around her, pressing his face to her hair, and breathing in hitched sobs.

"Because she took what I said and twisted it. Gabby came to Waterton to kill you, Lou. She believed, in her damaged way, that she could make that come true. I'm so sorry. If I gave her that thought and she followed through, I'd never forgive myself. I—"

"Stop."

Rich blinked. "What?"

"You can only control your own thoughts, your own behaviour." She leaned in. "You have to live for what you want, not stand on the outside, waiting, fearful that you'll mess it up." She smiled. "Know who taught me that?"

"Who?"

"You did."

He smiled. "Really?"

"Uh-huh." She nodded, and Rich leaned down, sliding his hand into his hair as he kissed her. For as long as Louise Newman could remember, she'd searched for her place, for her reason for being. She'd stood on the outside looking in. But here, in the heart of the Rockies, wrapped in the arms of her husband—a man she loved more than anyone in the world—she *knew* where she was meant to be.

Rich broke the kiss and pushed a strand of hair back behind her ear.

"I love you, Lou. So much. You're my everything…" He brushed his lips against hers. "My wife."

"Love you too." She nodded to the horizon. From peak to peak, dawn had broken, all of Waterton was bathed in a warm morning glow. "Now let's go home."

"Yes. Let's."

CHAPTER TWENTY

It was summer and the night air was heavy with the scent of flowers, both outside the screened windows of the Lion's Hall, and inside on all the tables where Louise Newman and Rich Evans were belatedly celebrating their wedding. Over the speakers, a rock song roared to life, and knots of townsfolk tumbled out of the chairs as they took to the floor. As Murray and Arnette headed off to dance, Sadie found herself without anyone to talk to.

She scanned the crowd. Vasur sat next to Margaret, the two of them deep in conversation. Audrika, their centre in life, was much the same in death. Next to them sat Sam and Jeannine Barton playing a drinking game alongside their table-mates. Sadie's gaze moved on. Jordan and Mila sat at the next table and she leaned in, saying something that made the young officer's face turn blotchy red in a matter of seconds. Mila laughed, grabbed his hand, and dragged him up to the dance floor. Sadie's eyes moved on. Liz Moran caught Sadie's gaze. An angry look passed across the hall between the two women and Sadie looked away. *You made those choices, Liz.* Sadie thought. *I just did what had to be done.* But knowing it and living with the consequences of Liz's voluntary retirement were two different things.

Around Sadie, more couples joined Mila, Jordan, and the others on the dance floor. She frowned and stepped back. For an uncomfortably long minute she waited at the side of the hall, uneasily crossing and uncrossing her arms. She didn't really want to be here, but it felt rude to leave.

"You're not going to dance with the rest of them?" a man asked.

Sadie turned to find Hunter Slate standing next to her. He was dressed in his Sunday best, which amounted to a brighter coloured shirt under a well-worn hunting vest. A shooting star flower twinkled in one of the buttonholes.

"Dance? Me?" Sadie rolled her eyes.

"Oh, come on," he said. "Everyone else is out there."

"Do I *look* like someone who dances, Hunter?"

He laughed. "No. But that doesn't mean you can't change."

"Don't hold your breath."

"I'll be your partner if you'd like." He lifted a glass of beer in a mock toast.

"Thanks, but no thanks."

"Oh come on! It could be fun!" Hunter laughed.

"Still a no." She waved and walked away. *Not a chance.*

Sadie headed to the side exit, avoiding a trio of mothers bouncing toddlers and babies on their hips, and a teenage couple so close the two silhouettes seemed like one person rather than two.

"Excuse me," Sadie said, sliding by. "I just need to get past."

She'd been seen now. She could go home. Hide.

Sadie had just reached for the door when a woman with long dark hair and a loose flowy white dress stepped from the washroom.

"Sadie," Lou laughed. "I was wondering where you were."

With a sigh, Sadie's hand dropped from the exit door. So much for her escape.

"Hey, Lou. You look great."

Lou reached out pulling Sadie into a hug, made awkward by the swell of Lou's belly. "You don't have to say that," she laughed. "But thanks."

Sadie smiled despite herself. "You do, actually. Pregnancy works for you. You look beautiful."

Lou ran her hand over her stomach, smiling. "Thanks. It's been interesting, that's for sure."

"Everything okay?"

"Oh, yeah, everything's good," Lou said. "But I've been having the strangest dreams."

"Ah..." This conversation had just slipped into that awkward place Sadie spent so much time trying to avoid. She glanced guiltily at the door; she just wanted to head home.

"You leaving?" Lou asked as if she'd said the words aloud.

Sadie jerked her gaze back. "I... no. I wasn't." She frowned. "I was just going to grab a breath of fresh air."

"You can leave if you need to. Honestly. It's no problem." Lou grinned as a new song echoed through the speakers. "The chicken dance isn't for everyone."

Sadie chuckled. "True enough."

"Thanks for coming though. It was good to see you. I'll tell Rich you had to run. G'night, Sadie."

Louise was halfway to the dance floor when Sadie shouted: "Lou, wait!"

She turned back. "Yes?"

"I... I need to ask you something."

Lou came forward, her hips rolling with the weight of her pregnant belly.

"What's that?"

Sadie frowned, fighting to find her words. "Lou, I... I want to ask you about something."

"Alright."

"When someone dies, do they—" Sadie took a shaky breath. "Do they—"

"Do they what?"

"Nothing. It's stupid."

"It's not," Lou said. "You can talk to me. I'm not going to judge."

Sadie took a deep breath and then blew it out. "Back in the fall, when Farrel tried to kill me, something happened…" She shook her head. "Oh, never mind. It'll sound crazy."

"Never mind *what*?"

Sadie was quiet for a long moment. Most other people would end the conversation, but Louise waited, smiling patiently. Sadie wondered how many *other* people she'd done this for. How many other stories she'd heard over the years? *Everyone came to Lou,* wasn't that what Jordan said?

"The night of the attack," Sadie said haltingly. "I woke up and I… heard something." She dropped her voice. "Something in my head. Like… a voice. But it wasn't mine."

"Whose voice was it?"

"It, uh… it was Jim Flagstone's."

"Ah… That makes sense."

"It— It does?"

Lou nodded.

"And later, when I got shot, I didn't just *hear* him." Sadie pressed her eyes closed, remembering. "I mean I *did* hear him, but it was more than that." She opened her lashes to find Lou waiting. "When I was trying to escape, he came to me. He was *there,* Lou. He was… real."

"And?"

A line appeared between Sadie's brows. "And that doesn't sound crazy to you?"

Lou shrugged. "Not really." She laughed. "I hear things all the time. I think of it as a gift."

"But is it—" Sadie's voice caught. "Is it…?"

"Is it really Jim?"

"Yeah." Her voice broke.

Lou stepped nearer, her swollen belly bumping Sadie's hip.

"I think it probably is."

"But how do you *know* that, Lou?"

"I don't," she said. "But it makes sense to me that it could be."

"But *how*?!" Sadie wiped tears away. "I don't understand what happened. I… I keep waiting to hear him again, but it's like he's gone."

"Maybe he did what he needed to do." Lou smiled. "Everything in life is a cycle. *Everything.* I see no reason that the part of a person that *is that person* would be any different. If I was to cut down a tree, then a new tree would grow from the seeds of the old. If water evaporates, it makes a cloud somewhere else." Her hand rubbed over the curve of her belly. "Humans are impatient. We're *young* in how we see the world, Sadie. But we're part of that cycle too. We just need to remember—" Lou gasped and looked down.

"What?" Sadie asked.

Lou reached out. "Here. Give me your hand." She pressed Sadie's palm against the curve of her stomach. "Feel that," she whispered. "He's awake again."

Under Sadie's palm, a movement stirred like a fish beneath water. She gasped.

"Wait," Lou whispered. "There'll be more."

For several long minutes the two women stood, caught in a private moment of magic, feeling the dance of feet and elbows under their palms. When Lou looked back up, tears glittered in her eyes. She let go of Sadie's hand.

"Everything is a cycle," Lou said. "Doesn't matter how long it takes, it always starts again."

"Then *why* do we have to die? What's the point?"

"We're learning," Lou said. "We're all unfinished, imperfect. And we aren't really alive if we don't die."

Sadie wiped her eyes. "Jim didn't deserve what happened to him."

"No," Lou said, "but he became a police officer, just like you did, *knowing* those risks. He knew and he still figured it was worth it."

Sadie tried to answer, but her throat was aching.

"We're only alive when we choose to live," Lou said. "Everyone's life is full of dangers, but the journey is the important part, not the destination."

"I—I miss Jim."

"We all do."

"I don't know how to go on, Lou. I don't know how to be *happy* again."

"You keep moving. Keep trying. You remind yourself that he died doing what he loved. And you keep watching."

"Watching for what?"

"For *him*."

Tears wet Sadie's cheeks. The rollicking music in the other room had risen to a crescendo and she leaned in as Lou continued.

"Things return," Lou said. "Ideas and thoughts too." She smiled sadly. "People even. We *all* get a second chance eventually." Lou pulled her into another hug and Sadie clung, tears soaking Lou's shoulder.

"How?" she croaked.

"Watch and wait. It's hard to do, but the universe has its own timing."

The song ended amidst cheers and clapping, and the M.C. said something inaudible.

"I should head back in," Lou said, stepping back. "Rich'll be wondering where I got off to, but if you want to talk again, I'm around."

"Would that be okay?"

"Of course." Lou grinned. "Swing by the garage. I'd be happy to talk."

Sadie gave her a watery smile. "I think I might."

Inside the dance hall, one song ended. Another began.

* * *

Lou lay in bed on her side, her body a 'C' around the new life that swam inside her. Rich's shape was an echo of her own form, his body stretched around her back, hand cupped protectively over their child.

"Tell me a story, Lou," he whispered.

She smiled as his chin brushed her shoulder, pressing a kiss against the bare skin.

"What kind of story?" she asked. "I think I've told you most of mine."

"Then one of your *other* stories. Something about this moment… about now."

"Hmmm… let me think for a minute." Lou closed her eyes, letting her thoughts spread out like a net, drawing the varied tales she'd read over the years. The one that returned was an old one. Her mother, Yuki, had told it to her more than once when she was a little girl, and she felt its truth tonight.

"How about this?" she said. "There once were two acrobats, a teacher and a student. They lived together—happy with one another's company—performing each day and earning money with their act."

Rich snuggled closer. "Am I the student in this story?"

Lou giggled. "Shhh... It's just a story, Rich."

"Sure it is." He nibbled the skin of her shoulder. "You going to teach me some new tricks?"

"Stop." Lou elbowed him and he laughed. "So one of their acts involved the student..." Lou paused. "Who happened to be a young *woman*—"

"Of course."

"—balancing on the top of a very tall bamboo pole. The teacher—a man, I'll have you know—stood underneath, with the pole balanced on his head."

Rich propped himself up on his elbow, grinning down at her.

"Did you just change the story?"

"No," she said with a giggle. "But I will if you keep interrupting."

"Fine." He leaned in, dropping a kiss on her lips. "I'll be good."

"Once the student was on top of the pole, she stayed there, balanced, while the teacher walked back and forth, demonstrating his skill for the audience." Lou rolled over so that she faced Rich, her stomach shifting with its own pendulous motion. "Each of them had to maintain complete focus for the act to work. One mistake on either side could mean trouble. If the student fell, there'd be no way for the teacher to catch her."

Rich reached out, stroking Lou's arm in the dark. "Sounds like they had to rely on each other pretty perfectly."

"They did. That part was its *own* balance, learning to trust one another," Lou said, shivering under his touch. "And most days that worked."

Rich smirked. "But…"

"But one day the wind was higher than usual, and the teacher said to the young woman: 'It's windy and I'm worried you might fall. Let's watch one another. You keep an eye on me, and I'll do the same for you. Then we'll certainly be safe.'"

"Did it work?"

"They never tested it, because the student herself was very wise." Lou grinned. "Wiser, in this case, than even the teacher."

Rich laughed. "I like this story."

"The student said to the teacher: 'I think it would be better if we watched out for *ourselves,* rather than each of us trying to watch the other. Because when we look after ourselves, we're already looking after both of us. We can focus on what we're doing, and trust the other is doing the same. And in this way, all will be well.'"

Outside the open window, the night air stirred the curtains, the scent of Waterton, of *home*, flowing into the bedroom. Rich pressed a kiss to Lou's lips and pulled her into his arms. "That was a good story," he said. "I liked it."

She nodded and closed her eyes. "Me too."

"Love you, Lou."

"Love you, too," she whispered to both the boy-child about to return and the man who held them both against his heart. And there, in a circle of beginnings and endings, and new cycles about to start, the three of them finally slept.

ACKNOWLEDGEMENTS

The writing of a book is a lengthy process, but I could not release Fall of Night without expressing my sincere gratitude to the many people who have shaped it along the way:

Thank you to my husband, my most enthusiastic collaborator, for supporting the writing of this series from beginning to end. You are my favourite human on earth. Thank you also to my three boys, for tolerating long periods of busyness as I shaped this series from a pile of notes into three distinct books, all while sitting at our kitchen table. I hope that the vacation to Maui was a fair trade-off for my distraction. Thank you to my mom and dad—one alive, one deceased—who raised me to be the kind of person who believed she could write a trilogy that mixed reincarnation, murder, and all the magical weirdness of Waterton... and get it published. Dad, if there's any book of mine that you live on in, it's this one.

A grateful shout-out to my fellow writers—far too many to name—who kept me going when my spark for writing was low. Thanks to Morty Mint, my agent, now retired, for his unwavering support and level-headed advice. Thanks also to Moe Ferrara, my current agent, for taking up Morty's torch. An enthusiastic thank you to my two editors: Dinah Forbes, for her ability to see the larger structure of a story, and Netta Johnson for being able capture and refine those microscopic details that dragged the unedited story down. Both of you made this book into something worth reading. A heartfelt thank you to my beta-readers readers who read the early versions of this book with an eye to details. My sincere gratitude and affection to the Stonehouse publishing team, especially Julie Yerex, Netta Johnson, and Lisa Murphy-Lamb, for their tireless efforts in bringing this project together. The Waterton series is yours as much as mine.

One final note of acknowledgement—for you, the reader. A story begins in a writer's mind, but it is not completed until it has moved into yours. Thank you for trusting me to take you on this journey. Thank you for rooting for Lou and Rich. Thank you for forgiving me for killing off Jim in book 2, and for trusting me when I brought him back in book 3. Your support is why I wrote this series, and why you are reading these words. I am eternally grateful for this gift of trust and I look forward to the next adventure we embark on together. I hope you do too.

ABOUT THE AUTHOR

D.K. Stone/Danika Stone is an author, artist, and educator who discovered a passion for writing fiction while in the throes of her Masters thesis. A self-declared bibliophile, Stone now writes novels for both teens: *Switchback* (Macmillan, 2019), *Internet Famous* (Macmillan, 2017) and *All the Feels* (Macmillan, 2016); and adults *Fall of Night* (Stonehouse, 2020) *The Dark Divide* (Stonehouse, 2018) and *Edge Of Wild* (Stonehouse, 2016). When not writing, Danika can be found hiking in the Rockies, planning grand adventures, and spending far too much time online. She lives with her husband, three sons, and a houseful of imaginary characters in a windy corner of Alberta, Canada.